Singer

Enjoy —
Kerry Casey

KERRY CASEY

SINGER © copyright 2012 by Kerry Casey.
All rights reserved. No part of this book may be reproduced in any form whatsoever, by photography or xerography or by any other means, by broadcast or transmission, by translation into any kind of language, nor by recording electronically or otherwise, without permission in writing from the author, except by a reviewer, who may quote brief passages in critical articles or reviews.

This is a work of fiction. In other words, I made it up and no one should get bent out of shape over content.

ISBN-13: 978-0-9769765-2-3

Library of Congress Catalog Number: 2012937558

Printed in Canada

First Printing: May 2012

16 15 14 13 12   5 4 3 2 1

Published by:
five friends books™
fivefriendsbooks.com

The best books come from friends. That's why Five Friends Books™ puts the destiny of a book in the hands of readers. Please pass along your bookmarks to five book-loving friends. How far this novel spreads depends on you. Find out more by visiting **fivefriendsbooks.com**.

To all of us who read because we are not sure.

There is ugliness afoot.

Sinister, with roots twisting down beyond hope of any kind.

It will find you, yes, by the throat, and rob you of all you dreamed and toiled for.

When at last it departs, it is without remorse.

Leaving your faith to shrivel and rot.

What is left is of greater darkness than its origin.

Because it is so, God sends His Singers.

BOOK

SPRING 1985

Love conquers all. Or does it?

PART ONE

Saturday

PAT

He never saw it coming.

The first punch fractured Pat's nose—ironically, in the direction opposite a break from years past. It's a detail worth mentioning because in the ensuing months, with the cotton packing removed and the swelling down, Pat's nose was again as straight as it had been in his fifth-grade portrait. Fate, it seems, is not without a sense of humor. Or at least a sense of symmetry.

Behind the force of the blow, Pat's knees abandoned him, leaving him on all fours in the mud of the sideyard. His attacker came at him like a placekicker approaching a football on a tee. As the foot blurred forward, Pat gathered the wherewithal to roll. The long tail of the untied lace lashed his cheek. The sting momentarily distracted him from his very basic dilemma: breathe through a broken nose, or gulp air with an open mouth, gagging on the blood streaming down his face.

Contrary to the immediate circumstances, this scene wasn't altogether abhorrent. The late May morning was a prize. The farmstead was caressed in a holy light that put out yawning soft shadows to the west. The morning soundscape was quiet, but not noiseless, as bees the size of candy root beer barrels worked the early flowering crab trees. In the farmyard, the fescue had come to be broad, the kelly green blades heavy enough to somersault. Newborn bunnies left the burrow with eartips reaching just above the grass. The shelterbelt hardwoods, always late to bud here near the Minnesota-Canada border, had leafed out in a wondrous silk of green where wind found sail, swaying branches long idle through the dead of winter. The day promised to be warm, unseasonably so, overdue after months of cold and dark. As Pat liked to say, spring was doing its thing.

Against this backdrop, the two adult men squared off. Counterclockwise, they slowly circled, dirt-stained sweat leaking down their faces. Each feigned punches, looking for an opening, their front feet not more than 10 inches apart. Pat held his fists higher, his right drawn back and loaded. His adversary, a Native American who Pat guessed was from the nearby Rez, sidestepped in front of him, shirt sleeves rolled up, revealing an open-winged eagle tattooed on his ropy right forearm.

Pat, six feet tall and slim, moved well on his feet. But what he wouldn't do to be free of his canary yellow sports coat. It was a size and a half too small, binding across the back, which would hinder the finish on his punches.

As it turned out, the sports coat was of little consequence with regard to the effectiveness of Pat's punches. The man on the receiving end was quickly heaped facedown in the slop of the sideyard where the spring runoff sluiced in deep tractor tire ruts. Pat straddled the man as he rolled him over so he wouldn't suffocate in mud. Bright blood dripped from Pat to the man to the mire.

How a 46-year-old ex-priest came to be so accomplished with his fists is a question any reasonable witness might ask. But there was no such witness. Except for the half dozen brown-headed

SPRING 1985

cowbirds that had collected on the powerline leading from the farmhouse to the barn.

A few other questions might fairly spring to mind, were you not familiar with Patrick O'Rourke's jagged life path. Beginning with, Why is an ex-priest brawling on a glorious May morning? And, for that matter, how did the "ex" get attached to Pat's religious resumè? And further, why is his yellow sports coat too small in the first place?

The catalyst of this unsightly event is familiar enough: a spirited young woman, a beguiling young man, a car's back seat and an irretrievably consuming, momentary engagement. But consequences trail in long after shirts are re-tucked and hair is straightened.

The young woman was Meadow FastHorse, an 18-year-old from the Ojibwe reservation just south of the farm where Pat lived. As sure as the sun will rise tomorrow, she was going to have a baby. Or she wasn't, if her father had his way. Not that he had lofty aspirations for his daughter, or himself for that matter. What he didn't need was the little whore and her bastard putting stones in his moccasins, fettering him with more inconveniences and burdens.

Pat first met Meadow working part-time as a counselor on the Rez—the same Rez where three and a half years earlier he was the residing pastor. He had left the priesthood, but he couldn't abandon service; he'd sooner lose his right arm than withdraw from the community with which he felt such common blood. They had accepted him, his white skin and well-documented faults, choosing instead to focus on his gifts. And Pat returned that perspective in kind. Judgment, both parties decided, was best left to a higher power.

He was offered a makeshift office in the community center where he volunteered three evenings and two Saturdays a month. Sometimes Pat's counseling took place in his two-chair office, across a wobbly desk pulled out of storage from the basement of the Rez school. But more often, his counsel was less formal. Much good can come of talks while shooting hoops in the community center gym or hitting grounders on the ball diamond or buying a couple vending machine Cokes and sitting outside on the brick half-wall.

Pat never second-guessed leaving the priesthood, but equally, he knew his ministry was unfinished. In fact, oftentimes his need to serve would outstretch others' need to be served. He recognized this, but his passion was hard to temper. So when Meadow rapped on his office doorjamb one evening, and was greeted by such a surge of enthusiasm, she wondered for a moment who was helping whom.

His offer of a chair, she refused. She looked disdainfully at the jumbo box of Kleenex on his scratched desk, there for some of the more emotional teens he counseled. She told him clear and straight of her predicament, and wasn't shy about mixing in an occasional expletive, but not for effect. I've been shit stupid, she had told him, saying little more than she slept with a boy a year older, but made it clear it was a lapse, not a pattern. She said so with her intensity, the tension of her body, the directness of her eyes and her unwavering voice. She stood before him asking not for compassion, but for options, she said. Choices. Ideas. Meadow swore him to secrecy, and put out a hand to shake to solidify their pact. Pat agreed. He wouldn't talk about her pregnancy unless her health or the health of her child were jeopardized. Everything in her bearing told Pat of the seriousness of the pledge he had entered into.

"I hear you help people," Meadow had said, leaning against the doorframe of his office.

Pat struck his knee on the bottom of the desk drawer as he went to stand. "I'd like to, yes," he said, wincing. "That's what I'm here for."

She'd made a mistake, a big mistake; on that point she was in accord with her father. She was angry for the expanse of the error. She spoke of the older boy, of alcohol, of not being true to herself, of how her old man said he'd kick her out of the house. That baby won't happen, her father had raged. He had spat on her shoes to punctuate his point.

Abortion wasn't an option. She said this with a strength that went right into Pat. She went to say more, but for the first time her voice caught in her throat. She stopped there.

Over the weeks the conversation moved to lighter ground. Pat asked of hobbies, how she was doing in school, about her friends. She was a swimmer, she told him. She said she loved music. She wrote songs that she never showed anyone. Pat asked if she would show him one someday. She said someday can be a long ways from now.

Pat didn't get into much about himself. He did tell her that he was a recovering alcoholic so she understood why he had to cut out early on Saturday nights for his meeting. And he talked a little about where he was living, a farmhouse that he built for a friend who had …. Here he had trouble finding the right word so he said "left." It was a longer discussion for another time, he had told her.

Yet as measured as Meadow was, she was unprepared for how Pat smiled at her. How his benevolence reached her. Even the little crow's feet radiating from the corners of his eyes reached her. His peace became her chance at peace. She found he helped her exhale, fully, for the first time in many weeks. But she was curious about the eyelashes over his right eye. They were white as snow.

The following month they talked about keeping the baby versus adoption. Meadow wasn't ready to be a mother, but she was smart enough to know that in some ways adoption was an even harder choice. The ache of separation scared her. And getting the baby adopted off the Rez was no easy task. But there could be no other way.

Most Tuesday and Thursday nights, they'd meet in his cramped office or on the basketball court, shooting free throws. Pat spoke of her baby's unrecoverable value to the world. Then, just about by the time Meadow worried others might notice what she called "Bulge," they made a promise to the baby: you will be adopted. You will fly over these broken fences. Both Meadow and Pat would see to it, no matter what.

Pat pulled who he guessed was Meadow's father into a semi-sitting position with one hand while using two fingers from his other to pinch off the blood flowing from his nose. Grasping a fistful of shirt, he shook him. "Mr. FastHorse?" The man's eyes were there one minute, rolling back white the next. He splattered mud from the man's cheeks as he slapped them, trying to bring him back to full to consciousness.

"Mr. FastHorse," Pat said as the man's eyes fluttered open. "Can you hear me?" The man half-grunted. Pat felt the musculature of the man's body begin to firm. The stench of gutter alcohol was strong enough to penetrate Pat's nose, even in its unfortunate condition.

His feet now under him, Roy Lee FastHorse wobbled, lifting his fists, baring his clenched teeth, bloody spittle running down his chin. He shook his fists, but his steps were in retreat.

"This isn't finished, asshole." He continued back-stepping.

Pat held his hands up, palms toward his adversary. "I have no fight with you, sir."

"Stay THE FUCK AWAY from my daughter." FastHorse spat what appeared to be a bloody tooth onto the ground. "You have trespassed, white dog. Into my family's home." The spring winds ruffled the cuffs of his jeans.

Pat squinted into the sun. "Sir, Meadow is 18. A legal adult. It was her decision not to speak to you despite my repeated requests that the three of us sit down."

"There is no three of us." FastHorse squinted. "You're a dog eating out of a garbage pile."

Pat tilted his head back for a moment, taking in the full blue of the sky. His nose wouldn't stop bleeding. "But she's afraid to come to you." Pat implored, taking a small step forward. "She's afraid to talk to you."

"The whore should be. Knocked up!" FastHorse took another step backward. "You stay where you are."

SPRING 1985

"I only want to talk." Pat kept his hands open, up in the air, continuing toward FastHorse, who had now made it back to his dilapidated sedan. FastHorse reached in the open window of the back seat and pulled out a shotgun. "I wouldn't," he said in a tone Pat thought too calm for the circumstance. "Not another step. Not another word. Not another helping hand."

Pat nodded, looking down the barrel of the shotgun.

At a moment like this, such a convergence of thoughts are simultaneously launched, it can overload the senses and leave one's mind frozen. For Pat, not so. One clear, true thought presented itself. Pat gave it voice, but he ventured not another step forward.

"You could be a good grandfather."

CORY

It was so Cory.
At once, he listened to the dean's opening remarks, eavesdropped on the conversation whispered behind him and shook his head in disbelief, thinking about his mother. Rigidly, he sat in the front row of the cavernous auditorium, waiting. Cory's polished shoe restlessly drummed the smooth cement floor until a discarded piece of chewing gum did its best to end that. It wasn't that he was nervous about the graduation ceremony or his ability to rise and present a perfectly serviceable valedictory address. It's just that crowds and ceremony were not in Cory's comfort zone—an area with little dimensionality to it.

Cory chewed the inside of his cheek, remembering his mother's brief note. She was sorry but she wouldn't be able to "make it up for the graduation thingy." Her note continued to explain, "As they say in the biz, real estate is weekends." Her uneven handwriting was pressed deep into the cheap office stationery for which employees paid a penny a page. She also included three business cards "in case you come across anyone looking in St. Paul." She inked a smiley face near the footer where her name and title were typeset along with the words bonded and certified. Actually, Cory thought, a slight edit was in order: bonded and certifiable. "P.S." she wrote, "Your father would be proud." Cory's mom was no stranger to underlining.

The dean continued his introductory speech, rolling up onto his toes whenever he wanted to emphasize certain points. *Where did college go?* Cory thought. One thing for sure, it didn't go as planned. But, smiling wryly, he recalled what Monsignor Kief said about the illusion of plans: Do you know how to make God laugh? he'd ask. Cory admitted he did not. Tell him your plans for the next three years, the Monsignor had finished. *Trite. But true.* Cory reached behind his ear and felt the small creek stone braided in his hair; felt its solidity, its cool certainty. He sat up straighter. He tried to blink into the present and let the past rest in peace.

At the rostrum, the dean finished with a rather pedestrian metaphor about how life moves in concentric circles, each milestone providing the impetus for the subsequent ring. The dean visualized his point dramatically, using his index finger to draw large circles in the air. Cory's mind jumped from the content of the speech to doing mental word scrambles with the words concentric circles: *icicles rot, eccentric Orion,* or the one that gave him pause, *inner loser.*

The dean was building toward his heartfelt close. As he prepared to introduce "the main event, our valedictorian," he gestured to Cory and spoke about the University's abbreviated time with this "exceptional talent." The dean clenched his hands together for emphasis, "In a mere two years he has given us so much."

Cory listened as out came the string of nauseating accomplishments: 4.0 GPA. Cory's commitment to teach math and coach hockey in the local school district. Volunteer work with the Down syndrome community. And last but not least, the heroics of last

August 15th. Here the dean took a moment to let the applause subside. Cory studied the floor, a slight frown on his face. A scar parted his right eyebrow, which he raised in introspection: *When would the fascination cease?* Could he not walk down the street without being stopped? Just wanted to shake your hand, strangers would say. Just had to. Some of the more intrepid teenage girls would insist on a kiss, but Cory would gently intercept them with a handshake. When you risk your precious life, that's heroics. But if you don't deem what's put at risk as precious, that's much ado about nothing. Cory's foot drummed the floor. His focus blurred. He was back at the dock.

The small single-engine Cessna buzzed over Cory's head. *Too low*, he thought, standing shirtless in cut-off sweat pants on the end of his dock, flip flops off, ready to swim. He was tanned, sinewed, muscles defined in his lean frame. He was a good twenty pounds below his college hockey-playing weight. The sun left his hair a wheat-colored brown, with loopy open curls that the wind would tousle.

The calm of a perfect August evening had settled on the lake. Water spiders danced in the reflections. Bluegills rose and gulped surface bugs. Above, the sky was suffused with the in-between shades of twilight. Even in this dimming light, the airplane was low enough for Cory to see the red piping along its fuselage. Suddenly, a yellow pinpoint flashed off the aircraft's right front wing; a split second later came a pop—like the report of a small-caliber rifle.

The aircraft jerked, banked suddenly and began to fade into a slow continuous turn. It looped the edge of the lake opposite Cory's dock, clearly losing altitude. Momentarily rapt by the sight, Cory then extracted himself and got to it. He sprinted up to the cabin, pulled on long pants, a long sleeved shirt, hopped into boots and yanked his Carhartt field coat from the back of the closet where it was stored for the summer.

Banging the cabin's old screen door open, Cory quickly came down the steps into the yard, pulling a ball cap tightly down on his head, inadvertently bumping the stone braided into his hair.

SPRING 1985

Holding his breath, he listened.

His heart pounded as he fully zipped his coat, the collar riding high around his neck. Moths ticked off the gooseneck porch light illuminating the outdoor thermometer. Eighty-eight degrees. Sweat dropped onto his boot tops, thwapp, thwapp, thwapp, in an eerie rhythm with the far-off sound of the failing engine. Cory deduced the Cessna had made it back around to his side of the lake.

In this beautiful still of dusk, Cory was a statue: head cocked, mouth slightly open. His throat was dry, in opposition with the twilight's mugginess.

The aircraft struck the trees in a gruesome, echoing mix of breaking branches. A heavy impact sounded before the engine was snuffed out. Cory breathed out. He turned in the direction of an alfalfa field not but a quarter-mile south of his cabin.

Held in the grasp of one final thought, Cory shifted his weight to his back leg. *August 15th, 1984. Every obituary has its date.*

Then he ran toward it.

Standing in answer to the applause, Cory approached the stage, which had no shortage of maroon and yellow bunting. His limp was noticeable because prolonged sitting stiffened his knee. It was the same knee for which the surgeon had done "everything medically possible," but during the same post-operative conversation, he had felt obligated to tell Cory that the joint was all but ruined. The injury ended Cory's notable hockey career, and then some. After taking two years off school, Cory transferred to the University of Minnesota Duluth, whose graduating class he was about to address.

He took the steps two at a time; Cory would have none of the stiffness. The stone braided behind his ear tapped lightly, but this too he ignored. Briskly he approached the dean, put on his best enthusiastic-graduate face, exchanged obligatory handshakes, and took his place behind the podium.

"Good morning esteemed faculty, parents, and future superstars of the American workforce." This brought raucous fist-raising appreciation from the 1700-plus graduating class of 1985. And then, just as instantly, he brought them to edge-of-the-chair silence.

"I'd like to speak today about a four-letter word." He let the notion hang in the air. "A four-letter word that has struck fear in emperors, kings, dictators and presidents. This four-letter word has left many aghast—but curiously, never once have you seen it written on a bathroom wall." In response to a squeal of microphone feedback, Cory leaned back from the rostrum.

"The word I'm thinking of is will. Not will? with a question mark, like 'will I?' Not little lowercase w-i-l-l like 'maybe I will.' But capital W-I-L-L. WILL. Your internal vow."

Letting that thought take root, Cory looked out upon the crowd, seeing only shapes in the glare of stage lights. "A dividing point awaits each of us: Will. Or won't. Waiting outside this auditorium, you'll come nose-to-nose with defining decisions. Life insists on a choice, without telling us which is right. The choice you make becomes you. Comfort or challenge. Wrong or right. Wait or go. How will you answer?"

Cory licked his lips and took a deep breath. He peered through the hard lights. Toward the back, the two overweight security guards had taken a step closer, listening. The overhead stage lights hummed.

"Will carries the day. The difference between advancing and not is will. If I were asked to choose between an abundance of talent or the same share of will, the choice is already written. Where there's a will there's a way.

"When people ask me what I've learned in my 24 years, what have my experiences, good and bad, taught me? Will beats skill. When decisive moments confront you, meet them with all your will."

Coming out from behind the podium, Cory walked to the front of the hardwood stage and looked out into the audience. Away from the microphone, he now raised his voice.

"This begs one final question …" he paused, "and it's not, can you hear me in the back?" The students laughed, a few in the last rows raising their hands to confirm they could. "The question is, what merits your will? What deserves *you*? Medicine? Business? Sport? Service? Art? Education? Knowing, truly knowing, the answer to this question gets you so far ahead that when you arrive to an interview, you'll leave your prospective employer rubbing his eyes because he's never seen anything like it."

Cory took two more steps forward, leaving his feet half over the stage edge. He stood there precariously balanced. A murmur rose from the student body. Then Cory lifted his right foot off the stage. He stood balanced on his left leg.

"At the risk of seeming clever, I'd like to demonstrate that will is not an abstract concept. It's as real as my standing here, on one leg. My sophomore year, playing hockey for Wisconsin—I know, boo! Wisconsin, boo!—I suffered an injury to this knee. The leg I'm standing on here before you." Cory touched his pant leg. "After surgery I said to the physician, 'Give it to me straight, doc. What are the chances I'll play hockey again?' I could tell by his face I'd asked the wrong question." Cory remained balanced on one leg. "The doc gave it to me straight. He said despite his best efforts, I'd walk with a cane the rest of my life and never have the strength or the joint stability to run, let alone skate."

Cory scanned the crowd. Then, with all of his weight on his left leg, he extended the right, straight out in front of him, arms out from his chest. Cory then lowered himself to a squatting position. "This is called a shoot-the-duck squat. I can't tell you how many times I fell on my ass trying to do this. First I used two chairs for balance. Then one. Then, after six months, no hands."

It was pin-drop silent. Squatting, holding that position on the edge of the stage, Cory continued. "I told the doc that I thought I would skate again. I said I recognized that he'd looked at hundreds, maybe thousands, of x-rays and no doubt, was renowned. 'But doc,' I told him, 'there are things that can't be x-rayed.'" Cory slowly began to rise to the standing position. When he was fully upright, the auditorium erupted in applause. Cory held out his hand for quiet. "I apologize for the stage calisthenics, but I wanted to make sure I had your full attention before introducing the very surgeon of whom I speak. He is here today. Doc, would you please stand."

Heads pivoted as the auditorium filled with the sound of shifting bodies. In the middle of the auditorium a distinguished-looking bald man stood and straightened his corduroy sports coat.

"Good morning, Dr. Pauley," Cory said loudly.

"Good morning to you, Cory" the doctor replied, holding out an arm and bowing broadly. "I, quite literally, stand corrected."

The crowd laughed in appreciation.

"And so do I," Cory bowed in return. "I'd like you all to give a round of applause to one of the best surgeons in this country." Cory began clapping and the auditorium joined. The applause died down as Cory walked back to the podium, adjusted the angle of the microphone, and picked up where he'd left off.

"The will of the man I just introduced found its way to my knee. This is a man who studied when others didn't. This is a man who left home to do his residency when others slept through re-runs on their parents' couch. He found a way to repair my knee so I, in turn, could have the chance to find my will.

"The point is, will moves. Will is restless. Will is inspirational. Will is one more page of the textbook. One more time down the ice for the puck. One more phone call to the company that wasn't taking interviews. One more attempt to tell those you care about how important they are."

Cory paused and glanced up into the lights to see where Hanna and Singer sat.

"Thank you, doc, for coming. I mean it. Thank you." Cory waited as the surgeon nodded, and then was reseated.

"Find what you have will for, each of you. Find what can't be quantified—what can't be x-rayed—and apply it wholeheartedly to the place that belongs to you. You will reach it. You. Will. Thank you. Now could someone please wake up the guy in the last row?"

SPRING 1985

First laughter. Then applause. Then a standing ovation. The din escorted Cory back to his seat. The applause did not buoy him. Instead, appreciation piled on the valedictorian's shoulders, causing his posture to begin to close down.

But ever playing the part of invincible athlete, Cory straightened, faced the auditorium, produced a compulsory smile, and offered a last quick wave.

Then to himself: *Good thing admission was free.*

HOMESKY

HomeSky puked.
Odd, she thought, pulling her hand along her temple, finding little hair there to pin back from the next wave of nausea. One would think that more than three years of short-cropped hair would replace the memory of a lifetime of wearing it long, but it did not. The long shimmering hair of love can be shorn and shorn and shorn again, but not altogether cut.

HomeSky retched again. This time, her head lurching forward, struck the porcelain bowl. A small knot raised purple on her forehead. The thread of bile in her stomach now hung from her open mouth. Cold perspiration beaded her forehead, wiped away with trembling fingers. HomeSky examined the cold sheen on her pale fingertips before closing her eyes to the yellow throbbing inside her head. *I'm so sorry.*

She wobbled to her feet and stood barefoot. The bathroom tile left square impressions on her bare knees, which she rubbed absentmindedly as the shower warmed. Not sure if her uniform was clean or dirty, HomeSky went to find the most recent mound of laundry. As she stepped from the bathroom into the bedroom, her foot struck an empty bottle and sent it careening into another, next to the mattress, which also lay on the floor. HomeSky's head jerked in sharp recall of that hollow, glassy note. She recognized the sound like a dog knows its master's voice. Childhood. Her father. Their trailer on the reservation. His boots scattering empty liquor bottles to make a path as he weaved for the door to empty his stomach just as she had. *How can this be my sound after I ran so far from it?* She dropped her face into her hands but rancid breath forced her head upright.

HomeSky blinked her waitress uniform into focus, cast atop a pile of dirty clothes across the room of her efficiency apartment. She was late for work. Again.

Saturday was no day to be late at Mick's Diner. The weekend breakfast rush was a well-established event. All the patrons knew it, which served only to push the rush earlier in an attempt to beat it.

At the diner, you'd find the limited booths, tables and counter space claimed by a ragtag, eclectic mix—a downtown mix. There'd be the local empty nesters with little to say to one another as they silently handed newspaper sections back and forth. The paunchy salesmen with beepers and neckties loosened against white shirts with reports to look over, leaving in a hurry with food between their teeth. The elderly and the dispossessed, paying monthly rates to live around the corner in the rundown motel. By HomeSky's scheduled clock-in time, the early regulars, the unshaven third-shifters at the newspaper press and the hoist manufacturing plant would have come and gone. Tables would be wiped down and ashtrays cleaned as a few hungover college sharpies would slide in a booth, shoulder-to shoulder, rumpled, laughing, enshrining last night's conquests, craving grease.

HomeSky brushed her teeth, choosing to stare down the drain hole. Had she cared to use the small mirror that doubled as the medicine cabinet door, she would have seen that her short-cropped black hair was now beyond flecked with gray, bringing her closer to looking her 45 years. Her reflection would have startled her. She chose not to witness it.

Was it so long ago that she sat in the embrace of her farmhouse, at her bedroom vanity, her grandmother's mahogany hairbrush in hand? Her moccasins off her feet as her bare toes rested on the cool plank floor, her head canted opposite the side of her long brushstrokes, which only occasionally teased a single gray hair out of the silken blackness. Her humming would cease as she plucked it, smiling at her reflection and the old Ojibwe myth that for every gray hair pulled, another beautiful girl is born to steal the eye of your husband.

HomeSky flipped off the lights and left her apartment wondering how long it had been, or if it had been. She winced. Yes, it had been, evidenced by her purse, and what was inside. These things—the clothes on her back when she left, and the picture—were all she took.

Outside HomeSky's apartment was a bus line that emptied into downtown St. Paul, the lesser-regarded of Minnesota's Twin Cities. St. Paul has a blue-collar sensibility that eased HomeSky's anxieties some. It was closer to what she'd known. It was also the city she once traveled to when her son, Joseph, led most of their hometown of Baudette on a journey south to play in the State High School Hockey Tournament. It was here that Joseph came up against Cory, and his hometown team, for the state championship.

St. Paul was as unpresumptuous as brick. It was a place that left you alone if you so wished. She could think of nowhere else to go with the smell of burning rafters in her hair. And where shampoo failed, scissors and alcohol succeeded. Somewhat.

The nine-fifteen city bus looked to be on time, bright sunshine leaping off its arced windshield as it approached from two blocks off. The weather was warm, but she wrapped herself in a coat. Cory wouldn't be taking the university stage for a few hours yet, she thought. He had sent a note to her PO Box. Cory had been good about respecting her wishes to keep her address private. He understood privacy.

HomeSky stepped onto the bus. She moved toward the back seats as a few smiled kindly her way. *Take your eyes off me. I am not here.*

On this magnificent May morning, she was dressed in a stained blue winter coat. The morning sun played through the windows, flickering off her as she went—like the slow projection of movie frames. This gaunt woman, head down, her hands holding her coat closed where the broken zipper could not, the socks with their tired elastic, the faded jogging shoes spotted with grease, the darkness under her eyes. Frame by frame, window by window, she passed.

And then, HomeSky smiled. Why she might was as mysterious as the smile itself. She took her seat as the bus jerked forward. She had found her place, in the back, next to a left-behind glove.

SINGER & HANNA

Singer clapped and clapped and smiled his lovely smile.
He heard Cory's name introduced, big and loud, rising up. He loved Cory. Love love loved Cory. More than 50 chocolate pies. More than 200 trains. More than 1000 rainbows. This was a game they played—who loved whom more than what.

He could see Cory walking to the stage, climbing the steps. Applause filled in everywhere. How Singer enjoyed clapping, especially with others. He clapped his small hands red.

Hanna had him on her lap, but excitement moved through the boy like voltage so she set him free, back onto his own seat next to her. He was a big boy now. Almost four. He'd be fine there, even in the first row of balcony seats, so close to the railing.

Hanna clapped too, but less fervently. With her journalist's eye she had attentively watched Cory stand upon introduction, as his hand reflexively moved behind his ear to the stone she knew was braided there. She had felt this stone many times. When in the dizzying center of their embrace, her hands moving up his back, her fingers passing through his hair, the stone would brush her fingertips. But upon touching it, she'd abruptly divert her hand. It was a trespass.

Cory and Hanna had been together for over three years. Although *together* is a relative concept. Despite her uncertainties about their relationship, there was no questioning Cory's love for her son. Cory and Singer could not have been more together. Hanna recognized this was necessary. Singer was working his miracles.

During the first 18 months of Singer's life, when Cory finally agreed to trust his arms and reach for her baby, he and Hanna took careful steps toward one another, too. But as time went on, she had started to wonder if their relationship was more about Singer.

Cory had come to enjoy helping Hanna. Giving the baby a warm bottle. Trusting himself to bathe the child. They were together, surely, but when he kissed her, did he look past her? Could she feel Cory moving beyond her—around her? Certainly, she had known no one like Cory, so it was impossible to interpret his ways. On the other hand, the sight of Singer visibly changed him—released a part of him strictly guarded. He'd scoop up Singer and they'd look at each other in their sparkling secret.

Then he'd smell Singer's backside and change his diaper. He'd take it personally when losing to diaper rash. He learned to swaddle Singer and put him down for a nap. And more and more, they'd end up napping together on the living room carpet, the worn yellow shag, laying in the room's very center, the safest distance from stairs or sharp-ended tables should Cory sleep soundly, too. Cory was short on sleep. These naps made the world stop and the thinking cease. Simplicity would spread through the room like a fragrance.

Oftentimes, Singer would fall to sleep on Cory's chest, to the low soothing reverberations of Cory's humming. Cory had never been much for humming, or for any type of music, but he had discovered how it reversed the boy's worst moods. Singer's eyelids would grow heavy, remaining closed longer each time they shut, fighting, trying to keep looking at Cory. Then sleep. There in the center of that room was pure interdependence.

Hanna learned to quietly close the front door when she came home from the news station. She'd slip into the perimeter of the room and breathe it in, her coat still buttoned. The sight of them settled her, slowing her breathing to match theirs. She'd be between the six o'clock newscast and the 10, and bearing witness to the two of them sleeping took the tension from her neck. More so, it made her want to cry. But she did not, unsure what emotion to designate to the tears.

Hanna had arranged a three-month leave of absence following Singer's birth. After that, even to her surprise, Hanna transitioned back to the anchor desk at Channel 6 with hardly a hitch. Only 26, her career gaining consistent upward momentum, she couldn't help but wonder where it might lead. Phone calls from larger-market stations came in on average once a week. She put them off. But there was one particularly bold station owner in Philadelphia who told her he didn't take no for an answer. Just when she thought he'd moved on, another bouquet of roses or bottle of obscure wine would appear.

Despite her apparent confidence, the mother-career conflict tormented Hanna, beginning in pregnancy. But never did it express itself as starkly as in the first night after Singer's birth. The moment remained vivid, despite the passing years. She could pinpoint the night because she attributed the event to trace medication left over in her system.

The dream began with Hanna standing on an empty sidewalk. Then came a gruesome sound—low, grinding, chewing, getting louder and louder and louder. She didn't know what was coming at first, but because this dream recurred, she soon knew that this awful sound was followed by the appearance of a massive boulder, rolling down the sidewalk. The boulder came toward her and stopped. She took a few steps away, again it would roll, following her. When she stopped, it stopped. In her dream she wanted to run, but dared not. She feared she couldn't remain in front of the boulder's momentum. Hanna was an objective journalist, not prone to psychoanalyze or to label the symbolism of dreams. Leftover drugs and raging hormones were her explanations as she sat up in bed, sweat-soaked. But long after hormones balanced and drugs departed, the dream persisted.

Cory's transition from college hockey prodigy to hobbled afterthought was quietly turbulent. He transferred his college credits and registered for his junior year at the University of Minnesota Duluth, but then decided not to attend classes. He put together a few part-time jobs. He worked his knee and body back into enviable shape. He found a cabin to rent on a lake 30 minutes from Duluth. This got him away from his past, and closer to Hanna and Singer.

There was a lot of back and forth for Cory, between staying with Pat for weeks at the Baudette farmhouse, and living out at the cabin, and keeping a few things at Hanna's. He was searching for a home. His return trips to Baudette became fewer and further between. To all appearances, he seemed to be out of the woods. But he made no friends.

In that first full summer after Joseph's death, when Singer was about to turn one, Cory began taking the baby for walks up and down the steep hills of Duluth. Cory said that carrying the boy up such terrain was conditioning for his knee, but the therapy went deeper. To hold a child, to have him sleep in your arms, it lifted something from him.

Spending weekend nights at Hanna's became a regular occurrence, but Cory wasn't sleeping well. Then, somewhere around month 11, Singer went from sleeping like a college student to showing all the symptoms of advanced colic.

Cory would take the wide-awake, very vocal child out for long nighttime strolls. "We're going out to hit a few bars." Cory would smile, squeeze Hanna's tired hand, pull on a baseball cap, lightly wrap the boy, and head out the door.

As more teeth pushed through, sleep became more elusive. Nothing seemed to work, so Cory went to the library, looked up colic, and there at the top of the page was a word: humming. The hell, he thought. He'd tried everything else.

Cory's walks stretched into the one- and two-hour range. This called for a change in strategy. He fashioned a papoose by knotting the arms of a sweatshirt, slinging it around his neck and creating a front pouch that cradled the boy there against his chest. After a few hills the wails would lose steam and there would only be the sound of footfalls mixed with Cory's humming. It was here, with the houses black and the town asleep under the kind summer sky, that this sleeping child had the music gifted to him awakened. Singer would stir, stretching out a little fist, his body atremble, and a tiny sound would leave him: a perfectly pitched musical note.

Not long after, the child didn't speak his first words, he sang them.

As Cory approached the stage, the auditorium surged. The applause built layer upon layer. Each consecutive row stood, like a rose opening. Hanna's eyes moistened. At her side, Singer clapped with no small measure of his heart. The boy stood at the balcony railing. He balanced on one foot. A simple act of faith.

Then, swept up in the jubilation, Singer peed in his big-boy underwear.

SPRING 1985

LU ANN

Garlic.

Lu Ann cupped her small hand over her mouth and nose and breathed out. *Oh God, definitely garlic.* Into her handbag she went for a half stick of sugar-free gum. But no sooner was that portion in her mouth, was she was back in the purse, doubling her decision.

Her mind was going faster than cows on roller skates, an expression she typically saved for the more distractible customers at the diner she owned in Baudette, Minnesota. She blinked. She leaned into the words of Cory's commencement address. She pinched her thigh. But her mind sat squarely on the empty seat next to her. *Where was he? Had she gone and scared Pat off?*

"Are you and Pat an item?" was the question she was hearing lately from her more elderly customers at the diner. They asked with sparkling hopefulness. As a 39-year-old woman, mother of two grown children, she couldn't help but blush. Were they? More and more, she found herself looking out the window intoxicated by the lightheadedness of a full-on crush. Or was it more? Not that she had much experience to say. Lu Ann encountered the one and only love of her life in high school, and it led to her beautiful baby twins. Strange though, when an intense experience resides in life's distant landscape, separated by such emptiness—you begin to question ever being consumed by the feelings in the first place. Lu Ann knew little of touch, outside the touch of her children. No wonder she was unsure in defining what she and Pat had or were or might be. And considering *his* past, he was even less qualified to speak to it.

At the diner, Lu Ann would allow her mind to drift to thoughts of them together, warm in each other's arms. Such mutual need—each with their catching up to do. Together, she thought, they were like a beautiful black-and-white photograph, like it had been this way for years. Then, absentmindedly, she would overfill a water glass where the Swenson bachelors were having egg salad with chips. She'd pop back to the here and now, holding a handful of wet napkins.

Where was Pat? It couldn't have been more unlike him to miss Cory's valedictory address; today likely meant more to Pat than to Cory. Was there anything unusual about him last night, she wondered?

They had had dinner at the farmhouse. Oh, what beauty when May bumps up against June on a farm in northern Minnesota. The homecoming, so long in coming. With treetops painted greener by the day, now fully leafed and holding a new hatch of finches testing sunlight on their wings. The sky seemed lifted, offering more fresh air to breathe. The grass on the south-pitched hillside, now tall enough for wind to tumble down.

It was, to her recollection, a perfect evening. They talked of Lu Ann putting through a twenty-five cent price hike at the diner, of overdue errands and about a neighbor's teenager who had a scrape with the law. They talked almost as a married couple might, comfortable, occasionally inattentive.

She'd surprised him with a gift of a sports coat for Cory's commencement ceremony. The bright yellow color, she thought, would offset Pat's blue eyes nicely. The coat might indeed have been a bit small, but she had driven to the Twin Cites for it, he knew that. He insisted it was perfect.

As the evening closed, would he invite her to stay? She'd been coming for dinner to the farmhouse for months now, an overnight bag always stolen away in her trunk under the emergency blanket. After the dishes were put up, Lu Ann had stepped into the bathroom, put on lip gloss, pulled back her hair, giving the wrinkles around he eyes a short massage before taking a deep breath. On the porch they sat centered on the white painted swing that Pat had taken out of storage and re-hung for the season. They sat close, Pat's new coat opposite them, folded over the swing's arm.

But once again, he kissed her with finality, standing on the porch after saying goodnight. Lu Ann had heard it said that if a man kisses you just before he utters the word goodnight, he doesn't mean it. But if he kisses you after goodnight is spoken, the decision to part has been made.

Pat had flipped on the overhead porch light, its brightness muting the stars. They stepped off the porch in the direction of Lu Ann's car. This was the porch, a thought reminded Lu Ann, that Pat had rebuilt with his hands. For HomeSky. So too, the house. Was he able to truly share this with any other? And what about the stars? Were they, too, for HomeSky, once, again, and forever?

SHERIFF HARRIS

"Son of a tailor," Sheriff Thurgood Harris half-cursed. He had twice tapped the right pocket of his pressed uniform shirt, and finding no pack of Camel Straights there, he used one of the amended expletives from a list approved by his deceased wife, Amanda. She had always been clear about one thing: a sheriff stands in front of his community as a role model. Once words leave your mouth, she had warned, they can't be withdrawn, just as a bell, once rung, can't be unrung. So be careful my dear, she'd say. Keep your badge shined and your elocution spotless. She would look up, directly into his eyes, cock her head and raise her eyebrows, signaling that a prompt response was required. The Sheriff would comply with a reluctant nod before leaning down to accept a soft kiss on the cheek, his compensation for being attentive to her scolding.

These days, though, the Sheriff found himself more prone to string expletives together like boxcars. Not here, though; not now.

SPRING 1985

There was something about the aura of the auditorium—the pageantry. It put him on his best behavior. He tapped his left pocket. The Vantages weren't residing in their usual place either.

No guns in either holster. The Sheriff frowned. For most of his adult life he had kept two brands of cigarettes in his front shirt pockets. Camel Straights on the right, Vantage on the left. He had promised to cut the Camels out of the rotation, to go just with Vantage, but that never quite transpired.

It wouldn't be easy to slip out for a smoke, anyway, the Sheriff consoled himself. Both the uniform and the Sheriff's size guaranteed that. This wasn't a man who blended into woodwork. Nonetheless, now with Cory's commencement speech finished—which, to the Sheriff's reckoning, went damn fine well—and the ceremony advancing to the presentation of diplomas, flashes popping, there was something lightheaded in this sensory mixture that triggered a craving.

The hell, he steeled his resolve. He'd made a bet—and he'd rather quit smoking than lose a bet to Pat. He'd never hear the end of it. Sheriff Harris wondered again where Pat might be. Strange.

The Sheriff had driven the police cruiser down from Baudette to the campus with Monsignor Kief, the retired priest from his lifelong parish. The Sheriff always preferred company when embarking on an extended trip by car. There was a time when he couldn't have made the drive alone, but thankfully, those days were behind him. Still, getting inside a vehicle wasn't his cup of tea. To this day, he couldn't bring himself to buckle in. That metallic click sent a jolt of fear through him.

Of all those claiming to be proud of Cory today, perhaps none topped the Sheriff. He'd watched Cory struggle back to his feet after the repeated kicks that life had landed. In Cory, the Sheriff saw a boy pulling himself up from an abyss. And just as the boy's fingers clawed over the ledge, there stood the good Lord, ready to stomp on his hands again. "The boy's been given shaved dice to throw," the Sheriff told his dear Amanda. He apologized for saying so aloud, but things were what they were. When he looked at Cory, he saw things that made him angry with God. Being a man of justice, he could find little in Cory's case.

As the diplomas were handed out along with sturdy handshakes, the Sheriff's thoughts carried him back. To the inescapable cold of Lake of the Woods. To the body under the rustling tarp. To the 13-year-old with his bandaged hand and eyes looking fiercely past him. *Had the boy seen too much?* the Sheriff wondered. He'd known a few men in the war like that. As the Sheriff wondered, he unconsciously tapped his prosthetic fingers against the handrest of the chair next to him. Tap tap tap tap tap. Until Monsignor Kief gently laid his hand on his friend's forearm.

SPRING 1985

MONSIGNOR KIEF

And, good Father, for this boy, a modicum of peace.
The Monsignor finished his prayer on Cory's behalf. The blind priest opened his eyes, remembering an innocent question once asked some forty years ago. A inquisitive young girl sitting in their Sunday school circle tapped his leg and asked, "If you're blind, Father, why do close your eyes to pray?" Hmm, a fair and wise question, he commended the child. Closing your eyelids, he explained to the group, tells us it's time to look inside, not outside. Blind or sighted, we all need to start our search for answers by looking here. Monsignor Frank Kief touched his chest. The children found that to be among the funniest of notions. Looking inside. What would you see, they laughed? Pancakes! Bacon! Juice!

As years passed, when someone would happen upon Monsignor Kief, his eyes closed in a moment of reflection, they'd devoutly apologize for the interruption. He'd merrily reply: not to worry. I was just admiring this morning's pancake breakfast. He'd again close his eyes, leaving the person flummoxed as he or she tiptoed away.

Frank Kief was born sighted. He had almost 18 years of excellent vision before a degenerative retinal disorder gradually consumed his eyesight. During the final year of the disease, his world crept inward as the aperture of his vision narrowed, leaving the edges darkly muted. It was then that the first thoughts of the seminary graced his consciousness. How unlikely, he thought, for he was little for religion, or prayer. The same could be said for his parents. On my life, he could remember telling people, I don't recall mustering a single prayer in my early years. Never. Suddenly, he was more than making up for lost time as prayer became as much a part of him as his inevitable blindness. As he aged, it became more and more clear to the Monsignor how alike prayer and blindness are. You must trust things unseen.

About the same time, he was putting the finishing touches on what he called Big Scrapbook. Visual images he'd mentally collected in hopes of saving forever. The cloud-rippled sky five minutes after sunset when the orange is absorbed by the undersides of the clouds and the blue and violet and purple separate over the horizon. Or a sky so full of stars that to look up is to be equally shocked by their number, their proximity and their mystery. Or how the full gray of low morning clouds pulls green's ideal hue out of a rolling pasture, as though the color were still wet from creation. The Monsignor's Big Scrapbook was full of what he called "nature showing off." As his sight left him, he began thinking more and more about the Maker of these pictures and how outstanding it would be to get to know Him better.

Finishing his silent petition for Cory, the Monsignor wondered how the acoustics in the college auditorium could be so inadequate. The Monsignor had been concentrating on Cory's speech about will—a concept he was no stranger to—and was moved to prayer. But it wasn't a joyful prayer.

Cory worried the elderly priest. He'd cherished the boy, from the first words they shared when Cory was 13, having hitchhiked to his rectory in disobedience of his mother. Yet tonight, as the Monsignor listened to the litany of Cory's accomplishments, the confident rhetoric, the wallpaper of words—what caught his ear was something hardly perceptible. Something in the boy's tone. Words can deceive. In the tone, one finds the bare expression of the heart.

Monsignor Kief closed his eyes. *Give the boy some happiness now, Father.*

The Monsignor searched for the precise word to label the subterranean quality in Cory's tone. During such moments of concentration, the Monsignor would unconsciously pull at the hair on his forearm.

The label he found was neither profound nor complex, but it was fitting. Cory's tone was joyless. Monsignor Kief wondered how he could help Cory find the happiness God intended him. How to tell him that faith isn't so hard for those who have lost much. For people like us, he knew, faith had ironic inevitability.

Monsignor Kief had abundant faith. More so, he had faith that Cory, finally, was on the forward edge of the muddled shadows. Cory, with Hanna in his life, and the boy—his Singer. He was a sunray, the child, pouring through a fissure in the clouds.

But why was it the Monsignor felt such a presence of darkness? He shivered and tried to cast the feeling out. But darkness moves unexpectedly. It sat among them. Foul, dithering, uninvited.

STU AND DARLENE

A brown bag holding a meatloaf sandwich in wax paper sat on Darlene's lap.

She had made it for Cory in the long dark of the morning, before she and her husband, Stu, had left the resort they owned on Lake of the Woods. They would come to see Cory have his day in the sun—at long last. He might need a little something to eat after his speech, she had told Stu, as he watched her halve the sandwich with a butcher knife. Stu thought about that. Agreeing, he said that he too might be hungry and maybe she could—but her look stopped him there. Can't fault a guy for trying, he told her with a shrug, walking off to watch the coffee pot percolate.

How they loved Cory, these two. How something as small as two human hearts could contain such expansive love is a mystery answered in another place and another time. Less mystifying, though, was the *why* of their love. As is often the case, love this unbounded is dropped from high. You happen to be standing in the right place, as they were, when Cory rowed his boat out of the vastness, with his daylong-dead father under the wind-torn tarp. A red-cheeked boy with his runny nose and vacant gray-green eyes that wouldn't meet theirs. Innocence drained. Thirteen years old. My Lord. The theft in those 24 hours. Cory landed and their hearts made space.

On the stage, Cory stood before them now. Valedictorian. Handsome and grown. His hair, which Darlene thought the color of wet sand, had a wisp of curl to it. When he did smile, the short-lived appearance of his crescent-shaped dimples left her aching. Cory. Sure. Strong. A smidge too thin to Darlene's liking. But he looked good. She hoped he was good.

The effects of the day's early start and long drive were at work on Stu. His head bobbed. The kick in the shin he received from Darlene carried just the right mix of discretion and force. His eyes snapped open and he sat up straight once again.

Stu had successfully groomed his hair but he'd inadvertently missed a few spots shaving. Handling predawn toiletries will do that to a man as he ages. The tufts of gray on his chin and neck stood out, but fortunately Darlene's eyesight wasn't what it once was, either.

He wore the shirt that she had ironed and put out. Rarely did Darlene have cause to heat an iron, but on one such occasion when she was at the ironing board, Stu happened into the room behind her. Humming, unaware of his presence, she remained at work on a particularly stubborn wrinkle. Her tune ceased just long enough for Darlene to put down a little spit on the fabric. That seemed to do the trick as the iron hissed and she pressed the wrinkle smooth. Stu quietly backed out of the room, secretly pleased. Darlene would have been mortified had she been caught improvising so, but for Stu, ironed shirts were never again the protest they once were. For the necktie he wore, Stu had little patience. They would all be outside soon. He'd get that lawyer's noose off and stuff it in the glove box when the coast was clear.

Before leaving their resort, they had visited Cory's tree. In the awakening sky, the dark shapes, backed up against the horizon, were just beginning to separate and come forward, identifying themselves as trees and outcroppings and islands.

Standing before the 12-foot pine, it was made clear to Darlene and Stu how time marches on. They had joined hands, each silently revisited memories from 12 years ago. It was the day Cory and Stu had returned from the big water with the very tree they stood before now, then but a freshly dug seedling to transplant. Cory had his reasons for this planting; it was left at that. They covered the hairy ball of immature roots in the sandy soil mix, drove a stake next to it, and twined it straight and toward the sun. Stu had said that in that first week, he'd watered that seedling enough with tears alone. In the months following, with Cory back home, Darlene and Stu would regularly visit this place, each with a half pail of lake water. Through that first summer, they nurtured the bent seedling, tying and retying it to the stake, hoping to orient skyward. It was as though the tree's survival and Cory's were linked.

Cory returned the resort more regularly in those first few years, and they'd all come to this spot, with Cory carrying the water pails. Stu could conjure up little to say beyond the platonic: who's growing faster? Or the laconic: who's more talkative? Darlene remembered there was a second seedling, one that Cory took home with him in an old minnow bucket. She always meant to ask about it, but when the moment arrived, she surprised herself by remaining silent.

Now, the resort owners looked at Cory at the podium, proud as they could be. Cory had grown straight and tall and strong. But as Cory addressed the crowd, Darlene's thoughts receded from the stage. She wondered about that second tree that Cory took with him. And try as she did, Darlene couldn't help but wonder what else Cory took with him that day. The interior stuff, as Stu called it.

SPRING 1985

REG

It isn't exactly clear when Reg Cunningham started hearing things.

Despite significant hearing loss in one ear, sounds were often there. Clear and near and breathy. A voice. Of the shivering sort. For him alone.

Maybe it was childhood when it began, or early teens—Reg had repressed all memory of its initiation. Yet the sounds would pin him, despite the room being empty. The yard, empty. The garage, cluttered, but empty. No other soul. It came and went without regard for predictability or pattern. In the last year, it was behind him more and more. Ready to pounce.

It was the voice of Kemp. That nasal bastard with his pinched-in nose and close-set eyes and hands like stones. But he heard more than Kemp. There were the associated sounds that refused to dissipate with time, but rather, clung in his consciousness like bats.

He'd hear, for instance, the quiet way a boot approaches on grass. He'd hear the rusty creak of a shed door. The nearby church bells. Glass breaking. Empty gas cans kicked aside. And the laughter. Regardless of what they put in his ears, no matter how hard he clamped his hands there, he heard the high laughter.

Oftentimes these sounds didn't trigger an obvious physical start in Reg Cunningham. That's how paralytic fear strikes. Freezing. Shoulders tensely drawn. Eyes clamped shut. Slowly, he'd reopen to the world, expecting fully to find the source of the sound hulking over him. There was nothing. He'd scoff then, filling the dead air with curses. If it were in reach—and it often was—he'd take a drink. Eventually, he'd uncoil, and get back to what he had been doing. Maybe he was taking a rake down from a garage nail. Perhaps stepping into the shower. It was especially bad when driving. Hearing the voice reach out from the back seat. He'd hunch down, getting small, letting off the accelerator and coasting to the side of the road, only to find the seat behind him empty when he eventually braved a look in the rear view mirror. Reg would curse, give the back seat a hard middle finger, and reach under his seat for the brown paper bag of amber courage. There he would have a taut swallow. Fight fire with fire. That was Reg's motto.

His cane hung on the back of the empty auditorium seat in front of him. As Cory took the stage, Reg was motionless in his chair. He sat in the last arcing row of seats, blending in with parents and friends who hustled in late. Reg was sly enough to melt into a group.

Cory spoke and Reg took out his billfold, pulling out a folded rectangle of newsprint from the *Baudette Region*. The article was creased and well-worn from repeated handling over the past week.

CORY BRADFORD TO GIVE COLLEGE COMMENCEMENT SPEECH.

Baudette's favorite adopted son, Cory Bradford, will give the valedictory address to the University of Minnesota Duluth's class of 1985 next Saturday at Fink Auditorium.

SPRING 1985

Most in our community will remember Cory as a close friend and college teammate of Baudette's pride and joy, Joseph Blackholm. Cory and Joseph were part of the NCAA hockey championship team in 1980-1981.

Many of us will also remember that these boys met as high school rivals in one of the most fabled Minnesota state hockey tournament championship games ever played—a game covered by the national media, including Sports Illustrated!

Cory will graduate with honors from the University of Minnesota Duluth, and plans to make his home in the area, teaching high school math and coaching hockey.

Any and all interested in attending the commencement speech this Saturday should contact Sheriff Thurgood Harris or Monsignor Frank Kief. They will be leading the caravan driving to the Duluth Auditorium, leaving from Lu Ann's diner. Breakfast at 8:00. On the road promptly at 8:45. Sheriff Harris has warned that all who are late will be left behind.

Favorite adopted son, my left one, Reg seethed. He looked at his cane dangling from the back of the seat in front of him.

Reg meticulously folded the clipping and slid it back into his wallet. He took a moment to adjust his shirt, smoothing it across his thin chest. He quite liked the shirt, liked how it said he was a man with places to go. It was short-sleeved, a polyester blend, if he correctly recalled what the shop girl had said. He'd found it on the discount rack at Night & Day, a clothier on the second block of Main Street in Baudette. Even the clerk who worked there had to admit it looked sharp. He'd come to know her a little bit from shopping there over the past months. Once a week, maybe twice, he'd look over the bargains, pull out a few hangers, try on a thing or two, ask her opinion. She was nice, unlike most high school lowlifes. Certainly not like his daughter, Lu Ann, who at that age couldn't keep her skirt down in a still wind. They're all no good. Except maybe this one at Night & Day.

Over time, the record would show, Reg Cunningham purchased eight shirts and seven pair of dress slacks from her. He had no occasion to wear most of these things. Hell, that's not why he bought them. He had his reasons. When they came to clean out his closets, he wasn't going to be labeled a bum. He was going to have respectable things on hangers.

SPRING 1985

HANNA

Hanna wasn't born with the cleaning gene. But there are times when one's nature doesn't win the day. And today, Hanna left no dust speck unturned. Methodically, mindlessly, she'd moved through her house, cleaning everything. It was only when she found herself outside, wiping down the doorknob, that she recognized she'd gone off the deep end, and tossed the rag down the laundry chute. Actually she let Singer throw it down the chute. It was part of the routine Cory had started him on. Ball up the rag, stand back a few steps, toss it down the chute. Same with the socks. Working on hand-eye coordination. Always.

There would be 10 coming to celebrate Cory's graduation. For the moment the guest of honor had gone out for a few bags of ice; the late May afternoon had edged into the seventies, a temperature that Duluth summer days are lucky to flirt with, what with Lake Superior lording over such matters.

SINGER

Singer was transitioning out of regular naps, but the morning's event left him out cold on the couch. What a big day of car rides and clapping and running down long auditorium hallways playing Hide Cory's Tie. Sleeping, Singer's curls were momentarily restrained, held to his forehead by droplets of sweat. The boy couldn't have been further from the dervish he was just hours ago.

Hanna gently sat beside her child, her darling, dreading disturbing this peace. She watched his little checked dress shirt rise and fall and wondered why God chose to bestow such a miracle upon her. Every mother sees her child as a miracle, but few have outright evidence of it. She let her fingers rest against his warm cheek.

Singer's father was out of the picture since birth, thanks in no small part to Hanna. Their relationship had been one of convenience, and it turns out, there's very little that's convenient about a baby wailing at two in the morning. They both recognized this. They went their separate ways.

"Hard to wake him, isn't it, hon?" Hanna's mother had stepped into the room.

"If I don't he'll be a hornet later."

"I wonder where he gets *that* from," she said, teasing. "When do you expect folks to start showing up?"

"Any minute now. I told them 2:30. Where's Dad?"

Hanna's mother looked at Singer. "He's doing his best impression of our dear little one here. Except your father's shirt is more wrinkled and he's snoring."

"Well, let's get our men up." Hanna slid her hands gently under Singer's back. He had sweat through to the couch. And he wasn't at all pleased about being moved.

Cory turned off the ignition and sat in his old yellow pickup a few blocks from home. Hanna's home, he was quick to correct himself. It wasn't that he didn't keep a few things at her place, he had a few drawers now, but it was just that: a few. Hanna had asked him about it once, but there had been no talk of it since. "I have a hard time moving things into a place," Cory had said in response to her inquiry. Hanna had frowned. "Stuff goes into a closet, Cory, or a drawer. It can come out again." She tried to keep the discussion light. But Cory had looked away. Hanna recognized the gesture. Cory had hung up.

He went through the guest list in his head. Hanna's parents, Ed and Jill. They were good people. Social. Happy. Somehow they mastered the mystery of "where do we fit in this world?" and that kept things simple. Even after 30-some years of marriage they knew when to tease, when to argue, how to make up, and how to keep a relationship from becoming cordial agony. You might even catch them outside on the door stoop sneaking a kiss and splitting a beer. Cory wished he could find some affiliation with the pair, but they were as much a mystery to him as he was to them.

Pat should be coming, but he'd been conspicuously absent from the morning ceremony. The unoccupied seat next to Lu Ann had been gaping. Cory noticed it almost immediately despite the near white-out conditions of stage lights. In the milling about after the diplomas were handed out, Lu Ann grew increasingly distracted. Sheriff Harris assured her it was a flat tire or an unexpected emergency on the Rez. He'll show, he said, doing his best to sound commanding.

Aside from Pat, the contingent from Baudette included Lu Ann, Sheriff Harris, Monsignor Kief and Radio Voice. Darlene and Stu had made it down from Lake of the Woods, for which Cory was deeply grateful. Late May and June were a busy time at the resort, with a million things to do before the onslaught of summer renters. The late spring walleyes were always going good, so a few cabins would have regulars, but more, it was the busywork of getting boats running, pounding down nail heads on the dock, getting leaky roofs shingled, cleaning grit out of weak-running showerheads, patching holes in landing nets—little jobs that were day-eaters.

Hanna and Cory had decided to keep it "just to family," a choice of words that made them both stop and look up from their to-do lists. In fact, only Hanna's parents fit the bill. Cory's mom and sisters stayed back in St. Paul "to work," his mother had informed him. We have to support <u>ourselves</u>, you know, she had underlined in her note. Cory had decided not to mention the money he'd sent every month since he'd "left her for college." We all live in our own little worlds, Monsignor Kief once told Cory. As pedestrian as that may sound, this nugget explains more behavioral oddities than a psychologist with a stack of degrees. Cory's mom, for example, lived in a world known as Woe Is Me.

He thought about his valedictory address. A bloom of heat rose through him and his back began to perspire. What was the word for what he did on stage? He ransacked his vocabulary for *le mot juste*. A stunt. That was it. Resolve can't be acted out, he chided himself.

Then it was on him. He yawned. His eyes watered. His shoulders slackened. The focus demanded by the morning's speech had turned to lead. It pulled him down, under the surface. His eyes shut, and for a moment he nodded off.

Snapping back to alertness, he was disoriented. Briefly, he'd been on the water in the small boat, pulling through the chop. "Snap to it," he commanded. "The ice is melting." He blinked and turned over the ignition. The truck in gear, he pulled away from the sidewalk in front of the church. He watched as the cross on the spire grew smaller and smaller in his side-view mirror.

Hanna and Singer had moved into a brick bungalow on Chelsy Avenue in the old north side of Duluth. The pre-World War One era homes were tilted high on the hill and came with a view of Lake Superior that would mesmerize you long after your coffee went cold. Hanna's modest home had a second story dormer with a window seat in Singer's bedroom that faced the big water. That was her selling point; she had always dreamt of a house with a window seat. Here, she and Singer would sit, cuddled, watching the sun rise over the endless silver lake. To have an early riser had become an unexpected fortune—it made Hanna shudder. To sit with a life that is new, blanketed in your lap, and watch the day start, this Hanna knew she must find time for. But there was career. Relentless,

relentless career. She wished to pretend otherwise, but a career can move like a cloud between you and the sunrise.

They called their sitting place the spider window because more often than not, a spider would make its way up the dark varnished window trim. As the years passed, a box of Kleenex became a mainstay there. Now, when the bug made its quiet entrance, Singer would pull a tissue out and hand it to his mother. He would then apologize to the spider for what was about to take place.

From their window seat they saw Cory's truck pull up.

"Where's Cory going, Mommy?" Singer asked.

"No, honey. He's coming back. He went for ice … to the store."

"Why's he going there?" Singer pointed to where Cory parked, well up the street.

"I bet he's leaving room in front for our party guests to park."

"So they'll get here sooner!" Singer beamed.

"Yes, honey."

Darlene and Stu were the first to step through the door, and they did so, formally, yet quickly, as if some critter might race in behind them. They immediately offered to remove their shoes. Hanna assured them not to worry, but they insisted. They didn't want to be tracking anything into her nice house. City houses are different from cabins that way, Stu told her, having trouble pulling off his right boot.

Sheriff Harris was the next guest up the front steps. Lingering on the stoop, squinting at the compact bungalow, he wondered if it might be incompatible with his mass.

"Darlene, welcome. Welcome all." Hanna's smile lit up the entryway. What a gift to have a smile like hers. Hanna greeted Darlene with a hug; they had all shook hands earlier at the graduation ceremony and Hanna wasn't sure her fingers could withstand Darlene's grip a second time.

Stu lined up for his hug. "I'll take one of those. I'm as likely to see a muskrat tap dance as find a pretty young lady offering hugs." He gave Hanna a hearty one-armed squeeze. "Here you are then."

Stu handed Hanna a tin canister. "Darlene's World Fair quality caramel corn." Stu smiled proudly.

"What's left of it." Darlene swung a stocking foot at Stu but missed.

Stu offered a big shoulder shrug and licked his fingers for dramatic effect.

Sheriff Harris came in next. He handed Hanna an envelope and a present covered in two times the wrapping paper required. "The box here is for Singer," the Sheriff said. "A puzzle," he whispered, sidestepping his way across the threshold with surprising stealth. Sheriff Harris was not a hugger.

Cory came into the living room holding Singer's hand. Hanna's parents trailed in behind, smoothing their slacks, straightening shirt cuffs. Everyone said hello at a volume above what was necessary.

"Any sign of Pat?" Cory asked.

"Harder to find than a grouse in a leaf pile," Stu said, heading for a corner of the room to his liking. He turned the floor over to the Sheriff, who was an expert in such matters. The Sheriff faced the group and crossed his arms across his massive chest, resting them on the ledge of his equally sizable stomach. "Lu Ann stopped in at the convenience store down the block to make another call."

"She could call from here," Hanna protested.

"Ah," the Sheriff held up a hand like he was directing traffic. "You try telling her that. Plus Radio Voice had himself set on a Bit-O-Honey so she said she'd get two birds with one stone. Monsignor Kief went along in too." Sheriff Harris leaned against the mantle over the fireplace. "I wasn't going to argue with that bunch."

Hanna's dad absolutely loved mysteries; he jumped in. "You said Pat had phoned Lu Ann early this morning?"

The Sheriff nodded. "Seems so. Said something had come up at the Rez. Said he'd meet us at the auditorium. Nothing specific. So Lu Ann brought her own vehicle, and Radio Voice for company. Monsignor Kief rode down with me."

Singer wiggled free and walked over to the Sheriff to have a better look. He'd never seen a man of such proportions. And a uniform, too! He pointed, almost too excited to speak. "Can I see that?" Singer whispered to the Sheriff.

The Sheriff bent at the knees, getting as low as he dared. He tapped his brass sheriff's badge. "This?"

Transfixed, Singer could do no more than nod.

"Well let's find a spot on the couch and see if we can't get it off." The Sheriff looked down at the boy with his head of yellow curls and eyes as wide as tea saucers. He had no recourse but a smile. "Do you think it's taped on or glued?"

Singer frowned. "Pinned, silly." They made their way to the couch.

Five minutes later Lu Ann made her way in. There was little to report, other than it was more difficult to move Monsignor Keif out of the candy aisle than Radio Voice, who quickly made his way next to Singer so he could try on the Sheriff's badge, too.

"Just got his answering machine at the farm again," Lu Ann told the roomful of guests. "And the phone at the Rez just rang and rang." She shook her head and clasped her hands. "Men," she said feigning less concern than she really felt.

"What does he do at the reservation?" Hanna's mother asked, trying to make friendly conversation.

"He's a social worker and a counselor. Mostly for the high school kids. They don't draw a hard line in that regard. He used to be the priest there, so he knows most of the families."

"Yes, Hanna mentioned that. He sounds like an interesting person. I'm excited to talk to him."

Lu Ann eyes sparkled. "He's very generous with his time and his life." Then her countenance hardened. "Too much so, sometimes."

"I gave a shout back to the office," the Sheriff said. "Nothing. The scanner has been quiet since morning."

Lu Ann went to the front bay window and looked out. The Sheriff sat on the couch as Radio Voice and Singer took turns

47

breathing on the badge and shining it before pinning it to their shirts. They had taken out the Lincoln Logs and made a prison. The three took turns apprehending balled up Kleenexes and throwing them in jail. The Sheriff taught the boys to speak lawman: "I wouldn't blow my nose with scoundrels like you." And, "You've been hanging out in the wrong pockets of town."

Singer looked at the Sheriff. "Why do you have hard fingers on your hand?" Singer asked, touching the Sheriff's wrist.

"Oh. Well, those aren't real fingers you're looking at there. They're artificial. I had an accident and lost three of them. This is called a prosthesis. It helps my whole hand work better."

"Where was the accident?"

"In Korea. In the war."

Singer was excited to know a sheriff and a soldier. But he was confused. "How do you *lose* fingers?"

The Sheriff smiled. "Ah, that's just a way of saying things. They were hurt so bad I couldn't use 'em anymore. So I got these new ones."

"Can I feel them?" Singer asked. Hanna was watching this develop and was about to intervene. Cory took her hand and gave it a light squeeze. "He'll be fine," he whispered.

"Sure thing," the Sheriff said. He held out his hand. He was aware that others were watching, but he kept his focus on Singer. He gave him a little smile. "It's okay."

Singer put his fingers on the Sheriff's artificial fingers. He didn't draw his little hand back on contact, but instead, wrapped his fingers around the Sheriff's and left them there, tenderly. He returned the Sheriff's smile. The Sheriff swallowed. He expected a curious tap, and that'd be that. Damn, if it wasn't the most curious thing. He was familiar with the phenomenon of phantom pain, the lingering feeling that a lost limb is still there, but as God was his witness, he *felt* Singer's touch. His fingers felt the boy's fingers. It was astounding. The Sheriff's mouth fell slightly open as Singer's smile continued. The Sheriff was overwhelmed with a sensation of comfort emanating from a place that had been long dead to him. Singer released the Sheriff's hand and went back to the Lincoln Logs. The Sheriff watched, eyes moistened.

A large bowl of Chex Mix sat on the dining room table next to Darlene's tin of caramel corn. The sweet and savory combination proved irresistible, and had pulled in Hanna's parents along with Darlene and Stu. They each took up a chair and went about filling paper plates, covering the colorful "Congratulations Graduate!" with snacks. Cory brought in a few beers and sodas and an ice bucket. Stu had a soda. Darlene, a beer.

"We better use coasters," Hanna's dad warned, handing them out. "Hanna's awfully proud of her new table." Her father rapped the oak veneer and nodded. "She's doing pretty well for a girl on her own with a little one." Cory wasn't sure what that said about his role in the relationship, but Hanna's mother was quick to translate. "Yes. Quite well for a young mother without a husband." She rested her hand on her husband's forearm.

Darlene was on the verge of saying something on Cory's behalf but Stu ran interference by way of pouring a splash of beer into her glass. "Great Chex Mix," he said. "I love the light brown ones." He showed his favorite member of the Chex family to all before popping it into his mouth.

Cory reached for a handful of Darlene's caramel corn.

Hanna's mother leaned in and continued in a hushed voice. "Tell me about your friend, Radio Voice. He seems a bit ... you know, delayed."

Cory looked at Radio Voice. A lightness came over him; few people engendered such a response. In concentration, Radio Voice had the tip of his tongue slightly out, building the world's tallest jail with his friends, Singer and Sheriff.

"Radio Voice has Down syndrome," he explained to Hanna's parents. "We met at a wood pulping factory I worked at in Baudette a few years back. Pat and Radio Voice still work there together." Cory took some more caramel corn. "You should make a point to ask him about his job; he's really proud. He's got a business card: Head of Custodial Services. Pat and I printed him up a box. He doesn't want to use them up. The one in his wallet is so ratty it could be the first one he took out of the box."

Cory leaned back in his chair and winced, thinking about the days at the pulping plant. That was when he pretty much went off the deep end. On the plant floor, Radio Voice was easy pickings—the butt of endless practical jokes from a pack of imbeciles on his shift. It went beyond joking around. It was cruelty.

"The guys at the plant used to mess with Radio Voice," Cory continued. "Hide his time card, put an egg in the hood of his jacket, glue the zipper of his coat shut, take the batteries out of his radio. Their idea of entertainment."

Stu's ears went red. "Lousy cowards. Is that when you punched that guy's lights out?"

Hanna's mother looked aghast.

"That's another story," Cory said in a clipped tone that made it clear he didn't want to go there.

"Good thing he's probably oblivious to it all," Hanna's dad interjected. "He looks like a happy guy." The group watched Radio Voice sharing some Bit-O-Honey with Singer.

"He is happy," Cory said. "But you'd be surprised by how much he knows, or what he believes he knows. One day at work, Radio Voice and I were were having lunch in the break room, and I asked him if he knew what caused Down syndrome. He said he did, but he said it like he was ashamed."

Hanna's parents stopped munching their Chex Mix.

"'What's wrong?' I asked him. 'You don't have to feel bad about it.'"

"Quietly he said, 'I wish my mom didn't do that to me.' I asked what he meant. Turns out one of the guys told him that you get Down syndrome when you're about to be delivered and your mother sees how ugly you are so she squeezes her legs shut and forces you back in. She keeps her legs squeezed as long as she can

SPRING 1985

because she doesn't want you." Cory swallowed. "Radio Voice told me, 'Mom squeezed till she can't hold any more. I couldn't get enough air. It hurt my brain. That's why my brain's not very good.' I told him no, Radio Voice, that is not how it happens. 'Yeah,' he said. 'All that squeezing made my eyes squishy.' Then he touched under each of his almond-shaped eyes to show me."

Cory looked at the two couples at the table. There was just the noise of the boys playing and the clock ticking on the mantel. "He's not oblivious." Cory took a breath. "How many years did he walk around with that until we talked—until I explained things to him?"

Darlene's brow crossed. "Why on God's earth do these things happen? Where do people come from who would say such a things?" Stu rubbed her back; it was the only response available to him.

Radio Voice was now handing Lincoln Logs to Singer. He would clap when Singer notched one into place. They were building Cory's cabin.

Hanna's father asked, "I don't understand the name. Radio Voice?"

Cory chanced a smile. "Come here. I'll show you."

They walked over to where the boys were building.

"Hey, Radio Voice. Do you think you can do today's weather for us?"

"Really?" he asked excitedly.

"If you're up for it."

Radio Voice clapped his hands together and grinned. He stood up and took a swallow of soda. Then, as if a switch was flipped, he began to talk in a deep baritone voice that you'd expect from a radio personality.

"We're in for a record-breaking May doozy today so be sure to get out and soak it in. A low-pressure trough from the south has spun up a batch of perfect southern air bringing today's high to a record 77 degrees. Average highs and lows for this time are 68 and 51 degrees respectively. Break out the shorts and the grills,

Hawaii—I mean Baudette—and enjoy your first nibble of summer in nine months. Weather today is sponsored by Honey Pot septic, reminding you that a flush beats a straight every time."

Radio Voice broke into a full-face smile and joined in as the group applauded.

"I can change my voice," he enthusiastically told Hanna's parents.

"You sure can," Hanna's mother said, giving him a happy handshake. But that wasn't nearly enough compensation for Radio Voice. He pulled her in for a big hug.

In the kitchen, Hanna and Monsignor Kief partnered on the menu: pork chops, green beans, Parker House rolls, applesauce and chocolate bundt cake, a staple that Cory had come to love from working summers at Darlene and Stu's resort. Food has the power to conjure traditions of youth, but Cory had little to draw from. Hanna made it a point to serve something nostalgic.

Lu Ann, certainly the cook among the three, moved fast. From making suggestions in the kitchen to blurring to the front room's bay window. Still no sign of Pat. *Where could that man be?*

Darlene popped her head into the kitchen to see if she could be of help. "I don't want to get under your feet, but if there's anything I can do?"

"I think we're okay," Hanna said, "but I do have a question."

"Sure," Darlene said, anxious to be of help.

"Is this meal we're having considered dinner or supper? Cory told me about the difference but it's a nuance I always mess up."

"In our neck of the woods, we're having supper," Darlene explained. "Supper is more like a late lunch, usually lighter than dinner. And dinner is dinner as you know it. Is that how you refer to it, Monsignor?"

"Supper and dinner, ah yes." He smacked his lips. "As the song goes, these are a few of my favorite things. My housekeeper at the rectory," the Monsignor explained, "is quite accomplished in the way of Sunday supper, of which one particular recipe immediately comes to mind. The farmer's casserole, she calls it. A dish from her childhood. It's egg-based, with potatoes—almost au gratin style. Cheese, not sure of the particular variety. And kielbasa, I believe. Always served at 1:30 with a bottle of beer, just as her mother did. A banquet. I'm quite sure she sneaks in a few libations preparing the meal, but what I can't say with absolute certainly is whether it's the beverages or the youthful memory that makes her voice so light and bouncy. Oh, the look on her face when the lid comes off that casserole and she spoons …. I'm sorry; I'm off in the weeds. What was the question?"

"Supper or dinner," Hanna reminded him.

"Yes, of course. Supper is the short answer. Although I've never found short answers to be very satisfying."

The small kitchen was crowded with voices and tasks and the faintly sweet aroma of potatoes and carrots baking. Lu Ann checked under the kitchen towel to see if her sourdough bread dough was rising. She had used her rising trick: heating a towel in the dryer before entirely wrapping the bowl and placing it on top of the oven where it was warm. Monsignor Kief stood ready at the sink on washing detail, keeping the prep dishes from stacking up. He had finished the mixing bowl and spatula used to make the frosting for the bundt cake. The two beaters from the electric mixer were covered in chocolate frosting. In a giant display of willpower, he set them aside for Singer and Radio Voice.

Darlene stole a look at Hanna. What a beautiful, beautiful girl. Hanna blew at a curl of auburn hair that fell to the bridge of her nose, her hands busy snapping off the ends of green beans. When from time to time she would glance up from the colander to add to the chitchat or laugh, that's when her smile would take over the room. Her dark hair and eyes offset her white smile, making it all the more entrancing. Darlene thought if the word famous could be used for someone in a town the size of Duluth, then Hanna Donnovan would qualify. She was the evening anchor of Channel 6 News, Duluth's go-to station, as well as the one news program broadcast to the outlying cities in the greater area. She was recognized everywhere, to the point where she was no longer surprised to be asked to sign an autograph in line at the bank or the grocery store. *She is good for Cory*, Darlene hoped to herself, as though an incantation. *She is good for Cory. Both she and Singer could walk him out of the past.*

Hanna caught Darlene's long look. "What?" she asked. "Do I have something on me?" Hanna brushed the back of her hand across her face. "I seem to leave a trail when I cook."

Darlene offered a warm smile. "No, no. I was just thinking what a beautiful hostess we have for this important day for Cory. He's darn lucky, I'd say."

Hanna blushed. "Thank you. Although the kitchen is not my bread and butter."

"Very good," the Monsignor clapped his sudsy hands together. "'Not my bread and butter.' I just love a well-turned pun."

Hanna chopped an onion and brought the conversation back to the meal. "Does Stu like onions?" she asked Darlene.

"Never met one he didn't. But," Darlene said in a whisper, "they give him a gassy chassis." They had a good chuckle over that.

Something reached for them just then, carried on an eddy. Cutting knives halted. Drying towels were set down, Conversations ceased mid-word. Heads turned as he kitchen went still. Notes of a melody wafted in from the front room. Singer had begun to share his miracle.

Without a word the group slipped into the living room. In single file, closely spaced, those in the rear on tiptoes, they tried to not disturb a molecule of air.

There was Singer. Sitting beside the Lincoln Logs. He had looked away from the miniature cabin, his chin raised, his large eyes wide and sparkling and fixed ahead as though something other than the wall stood before him. He sang, not so much to himself as to whatever it was he gazed upon. In beauty, in richness, in pitch, his singing was otherworldly. His tiny voice rose above the mundane of mid-afternoon.

SPRING 1985

Goosebumps ran up legs. All thoughts were stilled. Soon the music had a few of them looking through tears, which had the effect of putting an aura around the boy sitting there on the carpet. His song seemed to be a hymn, and it slipped in and out of Latin that none recognized, except for Monsignor Kief. It was an ancient hymn, the Monsignor recalled, from his early days in divinity school. But the Latin verse he couldn't immediately place. He stood holding the two frosting-laden mixing beaters he had saved for the boys.

In my heart
There is forgiveness
In my soul
There is light

On my path
I move forward
I turn toward
what is right

exspectate minime plus
progrediore iam
antequam lucis evadat
sub ianua

exspectate minime plus
progrediore iam
antequam lucis evadat
sub ianua

As spontaneously as the singing had started, it ended, ringing out in innocent majesty. Silence closed. A silence profound enough to make the group distrust all memory of what they had just heard.

Singer looked up and smiled, seeing the faces trained on his. He stood and walked across the room toward Monsignor Kief. The Sheriff exhaled, whistling softly through his teeth. "That boy knows music, sure as middle C."

"Amen," Darlene added. Singer stood before the blind Monsignor and pulled on his hand. The elderly priest knelt. Singer kissed his cheek.

Now if you asked the different people in the room about the significance of this act, you'd hear different explanations. Some would say Singer's kiss was typical for a child, because he proceeded to take one of the two chocolate-covered mixing beaters and commenced to lick it clean. But others, the Monsignor among them, felt the explanation wasn't as simple as chocolate.

"Someone's at the door, Mom," Singer said between licks.

"What, honey?"

Radio Voice came over and got his frosting-caked beater.

There was a sharp knock at the door.

Hanna looked at Singer, and then went to the door. Lu Ann caught up with her. Cory watched from the back of the room.

Another knock.

Hanna pulled opened the heavy door and there was Pat. He held a brightly wrapped gift at his side and a bouquet of flowers in front of his face.

"Pat?" Hanna said.

Pat lowered the flowers. His badly swollen broken nose was taped across the bridge, cotton packing apparent in each nostril. The first tinges of purple showed under his eyes. He managed a smile. "Sorry I'm … late." He reached out to Lu Ann with the bouquet of flowers.

Lu Ann was rocked by the entirety of the situation. Swaying on her feet, she swallowed her half stick of sugar-free gum.

SPRING 1985

DESSERT

Bundt cake was Singer's favorite, too. He called it big donut cake. A neighbor who daycared for the boy gave him his first taste, and he was hooked. Ms. Kortuem lived to bake, and it was her considered opinion that of all the cakes in all the recipe books across the world, the bundt cake had no rival. "Delicious ... simplicity," she would say, holding two fingers in the air to sum up her case. "No cake epitomizes those words like the bundt cake." And no one ever disagreed. Not if they wanted to plate a decent serving size.

By the time the gathering at Hanna's finished dessert, Pat had been over and back through his morning in more detail than he had hoped to. His story didn't exactly make for light mealtime chitchat, but it had that curious pull, like driving past a traffic accident. Pat offered to take his plate to the corner of the living room, claiming he was tough on appetite appeal, but Lu Ann, for starters, would hear nothing of the kind. She would have had him stationed at the head of the table if Cory hadn't saved him by assigning seats.

Lu Ann was certainly shaken by the state in which Pat had arrived, but she had nothing on Radio Voice. Radio Voice was a person who was deeply affected by another's pain. When someone was hurt, he would cry. When someone laughed, he laughed harder. When he saw Pat's face, he bolted behind the curtains where he sobbed. Pat went to him and talked to him gently. Together they formed a large bulge, Pat on his knees with his stocking feet sticking out beneath the curtain hem. By the time they rejoined the others it had been 15 minutes. It might have been sooner but Pat had told Radio Voice to touch his nose as proof he was okay. Radio Voice had gone a little rough and the yelp Pat let out was a setback.

Radio Voice sat at the dining room table with Darlene, Stu and Cory, polishing off the last of the cake. Darlene had tried to help with the dessert dishes, but was politely evicted from the kitchen by Monsignor Kief and Hanna. The Sheriff converted the snack table into a puzzle table; he and Singer began the 100-piece sailboat he'd brought as a graduation gift. Pat and Lu Ann had gone out to walk off supper. Hanna's parents returned from clearing the table and sat down with fresh coffee.

Hanna's father leaned across the table. "Radio Voice, how is it that you can talk in such a special way?"

Radio Voice looked shyly down at his cake crumbs. Cory put his hand on Radio Voice's shoulder. "Radio Voice has a great talent. When he hears something he can impersonate it. And he's a big radio listener—"

"Cory said I had to leave my radio in the car," Radio Voice told them, disappointed.

"His transistor radio is his constant companion. He even has an earpiece he can plug in the side, right?"

Radio Voice smiled broadly, nodding.

"When he hears a broadcast, he can repeat it, right down to the last inflection. Pretty cool." Cory smiled at Radio Voice who scrunched up his shoulders and eyes in pure happiness.

"Should I get it, Cory?"

"Maybe not right now, buddy. Let's just talk."

Radio Voice quickly rebounded. "Can I show my dollars?"

"Yeah, sure."

Radio Voice pulled out his wallet. "They're all in order," he said, referring to the bills. "See. Here's ones, then fives, then tens. And," Radio Voice whispered, "a twenty. I don't like change. I turn it in for dollars. When I get enough to do it. Right at Mark's Convenience Mart on the way to work."

"Except for bus money, right?" Cory raised his eyebrows, in soft reprimand. Too often Radio Voice wouldn't keep change for the bus and would slog through rain rather than break a dollar.

"Right. Except for the bus," Radio Voice nodded earnestly.

In the kitchen, Hanna and Monsignor Kief slowly finished the dishes, enjoying each other's company. But uncharacteristically, the Monsignor would slip away from the conversation, humming the hymn that Singer had sung. *Exspectate minime plus.* If the Monsignor's Latin was correct, that was *Wait no more.*

"Monsignor, how are you on the subject of love?" Hanna all but blurted out, breaking his spell.

"Love? Love." He centered his thoughts. "A complex one, that subject. I would say, with no false modesty, that I am an expert in the turbulent waters of love. And why not? I've been in love for 50-plus years."

"But Monsignor, you must admit, that's a bit different. That's with God. With God, love is unconditional."

Monsignor Kief flicked his drying towel up onto his shoulder where he let it lie. A conversation such as this required both hands.

"Hanna, my dear, love, by its very definition is unconditional. Not to be mistaken for like, which is conditional. Friend is conditional. Um, a hobby—conditional. But love, that's a different league."

Hanna furrowed her brow. She started to say something, but stopped; a habit she had picked up in reporting. Let them lead. Be a counterpuncher. If you allow the other person to fill in the silence, the unguided thoughts produce the richest material. But Monsignor Kief just let the mystery hang there for Hanna to examine.

She tried another way. "So the love you have with God is like human love?"

"Love is love, Hanna. Just as bread is bread and morning is morning."

"But with God, love is less challenging because on the other end there's divinity, right? Not humanity? The mathematician would argue that makes it only half as challenging."

"Not the mathematician who loved God. Not the mathematician who struggled while his peers were publishing world-acclaimed papers. Not the mathematician whose child has a rare disease. Not the mathematician who woke up one day to find he was going blind."

Hanna looked at the wise face of the Monsignor. Certainly his relationship with God could have been precluded by the loss of his sight. How many obstacles had he risen above because he held tightly to this ideal of unconditional love? For the moment, Hanna's emotions swelled. She didn't know if she wanted to cry or laugh or just let the whole thing drop.

"What is it, Hanna?" the Monsignor asked. "What are you really asking me?"

"I'd like for us to talk, sometime," she said. "Can I come see you? I don't think this is the time or the place."

Monsignor Kief put his hands out, searching the space separating them. Hanna took them. His hands were warm and soft and broad. "Of course you can come see me, my dear. Anytime."

Hanna looked at the dishtowel resting on the Monsignor's shoulder. She couldn't help but wonder if the Monsignor knew all along that this is where his hands would end up.

SPRING 1985

Back in the living room the Sheriff was passing down the finer skills of puzzle protocol to Singer as he tapped in a piece.

"Find your corners and your straights. Okay? Look over in this area." He gestured using his prosthetic fingers. "See any?"

"Did it hurt when you got new fingers?" Singer asked, looking up from the thin border of puzzle they had assembled.

"No. The accident hurt, but everything got better eventually."

"Like when you fall when you're running?"

"Yep. Like that."

"Except yours was worse?"

"I guess so. But I'm used to it now."

"And you can do stuff, just like before?"

"Pretty much. I can play the piano. Did you know that?"

"I love piano," Singer brightened. "It's my favorite other than singing."

"I have a piano. You should come see sometime. When I was younger I played all the time. My piano was like my best friend."

"I bet you're good."

"Well, I'm pretty rusty."

Singer was confused. "You mean your fingers stick?"

The Sheriff laughed. "No. I mean I'm out of practice."

"I still bet you're good," Singer said. "I can tell."

"How can you tell?" the Sheriff teased, looking more closely at Singer.

"I can tell things." He paused. "And you tap in pieces good. That's like playing the piano except you make a puzzle instead of a song."

"You are a smart one." The Sheriff shook his head, and allowed himself to touch the boy's back with his prosthetic fingers. For as long as the hand had been mangled, it had been something he instinctively hid. "I think I see a straight-edged piece over there," the Sheriff said referring to a one of the few remaining border pieces that had eluded them.

"You have that one," Singer offered.

The Sheriff picked it up and tapped it in.

"Way to go," Singer told him.

"Thank you," the Sheriff said.

They gathered at the open door saying goodbyes.

Darlene had freshened her lipstick and brushed a crumb from her sweater in the bathroom. She told her mirrored reflection that under no uncertain terms would she begin blubbering on the way out. Parting with Cory always turned her inside out. Ever since that boy first walked in off the lake and sat silently wrapped in her Hudson Bay blanket, something inside her had been roused. Leaving Cory, or Cory leaving her, felt wrong. There she stood in the doorway with the breeze touching her cheek, gripping her empty tin canister with "Darlene" neatly markered on masking tape on the bottom. She tried to hold a happy face. On the inside, lights were being put out.

Darlene handed Stu her tin and embraced Cory. She spoke quietly, for just the two of them. "So proud of you." She held him with such strength. She smelled of bark and hairspray. "I don't have words."

Hanna, watching the two, saw something that cocked her head in the way a revelation will. *It's like he's gotten smaller,* she thought. Cory, hugged, seemed to sink into Darlene in a way unfamiliar to Hanna.

When the last of the group had finally waved goodbye before driving off, Cory, Hanna and Singer tried to adjust to the quiet left behind. How, at times, can quiet be so inescapable?

They collected the last of the dessert plates and tossed the wrapping paper. It seemed later than 5:00 and Cory and Hanna didn't know what to do with one another. Everyone was bushed.

Cory went through the living room. His mind wasn't on anything in particular as he slid objects safely back from the edges of tables. There was a framed picture of the three of them ice skating. A table lamp. Two of Singer's picture books. A newly sprouted potted plant on the window ledge. He went into the kitchen and pushed back a bowl that was drying near the sink. A notepad on the countertop. This practice was more than the result of having a preschooler buzzing about with hands like wrecking balls. It was Cory's way. Objects near an edge called out to him.

He made up his mind to leave for the evening, to give Hanna some time alone with Singer. Her Singer. Her child. Was Singer just hers? Of course not, but biologically Cory wasn't involved. Cory wondered how much more connected he was than the daycare neighbor across the street. Then he cut off this useless line of interrogation. He stacked his graduation presents on the dining room table.

"I'll stay out at the cabin tonight," he whispered to Hanna, coming up behind her, smelling her hair. As soon as he said it he wished he hadn't.

"Are you sure?" Hanna asked.

"You and Singer should get some alone time," Cory said. "Sometimes that's really important."

"Okay. Thanks. I guess." Hanna smiled. "It's hard for me, being away so much with work."

"You're doing a fantastic job," Cory said. "Singer stole the show today."

"Did *you* have fun?" Hanna said, moving into Cory. They held each other.

"I did. Thank you. For everything."

Parting is awkward. You stand and shake hands and lightly hug people, but in your mind you've already departed. Your standing there is like a lie. Voices are muffled as promises are made about getting together more often and how you'll see each other soon. But who really knows? What if it isn't meant to be? What if fate says otherwise?

The sun had slid to the far side of the house, putting the cement stoop in shadow. May in northern Minnesota is temperamental. The cool of evening made it clear that this gorgeous day was to be replaced. But there was one last ray of sunshine. Singer pushed past his mother. His bright, high voice brought Cory back to the moment.

"Who will take me to Ms. Kortuem's tomorrow?"

"Tomorrow's Sunday, bud. You don't have daycare. Sunday's church day."

"Church day? Will you come with us?"

Hanna stepped forward and knelt next to Singer. "It's a long way to come. Cory might have to do some work."

"Well," Cory said, "if you tell me a joke, I'll come." Cory, too, got down on one knee. Singer now stood bookended by the two people he loved most in the world.

The boy, looked upward, thinking. A satisfied smile hooked the corner of his mouth. "Okay. What is round and blue?" Hanna and Cory had heard this one more times than they could count.

Cory played along. "Round and blue. Round … and … blue?" Singer's smile deepened with every pondering moment. Cory shook his head. "I give up."

"A very cold orange," Singer blurted, thrusting his hands up as if to give the answer to them.

"Man, you got me! A very cold orange."

"You'll come to church then? We'll sit by the piano."

"We'll sit by the piano," Cory assured the boy just as his little arms roped around his neck. Cory stood, bringing the boy up with him.

"Hold on, elevator going up." As Cory straightened he could feel a twinge in his knee.

"Ding. Okay, pal. This is your floor." He handed Singer over to Hanna, but not without resistance.

This was life. A small accumulation of moments and quirks that become customs and traditions, that become foundation, that become *them*. On the stoop, in the shadow of the house on the hill, they stood. Quiet. There were no witnesses to their simple joy, wrapped in the warmth and the coolness of the last days of May.

SPRING 1985

MICK

Most diner owners don't lay bright green paint down on the walls, especially the electric shade of green that you'll find at Mick's Diner in St. Paul. It's a color you might encounter on a toddler's spring rubber boots, the ones accented with flowers or frogs, made to romp through puddles. Or a green you might find on a yo-yo. But Mick's theory on paint was like all his life theories: uncomplicated. Lime green wakes a person up. When you open as early as he did, coffee alone isn't adequate. "A person needs caffeinated colors," he told anyone who challenged his palette.

At four a.m. the lights would flicker to life inside Mick's brick walls, long fluorescent ceiling bulbs buzzing for a few minutes until they fully warmed. The sound of his own feet would slap around the place as he went about his morning routine. Get the griddle heating. Start a few pans of rolls in the oven for the lunch crowd.

Bake his famous gingerbread, the secret of which is in the molasses. Mick would only bake three loaves. His homage to early risers.

Mick loved the first 30 minutes of the early morning. The old steel Farmers Brothers six-station coffee maker would sputter and percolate. He'd watch out the large front window as an occasional car rolled through the blinking stoplight at the intersection where his place stood sentry on the corner. He'd splash a little milk from the stainless steel dispenser into a coffee cup; the authority of the stream telling him how his milk supply was. He'd unlock the till and ring up a trial order to make sure his receipt paper was feeding. One million dollars came chugging up on the receipt roll.

A hole in the wall, that's how Mick described his place—with no false humility. It was small and canted. The long counter in front showed its age where elbows had worn the Formica countertop. Fourteen soda-fountain-style stools ran its length. The booths were comfortable, but you had about as much room as eating on an airplane when you squeezed four adults into the space. Ceiling fans spun with a wobble. Perhaps it was the imperfections that attracted the castoffs and the disheveled. For that matter, the humility of the place had pulled Mick in as well. Enough, eventually, to have him quit his job pushing small business loans at an anonymous bank chain and buy the diner. One didn't need to pre-qualify here. Mick's Diner was comfortably off kilter, revival for the hungry and overlooked.

His first Saturday morning customers were about 45 minutes from shuffling through the door, and Mick settled into the dark gap before the morning transitioned. He took up a stool in the middle of his counter with a cup of coffee. Centered, he joked with himself. He found the rhythm of the day. He ate his toast in his preferred fashion: burned with peanut butter and honey. Meanwhile the sleep- and otherwise-deprived radio jock bantered about which sports coach should be run out of town in his underwear. It was background noise that helped Mick simplify thoughts that he'd jot down next to his coffee. He'd extract a napkin from the stainless steel dispenser and ponder things he'd never say out loud. Fulfillment? God? Illusions? Then he'd flip the napkin over and pen a triangle, placing dots where the lines of the triangle joined, writing an F next to each of the three dots. He called this his happiness triangle, and the three words beginning with F were a riddle to solve. "If you can figure out what each of those Fs stand for," he challenged his customers, "you've pegged the secret to happiness."

Mick was a good man. His hero was Abe Lincoln. He cried at movies when pets got lost. He never took the last cookie. Most of all, he wanted to give people a little joy and comfort and companionship. When his customers sat down he told them, "I'm lucky to be here, but not as lucky as you."

Customers started to make their way in, past a front door covered with union stickers that regulars had left with Mick. Many a machinist, mechanic and pipefitter would touch his union number, just like the devout reach for holy water at the doors of a church. The shifts were still an hour or so away from changing at the downtown factories, but there was always a straggler leaving early, or the insomniac taking in the newspaper with coffee before clocking in down the street. Mick thought about HomeSky as he ladled the day's first pancakes on the griddle. What kind of shape would she be in when she showed up for work today? If she showed up today.

"Hey Mick, change my links to patties if it ain't too late," a customer shouted from the counter. The kitchen was in the back. Mick looked up through the order window. "It's never too late for you, Willy. But you better change your ways soon."

"Yeah, yeah," he said. "You'll make someone a fine wife someday."

Relationships weren't really Mick's thing. But when HomeSky first showed up over three years ago, broken and enigmatic, he wondered if the winds hadn't shifted in his favor. He gave her a job and patiently waited her out. Waited for her to move beyond whatever it was that kept her eyes looking away. From HomeSky, he uncharacteristically tolerated absenteeism, spells where she simply walked out the door and disappeared for 30 minutes, and the cloak of alcohol that she dragged in mornings as she scribbled on her order pad looking for a pen that worked. In return she promised nothing and offered little in the way of an explanation. For Mick, there were only occasional words beyond "onions in the hash and eggs over hard." But he did sometimes see a rare glint in the distant dark of her eyes—a glimpse of a half-smile. That was all, but Mick wasn't a greedy man. Nor was he going anywhere soon. He waited. The seasons changed. She was still much the same as when she first walked through the door of his diner. Mick distinctly remembered writing on a napkin, *Can someone die of loneliness?*

Things quickly got busy, and there was little time to think about anything but keeping up. One minute, it had been dark outside the window, and the next it was all hustle and bustle. Again, HomeSky was late. Mick was cooking and running food out to tables. He got impatient looks from customers, and the waitresses were no less thrilled about covering for her. Mick kept the food and the smiles coming. Life is 10 percent what gets thrown at you and 90 percent how you deal with it—another Mick motto.

HomeSky had to sidestep through a line at the door when she finally arrived. A few of the regulars, recognizing her, gave her mock applause. "Hey, hey!" they kidded. "Now we can get some service." The restaurant was a cacophony of low voices accented by the bright tinking of silverware and plates.

Mick stepped away from the griddle and came over to check on HomeSky as she found her apron hung on the peg near the back door of the kitchen. A welcome breeze came through the screen. The industrial-grade steel door was held open to the alley by a grapefruit-sized rock that someone once tossed through the back window to rob 22 bucks from the till. A warped tennis racket leaned against the door trim. Occasionally a bat greeted Mick when he opened.

"How are you?" Mick asked as HomeSky knotted the tie strings of her apron. She briefly made eye contact. "You ought to use that thing on me." HomeSky looked over at the racket.

Mick smiled. "Have a cup of coffee before you step into the ring with those heavyweights. Full moon last night."

HomeSky looked up at Mick. She wanted to say something to him, and keep saying things. It was no use. "Your French toast is burning." She touched his forearm. He turned away, muttered an obscenity to himself, and quick made for his spatula. By the time he flipped them and turned to find her she had disappeared into the front section of the diner.

After the breakfast rush, the ensuing lull took on an unreal quality. Quiet echoed off the few remaining customers whose folding and unfolding of newspaper sections sounded amplified over loudspeakers. The replenished coffee station hissed as an occasional drip fell to the warming burners. Champ, who bussed and washed dishes with never a complaint, clattered plates and cups in plastic tubs, moving without a word to the dishwasher in back. No matter how long you've been in the restaurant business, you don't embrace the lull. You wonder, regardless of how busy you were, if you just saw your last customer.

Mick came out from the kitchen and wiped down a table. "Here's what ticks me off," Mick said to HomeSky, who was drinking her third glass of water as she sat with Paula, the other morning waitress. "Why is it that no matter how many Saturdays you've opened to a rush like that, when it slows down you feel like your business is just about to go down the crapper?"

Paula jumped in, true to her nature. "Here's what ticks *me* off," she said looking at HomeSky. "Why is it that every Saturday she gets to stroll in whenever she damn well pleases and then gets to sit here splitting tips with the rest of us?"

HomeSky looked down at her stacks of quarters on the table. The till was low on quarters and dimes, so the waitresses were exchanging coins for bills.

"Dammit Paula," Mick glared at her. "Is that necessary?"

She continued like nothing was said. "Champ brings the tip jar over, we sit here like a happy little family splitting them, and I ain't happy and it ain't fair."

"I've seen your way of … *splitting* them." Mick made air quotation marks around splitting for emphasis. "You come out okay on your end."

"She's right," HomeSky said lowly. She put her elbow on the table, rubbed her forehead, then her eyes. Speaking down through her hand, her voice had an eerie canned quality. "She's 100 percent right, Mick." HomeSky shook her head, which remained cradled. She leaned back from the neat stacks of quarters and dimes and ones on the table. Her eyes were red-rimmed. HomeSky blinked Mick and Paula into focus.

"All right," she said, looking from one to the other as if they'd presented a question. Then she stood and walked out the door.

"Are you pleased with yourself!?" Mick blurted. His face was a shade of red that silenced Paula. Mick got up to go after HomeSky. He stopped, halfway, there in the center of his diner. The few customers eating lowered their newspapers to observe. He stood slumped on the scuffed linoleum tile floor, his head hung. The door had opened and closed and HomeSky was gone. Mick's shoulders rose and fell. His arms hung at his sides. One hand choked a dishtowel.

Then, like a gun going off, he stomped his foot on the floor so hard that he walked with a limp for the next three days.

SPRING 1985

WILDFLOWERS

It was not yet past one in the afternoon. The day had become unseasonably warm. Leafed out branches lolled in a steady breeze. The sun at this late May angle made HomeSky think about things that grow. She had coaxed so many seasons of crops from the dirt. The memory of it was an old friend, but for her, a lost companion. Eyes closed to the sun, she inhaled. She was a wildflower seed back home in the pasture. The direct sunlight on her eyelids left her seeing yellow-orange, not black like beneath the topsoil. She longed for the colored light of hope, just as the seedling stretches for it, burgeoning. But it takes so much energy to break through. It's every day, it's every hour.

There were too few occasions that brought back the wildflowers of home. HomeSky left her palms open to the underbellies of the clouds, the breeze twined through her fingers. Soon pastures would be awash in color. She heard the wind as it rustled. She strained to hear the bumping of the porch wind chimes. But no. Where was the companionship of the distant tractor on the back field? Where was Lick barking at a treed squirrel? And Joseph?

She had come to the river's edge without consciously making the decision to do so. The Mississippi swung along the edge of downtown St. Paul, and often HomeSky found herself here, standing before the ebbing water. "Misi-ziibi," she said, "Great river." She was drawn to the diversity of the water's movement. How in places it appeared still, in others, moving in opposite directions, wild, against itself. Rivers held such confoundedness. She thought of her husband, RiverHeart, and the words she had written for his eulogy: *There is a river / a strength / called serenity / I have swum in it.*

A wide buffer of grass and scrub was left uncut to the river. Stepping into its depth, HomeSky looked for a wildflower. Maybe there would be one premature bloom, the first muted pastel. She always kept a small scissors in her purse to cut summer flowers, but any spring bloom would be too precious to take. She just needed to witness one, touch it, to kneel and smell it. She walked for some time with her head down hoping to find something beautiful.

She found empty beer cans.

SPRING 1985

MICK

It was seven p.m. when Mick glanced up from his work at the dining room table to regard the surrounding rooms. His head cranked around, pausing here and there, as if taking photographs. Oftentimes, you're so close to a thing, you don't really see it.

This was the house that his mother and father had owned until they passed. Mick had lived here his entire life, for better and worse and all that is in between.

The oak floor beside his stocking feet lay sprinkled with torn, empty envelopes. This month's bills. His eyes traveled the expanse of floor, knowing where every squeak in the hardwood waited. How giant he used to think this house was. This floor, perfect for sock sliding. This wood, where the first precarious barefooted steps of Mick's life came slapping down. It lay in front of him, his past and his present. What about future?

Mick picked up an envelope from the floor and printed the word *future* on it. He looked across the room to the entryway closet. There he knew, inked on the inside of the door, was his growth chart: kindergarten to eighth grade. The first time he got the bed spins after prom and ended up retching in the toilet, that was upstairs, take a quick right. *What do you make of a man who doesn't venture out?* he wondered. He set his pen in the fold of his checkbook. *What about a man whose bills are always promptly paid and who waters his house plants every Tuesday and who bothers to print the first letter of his last name on his leather gloves should they be mislaid? Why would any man be so careful? Or should all be?*

He pushed aside the bills and went back to the envelope. Next to the word *future* he drew his happiness triangle and put an F at each corner. Can the mystery of life be explained by simple geometry and three Fs, he asked himself? Mick went with it. Just as he finished writing the words *why not?* inside the triangle, HomeSky rang his doorbell.

Guests to his house were few and far between. HomeSky could see surprise register on Mick's face as he swung open the door. She stood holding her folded waitress apron. The weak smile she offered did little to allay Mick's fear that something wasn't right.

"HomeSky. Hello. Do come in." His voice rattled nervously. "What a nice surprise," he said in less than convincing fashion.

"Sorry to bother you," she said, not advancing on his offer to come in. "I left earlier with this. Hadn't meant to." She reached across the threshold with the apron.

"Please, come in." Mick gestured to the front room. "It's not much, but at least my old pals at the bank don't own it."

She stepped in, noticing the house smelled like a meal recently cooked.

"Excuse the mess," Mick said. Aside from the envelopes scattered about in the dining room the place was neat as a pin.

Homesky laughed out loud, which surprised them both. "Sorry," she explained. "It's just, if you saw my apartment."

SPRING 1985

"Can I make coffee? I was just going to put on a pot. Are you hungry? I have leftover chicken." The low light of the entryway made HomeSky appear sunken.

HomeSky looked at Mick, his shirttails out, thinning hair slightly disheveled, evening whiskers. Outside the familiar context of his diner, Mick was less certain. He was a man you would see on the street, and immediately forget. Mick really didn't make a first impression. There were maybe three people in the world who could tell you the color of his eyes. Apart from his longish nose, he was the living definition of average. Outwardly, that is.

Mick waited for her response, getting self-conscious about the way she looked at him.

"Coffee'd be nice," she said. But she was thinking that something stronger was what she really needed—for a conversation they were about to have.

CORY'S CABIN

Cory sat on the warped wooden steps, flipping a silver dollar into the air with one hand and catching it with the other. Hand-eye coordination. Repetition. Focus. They were right up there with the word breathe on Cory's list of necessities.

The cabin he rented on Pike Lake was 30 miles northwest of Duluth. It was an easy drive to the city, with the exception of a handful of extreme days doled out by winter in northern Minnesota. Without question, the inconvenience of those days was worth the price of living on the water.

With his stack of graduation presents on the stoop next to him, Cory hadn't gone as far as inside the front door. Not yet. He forced himself to sit quietly; something Hanna had offhandedly said was absent from his ever-present schedule. He put away the coin and listened through the stillness. Bees hopped from clover head to clover head. Unaware of his presence, chipmunks scampered through the grass in front of him. The largest of the group sat poised on a rock and would pounce on the smaller two whenever they ranged into his space, chasing them to the weeds. Time would pass, and the process would repeat itself, with much chirping trailing each retreat. Cory looked at the dominant chipmunk who had returned to his rock perch, clicking his throat. "Careful, tough guy," he said. "There's always someone bigger out there." Cory took up a hunk of bark from the woodpile stacked by the front door and side-armed it over the chipmunk's head. He beat it to the weeds.

The log cabin had come up for rent, posted at a grocery store near Hanna's place. Turned out, a college professor who owned it was headed to Sweden on a three-year exchange program. When Cory saw the Polaroid attached to the posting, he got chills. The place couldn't have looked much more like the one he took refuge in as a boy, lost on Lake of The Woods. Cory had always smirked at the notion of fate, but Joseph told him, sooner or later, he'd get it. Cory pulled down the posting and rented the cabin sight unseen.

He carried his stack of gifts inside and set them on the dining room table. Cory couldn't help but be embarrassed by the fuss that people had gone to. He re-gathered the stack and left it on the bed in the spare bedroom.

The floor plan consisted of one primary room, 20' x 30', with an old oven and sink along one wall and a dining room table by the front window on the other. The fieldstone fireplace was the centerpiece of the third wall, a couch and a rocking chair facing it. A gas stove, used for heat in the fall and winter, served as a desk to the ninth-grade math texts that Cory was brushing up on. Two small bedrooms were just off the main room. Near the front door there was a utility room with a water heater housed in a closet that bumped up against a tiny bathroom with a shower.

It was an hour before dark, giving Cory time to run. He didn't want to push it too close. Running at night was something he'd not do again.

As he stretched his legs, working the stiffness out of his knee, he looked at a Crayon drawing held by a magnet to the front of the vintage Westinghouse refrigerator. Singer had made it for him last summer. It showed the three of them playing in wavy blue water under big loopy clouds. A deer was getting a drink near them. The proportionality of things was what so struck him. How big the faces and smiles were. How long fingers were, each hand with three. How large the deer was compared to the trees. No matter how many times Cory encountered that drawing, it moved something inside him, both happy and sad.

The drawing accounted for most of the decorating Cory had done since moving in. Other personal touches were an old Home Sweet Home cross-stitched needlepoint, about the size of a paperback book, yellowed in its scratched glass frame. It hung on what had been an empty nail on the wall near the kitchen table. And an enlarged photograph, framed and placed leaning on the fireplace mantel. Cory loved the shot. It was taken on the property at the circular stone fire pit. Hanna, Singer and Cory were roasting marshmallows. The boy had a long straight branch that he and Cory had hunted out of the woods. They had sharpened it with a pocketknife; is there anything more alluring to a young boy than the magic of a pocketknife? How the blade appears out of nowhere? Skewered on the tip of the stick were the next two plump white victims. Cory had put his camera on self-timer mode, placed it on a log and hustled into place just in time for the click of the shutter. Every time he looked at that picture he thought of one thing. Not of its simple beauty, of Hanna with her transcendent smile that lit up TV rooms throughout the northland, or of Singer, there between the two of them like some divine adhesive. He thought of how life is like a photograph taken on a self-timer. You have but a few seconds to jostle yourself into place. One pause too many, one mistake, one unforeseen event, and the picture is taken without you. Like what had happened with his father.

Out on the blacktopped road, it had cooled sufficiently to where a long-sleeved running shirt wouldn't have been overdoing it. As he ran in a t-shirt, Cory calculated the extra calories he burned in the early miles to stay warm. Worth it, he concluded.

SPRING 1985

A wall of pines, with intermittent birch and oak, lined the quiet road. He jogged around the slow bend as the strip of blacktop soon straightened into a rolling section of road that ran the length of the alfalfa field where last summer, Cory was willing to trade his life for that of three strangers.

The field. The dark green grass now lay in peaceful shadow. Cory jogged past the spot where not thirty yards away, in the hollow, the Cessna had cartwheeled after the attempted emergency landing. The landing gear sheared off—the wheel and shaft piked deep into the earth. The aircraft, twisted, on its back. The snapped powerline, which had stretched the length of the field, wrapped around the nose propeller as the plane came in low and desperate. He was there again.

> Cory crowned the hill and entered the field near the dusty rock pile that had been heaped long ago, back when the ground was first tamed for crop.
>
> Dressed in clothes inappropriate for a sweltering August night, he came hard and fast, breathing heavily, and then skidded to a stop that nearly left him on his backside on the long grass at the field's edge. There it was. Good Lord. In front of him in the shin-high alfalfa, the white crumpled heap of a small aircraft. It had gone down much where he visualized it might, judging by where the plane left his sightline at the cabin. He hesitated, heartbeats pounding out the seconds, hearing again in his head the sickening snap of distant treetops followed by the sharp crunch and bounce of metal.
>
> Sweat stung his eyes in the deteriorating light. The scene immobilized him. Less was it the sight of the prostrate woman, thrown face-up in the field, than was it the imploring voice from inside the wreckage. A father's voice, high and faithful. "My child. Oh God, help me!"

Cory shook off the memory. He spat and continued his run alongside the field. Spring alfalfa had filled in where the ring of fire had blackened. There were no sirens or red ambulance lights cutting through the night, bouncing off the pines. The shadowy reporters and the bright camera lights no longer lined the fields trying to siphon off a story—including, in her own way, Hanna. Just the harsh quiet that always slips in after.

Jogging required fifteen minutes for Cory's knee to fully loosen, allowing him to then run evenly, youthfully. Every half mile or so a chipmunk or field mouse would dart through the long grass at the road's shoulder, sounding out an alert. "You scared me more than I scared you," Cory would tell the critter. It was still too early in the season for horseflies, which served no good purpose that Cory could ascertain, other than to quicken his pace. The stone braided in his hair tapped with regularity. He savored the peace, alone, with his shadow running in front of him. Cory found himself wondering, as he often did, if others treasured empty space around them as he did. Certainly Hanna had made her way in, and Singer—and Joseph—but why had Cory made room for so few? He decided to drop the thought.

After his seven-mile loop, Cory stood just beyond knee depth in the lake, still wearing his t-shirt, a towel tossed around his shoulders. A shiver ran through him, but like a sneeze, it was gone almost the moment it arrived. The crimson sun rested on the curve of the horizon like a wax seal on an envelope. He had found an eagle feather to distract his mind from the temperature of the lake water. This time of year, the water temperature hadn't reached 60, so wading hurt, but soon numbed. Cory knew this would keep the inflammation out of his knee.

Cory stroked the crystal clear water with the tip of the eagle feather. It was majestically bowed with an alternating pattern of dark and light stripes. Cory guessed it to be at least 19 inches from tip to quill. As the tip sliced through the water, droplets beaded on the feather's broad surface. Impervious, he thought.

The evening light shimmered crooked and bent off the blue water. The wind stirred high in the restless trees. There'd be rain tonight, sure as dogs barking from across the lake. Cory had some burning to do. A large pile of boughs that winter had willed to him—limbs snapped under heavy snows. And dead pine needles heaped in piles near the fire ring. And some over-winter straw that had been laid on the perennials before the killing frosts descended. Cory had taken to looking after a small south-facing garden along the front of the cabin. At first he thought it would be more of a nuisance, lugging up pails of water from the lake and such. But he came to look forward to it. Keeping hostas and bleeding hearts and black-eyed susans and irises was good company. He found comfort in the predictability of their needs.

After the dinner dishes were cleaned and put up, Cory pulled on a long-sleeved fleece and leather boots. With the help of some old gas from the outboard motor, Cory coaxed a healthy fire to life. He threw pitchforks of dead needles onto the blaze. They were damp, so they landed, hissing, almost suffocating the blaze. Gray-white smoke streamed toward the skies as the fire gulped for oxygen. Inevitably, the fire would resurrect and consume the deadfall. The blaze launched brilliant orange sparks like tiny pieces of sunset into the darkness. Cory, leaning on his pitchfork, thought about Hanna and Singer. Over his shoulder in the east, the night's half moon was beginning to rise.

NIGHTFALL

Meadow's dingy bedroom was reborn in the late afternoon light. The sun swung low and west, painting her side of the house golden peach. A flow of sunlight pushed through her cracked window, setting down a warm swatch across her bed. Where she lay, the light fell across the bottom of her bedspread and was a welcome place for her cold bare feet. This left her wondering if poor circulation was part of the package.

The doc at the clinic told her to expect life to be very different now. Nausea. Hormones. Major appetite and mood swings. Meadow shooed away all of that as she lay on her back diagonally across her bed. She looked through the bedroom window at the treetops set off from the deep blue sky. *Will I follow the clouds?* she wondered. Small puff pastry clouds moved past her window, dotting the sky, seemingly only skipping distance apart. *Is there space there for me?*

SPRING 1985

"I should say, will *we* follow the clouds, right, Bulge?" Meadow had her shirt pulled up off her stomach and felt the hard little bump there. She didn't so much stroke it as inspect it with her fingers. For some reason she expected it would be more tender.

"Hey, Bulge," she said. "We've got shit to decide. The old man says for me to get it into my head that you don't exist. He says he's taking me to see someone who'll end this, and the longer I wait the worse the mistake gets. Says if we go in the morning, by the afternoon I can be back cleaning motels like nothing happened. How 'bout that for a prize? Peeling rotten sheets off of beds. Who-wee."

Meadow tapped her belly as if to induce an answer. "Hellooo? Are you a mistake?" Meadow looked carefully at her stomach. "Ah, take your time. Never trust anyone who answers right away."

She closed her eyes and thought about what Pat had promised. They would find a couple to love the baby. Adoption. Start by looking on the Rez. You never know, he said. But she did know. She didn't want her child on the Rez. They should both follow the clouds off the Rez, to someplace where windows aren't broken.

Meadow rolled on her side and pulled a folded song out of her back pocket—her song drawer, as she called it. This is where she kept the one that she was currently writing, or butchering, she often joked. The finished songs were rewritten in a blue spiral notebook. That notebook meant more to her than anything she had known. Before Bulge.

Her guitar stood in the corner of the room, but Meadow decided to compose with just a pencil. Sometimes she'd write songs while playing, strumming out the wrinkles in the words. She'd play a little, and then use the body of the guitar as a desk to jot parts of lyrics. Other times she went to the words—words, words, humming words, unaccompanied, on white paper, crossed out and underlined with arrowed lines connecting one stray to another. Sometimes the beauty of words alone made music.

Her bedroom door banged open. He father stood there in the shadow looking like he'd been in a car wreck.

He squinted. "Well there's a position you know well."

Meadow yanked her shirt down and sat upright on the bed. She pulled her knees to her chest. "Will you learn to fucking knock!"

"You pay bills, I'll learn to knock."

"I pay my share." She recoiled from the sight of her father's face. His left eye was a purple mess, and his upper lip was so swollen it looked like he'd been eating bees. "There go your good looks."

"Aren't you going to ask me what happened?"

"Fine. What happened?"

"None of your damn business. When's dinner?"

"Where's Mom?" Meadow asked, although she was pretty sure she knew the answer.

Her dad passed gas. "I'll give you three guesses and the first two aren't the library. Now get dinner ready. Your brothers will be home soon. You shouldn't leave them up at the rec center all day long. Nothing but drug dealers and lowlifes up there."

"Since when? You guys let me hang out there whenever."

"Yeah. Take a good look in the mirror. Model citizen. Now get dinner going."

"Why don't you call around and try to find Mom. It's Mom's job."

"Yeah, good luck there. Plus the damn phone's disconnected. They must not a got my check."

Meadow had a smartass comment for that, but her father's beat-up face made her swallow it.

Since Pat had driven to Duluth separately, he and Lu Ann each had cars to drive back to Baudette. Counting the cruiser with Sheriff Harris, Monsignor Kief and Radio Voice, and Stu and Darlene in their vehicle, they were a full-fledged caravan. By the time they had pulled off the highway into the motel parking lot at the edge of town, and said yet another round of goodbyes, it was getting close to sundown. Lu Ann didn't like driving without company, but she did have her bouquet of roses next to her on the front seat, and that helped. Plus she sang with the radio.

After the other cars went their ways it was just Pat and Lu Ann.

"Careful hanging out with guys with bandaged faces in hotel parking lots. It'll get a girl talked about at the women's auxiliary."

Lu Ann came over, picked up his arm and put herself under it. She hugged him. "Does that hurt as bad as it looks?"

"I don't know. Does my voice sound funny when I talk? Like I'm under water? It's like I'm in another world."

"How about I follow you home and nurse you back to health. By the end of the weekend you'll be good as grapes."

"I thought you had to go over to the diner and check on things."

"Well," Lu Ann said giving him a little squeeze, "I'll stop in quick, give Mary Alice the key, and let her lock up and open up in the morning."

Pat thought about how not to make this come out wrong, but frankly he felt worse than lousy, his head was pounding, and the last thing he wanted right now was another human within close quarters.

"Sweetie, I'm going to have to take a rain check. I feel miserable and contrary to the expression, misery does not love company."

Lu Ann looked away, but as was her constitution, she rallied. "How about I bring you out a nice bowl of chicken soup later? I could get away for an hour or so."

Pat rubbed his eyes. "Let's do this. I'll come pick you up for church tomorrow. It will be fun. We'll scare the elderly folks with my face. Tonight I just want to go home, take two of those horse pills they gave me for the pain, and call it a day. I hope that's okay?" Pat could see she was hurt. He smiled at her. "After church you can make me a stack of your famous chicken soup pancakes."

Lu Ann crossed her arms. "Chicken soup pancakes my eye." She did her best not to smile. "I was so darned worried about you today," She shook him a little for emphasis. "So many bad things went through my head. I was really scared, and I don't like being scared."

Pat took her in his arms. He was a little over six feet tall and she was five-five on her tip-toes so her head nestled nicely into his chest.

"Nothing to be scared about," he said. But as a pickup truck roared by with a muffler badly in need of service, something twisted in Pat's gut. He was pretty sure he hadn't seen the last of Roy Lee FastHorse. Nor that damned shotgun he drove around with in the back seat.

There was little more than an hour of good light left by the time Stu and Darlene got back to Darlene's sister's place where they parked their car in an outbuilding. That's the thing about living on an island on Lake of the Woods: not much cause for an automobile. Darlene's sister lived five minutes from the marina where she dropped them off after an extra-long hug for each.

To get back to the island before last light meant they couldn't dilly-dally at the docks—despite the grief the dockhand gave Stu. He said he ought to charge him a launch fee. Charge him double cause how Stu was dressed up so fancy and nice and looked more like a city slicker yachtsman, and yachts go for double. The tops of Stu's ears went red and just as he was about to set the dockhand right, Darlene moved in, started the boat and let it idle as she untethered the bow. Stu undid the back rope with a single swift yank. Then he trimmed up the motor, and left the dockhand under a rooster tail of water as he goosed the throttle, pulling away. They had a 30-minute run back to their resort in Monument Bay.

Stu stood at the wheel of his Boston Whaler, engine pinned wide open, the wind pulling back his gray hair. The big water was still blowing whitecaps, occasionally sending a splash of water overtop the bow, back his way. As Stu wiped the spray from his eyes, so too went the traffic lights and the parallel parking and the tangle of city road signs. He gave Darlene a relaxed smile. She gave him a quick wink, happy to be back in her element, pointed homeward.

SPRING 1985

As they tied up at their resort pier, the light was beginning to block and fail.

"Let's pay a visit to Cory's tree," Darlene suggested.

Stu took her hand as they walked down the dock. "Just have to duck into the house. Need a pipe."

Stu tapped out the remains of the last smoke on the heel of his boot, took a pinch from his tobacco bag, and thumbed down a fresh bowl. Darlene had gone to the lake for a pail of water, leaving Stu to his thoughts in front of the tree that he and Cory had planted years back.

Cory, my beloved boy. It was good to see you today in front of an auditorium of classmates, leading them. So good. But I wouldn't be honest if I didn't say I worry about you. Both me and Darlene do. More than we let on because we don't want to be clingy—especially our Darlene—but I send out this simple petition: be happy now. I know it sounds sappy, but it's finally gotten through my thick skull that that's the secret. Take time to see what's behind ordinary moments. There's more there, there's real goodness there. Like this simple grown tree. One of thousands, at first glance. But we know better. I know you're not much on faith, but faith brought that tree here. Faith in yourself, faith to set off. But it's beyond that. Beyond just you and the oars. Something put you on course with us. That's what's behind this ordinary tree. Your will ... your faith in yourself ... your Hanna and Singer ... they've shown you there's more. Gosh, enough blabbing out of me, it's just—

A twig snapped behind Stu. He was brought back to the here and now.

Darlene approached with her water pail and two old heels of bread for the chipmunks.

"Not like you to let a pipe go out," she said.

"Yep," Stu said, smiling at his wife of almost 50 years.

"What's got you grinning like a badger?" she asked, self-consciously.

"Not like you to feed chipmunks."

Darlene gave the tree a drink. "Remember how Cory used to look after those rascals?"

"Funny," he said, relighting his pipe, watching his wife scatter bits of bread under the skirt of the tree. "And the rabbits. Remember those crazy two, that summer he was with us?"

Darlene looked off, a small grin parting her lips, shaking her head. "Oh my gosh those two. How they'd run around the grass jumping over top one another like they were raised in the circus. We'd all laugh."

"Yeah," Stu said, reliving the moment.

"You know what I remember thinking, watching Cory watch those rabbits?"

Stu looked at Darlene.

"All I could wonder is how it felt for Cory to watch them, knowing he had no such brother to play with."

"I guess so," Stu said. "Until he met Joseph. They played like that."

Darlene swallowed. "Yeah. Met Joseph. And lost Joseph."

Monsignor Kief returned to the rectory, chewing his lip. Something was pressing on him, something like that first trace of a storm pulling itself over the horizon. He'd been quiet as a burglar the whole ride back, the Sheriff had commented.

It was the boy, that prodigy, Singer, that consumed his thoughts. Where on earth had he picked up a hymn like that? Certainly he and his mother and Cory were churchgoers, and Hanna had commented on how the boy liked to sit near the front on Sundays, up by the musicians. But Latin? He shook his head. The Monsignor concluded a mystery such as this called for an extra large bowl of chocolate almond fudge and a handful of vanilla wafers.

He sat with his spoon hovering above the untouched ice cream, and the words flowed to him like God Himself was whispering in his ear.

SPRING 1985

exspectate minime plus

progrediore iam

antequam lucis evadat

sub ianua

Monsignor Kief set down his bowl and wafers and went to his bookshelves. Extending upward from the floor, to as high as his hand could reach, the shelves had been custom built to fit both the Monsignor and his love of words. Books filled the walls on either side of the stone fireplace, accumulated over his many years, a good share from his sighted days. But most were Braille. His finger traced the hardcover spines until he located his Braille Latin dictionary. His brow creased in thought, Monsignor Kief began to piece the meaning of the hymn together.

Five minutes later he sat with his hands solemnly on his lap. He hummed the missing verse of the hymn. There was no questioning what it meant, nor his intent to follow through on it. He lacked only a precise plan to accomplish what these words called him to do.

Wait no more

Go forth now

Before the light is put out

Under the door

The elderly priest walked away from his full bowl of ice cream and stack of cookies. Climbing the stairs to his bedroom, with each ascending step, he was filled with more energy of purpose.

Packing a small suitcase, the Monsignor set his rosary atop of the folded items. Lastly he found the letter he'd long ago put under his socks for safekeeping. The letter was from HomeSky, the one and only she had sent when she first settled in her apartment in the city. She wrote to say she was fine, but made it quite clear she didn't want to be sent for. She apologized for not knowing Braille, but remembered that as often as not, the Monsignor's housekeeper read letters to him. When the housekeeper had finished reading

HomeSky's letter aloud, there was one question the Monsignor had for her: did the envelope come with a return address? She said it did. It was for this reason that the Monsignor had kept it all this time. He slid the envelope into his shirt pocket and closed his suitcase with a sure snap.

Despite the challenges of the task in front of him, he harbored no doubt. He could hitchhike out of town just the same in the dark of night as the light of day—likely easier at night because there was a smaller chance of being stopped by some good-intentioned local. He was unsure how much money there was in petty cash, which they kept stashed in the spare cookie jar, but he took its entire contents. It was money used when his housekeeper ran out of checks or just needed to make a quick run to the grocery store. More than occasionally, when the Monsignor was light a few dollars, he'd dip into it. Accordingly, the fives, tens and twenties were each folded to indicate their denomination. He carefully put the bills in his front pocket. No telling how long he'd be gone.

With red-tipped cane in hand, a light jacket to keep the cool spring night air at bay, Monsignor Kief pulled his cap down snug, took up his suitcase and descended the rectory's four front steps. He bothered neither to lock the front door nor leave a note. Filling his lungs with the brisk air of nighttime, he thought: *What will be will be. Note nor lock can alter that.*

Had Reg Cunningham been facing the other way at the bar, he would have seen out the front window as the Monsignor tapped by on the sidewalk under the greenish light cast down by the Mutineer's Jug's neon sign. But Reg had turned his attention to the TV over the bar. The 10:00 newscast signed on, flashing up the weekend anchor crew, who were sitting in for Hanna and her regular co-anchor.

"These two wax dummies," the bartender said, more to himself than the few scattered regulars in front of him. "There ain't a word in the English language that doesn't give them trouble." He set down a fresh drink in front of Reg.

SPRING 1985

"Better be better than the last one. Your drinks are for pussies."

"Then drink up," said the barkeep.

"Oh, ouch," Reg feigned. "You've hurt my feeling. My one and only."

"Why do I put up with you losers?" The bartender shook his head.

Reg straightened. "No wonder this place is empty. You treat your customers like shit."

"They ain't mine," was all the barkeep offered. To his way of thinking, any moron drinking in this hole on a Saturday night deserved to be insulted.

"Pretzels? For the fiftieth time?" Reg Cunningham held his palms up like a suffering martyr.

"Do you think you could move your hand six inches to the left?" The bartender pointed at the pretzels sitting there.

"Well kiss my ass and call me honey." Reg reached for the bowl. "When did you sneak them in there?"

"About three drinks ago. So get another ten on the bar."

"Don't worry, I'm good for it. Do you have a buck for the juke box?"

The bartender turned around to watch the lead news story. "Spend your own damn buck."

Reg objected. "The whole bar gets to listen and I have to flip the bill?"

A regular chimed in from the end of the bar. "*Has* to listen, is more like it. Play something from this century and maybe we'd care."

"Tim, the only music you listen to is made by the speaker you're sitting on."

"Very original, Cunningham. Haven't heard that since about sixth grade."

Cunningham left his cane at the bar and slowly made his way to the juke. He moved like a man closer to 80 than 60. Two quarters got him two plays. Plenty for those freeloaders. Now that the special on rail drinks was over, he'd be hitting the road once he drained his last one.

Johnny Angel started up to a reception of groans. "Not again!"

"Shelley Fabares, gentleman. Woulda loved to play with her sweater puppies." Reg reseated himself on his barstool and took down half his brandy 7, but not before he swished the drink around in his mouth letting the carbonation of the 7-Up bite the inside of his cheeks. Something in the stinging combination of brandy and 7-Up made Reg's hand fish a cigarette out of his pocket.

The lead local story rolled on after the national headlines, catching the attention of the bartender. "Hey, isn't that the kid that used to come up here and skate with Joseph Blackholm? Cory ah …?" The bartender snapped his fingers hoping it would summon the last name. "Shit. Cory…what's his face? Remember? Boy, those two could play some puck."

The story was about the valedictory speech that morning at the University of Minnesota Duluth. They cut to a location reporter who had done an interview with Cory on stage after the ceremony. "And here flanking the proud valedictorian is Channel 6's very own pride and joy, Hanna Donnovan, with her son." They waved to the camera. The reporter spoke over a final clip of Cory speaking from the dais. "Mr. Bradford told us he will be teaching math this fall at Duluth East High School, where he will coach the JV hockey team."

"Bradford," the bartender said, slapping his hand down on the bar. "I knew his last name started with a B."

"What did he say?" Reg asked, trying to act like he wasn't listening.

"Bradford," the bartender repeated. "He and Joseph got a national title at Wisconsin."

"Not that," Reg said, frustrated. "Never goddamned mind."

As the story wrapped, the lead anchor commented that it was a feather in Duluth's cap to be getting Cory to stay and teach in the area. His female co-anchor added that Cory appeared to be a feather in the cap for their colleague, Hanna. Guffaws all around the anchor desk.

Tim rambled on the subject from the far end of the bar; you needed guardrails to keep his thoughts on track. "It'll be great to have a kid like Cory teaching up north. We read differently up here, you know. Not as much time for it, and that hurts a guy in math. Now he's sniffing them panties of Hanna's. Boy, there's work I'd line up for. I think that kid worked up here a spell, didn't he Reg? Hell, at least the Cities didn't get him. Hate the Cities. Didn't you two work the plant together? Screw the Cities and all their traffic and fur coats. He's a real hero you know. Remember that thing with the plane last summer? Or was that two summers now? Didn't he work up there with you? Reg? Up at the plant?"

Reg's neck prickled and reddened. His hands trembled. "Shut up, dick-weed!" was all he could manage. He had had it for one day—all the Cory Bradford next-anointed-saint bullshit. His hand fidgeted with the newspaper article in his top pocket, but he had no stomach to look at it. His barstool squealed as he pushed back from the bar and reached for his cane.

"Ain't you going to listen to your other song?" Tim wiped beer suds and cheese popcorn off his mustache. The Everly Brothers sang harmony as Cunningham tossed a wadded ten on the bar and made his way erratically toward the door. Conversely, his thoughts were as unwavering as the flight of an arrow: *It's not a matter of if between us, it's when.*

HOMESKY

She fussed with a loose thread on the apron she had brought to Mick's home. In the kitchen there were the quick, neat sounds of Mick making coffee and putting M&M's in a glass bowl. She had come here to explain herself. But all attempts to arrange her thoughts in an orderly sequence resulted in HomeSky hanging her head. Such was the posture that Mick found her in as he brought their coffees and treat into the living room.

She was the picture of sadness.

Mick took a deep breath and came forward. "I was going to ask you if you wanted biscuits and gravy with your coffee, but you don't seem to be in the mood." Biscuits and gravy was the one item on Mick's menu that HomeSky had once mentioned turned her stomach, and he ribbed her about it because it was unlike her to make such a complaint.

HomeSky smoothed the folded apron on her lap, trying her best to brighten up.

SPRING 1985

Mick jumped in. "What is it, HomeSky?"

"I've brought your apron," she said, exchanging it for the coffee.

"It could wait till tomorrow, you know. I could get by without it until then." Mick grinned, trying to break the formality. Then his face changed. "But you won't be coming in tomorrow, will you?"

HomeSky swallowed. "No. Sorry."

"I don't know whether to scream or cry, and that's a fact." Mick's voice was tilting toward the latter. "HomeSky ..." Mick closed his eyes, standing before her with an apron in one hand and a steaming mug of coffee in the other. He lowered his voice to a whisper. "HomeSky, we've been good friends, yes?"

"Yes," she told him.

"I haven't pried. Your business is your business."

"No, you haven't pried." HomeSky watched Mick stand there with his eyes closed. A wincing furrow creased his forehead.

"What kind of a friend does that make me? Really? Real friendship isn't so ... sanitary."

Mick opened his eyes and he and HomeSky looked at each other. There between them was the look of real friendship—fully realized for the first time.

"Please tell me what I can do for you, HomeSky Blackholm." Mick's eyes began to fill.

"Sit down then," she said, with some energy now. "Drink your coffee. Have an M&M. Listen to what I have to say. But please, don't try to fix anything. What's done is done." She looked at him directly, and he responded with a nod before sitting in a chair across from her.

HomeSky raised her chin and looked at Mick. "I had a family, a home, a husband. Once. Forever ago. William RiverHeart was my husband, and my boy, my love of one thousand lives was Joseph Good Thunder. We lived north, near the Canadian border, off-reservation. Had a farm there, just a small one. Respected the land, and worked it for much of what we needed. Asked for no more than we gave." HomeSky took a breath, slowed down. "I know that looking back on life throws things out of perspective, but there was deep peace there, and there was real love. That I know." HomeSky clenched her fist and squeezed her eyes shut. "When you're happy, a gift is put on your bed every morning when you wake, and you're astonished by your fortunes, even if you don't pause long enough." She exhaled deeply. "And then when that gift is taken from your hands..." HomeSky's voice dropped low, "you wake up one day and there is no trace of it, not for as far as your feet can take you."

"Can you tell me what happened?"

HomeSky folded her hands tightly. "My husband was killed in an automobile accident. It will be 12 years this fall. My son, Joseph, died four years ago, in August. I came here after that. I left. You were kind enough to give me a job and put up with everything I've done." The walls buzzed in the silence. HomeSky waited for Mick to look up at her. His eyes were red-rimmed.

She spoke. "Why make any plans when these possibilities lay in wait? Why friends? Why lists? Why bank accounts? Why water flowers?"

"But you're a wonderful person, HomeSky."

"You don't know me, Mick." She knew how that comment stung, but it needed saying.

"We've known each other going on four years. Is that nothing?"

HomeSky refused to engage. "I thank you for your help. Most bosses would have fired me a long time ago."

"Please, HomeSky. I'm not your boss. I'm your friend. Let me help."

"Will you do me one last favor?"

Mick looked at her. He didn't like the sound of that question. "All right," he said quietly.

"Tomorrow, take me to the bus depot. I know Sunday is your only day off. I'm sorry to ask."

"Don't worry about that. What time?"

"Eight o'clock."

SPRING 1985

Mick didn't know where to turn. "Will you wait a week? Don't make this decision in haste."

"Mick, I've had one foot pointed this direction for a very long time."

Mick winced.

HomeSky wanted to apologize for the remark, but kindness was a complication that would serve neither of them. She stood to leave.

Mick looked at the faded, dirty fabric of the apron. "I have something for you."

They walked over to the dining room table where Mick had his stack of bills. "The girls gave me this." He picked up an envelope from the diner. "You left in such a rush. You didn't get your tips. Paula says she charged herself an asshole tax and put extra in. She requested that you please don't hate her." Mick held out the envelope with the tip money.

HomeSky could see it was useless to argue against taking it. "Okay."

Mick picked up his car keys. "Let me drive you home." She started to object. "So I can find your place easily tomorrow."

HomeSky nodded. "All right." She looked at Mick. "Don't feel sorry for me. Please. This is my undoing."

"I'm sure that's not so," he said. There was no getting through the wall she'd put up. "But I don't want to argue."

On the living room table lay Mick's doodle of his 3-F happiness triangle. HomeSky picked it up. "I guess I'll never know what those Fs stand for."

"You know the rules," Mick said, trying to find a lighter note. "You gotta figure it out. When you do, you'll want to water flowers again."

HomeSky's face tightened and she looked away. *If only it were as simple as a scrap of paper.*

MEADOW

Meadow put a plate of venison burgers on the table. Her father, Roy Lee, and two brothers couldn't have grabbed theirs faster if it were a contest.

"Could you please just pass the food."

"You're not the mom," the older brother said, shoveling steaming baked beans onto his plate.

"Yeah. You're not the mom," parroted the younger brother with his mouth full.

Roy Lee smirked. "No, your sister is no mom. You boys are more on the money than you could possibly know."

Meadow glared.

Her father laughed. "Hey, you remembered to grill the buns. I should break out my dancing moccasins." The boys had taken two patties each and Roy Lee took three, leaving none for Meadow.

"What?" Meadow hissed. "You're all dogs."

SPRING 1985

Her father used his t-shirt as a napkin. "Just chuck a few more on the grill. I'm sure the coals are still hot."

"They're frozen."

"The coals are frozen?" Roy Lee mocked. His oldest boy laughed so hard he spit out his bite of food, which caused the younger one to do the same.

"Worse than dogs." Meadow pushed away from the table and went to the freezer for more burgers. The laughing would almost subside, but then it would burst anew.

She sat in the backyard on the torn edge of the circular trampoline, her knees up close to her chest. Meadow's jeans had holes in the knees, and not because it was the style. Plus they weren't fitting too well these days. She tapped a cigarette out of an old pack she kept hidden in the garage in a rusty coffee can. "I know," she whispered. "I said I'd quit and I will, Bulge. Promise. But those hyenas make me so mad." Meadow left the top off the grill to revive the coals. Two frozen patties sat there. She lit the cigarette and blew out a thin stream of smoke. From her back pocket, she took out a folded song in progress.

Lying on the dock
Looking at the stars
Thinking of you
Whoever you are

You're lost in the millions
You're just like me
You're my hope
My beautiful maybe

In the hallway dark
With all those doors
Which one's mine
Which one's yours

We'll go together
See what we'll see
You're all I've got
My beautiful maybe

Meadow was returning the cigarette to her mouth to inhale when she stopped. Something inside her conceded. To the tattered trampoline. To the ripped jeans. To the rusted kettle grill with a substitute broom handle for a leg. To the shrunken house and the sagging roofline and the TV antenna steel-strapped to a broken chimney. To the yard uncut this spring. To her brother's bikes on the lawn like dead animals. Her eyes could have gone on, but they retraced their stops. Trampoline. Jeans. Grill. Broom handle. TV antenna. Yard. Dead bikes. Trampoline. Jeans. Grill. Broom handle. TV antenna. Yard. Dead bikes. Her unattended cigarette burned down and nipped her fingers, causing her to drop it.

"Bulge, it's always been hard for me to see myself here, but with you, it's impossible." Meadow slid down off the trampoline's edge. She made sure the cigarette was out with her tennis shoe before dropping it through the grill grates into the coals. "There are only two questions worth asking: Why? And Why not?" Her gaze swung around the backyard one final time. "Why not?"

When Meadow walked off the property, her full backpack was slung over her shoulder. The hood of her red swimming sweatshirt lay over the collar of her dark jean jacket. Her guitar case hung in her hand.

In the backyard, the burgers burned.

SPRING 1985

FROM BLACKNESS

Night pulled quiet over the day. It was black and profoundly still when Monsignor Kief stopped to remove his Irish snap-brim cap and wipe his brow. Night is different from day for a blind man, too. Not in its absence of light, but in its absence of sound.

His feet resumed their short sure shuffle steps and his cane lightly tapped out to the silence. He knew well the way to the highway south out of town, although he'd never had occasion to walk it.

Occasionally he would set his suitcase down and let both hands rest, listening, hearing his breathing. Then he would restart, suitcase in one hand, his other hand falling into the regular sweep-tapping. A smile crossed his face as he went, thinking about one of the little known advantages of being blind: you're never afraid of the dark.

He had sidewalk to take him past the post office, the credit union, and Ben Franklin, but the cement strip quit abruptly two blocks out of town where last year, Tom Crain put in an oversized parking lot for TC's Auto Body and Tanning. From what Monsignor Kief overheard at Lu Ann's diner, the town was up in arms about the size of that parking lot. "Could land a plane on it," they said. "And that ridiculous numbering system on the blacktop." It seemed TC had high hopes for the amount of business an auto body and tanning boutique could generate so he had lines put down to accommodate 40 vehicles. Every spot was given the number 1, because, TC said, that aptly captured how he valued each customer. The joke around town was, based on how he was doing, he could have added the number 2 to his parking lot and that would have accounted for most of his business.

After navigating the TC lot, Monsignor Kief found his way to the shoulder of the road, listening carefully for distant cars. He knew that less than a mile west of town, the highways intersected, one going south to the Twin Cities. A four-way stop was put in there years ago after one too many accidents. That was where the Monsignor would set up to hitchhike.

As he shuffled steadily ahead, the Monsignor let his concentration migrate to the boy, Singer, and the Latin phrase in his song. Where could those words come from if not God? For whose ears were they meant if not his? The words played over and over in his head. One's catechism can take many forms. Religion is lived, not learned in texts. Where some might call this journey into the night ridiculous—and dangerous—he knew God didn't share that opinion. When one has faith, doubt goes in search of an easier mark.

These thoughts filled the Monsignor with a gusto that was, in fact, distracting. As he approached the four-way stop at the highways' intersection, he'd begun to walk a line that angled him toward the ditch. He didn't hear the car approaching from behind. As he stepped beyond the shoulder's edge, the bottom suddenly went out beneath Monsignor Kief's foot, causing him to lurch forward.

SPRING 1985

Everything cascaded. His arms shot up in a desperate attempt to regain balance. The suitcase was launched in one direction, the cane flew in another. The Monsignor pitched forward, somersaulting headfirst down the ditch. Unbeknownst to him, all this was caught in the spray of headlights of the car behind him, which had slowed for the blinking red light that hung over the intersection. Here is what the driver's eye captured in a series of high-speed flash frames: Falling man. Airborne suitcase. And, if he wasn't mistaken, a long red-tipped cane, usually reserved for the blind, disappearing into blackness.

HomeSky entered her efficiency apartment, flipped on the light switch, and was shoved backward by the sight.

How can the truth of things escape you for so long, and then, there it is right before your eyes? The dirty piles of clothes scattered on the floor. The empty liquor bottles. The unwashed dishes heaped in the sink. The dust skinning every light fixture. The gray smudged windows.

"I'm lost, Joseph," she said. "I'm in the wilderness on strangers' land." Two of the front room light bulbs had long since burned out, but the one above shone brightly down on her. She looked at her hands, her jacket, the frayed cuffs of her pants, her grime-riddled shoes. "Who is this woman?" she asked.

HomeSky put her jacket over the back of a kitchen chair and set the envelope of tip money on her small dining table. She went into the hall closet for cleaning supplies, which had been untouched since she bought them. She took the sponge from its cellophane and put it in the cleaning bucket along with the Mr. Clean and a bottle of 409. She opened the box of garbage bags and picked a t-shirt off the floor for a cleaning rag. She set all of this in the middle of the efficiency apartment and sat next to it on the dirty linoleum. Eyes closed, she folded her hands on her lap and let her head hang. She listened for her breathing. She tried to visualize the gate to good thoughts. She strained to hear the wind chimes of the porch, the songbirds, the breeze in the treetops, the call of the tractor in the back pasture. Nothing. There was only the sound of water dripping into emptiness.

She took the soft, unused sponge out of the cleaning bucket. Defeated, HomeSky laid herself down, curled on her side in the middle of the poorly lit floor, and with the sponge as a pillow, rested her head, waiting for merciful sleep.

Meadow cursed both the craving for a cigarette and the fact that she carried none with her. A smoke could knock the edge off, embolden her, but she knew it was a fool's courage. "Oh, Bulge, just one, or a couple long pulls … SCRAM THOUGHTS!" she said, casting her arms apart. She refocused. "All we need to do is knock on that door. Nothing to it."

Three times now the young woman had picked her guitar case off the ground and moved through the night's cool darkness. She made it as far as the third stair tread on Pat's front porch. The squeaky one. Three times it sent her scurrying back to the side-yard, to meld into the deep shadows for her nerve to recharge.

"Plus I have to go to the bathroom, Bulge. Doc says you're going to give me the bladder of an old maiden."

Meadow shut her eyes tightly, but then let her face relax. She thought of the swimming races she'd won, how strong she felt getting out of the water, standing on the pool deck, knowing all the other girls' eyes were on her. She was hard and muscular and wouldn't take no for an answer. "Quit being a princess, right Bulge?" she chastised, opening her eyes, letting them adjust again to the poor light. "Just like morning swims. The longer you stand in knee-deep water the colder it gets."

This time she avoided the third step altogether and was still moving as she pulled open the screen door and rapped on Pat's front door. Meadow was a bit alarmed by the sharp volume her knocks generated. The tension spring on the screen door sighed as she gently shut it.

She set her guitar case down. Waiting. Waiting. Thinking it's not too late to bolt. Ironically, she would have run. Holding her feet to the boards was not the physical load of a guitar or a backpack, it was a less tangible presence. She sensed another life now, observing her, just one trimester into a lifetime. And so it was what brought her here, kept her here.

The overhead porch light snapped on. There was the muffled weight of another as the door handle was grasped from the other side. The door swung open. No one took a breath. Looking through the screen door, she saw in Pat's eyes first surprise, then confusion, then comprehension. They stood at the point of no return, and how long they would have remained motionless is hard to say. But the paralysis was broken when Meadow's stomach growled loudly, both from nerves and the fact that she never did eat dinner. They both glanced down at Meadow's midsection.

Pat reached to push open the screen door. He was holding a dripping dishtowel of ice to his nose.

"You look like shit, Mr. O'Rourke," Meadow said.

"And good evening to you too, Ms. FastHorse."

"Sir! Sir! Are you there?" The driver of the car ran through the black of night toward the ditch, one foot coming down on Monsignor Kief's cane. It rolled underfoot, nearly sending him to the same destiny as the man he'd come to assist.

"I'm here," a voice piped up. "Just ahead. I believe I've lost my cap."

Rodger Burke, the car's driver, scrambled toward the voice. "Yes, I see you. Here we go. Take my hand. I'll pull you up."

The elderly priest's foot slipped on the wet ditch grass. "You'll have to take mine, friend. I can't see."

Rodger had clicked the car's headlights to high beam. They threw just enough light for Rodger to make out a trickle of blood over the elderly man's eye.

"Have you been hurt? Is it your eye?"

The Monsignor stopped a moment and smiled. "It's my eyes, yes, but no, I'm not hurt. I'm blind, son. Now help me find my things. I've scattered possessions like a Sunday picnic."

"I'm pretty sure I have a flashlight in the car," Rodger told him as he set his feet and heaved the Monsignor up on onto level ground. "There you are. Why don't you just sit a moment."

"Thank you," the Monsignor said. "You're my Good Samaritan, but I prefer to remain upright. You get your flashlight while I do roll call on my various limbs."

Monsignor Kief heard the man's shoes jog along the loose gravel of the road's shoulder to his idling car. The door alarm dinged as he rummaged for the flashlight, which from the sound of things, was not where it was supposed to be.

Rodger came back and saw that Monsignor Kief held a handkerchief to the gash over his eye. "All I could raise is a Bic lighter. I did find your cane, though." He handed it to Monsignor Kief. "My name is Rodger, by the way. Rodger Burke."

The Monsignor took the man's hand and shook it firmly. "Rodger, you're a man of impeccable timing. I'm Monsignor Frank Kief. How are you at scavenger hunts? I'll say a quick petition to Saint Anthony, the patron saint of lost things."

The two clasped hands. Rodger was surprised that his own hand seemed to be one trembling, where the Monsignor's was cool and firm.

"Monsignor? You're a priest?"

"Yes. Semi-retired."

Rodger breathed out, catching his wind. "I've spent over 20 years on the road in sales, driving, flying, you name it. Just when you think you've seen it all …"

"Surprise is a firm reminder that there are plans that go beyond our own."

"Whatever you say, Monsignor. You're okay then?"

"All limbs present and accounted for. Now, we're missing a suitcase. Brown, smallish. And a cap. I think under the present circumstances, I make a better supervisor up here than a searcher down there."

"Let me see what I can find," Rodger said, flicking on his Bic lighter and turning up the flame. Dew had settled on the grass of the road's shoulder, so he edged his way down.

The search went exactly opposite of what they expected. The hat, which the Monsignor dubbed the needle in the haystack, was immediately located. The larger suitcase proved to be the mystery. There was much conversation back and forth about locating soda cans and a hubcap, then lulls of silence with little more than the sharp flicks of the lighter's spark wheel on the flint. The suitcase was finally found, sitting open, much farther from the road than expected. Everything seemed to be pretty well held in place by the interior straps.

"Monsignor," Rodger said, climbing out of the ditch with the bounty, "you gave this thing wings."

"Perhaps I missed my true calling … discus thrower," the Monsignor joked.

"Yeah. Or baggage handler." Rodger took another moment to catch his breath. His busy life in sales left him breathing harder than should be from coming up and down the side of the road. "Monsignor, you've taught me a valuable lesson."

"Please, call me Frank. What lesson is that?"

"I'm in lousy shape. I need to pack my running shoes when I'm out on the road." He wiped his brow. "I bet if I get back in those weeds I could scrounge up a pair."

The two men laughed.

"Frank?" Rodger asked. "Can I ask you what you're doing out here in the middle of the night?"

"Fair question," the Monsignor said in a pacifying tone that served to slow things down. It had been an alarming 15 minutes for both of them. "Of all things, I'm hitchhiking to the Cities."

Rodger took a moment. "Hitchhiking! Why?"

"Would you prefer I drove?" The Monsignor stood there with his patented wry smile. The small cut over his eye had dried up innocently enough. His hat was askew, suitcase at his feet, cane in hand. It made Rodger suddenly think of a boy going off to camp.

"But hitchhike. Why not just ask a friend for a ride?"

"Exactly, Rodger," the Monsignor smiled fully. "You have struck on the very definition of hitchhiking. We're all hitchhiking. Ask, and God will provide the ride."

"Can't argue with that," Rodger said. "Because here I am, and you've probably guessed where I'm headed."

The Monsignor picked up his suitcase. "To the Cities."

"To the Cities. And your company would be welcome. One condition, though. It's a long drive. Can we fill it with you telling me what's so important you're out here in the dark with your thumb pointed away from home?"

"Ah," the Monsignor beamed. "A drive … a story … and an unanswered question." He paused for dramatic effect. "We'll need coffee, Rodger. Plenty of it."

SPRING 1985

STORIES

Meadow's body tilted over her bowl at Pat's kitchen table. She hadn't removed her black jean jacket. She sat, legs folded under her, and ate without speaking, or even as much as lifting her head. Beside her elbow was a small plate that once held three pieces of buttered bread. A half-sleeve of saltine crackers was ripped wide open. She was ravenous, for which she silently blamed Bulge.

Pat turned from the sink to watch her at the small rectangular table. He was drying the Tupperware that had held Lu Ann's chili. Lu Ann always made sure he had a few meals waiting for him in the freezer. The Tupperware lid had a strip of masking tape atop with the words Rainy Day Chili / 2 Servings printed neatly on it. Pat smiled, thinking of how he teased Lu Ann about her perfect penmanship. She told him any waitress who can't write with precision ends up on the mean side of the cook. He put the Tupperware in the drying rack, watching Meadow devour her food.

She struck him as small, there at the wooden table. It was the first time for that. Maybe it was the light, which was spare, thrown from the room's ceiling fixture. This kitchen was designed for daylight hours, for morning sunlight flowing in from the many windows that Pat had carefully worked into his floor plan. Meadow's bangs hid her face. Her hair was tucked behind her ears, one of which had multiple piercings. She appeared to shiver. Cold had snuck into the farmhouse.

"Everything good?" Pat asked awkwardly. To this point their snippets of conversation had been stilted. They had talked fairly comfortably in the past. But this wasn't the rec center. The unfamiliar drew out Meadow's suspicious nature.

Now Meadow looked up. She pointed to the chili with her fork. "You make this?" She arched an eyebrow, as much as saying that she knew he did not.

"What if I said I did?" he said.

"Then I'd ask you if that's pineapple juice I'm tasting in the recipe."

"Oh," Pat said. "Then I'd say no. I buttered the bread, though."

Meadow went back to her bowl. "Tell me about this farmhouse," she said. "You never really went into any detail when you mentioned it before. Other than you built it for someone who left."

Pat let that sink in a moment. "Okay. Where do you want me to start?"

"Start at the end," Meadow said, watching him. "Start at now, and work backward. I mean I think I know how your nose got to look like that because my dad is wearing the same face. How about start with you and whoever's chili that is in the freezer, and work to you being on this land."

"Wow. That recipe should be called Curiosity Chili. Aren't I the counselor here? Aren't we supposed to talk about you?"

"We'll get there. Plus we've talked a lot about what I'm up to already. It's too one-sided."

Pat put a fresh handful of ice into his dishrag, holding it to his nose and eye. "I'm not sure what you mean."

"Too one-sided means too one-sided for trust. How can I trust someone I don't really know?"

"You've trusted me to this point."

"Up to this point. Correct."

Pat spoke in a non-serious, coaxing tone. "What about my lengthy experience … my gray hair? Is that good for nothing?"

"If I were buying a used car off your lot, maybe." Meadow looked at Pat as directly as she had all night.

Pat measured her comment and nodded. "I guess that's fair," he said.

"Can I ask one more thing?" Meadow said.

"You're on a roll. Why not."

"Got any more of that bread?"

"I hear the call of nature," the Monsignor said in a manner that led Rodger to believe it wasn't a distant alarm. "I erred in getting that extra-large at our last stop. You must admit, it was an extraordinary value."

"Extraordinary is one word for it." Rodger laughed. "It's a conspiracy. These truck stops shell out drinks in huge volumes at ridiculously low prices so you have to keep stopping all the way down the line. It's a perpetual business scheme based in biology. Dang smart."

They had been driving almost an hour now, and from no lack of effort on Rodger's part to divert the conversation, they had spent the majority of the time talking about him and his new family.

Rodger explained that he got married in his late 30s, and then got busy making up for lost time. He and his wife had two baby girls in 30 months. Of his old life, he missed nothing. Except sleep. Whenever he had to go out on the road it flat out knocked the wind from him, missing his family so.

Returning to the car after the pit stop, Monsignor Kief settled in with a Salted Nut Roll and a small bag of corn nuts. He opened both and worked back and forth as he renewed the conversation precisely at the sentence where they'd left off. "How much time do you have to spend away from home? Like now in Baudette, for example?"

"Less so since kids, but it can't be altogether avoided. My boss is great. A family guy, too. Came up through the ranks like me. Mostly we send the young Turks on the road, but I handled the equipment installation at your plant about, what was it, seven years ago. It's time for some pretty major upgrades, and I always see to those personally. So lately, the spacious Dew Drop Inn has been my second home."

"Have you gotten to know anyone in town?"

"The owner of the plant golfs, so we do that occasionally. A dinner once in a while. I keep to myself mostly. Back when we put the equipment in I did have a chance to meet one family. The Blackholms. Do you know them? HomeSky and Joseph? I looked for them in the phone book but couldn't find anything."

Monsignor Kief measured what he'd heard. He closed his eyes and let it sink in. "Could it be?" was all that he said, more to himself than to Rodger.

"Say again?" Rodger said, watching the road.

"You know HomeSky and Joseph Blackholm?"

Rodger noticed the abrupt change in the Monsignor's tone. He looked over. "I do. I did. For a short time. Why?"

Monsignor Kief took a deep breath and let the air blow out slow and steady. "Did you get to know them well in that time?"

Rodger studied the serious expression on the Monsignor's face. "Has something happened, Frank?"

"I'm afraid so." The car made its way through the shapeless night, cupped in momentary brightness when it passed under the hulking light poles. "I'm sorry to tell you this Rodger. Joseph has passed away."

Rodger's foot came off the accelerator. The car drifted before he quickly refocused, resetting his grip on the steering wheel.

"No. How, Monsignor?"

"He was struck and killed by a automobile. He'd been out running."

Rodger drove in numb silence as the Monsignor filled in the story.

Rodger finally spoke. "I knew Joseph for a brief few weeks. He was just starting his senior year of high school. It's funny how often I think of him, even as recently as this week." Rodger's voice tightened. "How about HomeSky? Tell me she's all right."

"Rodger," the Monsignor said solemnly, "would say you're a religious man?"

"I'm sorry, Frank. Not particularly."

"This will probably be all the more confusing then. You see, my hitchhiking, I'm on my way see HomeSky. To find her, actually."

Rodger shook his head, to clear it. "Frank, please. That doesn't make sense. Are you saying what I think you're saying?"

"Son, we are on our way to the Cities to find HomeSky. I fear she's not well."

"How? How could she not be well? How could *this* be ... happening?" Rodger gripped the steering wheel, to feel something real, to make sure he wasn't dreaming. "I can't believe we're having this conversation."

Monsignor Kief shook his head. His face had a wise peace about it. "Rodger, no one can explain God's will. There's an old saying: if you understand it, then it's not God. I must admit, though, this is a doozy."

"I don't know if that's comforting. You're a priest. Aren't you supposed to explain these things?"

The Monsignor smiled. "As I like to say, Rodger, I'm not management ... just in sales."

Rodger contemplated that. "So ... what? You just take it as it comes? Like the rest of us?"

"Pretty much. Of course there's prayer. So management understands our position on things."

All Rodger could say was a quiet wow.

"I agree," the Monsignor said, reaching over and patting Rodger on the shoulder. "You've had but one minute to catch up with all these years."

Rodger rubbed his hand over the day's whiskers. "It's that. And it's this. Me, finding you. I swear it's a dream. I'm about to wake up and be back at the Dew Drop Inn and the Baudette TV station will be off the air and there will be nothing but a test pattern on the screen."

They let silence settle in between them. A rest between the waves.

"Why isn't HomeSky home on the farm?" Rodger asked flatly.

"Perhaps we should stop and talk about all this? Get a bite to eat? I know it's a shock."

"No, no. Thank you. Please, go ahead. I'm fine. Confused, but fine."

"After Joseph's funeral, HomeSky was riven by grief. She didn't know what she was doing, I'm quite sure of that. She set the farmhouse on fire. By morning there was nothing left and she was gone. Our first fear was she had been lost to the fire. But the sheriff found empty gasoline cans and no trace of HomeSky."

"Forgive me Father, but I have a hard time believing any of this," Rodger said. "I know that farmhouse. I've been to it. HomeSky *loved* that place."

"Indeed. No one knew where she had gone at first. Then a letter showed up at my rectory. Just the one, over all these years, and it was brief. She said she was okay and had settled in the Twin Cities. She had a job. She made it clear she needed time away and there was to be no contact with her. She was unwavering on this issue. I respected her request, praying that something would change her mind."

"Do you know where she lives?"

"I have the envelope with the return address."

"But that was ... what? Almost four years ago. What if she moved?"

"Then I'll go from there."

Rodger was astounded. "Please, don't take this wrong, but you're blind, you're hitchhiking 250 miles in the middle of the night, with nothing more than a return address on an envelope that might or might not be current."

"I am."

Rodger shook his head and exhaled loudly. "Can I say it? Holy crap. Excuse me, but ..." The car rolled through the night, the rhythmic bump-bump of tires on pavement sections like a heartbeat. "Why, why, why?" he added.

"Rodger, never underestimate providence."

"Frank, all I can say is you're an amazing man of faith." Rodger looked over at the elderly priest, whose face, just visible in the light of the dashboard, held a perfect thin smile.

"Thank you, Rodger. Your faith needs to be greater than your fear. But also remember, just when you know the story, it changes on you."

"I'm not even going to attempt to interpret that."

"See, Rodger. You too are a man of faith."

The two drove on. And although the night blackened, their spirits moved in the opposite direction.

Pat spoke from a chair. Across from him, on the couch, Meadow was curled in the corner section.

"I've made a lot of mistakes, Meadow." She and Pat had been talking for about 15 minutes. "Had successes too. But I dwelled on my failings most of my life. Stuck there. Which, if you think about it, is like closing your eyes on a sunny day and saying it's cloudy. Right?" Pat looked over.

"I guess." Meadow pulled up a bit straighter on the couch.

"I could put it two ways: 'I didn't make it a lifetime as a priest.'

Or, 'I made it 23 years as a priest.' How I choose to define it sets the course. Negative. Positive. Too often I chose the former."

"Why?"

Pat looked at Meadow. "Oh what a question, what a question, what a question." He took a sip of coffee. "But you asked that we start with the now and work backward, right?"

"Uh-huh."

"Then that's where we'll start. I built this farmhouse for HomeSky Blackholm. Do you know her?"

"I know her story. At least I know what's said about her and her kid, Joseph. Everybody knew about him."

"Am I in that story, too? Have you heard what was said about me?"

Meadow nodded sheepishly. "I guess she lured you from the priesthood or something. And then Joseph died."

"Do you think those two events are connected?"

"I'm just telling you what I heard," Meadow said defensively.

Pat looked at her, quite directly. "I understand that. But do you think those two things are related?"

Meadow tilted her head, searching for the right phrasing. "Maybe she took you, so God took Joseph."

"Do you believe God would do such a thing?"

Meadow looked at the ceiling. "It's none of my business either way."

"So you have no opinion?"

"I don't think so."

Pat leaned forward. "You don't think so on having an opinion, or you don't think so that God would do such a thing?"

"I don't think the Creator would do that. Take something for something took. That seems like a human reaction."

Pat smiled. "I'm glad to hear you say so. The truth is I had decided, independent of HomeSky, that I couldn't be a priest any longer. As hard as I had tried—and I've never been more determined about anything in my life—it wasn't my true calling. Meanwhile I had fallen in love with HomeSky. And with Joseph. And there was something in all of that—a sense of family—that felt more right to me than I can articulate. Did you ever meet Joseph?"

"No. Just heard about him. They say he was a great hockey player. That he would have gone pro."

"Is that all they say?"

"I hear he is *jaasakiid.*

Pat thought about the Ojibwe word. "A saint?"

"Kinda. More like a prophet who's closer to the Creator than we are."

Pat nodded, thinking back. "I'd have to agree with them. After Joseph died he was laid to rest on the property here." Pat looked out the window. "Up on the ridge, next to his father. In her grief, HomeSky burned the house down. I can only guess that the memories were too strong and the loss too unbearable. I can't say. She disappeared without a word. We haven't spoken since."

The sounds of house closed in around them. "Sorry." Meadow said.

Pat put his finger in his coffee. It had gone cold. "Thanks. More coffee?"

"I'm good."

Pat walked into the kitchen, away from the past.

Meadow sensed he needed a break from his narrative so she waited until he was settled with his coffee to pick it back up.

"So this is where the old farmhouse stood? You built this for HomeSky?"

"For HomeSky. And for Joseph. And for his father, RiverHeart. Memories need to stand."

"It sure is cool." Meadow looked around at the care and craft of the space. "Really nice."

"Thanks. A little too new for my tastes. Needs to be more lived in. Needs some dings in the paint and things left out of their places." Pat was saying this as much to himself as to Meadow.

"I can see that …" Meadow said. But she didn't go any further.

Pat looked at her. There was something about her voice in that sentence that grabbed him, something alive and light. What was there, Pat wondered, before the sentence fell apart in mid-air? And then he knew. Hope. She sounded hopeful.

Finally and at last, good nights were shared.

Monsignor Kief and Rodger Burke parted after they had quietly made up the couch in Rodger's home, careful not to stir his young family upstairs. Cory phoned Hanna from his cabin and before hanging up he said goodnight to Singer, who informed him he no longer put boogers on the banister, but on the carpet because they go away there. Stu gave Darlene a little pat on the hip and Sheriff Harris kissed his finger and touched his dusty wedding picture. Lu Ann sent out a goodnight wish to Pat as she hugged the empty pillow next to her, careful not to get night cream on the pillowslip. Radio Voice said goodnight to God and sat up one more time to triple check that his transistor radio was there on his desk, standing by for the morning weather. Pat made sure that Meadow was comfortable in the guest room. Reg Cunningham had long since said his goodnights as he left the Mutineer's Jug, giving the collective bar the finger over his shoulder. And Mick closed his eyes, trying to erase all thoughts of bus depots by whispering, "Goodnight, HomeSky."

But it was not to be.

HomeSky lay curled on the floor of her kitchen. Suddenly, she sat bolt upright out of sleep. Her heart pounded, her breathing short. She swallowed, ears straining to hear it again. Was it a dream? Surely it was. She craned her head around, desperately listening. She swore she heard Joseph say *Gi zah gin*. "I love you," she said in return.

But when no other sound came, she doubted hearing anything at all. Then someone was yelling on the street below her apartment. *That's all there is,* she told herself.

She stood and began to scrub her apartment clean.

PART TWO

Sunday

MORNING

Mick couldn't sleep past five a.m. if his life depended on it. Sunday, the one day he didn't personally open the diner for business, allowed him to stay in bed. It was no use. All the years of rising before the cardinal's first call had wired his internal alarm clock with no snooze button.

At 4:45, his hair was almost entirely dry from the shower and his coffee was ready. In the predawn of morning, before light gives shape to landmarks, here is a time when the world has forgotten how far it has progressed. Simple, primitive sounds rise out of blackness. The creak of a tree. The gentle rustle of leaves. Followed by utter nothingness. It could just as well be 100 or 1000 years ago. Or so Mick thought. Simplicity is what Mick liked about this early hour.

Every day, Mick beat the sun in its race to find the day, but only on Sundays, when the weather was right, would he indulge in a sit on the stoop, his hair drying, his coffee steaming. He'd listen to what peace had sounded like since the beginning of time. His cup held to his cheek, warm as leaning against God's shoulder, Mick had to smile at himself, of the thoughts this time of day conjured. Some might call them silly, but what is silly except for a happy truth that some have yet to discover?

There was much truth injected into today, but for Mick, none of it happy. He spent time with the newspaper, he thinned a few stacks of paperwork, tidied a drawer, started a load of laundry—killing time until 8:00. He would pause from his particular chore, "Oh, HomeSky," he would slowly say aloud, in reluctant acceptance. Or, "Ah, shit!" spoken sharply to the countertop he was wiping down.

But now the time had come. He strode to his car as though he planned to kick it. As he turned over the engine, and backed down his driveway, he stopped and shook his head. "Going backward," he said, ironically. There was nothing he could do. He pulled onto the empty street and drove away. Leaving behind the one desperate hope he had allowed himself in his adult life.

At the farm, Pat stood at the kitchen sink, eating a half-bowl of corn flakes. The perfect amount, he told himself, to give his run sail, not anchor. He had gotten into the habit of eating while standing. In fact, he took few of his meals sitting down. *Good for the digestion,* he kidded himself. He knew the real cause was a never-ending schedule. It was like a perpetual-motion painting where water flowed upstream and small gears somehow managed to endlessly crank larger ones. In Pat's case, this picture wasn't entirely unrealistic. Tasks did give him more energy than they consumed. The underlying friction of life was not force enough to stop him as long as he kept moving. But in the back of his mind, he feared if he paused too long, inertia might swallow him whole.

He was wearing sweats, a ball cap and running shoes, ready to get out for an easy five. Pat tipped the bill of his cap up so he could drain the remains of the milk from his cereal bowl. He consulted his watch and left a note for Meadow:

SPRING 1985

Good morning.

8:15.

Went for a run.

Made you breakfast, wrapped in fridge.

Pancakes the size of wagon wheels.

Befriend the microwave.

Coffee's on.

Pat

Next to his name, he penciled a stick figure running, and made his way out the door thinking of Meadow. What an interesting girl—he caught himself—young woman. A conundrum in full. Cautious in every direction, especially with her words. She would look at Pat long after a sentence had been left open to her. She'd glance away, thumbing through some internal file drawer of replies, measuring, sometimes answering, sometimes leaving the question to hang there for both of them to silently resolve.

Pat jogged down the gravel service road that wound past the back pasture and would eventually bring him to highway. He smiled at the mailbox he built, a miniature of the farmhouse. His legs were loosening as he went around the north end of the quarter section, past where the stone foundation of the one-room schoolhouse stood grown over. He followed the highline wires leading to the main road. Over his shoulder, their lone silo stuck up on the horizon like a thumb.

So many experiences resided here, in the rising slope of the adjacent ridge, in the flat of spring pasture, in the sound of gravel under his running shoes. Time had made this space a memory gallery. The sun cleared the ridge, illuminating how lucky he was to have had this life. Despite the range of emotions that hung here, on both sides of this narrow gravel road, he cherished the chance to move through it, and find some new interpretation each time through.

Taking it all in, Pat drifted a bit too far onto the shoulder and stepped in a small sinkhole that sent a flash of pain up his ankle and jolted him to the present. He stumbled forward and nearly fell, firing an uncomfortable rush of pain through his sinuses, which were packed with cotton. He limped through the next mile waiting to see which pain would remain more present. Adrenaline is a wonderful thing. Soon he felt none of it, from his nose to his ankle, although he was quite a sight with his gimpy stride, his blackening eyes and his going-to-a-birthday-party smile.

HomeSky had cleaned her apartment to where it looked like it did when she moved in, except for the single mattress, which she leaned on the bedroom wall. The few dishes, pots, pans, silverware and coffee maker that she had acquired, she washed and left in a cardboard box outside her door with the word FREE written on it. She doubled up two paper grocery bags to carry a change of clothes and a second pair of shoes. This was all she'd take with her to the bus depot. Everything else she had acquired in her years here she stuffed into two large green garbage bags and hauled to the dumpster in the alley. She had arrived with the clothes on her back, and her purse, which held little more than a picture of Joseph. She would leave in much the same way.

She took the tip money from the envelope that Mick had given her the day before—$23 paperclipped to a guest check. Mick was proud of his custom guest checks with Mick's Diner in a slash of cursive across the top, followed by an address and his slogan below: Mick's Diner. *Come scrambled. Leave sunny-side up.* Mick had handwritten a note on the check.

HomeSky,

Twenty-three bucks. Paula says she's sorry and she'll do

the sugar packets and the creamers all next week for being

such a shit (her word not mine).

Mick

SPRING 1985

It made her smile sadly. She held the note to her nose and it was cool and smelled of bacon. HomeSky didn't have the heart to throw the note away, nor keep it. She stuck it in the envelope, and then used the back of the envelope to leave a note for the apartment super.

Mr. Dvorak,

I won't be in apartment 305 any longer.

Sorry for the short notice. Keep the damage deposit.

HomeSky Blackholm

HomeSky put her two keys inside the envelope and checked her watch. It was 7:45. She would wait for Mick outside. She didn't want this empty apartment to be how he remembered her.

"Heavens to breakfast, Mary. What a meal!" Monsignor Kief smiled fully at Rodger Burke's wife. "Just wonderful. Tiny confession: I do like to eat."

Rodger pushed back from the table and patted his stomach. "Tell me about it. This is why I can't ditch those 15 pounds that follow me around everywhere." Rodger sat grinning at his wife. His two-year-old daughter wriggled in her highchair, Cheerios stuck to the top of her soft little hands and cheek. The youngest, who had been up most of the night, now slept without so much as a peep. Such is the defiant time zone of an infant.

"Honey, Frank and I should shove off. We need to see where his envelope leads us." Rodger kissed his wife and child.

"Sorry to take him away from Sunday Mass like this, Mary," the Monsignor apologized. "But the good Lord has seen to it that I have a chaperone on this journey."

Mary came over and found Monsignor Kief's hands. They were strong, but gentle. "He's getting a little better at making it to Church, but we need to work harder. I hope this week's absence won't be counted against him."

"Certainly not," the Monsignor reassured her.

Mary continued. "It's so good to meet you. It's beyond amazing that you and Rodger met the way you did. I hope he can help in some way." Mary looked at her husband, thinking about the story he had shared and how HomeSky's suffering was at its center. "For a mother to lose her husband and her child …" She shook her head and spoke reverently. "I pray you find her. I hope she finds peace."

Monsignor Kief patted her hands. "Say an extra prayer and think positive thoughts. She'll find her way. I just know it."

The upper-floor windows of red brick high-rises were aflame in sunrise. Below, the streets were padded in a silent gray called early Sunday morning. Mick drove in a fog of thought, going through the motions but not all there as a driver.

He abruptly swung to the curb two blocks short of HomeSky's apartment. He threw the car into park and slapped the steering wheel. "Damned if I won't just do it!" He blurted out a short laugh. He knew. At that moment he knew. Or maybe he'd known from the moment HomeSky walked into his diner in response to the Waitress Wanted sign in the window. "I'll ask her," he said. Then talking to his reflection in the rear view mirror, "You just watch. I will. I'll ask her!" As he pulled away from the curb, the knot that had gathered in his stomach was busy doubling and redoubling.

The conversation with himself continued in earnest as he drove down the block and unwittingly ran a four-way stop, which earned him a one-finger salute from a driver who had already started through the intersection. "A little early to be drinking, idiot!" the driver shouted as he put down his window. Mick took notice of none of this.

He would walk straight up to her room, knock on the door and ask her. "Why not? She might say yes—"

Mick touched the brakes, his internal conversation interrupted. HomeSky was sitting on the cement steps of the apartment complex. The sight of her, waiting there, with her brown grocery bag and her pale blue winter coat, was a hard slap to the face. His optimism turned over like a coin.

SPRING 1985

"Am I late?" Mick asked a bit desperately as he hustled around the car to help Homesky with her bag. "I thought we said eight."

HomeSky told him he wasn't late, but the sound of her voice told him he was indeed too late. Far too late for any of the plans he held. Looking at her was to watch them vanish.

HomeSky misinterpreted his delay. "I know we're past winter coats, but I ran out of space in my luxurious travel bag." HomeSky tried to set a lighter tone as she lifted the double-lined grocery bag.

"It's not that," Mick said more abruptly than he would have liked to. He looked at the coat, then its broken zipper, frayed cuffs, the stains that went permanently into the fabric. "I guess we should be going," he said. They looked at each other across the empty sidewalk. The light around them was shapeless. The sun was lost, far back behind the urban high-rises.

"Yes," HomeSky said. "We should."

Meadow lay in bed with her eyes open, not sure why she was happy. She didn't trust it, but there was a stronger call to relish it.

The essence of her happiness was embedded in the small sounds and sights and smells surrounding her. Laundered sheets. Singing birds outside her window. A ceiling above her that wasn't festered and cracked. The aroma of coffee … and what? Bacon. The yellow flood of sunlight on the smooth white wall of her bedroom. "I don't want to move, Bulge. Tell me we're not still sleeping? Pinch me."

Her baby kicked on cue.

"Not exactly a pinch, but it'll do."

Meadow sat up. Her dinged-up guitar case leaned against the wall next to a high-backed chair. The door was closed but for a crack. On the chair, folded and neatly stacked, were her red swim team sweatshirt, a bath towel, a washcloth. Perched on top, a fresh bar of soap.

"The cherry on the sundae," Meadow said. "No more sharing soap." She rubbed her growing stomach. "I'm not whining, Bulge, but can it be, for the first time in our lives—yours notably shorter—

that we haven't drawn the short straw?" She pulled her hair back in her hands. "Well, time to shower. Then downstairs to see what Sundays are like in Camp Hideaway."

Meadow came padding barefoot down the steps *differently,* she thought. It wasn't a physical thing, even though lately she had noticed she was walking "kinda pregnant," especially down steps—going slower, safer, using the handrail, descending slightly splay-foot. *No,* she thought, *this is a different different.* She frowned at herself for having goofy thoughts, but the sensation was real. The exact what or why escaped her.

"Must just be hungry, Bulge." Meadow's ink-black hair, wet from the shower, was combed back, bringing out the strong features of her face. Her high cheekbones. Her smooth tan skin. Her thick, rather flat nose—which she despised. And her fiery black eyes, the one feature she admired. She liked her eyes because few could withstand their intensity.

It had been some time since she felt warm. What an indulgence a long hot shower is; for that matter, a hot shower of any length. Back at her house, *if* the hot water heater was functional, the boys or her dad took all it had to give. This meant Meadow's hot showers came only after morning swim practice, and she had to hurry so as not to be late for first period.

A brightness surrounded her. Again, a simple pleasure. The clean of white painted walls and white painted trim. The fill of sunlight in the eastern-facing windows. This was a calm her mornings had not known. She quietly acknowledged Pat's foresight in building this house with its oversized kitchen windows reaching out to the front pasture. *Was it the brightness?* she wondered. Was that what she was feeling?

Or was it the quiet? Again, a pleasure she couldn't recall, not in her house. With the ever-constant arguing and her brother's voices set on level nine. The quiet here wasn't lonely, as quiet can often be.

She closed her eyes to this kitchen and pressed into it.

"Hello?" she finally called out. "Anyone here? Pat?" She paused. "No Pat," she said to Bulge. The aroma of coffee pulled her to the warm coffee pot where he had left a note. "Well," she said after reading it, "Pat is a runner. There isn't a worse way to start the day if you ask me."

She poured coffee into the cup Pat had left out for her. It was a small act of kindness but one that returned her to earlier thoughts, of trying to find the word to express how she felt in this farmhouse. "Not bad, huh Bulge?" she said. "A place like this." She put her hands on her belly and took in a deep breath. "It's weird. I can't tell you what it is … but it's like when someone changes something in a room and when you come back in, you know something's different but can't figure out what." Meadow moved her hands to her hips and looked around. "Whatever."

Meadow found a plate in the refrigerator with three pancakes, three strips of bacon, and a quartered apple under Saran Wrap. "Trying to fatten us up," she said, munching on apples as the plate spun in the humming microwave. She pulled an in-progress song out of the back pocket of her jeans. "Harsh," she laughed at her lyrics. She turned over the sheet and wrote something new.

Who could have dreamed
houses so white
days this quiet
rooms so light

Where to go
to lay your head
tired and cold
a stranger's bed

Who could have dreamed

*could have dreamed
it so
Who could have dreamed
could have dreamed
could have dreamed*

*Dark to light
sand to pearls
first I'm alone
now you're my world*

*All these windows
replaced my walls
light becomes you
you are my world*

"Maybe a start," Meadow shrugged. "Maybe not." She returned the folded page to her back pocket. Just then, through the kitchen window, she watched Pat jog to a trot, finishing his run by the mailbox. He stretched at the far end of the driveway on the sun-sprayed gravel.

"I know!" Meadow snapped her fingers sharply, now in full grasp of what was *different*.

She was relaxed.

SPRING 1985

SHERIFF

Sheriff Thurgood Harris sat in his favorite booth at the back of Lu Ann's diner, as alert as a lifeguard. Little remained of his delinquent breakfast. He forked his last bite of sausage, pushing it across his plate like a mop head. At the same time, he tried to assemble some logical explanation of the morning's bizarre events. His sausage snagged a last string of hash brown potato. He finished it quick-like.

His coffee cup had gone empty and he let Lu Ann know about it.

"Where's the service in this place?" His voice rattled the silverware. As Lu Ann made her way over with a fresh pot of coffee, she was greeted by the Sheriff's cup, extended at arm's length.

"You checking the roof for a leak?"

"Just fill it. I'm busy thinking."

Lu Ann poured. "Oh. I thought that was burning toast I smelled." She turned and went off, looking, she said, for more agreeable company.

What a morning it had been for the Sheriff. He considered talking to Lu Ann about it, but at this juncture in the case, the Sheriff knew talking would produce more questions than answers.

A phone call from Monsignor Kief's housekeeper had awoken him just before 7:00. It was high-octave hysterics, yet due to the deep sleep he was emerging from, it took multiple repetitions of the same sentence for comprehension to find him.

"The Monsignor's been kidnapped!" By the third time, he was sure he had heard the housekeeper right.

And evidence consistent with such a statement did seem to exist. She told him how she had risen early, as usual, to start Sunday breakfast and found a stack of uneaten cookies and a full bowl of melted ice cream. "Something unheard of for the Monsignor. Unfinished!" She had been in the employ of the Monsignor for over 20 years, she informed the Sheriff, and never was there a bowl of ice cream started that he did not finish. She hardly took a breath before jumping into how the petty cash had been ransacked from the cookie jar, which sat lidless on the kitchen countertop. His coat and cane were missing, too. "Hurry!" she had implored. "The kidnappers could call at any moment."

The Sheriff chewed the last bits of sausage. He was suspicious of all of it from the moment he set the phone back in its cradle and dressed to go have a look. Suspicion came with the business, and more so, to the Sheriff. He liked to kid that he was born of an untrusting mother. *Who would kidnap a Monsignor?* he remembered postulating as he hiked the four blocks to the rectory.

If the evidence found there wasn't conclusive, it certainly was confounding. All signs pointed to a hasty exit. The abandoned bowl of melted ice cream indicated some late evening interruption. The bed—the housekeeper had run her palm across its unwrinkled condition, emphasizing her point—was still made up from the day before. And from the Monsignor, no sign or note. It was indeed a puzzle. The Sheriff had stepped out of the rectory in need of fresh air and a cigarette to help him mentally whittle down the knobby particulars of the scene. But as quickly as the Sheriff's hand moved to the front pocket of his shirt, he winced in recollection of his unfortunate situation. As of last week, he had wagered Pat $50 that he could quit smoking for a month. Consequently, the two front pockets of his uniform shirt harbored not cigarettes, but a pack each of pull-and-peel Twizzlers licorice. Red in the right pocket, black in the left—a sugary countermeasure to the call of nicotine.

Or so that was the theory. But when he stood facing one of the most extraordinary mysteries to strike Baudette, to have his acuity aided only by red and black licorice? Ridiculous, he thought, as he pulled a string of black licorice off the bar and stuck it in his mouth. It hung there like an old bootlace. That wouldn't work. He halved it with his front teeth, reducing the length to cigarette size. The other half went into the bushes. He found himself inhaling through the hole as his mind tried to traverse the details of the disappearance. "Shitfire," he growled. "I should know better than to wager with anyone who'd forswear alcohol."

There had been no further discoveries of foul play in the rectory, all of this penciled neatly onto a square of folded paper that the Sheriff slipped into his front shirt pocket behind the licorice. The Sheriff announced he needed some time alone with his notes before formulating a next move on the case. He delegated the responsibility of waiting for the rectory phone to ring to the deputy. Meanwhile, he went for breakfast. And that brought him to Lu Ann's for the egg and sausage scrambler, a local stronghold that combined four eggs, hash browns, shredded cheddar cheese, onions, green peppers, and a spice that Lu Ann would not relinquish, all brought together in a fry pan to give the dish a pie-like structure.

And so with the last of his scrambler hardly swallowed and the Sheriff no closer to the whereabouts of the Monsignor, the front door of Lu Ann's flew open and in came Mark Haumersmith, a local cabinet builder of German descent who kept mostly to himself except for the three dozen heirloom chickens he raised on his farmstead. He was nearly pushed through the door by the close-following deputy, who was subsequently pushed by the housekeeper. Once inside, this human train of people cast a hush through the diner. The silence was pierced by the out-of-breath housekeeper.

"Mr. Haumersmith has found something." She clasped her chest for a breath, or maybe just for the drama. "Evidence!" She spoke with such import everyone's head swiveled to the laconic cabinet-maker who, true to his nature, said nothing. Instead he lifted his find above his head for all to see. A murmur boiled through the diner. The deputy did nothing more than point at the artifact raised toward the ceiling.

The Sheriff's eyes weren't what they once were.

"What in Hades is it you have there, Haumersmith?" the Sheriff bellowed, twisting impatiently from his back booth. "The glare's a bugger from back here."

Haumersmith answered by holding the item higher, confident that would resolve things.

"Is that what I think it is?" Lu Ann questioned, as she approached the group in the diner's front section.

The deputy, still pointing, said yes it sure was.

The Sheriff squeezed his hulking frame out of the booth and walked toward the group. "Christ on a crouton," he muttered in frustration, trying to bring the item into focus. "A shoe?" he scoffed in disbelief.

"Not just *a* shoe," the housekeeper gasped, unable to restrain her tears any longer. "*His* shoe. That's Monsignor's Allen-Edmonds Weybridge leather loafer. Found …" she choked, "… found in the ditch where the highway leaves town."

Haumersmith vigorously nodded it was so.

The deputy added, "Appears he put up quite a struggle. Found this, too."

"The Monsignor's sock," the housekeeper verified. "I do the laundry Tuesdays and Fridays. I'd know his argyle anywhere." Then, like a volcano overwhelmed, out it came, loud, full-throated and spectacular. "The Monsignor's been kidnapped!"

SPRING 1985

The deputy sniffed the sock for freshness as the patrons of Lu Ann's hastily tossed money next to unfinished breakfasts to cover the costs. They pushed like cattle toward the door in possession of the biggest news to hit Baudette since the water tower got dropped on the bank in the '61 twister.

"Kidnapped," the housekeeper repeated, sobbing, covering her face.

"Just a crap-damn minute," the Sheriff called out.

Haumersmith continued, to no one in particular. "Know it's his shoe, yep. Did a cabinet for the good Monsignor last year. Nice cherry inlays."

"Everybody, hold it ..." the Sheriff's voice was rising against the rush.

Haumersmith added to the cacophony. "Always take off my shoes to carry in a piece. Noticed the Father's shoes right away there in the entryway. Allen-Edmonds. Quality leather. Pay a pretty penny, but worth it to get your quality."

"Keep your shirts on, people!" The Sheriff stepped forward and hiked up his trousers. "This is a direct order!"

But it was too late. The avalanche had come loose.

And so the word spread. Like so many proclamations made at Lu Ann's over the years, once something is spoken here it might as well have been printed in the *Baudette Region*. Before the hour was out, the town was buzzing: while our quiet God-fearing town had slept, the Monsignor had been snatched.

CORY

The idea of living happily hadn't occurred to Cory. Not that he was miserable, that wasn't it. But life's touch was not light on him. Days didn't sparkle nor did they shine. They pressed.

He walked out the door of the cabin with a cup of coffee and stepped heavily into the morning's magnificence. The serenity here, something that would make most inhale deeply and look around jaw-struck, this was lost on him. His knee was stiff from yesterday's theatrics on stage and the run last night. The cool of the morning was no help either. With a slight limp, he made his way down the steps, tangled in quiet thoughts. Sometimes just moving helps, this he believed.

As Cory came out of his wooded driveway onto the uneven blacktopped road, the sun verged on peeking over its bedcovers. Cory's footfalls came down on the scattered pine needles that softened the road's shoulder. Giant Norways hovered on either side of the road, sculptures pulled out of the earth by rain and sun and perseverance. The morning winds were so slight that the boughs seemed less to move than to breathe.

Rounding the bend, Cory stopped to take his last sip of coffee and stretch, aiming to unlock his knee. In front of him a deep green rectangle of alfalfa spread open to the sky. Muddy bear tracks, fresh from last night's stroll, exited the field, crossed the blacktop, and vanished into the woods. A paper-thin fog whisked the lowland—ghostly, rising, blue-tinged—momentarily held by the stored warmth of the earth below.

The sun broke hard over the horizon, finding the field's dew, touching off life there. A dress of golden beads sparkled across the terrain. A doe and a fawn, now rim lit, were carved out of the backdrop. They looked up from the grass, chewing. Cory returned their stare. Neither had noticed the other until this moment. The day was opening up.

Cory had to be to church by 11:00. As he walked, his mind processing the math of the morning's logistics. Walk: 40 minutes. Shower and shave: 15. Breakfast: 30. Drive time to Duluth: 40. To church from Hanna's: 10. Add ten more minutes for the Singer factor.

Total: one hour and 45 minutes. Cory had plenty of time thanks to the season's early sunrise.

Cory relished the sturdiness and dependability of math. Formulas. Rules. Certainty. *Math. It's something you can count on!* was the text on a poster back in Cory's third-grade classroom. For Cory, this wasn't a mere play on words. The message assured him. Math could be trusted.

The birds were busy in the sumac. Cory left the blacktop and walked into the field where the scrub and brush had been cut away for tractor access. The pile of rocks near the old, unstrung fence post had grown large over the years. Cory stood on the field's fringe and the memory rose out of the dirt and took him back:

Cory sprinted to the edge of the alfalfa field. Even in the dim evening light, there was no mistaking the shape of the belly-up single-engine plane. One wing was snapped off halfway along its length. A powerline was wound in the propeller, and despite it being torn down, it was live. Yellow sparks danced out of the frayed end on the plane's nosecone. A woman, thrown from the cockpit, lay unconscious 20 yards from the wreckage. The oppressive heat from the August night was combustible.

Kneeling next to the woman, Cory removed some grass and dirt from her mouth and put his ear to her lips. She was alive. A male voice rose out of the heap of twisted metal. "My child. Oh God, help me!" Cory knelt, stock-still, transfixed by the jumping sparks. The odor of gasoline was pungent. It was like watching a lit fuse.

The whoomph of ignition was insidiously quiet, but it broke the spell. Cory clicked into go-mode. He double-checked that his field jacket was zipped high up round his neck, turned his baseball cap around backward, pulling it low over his eyebrows, made a fist with each of his gloved hands and sprinted toward the fire which was spreading down the length of the plane. "Me, myself and I," he said, under his breath.

Crawling over the fire, Cory quickly squeezed in through the broken windshield. His heavy canvas coat protected him from the shards of glass. Smoke whirled inside the fuselage. Cory wiped away tears while the fire provided enough light for him to size up the situation. Because the plane came to rest on its roof, the pilot, strapped in his chair, hung upside-down, hands hanging limply. He was unconscious, with blood leaking from the corner of his open mouth. Cory put his ear there. At first all he heard was the chirp of crickets in the field, but then he detected breathing. In the back, a boy, who appeared to be about eight years old, looked at him, eyes wide with panic.

"Don't worry, buddy. I got you." Cory crawled to him. "Are you hurt?" The boy stared back, mute. "You're okay," he assured him between coughs. The boy was pinned, either by fear or injury or both. "Is that your dad?" he said, pointing to the pilot. The boy nodded yes.

SPRING 1985

To reach the boy in these compressed quarters, Cory rolled and slid himself on his back under the child. He unbuckled his seatbelt, lowering the boy down on him. "I'm going to give you a horsey ride out of here, okay?" He and the boy were face to face. "But first I have to roll over, so you climb on my back and hold around my neck." The boy wouldn't let go of Cory. "You need to slide off, buddy, while I roll over." Cory coughed through the thickening smoke. "It'll be okay. I know you know how to do horsey rides, right?" Cory looked into the boy's deadened eyes. A glint came to them as the boy nodded yes. "Nice job, buddy." The boy slid off as instructed. Cory rolled over on his stomach. "Okay, hop on." Arms came around his neck, taut as leafsprings, pushing on Cory's Adam's apple. He adjusted the boy's arms as he crawled out the way he entered, but not before his gloved hand cleared the windshield of the remaining toothy shards. Once they had exited the windshield, Cory told the boy to hang on tightly as he stood and ran-trotted away from the flames with the boy secured on his back.

As they passed the boy's mother, the boy didn't react. Cory sat him down by the rock pile on the field's edge. "I'll be right back. Don't worry, okay?" The boy just stared. "I'm going back for your dad."

Back inside the plane, a slashed rear seat was burning. The billowing acrid smoke clawed at his lungs. Cory estimated the heat was over 150 degrees. He could take nothing more than quick, sharp breaths. There was the ugly smell of scorched hair. Cory raked his coat sleeve across his eyes, removing the stinging sweat. To breathe, he had to stop coughing, which was bordering on impossible. His head ached, pounding for oxygen. He reached for the visor over the pilot's head. The paperwork clipped there had caught fire. Cory snapped the visor off and threw it out of the way.

The weight of the pilot hanging upside down made releasing the seatbelt impossible. "Think!" Cory commanded himself. Again, he rolled onto his back. Then, wriggling his way under the unconscious pilot, he placed one foot on each of his shoulders. With the pilot directly above him, Cory leg pressed him upward,

137

taking much of the dead weight off the seatbelt buckle. Then, doing a stomach curl, Cory reached for the seatbelt and unlatched it. The full weight of the pilot dropped onto Cory's legs and arms. He had no other choice but lower him down on top of himself, much like he had done with the boy. Blood from the pilot's mouth splattered on Cory's face. Smoke cut visibility to inches. The fire snapped, hungry for a fuel source. It had found the curtains now, and seat batting, as it inched its way toward the gas tank. Won't be long, Cory thought. The fire was consuming most of the oxygen, as well as the majority of Cory's strength and focus. His limbs were heavy with a numbing tingle and his vision moiréd. *Just take a short rest*, he thought, closing his eyes. In his mind, he saw the boy left by the rocks. Cory grit his teeth and rolled the pilot off him. On all fours, Cory began backing out of the windshield, using what was left of his strength to inch the limp body out behind him. Once outside the fuselage, Cory was revived by clean, pure air. Wobbly, he stood, hooked his arms under the pilot's armpits and began dragging him just as a blinding explosion illuminated the field and the surrounding trees in a flash of white.

When Cory regained consciousness he was 40 yards back from the burning wreckage. How long he'd been out, he didn't know. The pilot lay next to him. To his right, the boy sat next to his unconscious mother, stroking her face. Cory sat upright. The sticky chill of cooled sweat sent a mini seizure through him. Had he pulled the pilot this far from the wreckage before the explosion? Or had the explosion sent them both back? He had no recollection.

Two ambulances and a sheriff's vehicle were accelerating up the road that bordered the far end of the field. A neighbor had called upon hearing the crash. The flashing lights of the emergency vehicles splashed on the trees paralleling the road. Cory got to his feet, testing his limbs, and went to the little boy. As Cory knelt next to him, he saw the face of the child was no longer owned by a blank expression. In fact, his look of calm caught Cory off guard.

SPRING 1985

The ambulances skidded to a stop, doors flew open and flashlights and voices of the EMTs hurried into the darkened field. The boy whispered to Cory, "You saved us." He put his arms around Cory neck. "Horsey ride." The field was ricocheting with voices and flashing lights. The scattered flames burned innocently now on plane parts that had been dispersed throughout the field. "They look like candles," the boy said.

Cory stood and piggy-backed the boy toward the emergency vehicles. A few other cars had pulled along the shoulder of the road, their drivers silhouetted in the headlights as they strained for a glimpse. Cory directed the EMTs to the boy's parents. They shouted vital signs to one another as they assessed their conditions. One EMT reached for Cory's arm and asked him to please sit so she could examine the two of them. Cory said they were better off doing that up at the ambulance and proceeded in that direction. "What about your friend?" the little boy asked from Cory's back as they were stepping out of the field. Someone with a camera took a flash picture. Dark shapes out of their cars murmured to one another. "What friend, buddy?" Cory asked as he knelt next to the ambulance, helping the child slip safely to the ground. They came face to face. "Your friend back there," the child said, pointing to the spot where the wreckage burned. The female EMT approached. "Sir, please, I need to examine this boy. Step back, now," she insisted. "The one who helped you," the boy said as his eyes began to flutter. "He's quite pale," the EMT said. "I don't feel good," the boy told Cory as his knees began to buckle. Cory caught the child just as he lost consciousness. Carefully he lifted him into the ambulance. The EMT brushed past Cory. "Sir, you have to step aside. Now!"

Cory stood in the field. Spring alfalfa rose in neat green rows where the wreckage burned the summer before. What took place here was like something out of someone else's life. There was little trace of anything ever visiting this spot aside from rain and sun and field mice; look closely and you might be able to find a small depression in the earth. Cory squatted and quietly lay his hands on the ground. Here, like this, this place took hold of him, and asked the unanswered question. He heard the soft, high-pitched voice of the boy who he had come to know after the rescue. *What about your friend?*

Had someone helped him? Cory remembered nothing of how he escaped the plane's explosion. Or had the boy witnessed only Cory going in and out of the wreckage, seeing him as the light changed, as the fire intensified, thinking there was more than one? What was not in doubt was that Cory, alone, was lavished in honors. Hero Saves Three From Plane's Burning Wreckage trumpeted the headlines. There was the weeklong string of television interviews, beginning with Hanna's national exclusive, propelling her career with further exposure.

There was also the never-ending parade of handshakes and claps on the back. "Just wanted to say thank you," strangers would say. "You're an inspiration to us all, Cory." Through the media's overplaying of the story, they felt as though they knew Cory, greeting him like lost family. What ate at Cory, beyond the little boy's question, was this issue of heroics, which Cory dismissed—and not out of false modesty. He knew it wasn't so. A true hero, he told himself, put something precious at risk. Cory hadn't done this. *You ran toward that plane. Heroics didn't carry you there; it was inevitability. You've been on borrowed time since 13.*

Cory got up. The morning's beauty stood ready to embrace him, but he had to go. He walked on, limping noticeably only to those who knew to look for it.

SPRING 1985

HOMESKY

HomeSky needed a drink. She waited for her bus's departure, watching the clock, turning her ticket over in her hand. The brown paper bag with her things sat crumpled at her feet. A whistling janitor pushed a wobbly-wheeled bucket across the concrete floor, stopping now and again to mop a spot clean. A young boy and his mom made a game of getting a few vending machine snacks. The bus depot was dank, the sting of mold in the air. Every person's mood wasn't just present, it echoed.

Mick had walked her in. Stood with her as she bought her ticket, trying to make conversation, but failing. HomeSky told Mick she'd been in contact with a cousin in Des Plaines, Illinois. There was work there for Native Americans—at the hotels near O'Hare airport. The overtime pay was good, she assured him. She'd stay with her cousin until she got settled with a job and her own place. Nothing to worry about. Mick struggled with the right thing to say, but he felt like he was going to be sick. Finally, he relented, handing her his phone number on a scrap of paper. Mick made her promise to call if it wasn't working out—to call regardless. He wished he could help, he told her. He offered her money, but HomeSky said she was fine. She smiled and said he had been a good friend. Mick didn't care for the finality of the remark.

They sat together on the hard bench until at last, Mick couldn't bear it. He told her it was time he got to the windows. Sunday was Mick's day off, with a caveat. He always washed the windows at the diner on Sunday. Then he went to church. He found the two activities harmonious. HomeSky, looking at Mick there, incapacitated, hugged him strongly and said she would call, ashamed to lie to him like that.

Twenty minutes later, they called her bus. Homesky got in line. The small group shuffled toward the loading area. HomeSky wondered if she looked as run down and out of sorts as the others in line. Then she caught her reflection in the depot window as she went out the door to the buses, idling in the shadows.

Sheriff Harris wasn't sure. Was it Monsignor Kief's mysterious disappearance or Lu Ann's greasy hash browns doing the number on his stomach? He leaned on his cruiser and let the moment pass, so to speak.

"None of this makes a hen shit of sense," he muttered. He looked at the intersection of the roads where the Monsignor's shoe was found in the ditch. It was desolate country. Ragged, scrub spruce flanked by deeper woods in every direction with nothing more than a length of highway cut through the wild. No traffic at the present, only the endless low-frequency buzz of the powerline and the monotonous electric click of the caution light wired across the intersection.

"Nobody in their right mind would kidnap an old priest," he said aloud, roughly rubbing his flat-topped hair before reaching for the cigarettes in his breast pocket. "For Christ—" He stopped himself and looked to the sky. "Sorry, Amanda. In honor of it being

Sunday, I'll keep it PG." The Sheriff took a red Twizzler from his pocket, bit it in half, chucked one end into the weeds and stuck the other in his mouth. It whistled as he inhaled. "Not that making sense matters to some," he continued his internal conversation. The Sheriff had seen his share of ugly in his days. "Some people take a I-don't-give-a-shit pill and never come back."

The morning was warming quickly, but the dew hadn't burned off. The hulking figure of the 300-pound sheriff skittered carefully down the back of the highway's shoulder.

The wet grass, combined with the gnats rising from the ditch, made the Sheriff grumble. "Flying pollution." His hand cut through a ball of bugs.

The Sheriff had put a call into Pat at the farmhouse to tell him of their missing friend, but got a busy signal. Surely he'd hear the news soon enough from Lu Ann, or in town. The Sheriff's eyes stayed trained on the ground as he incrementally traversed the ditch grass, looking for any further scrap of evidence or clues. "What would his shoe be doing out here with this crap?" He kicked a Schlitz beer can out of the way. When it came down in the grass in front of him, it made a hardly perceptible metallic clin-CK. "What do we have here?" the Sheriff asked, his shadow coming over the can. When he lifted it, his skepticism about this being a legitimate missing persons case abruptly reversed.

"Heaven help us," the Sheriff muttered, pulling a pencil from his pocket so as not to get fingerprints on the evidence. He walked briskly up the embankment to the highway carefully holding the pencil out in front of him. From his cruiser he called in a missing persons alert in on Monsignor Frank Kief. As he was providing a physical description for the alert, the Sheriff lifted the pencil to the sunlight streaming through the windshield. He was transfixed by what hung from the tip, sparkling: an onyx-beaded rosary with a golden crucifix. Slowly the crucifix rotated, front to back, the light jumping off it. On the back of the cross were the engraved initials MFK.

Monsignor Kief shifted in the front seat, frustrated that he couldn't be more useful.

"Finally," Rodger Burke exhaled, pulling curbside and putting the car into park. He had circled the busy city block three times before finding the apartment matching the return address from HomeSky's letter.

As they made their way across the sun-dappled sidewalk to the apartment complex's entrance, Rodger looked skeptically at the yellowed envelope. "This postage date goes back a long time, Frank."

"Faith, my boy," the Monsignor assured him, pressing down on Rodger's shoulder more firmly as he guided him up the stairs. A woman leaving the apartment saw the two approaching, concluded they were harmless, and held the door open.

"Thank you," Rodger said.

"What?" the Monsignor replied.

"This nice young lady is holding the door for us," Rodger clarified.

"Oh, thank you indeed," the Monsignor said.

In the entryway, Rodger found an intercom buzzer button with the name H. Blackholm. "How do you like that," Rodger laughed. "There she is, in 305."

"A-ha!" the Monsignor clasped his hands together. "Praise be! Ring it. Ring it!"

After the third ring went unanswered, Rodger found the apartment superintendent's button and buzzed him. A neatly dressed, rail-thin man came to the entryway. He stroked his small groomed mustache as he listened to their story about HomeSky, inspected the envelope's return address and looked at Rodger's driver's license.

"This is highly unusual," he finally said.

"We just need to speak to HomeSky," Monsignor Kief said. "I think she might be in trouble."

The super's eyes narrowed—more than they naturally were. "And you say you're a priest."

"Forty-seven wonderful years." Monsignor Kief assured him. "Being blind, I don't have a driver's license, but I can show you my diocese card."

"Highly, highly unusual," he repeated, but his resistance slowly melted away.

"She's a fine tenant. Keeps to herself. No complaints in either direction," the super told them as they took the steps to the third floor. His tone had become collegial. "Just three floors here. Plus a basement. No elevator, thank goodness. My last building had an elevator. Old fusspot. You can't keep 'em working. Worse than an old boiler."

"What's this?" the super said as they approached HomeSky's unit. Against the wall outside her apartment was a cardboard box with the word FREE markered on it. Inside it were what appeared to be her dishes.

"What is it?" asked Monsignor Kief.

Rodger stopped at the door as the super pulled out his ring of keys "It's a box of dishes outside of HomeSky's apartment." The Monsignor's face spoke to his concern.

"Hey, what's the program here?" the super barked, opening the door and snapping on the lights. "It's empty."

"Empty?" the Monsignor asked.

"She's cleared out," the super said.

"There's nothing here, Frank," Rodger informed him, stepping inside. Other than a mattress leaned up against the wall, there was no sign of life in the small, clean space.

"I saw her only yesterday on her way to work," the super said, biting his mustache. "She's some sort of a waitress I think."

"Sure," the Monsignor said enthusiastically. "That's what she did back home."

Rodger recalled meeting HomeSky at Lu Ann's. He took a few further steps in. "I feel like an intruder," he said. Footfalls echoed back at them.

"Here's something," Rodger said. On the countertop was an envelope with the name Mr. Dvorak written on it. In tight, neat script, HomeSky wrote she was moving out. "I take it you're Dvorak," he said, handing the super the envelope.

He grunted as he took the envelope. "The policy is a full month's notice," he said, squinting at Rodger like he'd done something wrong. "And policy is policy." The super shook the contents of the envelope out on the countertop: Two apartment keys were twist tied together and there was a guest check from a restaurant. He handed the envelope to Rodger. "You read it. I left my cheaters downstairs."

Rodger read aloud that HomeSky apologized, but she was moving out. Dvorak was to keep the damage deposit to cover the rent.

The Monsignor spoke up. "Is there any forwarding address, Rodger?"

"Nothing," he replied.

The super was examining the guest check from inside the envelope. "This might be of use." He handed it to Rodger.

"Looks to be from the restaurant where HomeSky works or worked." Rodger told Monsignor Kief. "It's called Mick's Diner, on West 7th Street."

"Do you know it, Mr. Dvorak?" Monsignor Kief asked.

"I know the street, but not the restaurant," he said.

"We should go there, Rodger. Maybe she's working, or they have an idea of her whereabouts."

"Mr. Dvorak, could you point us in the right direction?" Rodger asked.

The super was busy going over the walls with his hands, inspecting for damage. He disappeared in the bathroom. His muffled voice came out into the main room. "You gentlemen better have a look at this."

Inside the bathroom, the super had opened the medicine cabinet to make sure it had been cleaned out. Taped to the back of the mirror was a page torn from the bible. A passage was circled in red ink.

> My days are swifter than a weaver's shuttle;
>
> they come to an end without hope.
>
> Remember that my life is like the wind;
>
> I shall not see happiness again.
>
> —Job 7: 1-4

SINGER

Bedside, Hanna watched him. *Just a little longer,* she told herself, sitting on the small wooden horse she'd brought over from the corner of Singer's bedroom. She didn't observe Singer as he slept, she absorbed him. His open hand turned palm up over his head. His ringlets of curls spread out on the pillow cover with its printed trains and bunnies wearing coveralls and engineer hats. The press of rouge in his cheeks. His perfectly symmetrical lips slightly parted. And what held her most rapt, the dark, beautiful arc of thick lashes. *Why didn't I get those eyelashes, my little wonder?* Hanna's hand slid onto the blanket covering his tummy. Lightly, she stroked it.

"Singer," she whispered. "Singer, honey. Time for breakfast."

His eyes blinked open. He stretched so big it almost hurt to watch.

SPRING 1985

"What?" his little voice peeped.

"Breakfast time."

Singer's eyes flashed as the sleep left him. "It's church day."

"Yepper depper." Hanna helped him sit straight up. She rubbed his warm back.

"Cory's coming," he said, giving her the double-thumbs up, just as Cory had taught. She smiled at her little man in his wrinkled pajamas and his little thumbs-up fists in the air, arms poking out from sleeves rapidly getting too short.

"You're growing up too fast," she said touching his cheek. "Stop that."

His tiny voice replied. "Ten hours rest puts hair on my chest." Singer was delighted with himself. Undoubtedly, more of Cory's training.

"Don't you go becoming a teenager on me," she said, smiling through a twist of melancholy.

"Okay, Mom," Singer said brightly. "Puzzle pancakes for breakfast?"

"Puzzle pancakes it is," she said, lifting him out of bed and setting his bare feet on the floor. She groaned. "You are getting so heavy. How old are you, seven?"

He crouched down ever so much. "Lower."

"Six?"

He crouched a bit more. "Lower."

"Five?" she said in mock astonishment.

Singer smiled widely, crouching even more. "Still lower."

"FOUR?"

Singer laughed and straightened all the way up, getting on his tiptoes. "Almost as big as four." He proudly stretched as tall as he could go. He turned and skipped off to the bathroom, in a moment as beautiful as it was fleeting. He sang:

SINGER

See the pony gal-lop-ing, gal-lop-ing, gal-lop-ing
See the pony gal-lop-ing
Down the country road

"Don't run down the stairs," Hanna's voice raised. Her admonition worked until the first landing but Singer couldn't hold back. He bounded down the second flight.

"Gotta check the window garden," he yelled, jumping from the third to last step to the floor.

"Use the ... banister," she called out to the empty staircase.

Hanna came into the living room where they kept their plants on the two south-facing windowsills. Singer carefully checked each. They had started from seed last month. All had sprouted except for Cory's lollipop plant.

Side-by-side, the plastic cups were wrapped in the first traces of morning light. Taped on the cups were the words Singer had proudly written using Hanna's letters as a guide. CORN in yellow. BEAN in green. In all there were six cups.

"When do you think the lollipop plant will sprout?" Singer asked, frowning.

Hanna looked at the empty black dirt in the last cup wondering what Cory had planned. "Remember what Cory told you."

"Singing is water," the little boy said brightly.

Singer sang a quick song to the unsprouted plant and then met his mother in the kitchen as she stirred the pancake batter.

"Did you stick your tongue out at it?" she asked.

"Twice," Singer replied.

"That should help," Hanna said. Cory had told Singer that nothing gets a lollipop plant blooming like the sight of a little boy's tongue.

When the pancakes were ready, Hanna took two of them aside and cut each into four different pieces. With the eight pieces mixed up on a plate, she set the pancake puzzles in front of Singer. He quickly used clues like matching round edges and which pancake was cooked browner to make the two pancakes whole again. Feed the boy and the mind, Hanna thought. Singer let out a hooray! before the disassembly began with the aid of syrup and a fork.

Hanna looked at her little king with his crown of curls, sitting in his white t-shirt while his Sunday dress shirt and clip-on tie waited patiently on the couch. How many boys going on four years of age would ask to put a dress shirt aside so as not to get syrup on it? How many would get excited about a clip-on tie from Grandma? How many would look forward to attending church? And certainly, how many are given a gift like he's been given? She watched as he ate. *Am I just along for the ride on this miraculous journey?*

Her thoughts were interrupted by the sound of the front door being opened and closed. "Hello?" Cory's voice called out.

Singer pushed back in his chair so fast that he almost went over backward. Out of the kitchen he went.

"Cory!" Hanna heard Singer's excited shriek cutting through the house. "I got my puzzle pancakes done already so we can play before church, right?"

"We're pretty short on time, bud," Cory said, picking him up and carrying back to the kitchen. "I missed you last night. One of these nights it's going to be just you and me."

"Yeah, Mom," Singer said hopping down. "When can I sleep over at the cabin? Just the boys, right Cory? Brigadiers."

"You mean bachelors," Hanna said. She kissed Cory good morning. "Singer, you've got too many questions going at once."

"But I want to go to the cabin."

"Cory and I will work out a time," Hanna said.

Cory jumped in. "I think it will be more fun in the summer. When it's steaming hot."

Singer's eyes flashed joy. "And we can play in the water like last year?"

"For sure," Cory said, charmed by the boy's zeal.

"I'm going to clean him up and then we'll go." Hanna took Singer by the hand. "Did you eat?" she asked Cory. "There are a few extra pancakes you could warm up quick."

"I'm good," Cory said. He looked at Hanna hand-in-hand with her child in the Sunday morning quiet. "You look nice," he said to her.

She smoothed her dress and stood in profile. "This old thing … thanks. It's not too tight, is it?"

"Not from where I'm standing." They looked at one another until Singer gave Hanna's arm a mighty yank. "C'mon. If we don't get to church early we won't get our good spot."

"Your wish is my command." Hanna was pulled past the refrigerator, out of the room and up the stairs.

Cory stood in the quiet of the humble kitchen. He felt good, surrounded by the smells and sounds of family. For him, such memories were dismantled, but not altogether lost. He walked into the living room and went to the window garden where the unsprouted lollipop plant sat. He took a bare white Tootsie Pop stick from his coat pocket—the candy had been cut from the stick. Pushing its length into the dirt, he left just an inch of it exposed above the black soil line. He went to the couch and sat down.

"Don't run down the … stairs." The smack of Singer's shoes making a perfect two-point landing punctuated Hanna's voice. She came down after him holding a brush. Singer ran over and sat with Cory.

"Whatcha doin'?" Singer asked, picking up Cory's hand.

"Thinking," Cory said.

"'Bout what?"

"About your plants. Have you been watering them?"

"Yes, but if they drink as much as me they'll get sick."

"Not too much, right?"

"Just this much." Singer showed Cory a tiny space between his thumb and forefinger.

"Did you sing to the lollipop plant?"

"Uh huh," Singer nodded.

"Is it growing yet?"

"Nope."

"Well what's that I see?" Cory gestured to the windowsill.

Hanna came over and joined them on the couch. They watched Singer's eyes scan the plants until settling on the cup with a tiny white stick rising just above the soil.

"Hey," Singer said getting off the couch, pulled toward the window by the sight. "Hey look! It's growing!" Singer waved them over, not trusting to take his eyes off the stick for even a moment. "See?"

"Would you look at that," Cory said. "It's small, but it's growing. What flavor do you think it'll grow up to be?"

"Cherry," Singer said confidently.

"Oh. Cherry grows fastest," Cory told him.

"Will it grow into a lollipop for sure? I don't see the candy part."

"Once the stick gets big, the candy blooms. *If* you take good care of it."

"I will. Promise."

"I know," Cory said, seeing magic in the boy's eyes.

His mother steered him back to the couch to brush his hair. "You look like a blonde lollipop, do you know that?"

"Mom," Singer complained. "Why do you have to brush my hair? It hurts."

Hanna tried to gently work out the tangles. "Just think about all the fun we're going to have today."

"What will we do?" Singer took Cory's hand again.

"Well," Cory said, "there's a nice farmer who lives by my cabin and I was talking to him the other day about you."

"About me?"

"About you and your mom." Cory continued. "He said if we wanted, we could come over for a real farmer tractor ride. Guess what day?"

Singer was too excited to guess.

"He said come on Sunday."

"This Sunday?" Singer said, squinting, just hoping it could be true.

"This Sunday," Cory confirmed.

"For real?" Singer said, almost breathless.

"Real deal. If your mom doesn't have plans for us."

They both looked at her. Singer saw the mom he so dearly loved; his body quivered to hear her say they could go. Cory saw a stunning woman who had freshened her makeup and let down her hair since she was in the kitchen. *It's no wonder,* Cory thought, *that everyone tunes into the news.*

"Why are you both staring at me like that?" Hanna blushed.

"Can we go?" Singer implored

"Your mother sure is pretty, isn't she?"

Singer scooted up on Cory's lap. "That's called buttering her up," Cory said in a stage whisper.

"Come on, Mom," he said. He could hardly focus. "Say yes. Real farmer tractor rides." Singer made a very earnest face and nodded for her. "We'll change our church clothes first."

Hanna got serious, too. "Hmmmm …" All eyes remained on her. "What's planned for today? We have a meeting with the president. The rocket ship needs to be washed and waxed and my magic carpet has to be vacuumed …." She paused. "Ah," Hanna tossed out a dismissive hand, "for real farmer tractor rides, we could cancel everything."

Singer jumped over to his mother and threw his arms around her neck and took her breath away. "Thank you thank you thank you Mommy!"

"And …" Cory's inflection told them there was more to come, "the farmer said he has a HUGE tractor tube he can fill so we can have a giant inner tube to use this summer at the lake."

Singer's eyes widened. "How huge? So I can stand on it?"

Cory's voice lowered like he was giving away state secrets. "So huge that we can all three stand on it."

"Really?" Singer was on the verge of peeing himself.

"And jump off."

Singer couldn't speak, only hold tighter to his mother.

Cory continued. "So big that we have to bring rope. Guess why?"

Singer slowly shook his head, struck mute.

"So big that we have to tie it down in the bed of my pickup."

Singer jumped off his mother's lap and danced on the floor. He sang and jigged.

> *This is the best Sunday ever.*
> *This is the best Sunday ever.*
> *Don't want it to end, never.*
> *Never. Ever. Never. Ever.*
> *The best Sunday ever.*
> *The best Sunday ever.*

Singer shook his hips and twirled. He had Cory and Hanna laughing till tears ran down their faces. Hanna got off the couch, trying not to disturb the performance. "I'll be back," she said. "I have to redo my mascara."

MEADOW

"How was your run?" Meadow was leaning on a post of the wraparound porch, wearing her ripped jeans and her hooded sweatshirt. Pat's palms were against the gnarled girth of the century-old oak that stood majestic in the front yard. He stretched his calves. His right one had a tendency to bite lately.

"What a day to be lucky enough to be a runner." Pat beamed, despite a nose and a pair of black eyes that would have stopped a parade.

"Running is self-imposed torture," Meadow observed. "Our coach made us run … until we threatened to drown him in the pool."

Pat wasn't listening. "It's spotless out there."

The wind picked up, but the day was warming nicely. The sun had climbed high enough to find the east-facing roof of the barn; steam rose as the dew burned off. A pool of shade stretched over the old hand pump, which was tapped deeply into the property's aquifer. Pat levered the squeaky handle. He reflected on how over the years, owners of this farmstead stood in this very shadow, and how the shade had widened as the oak's canopy had grown, and how shade from a tree is like compassion that a person can develop as he or she grows. He cupped water and brought it carefully to his face. The numbing cold was God-sent.

"What do you say to going to church with me today?"

Meadow gave him a smirk. "More self-imposed cruelty."

"Seriously." Pat looked at her earnestly.

Meadow crossed her arms. "I'm kinda unchurched."

Pat frowned, but his run left him endorphin-filled. He wasn't going down without a fight. "Come on." Pat took the porch steps two at a time. "It'll be fun."

Meadow walked across the porch to the door. "Church?" She put out one hand. "Fun?" she held out the other, as if weighing these two entities in the palms of her hands. "Can't see them together."

Pat stood in front of her, the cooling sweat now shooting quivers through him. He smiled and folded his hands like one does to pray. "Church and fun." He raised his eyebrows. "Just like that."

Meadow held the door open for Pat. "That's a new one."

"Thank you, ma'am," he said, walking through the doorway. "When was the last time you went to church? If you don't mind my asking?"

"Can't say, off the top of my head. Couple years. Couple lotta years."

"You're an adult now. With a beautiful child on the way. You're going to need God more than ever. A friend."

"Friend?"

"Yep. Somebody to talk to day or night."

Meadow turned away. She wasn't used to this much conversation ever, let alone so early in the morning, and the religious stuff to boot.

157

Pat sensed her pulling back. "Meadow, I'm not trying to lecture, or plan your life. Just start thinking of what's coming so it doesn't hit you all at once."

She re-engaged. "Like what?"

"Well, baptism, for one. I know you want what's good for the child. You'll want him baptized."

"How do you know?" she asked

"Every child should be baptized."

Meadow shook her head. "Not that. How do you know he is a he? You said 'you'll want to have *him* baptized.'"

Pat stood there with a puzzled look on his face. "I did say him. Hmm. I don't know. I just know. He's a he." Pat shrugged.

Meadow smiled. "I know what you mean. Bulge is a boy, no doubt."

"Bulge?" Pat winced.

"It's my nickname for him. Bad choice. I started calling him Bulge, it kinda stuck."

"I baptize you, Bulge," Pat cringed.

"I'll work on that," Meadow said. "Do you seriously think church would be good for him … for us?"

"Good?" Pat said passionately. "Great! Sitting on hard wooden benches, standing for hours, kneeling on cement floors. Sit, stand, kneel. Sit, stand, kneel. We'll have you two whipped into shape in no time."

Meadow remained serious. "Do you think of church differently now that you're an ex-priest?"

That hit Pat like the cold well water. "Yes and no," he said after some deliberation. I feel more drawn to it, now, than responsible to it, I guess. I never thought about it, exactly, until you asked. Interesting. In a way it's cool to hear my answer." Pat paused. "I wasn't the quintessential priest."

"I doubt there's such a thing," Meadow said. "You were a good one, though," she added quietly. "I used to go to church in grade school. The sisters made us, upon penalty of burning holes through us with their eyes if we skipped. You were good to listen to. Told good stories."

"Thanks. I had my failings, as I'm sure you heard."

"I guess," Meadow said.

Pat's mood lightened. "The glass is cracked but it still holds water."

"Huh?" Meadow said.

"Oh, just something a dear old Monsignor used to tell me." He smiled.

They were quiet for a moment, there in the entryway of the farmhouse, with little more to hear than the wind through the leaves and the laughter notes of the wind chime. An unusual space for such a discussion, but a good discussion. An inching forward.

Meadow spoke up. "Tell you what. Let's see how this week goes. Maybe we'll do church next week."

"General Patton couldn't have laid out a better plan," Pat answered enthusiastically. "I'm going to jump in the shower and get ready. Do you have anything you need to do? Homework?"

"There's just two weeks left of school." Meadow frowned. "I guess I have this one totally meaningless paper to write."

"All right. Try not to make it too meaningless. The last weeks of your senior year are supposed to be memorable and full of anticipation."

Meadow gave Pat a measuring look. Her eyes said everything she was thinking.

"Okay," Pat confessed. "I don't remember a thing about my last weeks apart from counting days like I was in a maximum security jail."

While Pat was upstairs cleaning up for church, Meadow found a writing desk in a small room off the kitchen. She set down her backpack and took a brief survey of the space. It was filled with psychology, sociology and theology books, and a number of keepsakes that Meadow tried not to linger over. "That stuff is private, Bulge," she told him. But one picture in particular held her gaze. It appeared to be taken a few years ago. Pat stood in the middle of the enlarged snapshot with his arms around the shoulders of a Native American woman on his left and a broad-shouldered boy an inch taller than Pat on his right. They were all three laughing, which made the photo unusually alive and captivating. Behind them was an old farmhouse, crooked with age, with a large wraparound porch. "It's just like this one, Bulge." She allowed her fingertip to gently touch the glass of the framed photograph. "That's HomeSky. She's beautiful, isn't she? And that's Joseph." Meadow studied the young man's face, how the joy radiated. He looked to be about her age. She lost track of time, gazing at that photograph, and might have been longer had it not been for the phone on the desk. When it rang, she jumped. In between rings she could hear the shower running upstairs, so she picked up the receiver.

"Hello?" she said.

The phone line crackled with emptiness. Finally, "Um ... hello?" said a voice from the other end. It was Lu Ann. Pat was supposed to have called her to make church plans 30 minutes ago. "I'm sorry," Lu Ann said. "I must have dialed the wrong number. I was trying to reach Pat O'Rourke."

"He's in the shower," Meadow said matter-of-factly.

Lu Ann's tone tightened. "What?"

"He's in the shower."

"Who is this?" Lu Ann demanded.

"Who is *this*?" Meadow snapped back.

And in that moment, one of the stickier misunderstandings of Pat's life was set in motion.

SPRING 1985

MICK'S DINER

With the guest check from Mick's Diner on Rodger's knee, he drove down West 7th looking for the address to match it. "I think I see it," Rodger said, excitedly. "Yep. Up on the right. On the corner. I think."

"Is it there?" The Monsignor had long ago made his peace with his blindness, but the last two days had been particularly trying. "What does it look like?"

Rodger pulled past the front. "Corner location. Nice. Nothing fancy. Hard to tell from out here. Looks like they're having the windows washed." He continued on, turning into the small parking lot clearly marked for Mick's Diner only. All others would be towed. "Pretty full parking lot. That's a good sign."

Rodger came around the car. Monsignor Kief was already standing, waiting for him. "I'm nervous as my first sermon … something sure smells good."

"I'm with you on nervous. I wonder if she'll look the same."

The Monsignor gave his shoulder a comforting squeeze. "She can't have changed that much."

Once inside, Rodger provided some color on the diner, literally. "Wow, it sure is green. A real eye-opener. But clean, neighborhoody."

"Any sign of HomeSky?" The Monsignor asked.

"Not that I can tell. Not yet. Hmmm—"

"Two today?" A waitress snapping gum approached the men.

Monsignor Kief broke in and took charge. "Good morning. Do you mind if I ask you your name?"

The waitress was momentarily taken aback. "Guess not, luv. It's Angie."

"Angela. A beautiful name. There was a Saint Angela who went blind, but whose sight was returned to her."

"Well I ain't no saint, but you sure are kind for bringing up the possibility."

"Angela, allow me to introduce myself: my name's Monsignor Frank Kief. And this is my friend, Rodger Burke." Everyone said hello.

"We're wondering if you know HomeSky. HomeSky Blackholm."

The waitress' face went slack. "Oh, God. Has something happened?"

"No, no, no. It's not that at all," the Monsignor said in an easy voice. "We're friends of hers from Baudette. Her home."

"Oh." Angie relaxed and put her hands on her hips. "Haven't seen her today, but that's nothing new. Mick, the owner, is right out there." Angie pointed to the window, but noticed the Monsignor's sightline didn't change. "OUT … THERE," she repeated, slower and much louder.

The Monsignor smiled. "Angela, my dear, I'm not deaf. Just blind. Rodger, do you see where this kind young woman is referring to?"

Angie's gum almost left her mouth.

Rodger looked to the window. On the reverse side, a man with a squeegee on a long rod was cleaning the window. "The man out cleaning windows?" he asked.

Angie was still looking at the Monsignor. "I hope I didn't offend you, sir."

The Monsignor smiled. "Heavens, no."

"Because I have plenty of marks in the wrong column of my book up there." She glanced to the ceiling. "Don't need no more."

Rodger interrupted her gaze. "That man outside?" he pointed.

Angie saw that Rodger was indeed pointing to the right man. "Yep, that's our Mick."

Rodger took Monsignor Kief's arm at the elbow. "Looks like we're headed back outside."

Angie suddenly grabbed the other arm. The Monsignor found himself in a mini-tug-of-war.

"Father," she said in a whisper, "will you say a prayer for me? I wasn't joking about my marks. Not so great. Well just the other night …" She stopped herself. "Could you send a prayer up for me?"

The Monsignor let go of Rodger's arm and found the waitress's hands. "By all means. But remember, God doesn't keep a scorecard. That's a human invention, and not a very good one at that. Throw yours away."

"Thank you, Father, I will."

"And one other thing, dear."

"Yeah?" she said.

"My prayer can't make it to heaven without yours to help carry it."

"I should say one, too?"

"Prayers travel better together." He patted her hands. "Now we must meet your Mick."

"Nice meeting you. The both of yous," she said, straightening her posture.

Mick's bucket of soap water had gone cold and he was about to go inside for a refresh when two men approached. They had the sun behind them making it impossible to see who they were. The younger one called out his name.

"Yeah, I'm Mick," he said. "Someone burn your toast?"

"No, not at all," Rodger assured him. Then he was silent, letting the Monsignor pick up the conversation.

Monsignor Kief made introductions, explained that they were friends of HomeSky and showed Mick the guest check he'd gotten from HomeSky's apartment. "This is how we ended up here," he said.

Mick tightened. "How, exactly, did you get this?"

Monsignor Kief heard the suspicion in Mick's voice. "Let me back up, Mick. May I call you Mick?"

"Everyone does." Mick remained on the defensive.

"We were let into HomeSky's apartment by the building superintendent. We were shocked to find it empty. HomeSky had written a note to the super on an envelope. Inside it were her keys and your guest check."

Mick blew into his hands. The glass was still in cool shadow, but the sidewalk was in hard light. "You say you've known HomeSky a long time?"

"Since she was a little girl," Monsignor Kief said with a warm smile. "And of course, her son Joseph, I knew him from a boy. She told you about him?"

"Never in great detail," Mick said. "There was great pain there."

Both the Monsignor and Rodger nodded. Mick went on. "I don't mean to interrogate you two. It's just that today has made no sense.

No sense whatsoever." Mick shook his head. "And now you show up and it gets more confusing yet." Mick paused again. "HomeSky has left," he said flatly. "She's left."

Rodger thought the man looked like he might cry. "What do you mean, left?"

"Left town. I took her to the bus depot …" Mick checked his watch, "forty-two minutes ago to be exact."

"Where on earth is she going?" Monsignor Kief asked.

"Father, that was my question exactly. Where? And why?" Mick's voice cracked. "There was nothing I could do, so I drove her to the bus depot just like she asked." Mick threw his rag into the wash bucket with a splash.

Cars drove by. Silence filled between the men. Inside the diner was the muted clinking of plates. A laugh escaped out the door as a couple entered for breakfast. To be here was to witness man's obliviousness to ever-present pain. We drive by it. Walk past it. Tracking our laughter through it. Clueless. It's there, should you bother to look. As hidden or apparent as three men backed into the shadows.

"You might be able to catch her." Hope lifted Mick's voice. "Yeah. If you go to the bus depot, which is an easy shot down 7th Street here, and ask about the route to Des Plaines. Maybe you can get one stop ahead and catch her before she goes and does this thing all the way."

Rodger spoke up. "Let's do it. We've come too far to only get this close."

"There's the spirit," the Monsignor proclaimed, clapping his hands together.

"Let me get you two road coffees," Mick said, the color returning to his face and disposition. He reached for his bucket, but paused to ask the one final question. "You guys came all this way. Why today? Why now?"

Rodger looked at Mick, knowing he had essentially asked the same question 12 hours earlier. "Monsignor?"

The Monsignor cocked his head. "Because something tells me it's time for her to come home."

SPRING 1985

BAUDETTE

Back in Baudette, word of Monsignor Kief's kidnapping spread faster than last summer's news that Elroy Eddelson's sow birthed a two-headed piglet. The local radio station, which typically found airtime to announce lost pets and update listeners on whether the walleyes were off their spawning beds, had dedicated much of its live commercial time to the description of Monsignor Kief, including his white Hoover cane with its red tip. Anyone with any news was asked to call the Lake of the Woods County Sheriff's Department.

Sheriff Harris was back at the intersection where Monsignor Kief's items were found. The wind caught hold of his tie and laid it over his shoulder. *Blowing a blue streak,* he thought as he stood on the rough shoulder of the blacktop. He stopped to make the sign of the cross before stepping into the road, something he did unconsciously—a habit from his youth.

What would he be doing out here? Sheriff Harris crossed the open road and stepped onto the opposite shoulder. He pulled a black Twizzler from his left front pocket, bit it in half, spit half onto the road, wedging the other half between his lips. He smoked it while unfolding a slim folded piece of paper that held the notes on this case. His printing was hard-pressed with a slight forward slant.

Melted ice cream, 6:45 a.m.
No forced entry.
Resident's petty cash fund raided.
Highways 11/72
Left shoe and sock, identified MK.
Rosary, also MK.

The Sheriff pursed his lips as he paced the highway ditch, thinking. *A struggle had to occur. The shoe and sock were pulled off? Why here? Had the car stopped at the intersection and the Monsignor attempted an escape? What other explanation could there be? Unless he'd come on his own accord, waiting for someone? Who? Why out here, away from town?* He puzzled over the case, turning over piece after piece in his mind until—FLASH—an a-ha!

The Sheriff looked up at the sky, licorice pinched between his teeth. He knew, then and there, that one immutable piece of evidence—or missing piece of evidence—back at the rectory would tell him if the Monsignor was going somewhere on his own accord, or if he was taken against his will.

The Sheriff again made the sign of the cross, double-timed it across the highway to his cruiser, spun a U-turn and flipped on his flashers. With authority, he sped back to town.

Reg Cunningham pulled his van to the side of the road and let the Sheriff's cruiser race past. "Where's the fucking fire?" Then, making the most of being curbside, he reached under the seat.

"Hello there," he said to the fifth of brandy. He slid the brown paper bag down, untwisted the top and had a grimacing swallow.

This was his travel companion. When it ran low, he'd refill it from the two-liter mother ship back home.

A splash of brandy ended up on his new shirt, one of five he'd bought over the past months from the nice-looking clerk at the Night & Day. Reg let the uncapped bottle linger on his lap while he thought about her. She wasn't like most of them wise-asses in high school. She had some respect, used the word sir. Plus she gave him a nice show when she leaned over, reaching below the counter to get a shopping bag for his purchase. *Like to sample that merchandise*, Reg grinned, giving himself a slow wink in the rearview mirror.

Reg was oblivious to his harsh reflection. His thin greasy gray hair was lucky to get washed twice a month, and then with bar soap because the only bigger rip-off than shampoo was conditioner. His pallid skin had a chalky gray tinge, deeply drawn and darkened around his eyes. There was something frighteningly dead about his eyes, which he kept in a constant squint. If you were to guess a color, you'd have to call them black, like an empty well shaft. Standing, Reg was still nearly six feet tall despite the incident at the pulping plant that left him stooped with three surgically fused vertebrae and a rod in his right femur. Looking at him, there was no hint of health. He was skin and bones and bile and booze.

Appetite was rare for Reg, but this was one such occasion. Maybe it was the new life opening up from every tree and on every lawn surrounding him. The spring air made his stomach growl. He gave half a thought to going downtown to his daughter's place but decided against it. The one time he turned over a coffee cup at Lu Ann's it was embarrassing, even for him. He'd taken his place at a table near the window and sat for 10 minutes, ignored. Then Lu Ann took the sign off the wall that said We Reserve The Right To Refuse Service To Anyone and walked over with it. She cleared his table of the coffee cup, silverware, salt, pepper, creamer, and napkin dispenser before slapping the sign down in front of him with such a bang, customers in back jumped. Reg remained there with that sign as a placemat for an additional 15 minutes before pushing back and leaving.

Screw her, he thought. *The tramp. Cracks out twins before she's out of high school. Higher-maintenance than a foreign car. Just like her mom. Ain't worth —*

SHUT YOUR MOUTH. The haunting voice of Kemp, from his youth, powered over him. YOU PIECE OF SHIT. SHUT UP. YOU TOLD.

Reg shrunk in the driver's seat. He balled his shoulders, squeezing his eyes shut. His hands went cold. "I didn't tell no one."

YOU TOLD, NARC!

"I didn't. I swear." Reg didn't dare look back.

YOURS IS COMING, REG-IN-ALD. GOT IT? YOU TELL ANYONE …

"Yes. I mean no. I won't talk." He cowered.

REG-IN-ALD. REG-IN-ALD. The voice laughed, booming off the van's windows. Reg grit his teeth. The laugh towered over him. It was there. He could smell it. Gasoline. Old paint. Dead mulched grass. Sweat. Grease. He hid in the driver's seat until his jaw ached from clenching. He finally dared to look up into the rearview mirror. The van's back seat was empty. Reg fumbled with the neck of the brandy, trying to unscrew the cap, realizing then it hadn't been replaced. "Son of a bitch." He tipped it high and left the brandy sit in his mouth, holding it. His breathing slowed. He swished it around. Slowly, back and forth, trying to rid the taste from his mouth. His rayon shirt was sweat-through. Reg swallowed.

When you have no ballast, you have no balance. Without balance, a human being degrades. Becomes wild. Nothing will slake the thirst. To be kissed by hate, from this, few recover.

Reg opened the driver's side door so he could reach down and pick up the gold plastic brandy cap that had fallen. He tightened it down and slid the bottle back under the seat. His hand shook as he lit a cigarette with the van's lighter. A beanbag ashtray sat on the dashboard. He emptied it at the curb and pulled away.

SPRING 1985

THE DEER

The cold that crept under the seats was damp and odorous. The Greyhound Superliner tracked southeast from St. Paul on its way to Illinois. Everyone inside the bus seemed to belong to a different world than the sun, which had climbed high enough to glance off the vehicle's long silver roof.

HomeSky had found two empty seats toward the back, staking claim to them. She sat sleeping against the window, her old blue coat softening her place there. Taking up the seat nearest her was the double-bagged grocery sack with her belongings. It was her Do Not Disturb sign. Or, she wondered before falling asleep, did it more say Beware of the Dog?

The busload had settled into the droning quiet of highway travel. The residual anxiety that comes with departure, with seat allocation, with the unknown, was behind them. They sat, empty. Many sleeping. Some staring blankly into the void ahead. A few tried to read a magazine or newspaper, scanning for someone's misfortune.

The driver was equally vacant of thoughts and sunshine. He put his sunglasses in their case, trading them for a few carefully placed eye drops. His eyes were light-sensitive and he abhorred this route later in the year when the sun wasn't so early to rise and he had to drive straight into its full morning intensity. He was about 20 minutes from his second stop: Rochester, Minnesota. From there he'd start pushing the nose of the bus harder east, the direction of Lake Michigan. Currently, he had the four-lane highway mostly to himself. Some elderly farm couples were making their way slowly to church, gussied up in their pick-ups.

HomeSky's right foot began to twitch. She had slipped into REM sleep. Her breathing quickened as a vivid dream opened.

Monsignor Kief and Rodger Burke were only 45 minutes behind the Greyhound. They had had difficulty convincing the ticket agent to divulge the destination and route of one of their passengers; it broke with policy, they were brusquely informed. But Monsignor Kief had a way of presenting the truth. That, and the presentation of his identification from the Archdiocese, not to mention his being blind, made for a story so compelling, by the end of the conversation the agent was mapping the route's stops and timetable. He also included his phone number should they need further assistance.

"Now I feel like we're getting close," Rodger said, glancing away from the road to the cup holder where he placed the cold dregs of his coffee.

Monsignor Kief had a flurry of powdered sugar donut on his shirt and lap. "Ah, faith has found you." He smiled at Rodger as the car wound southeast. The flat terrain on either side of the highway rose up now, giving way to majestic green vantage points as they traveled south.

"Where does faith come from, Frank?" Rodger asked the Monsignor. The car pushed ahead in silence. "Is it inside all of us, I don't know, like a package that some of us haven't opened? Or is it everywhere, but we all can't see it? Or is it like a book that we may or may not stumble across? I have trouble grasping the concept."

The Monsignor leaned back in his car seat. "Faith is."

Rodger slapped the steering wheel. "See," he said in friendly frustration. "Stuff like that makes us fence-sitters crazy. Faith is … what?"

The Monsignor laughed. "You're not going to like my answer."

Rodger mock braced. "Hit me with your best shot."

"Faith is everything."

"Oh, no!" Rodger struck the steering wheel again, not entirely in jest. "So, if I don't have faith, I have nothing."

"That," the Monsignor said quietly, "is absolutely correct. One of the few absolutes in this world."

"Meaning, I can have a job, and a wife, and a few kids, steaks in the freezer, a fishing boat in the backyard, a few buddies to golf with, and some money squirreled away, but if I don't have faith, I have nothing?"

"Sad, but true."

"So I have nothing?" Rodger spoke in a whisper.

"Are you asking me, or are you asking yourself?" the Monsignor said. Now they were getting somewhere.

In silence they drove on. Rodger spoke up. "Tell me about your faith." He looked over and saw the peace and calm that resided on the Monsignor's face. "It couldn't have been easy for you, losing your eyesight."

The Monsignor nodded. "Easy has no place in a conversation of consequence. But to back up to your first question about faith being a package or a book or carried on the air: yes to all of the above. But allow me to rephrase the question. It isn't a question of where does faith come from, but more so, where does it start. What is 'faith's fountainhead' is how the concept was first presented to me.

"When I was in the seminary, barely 20, I struggled mightily with a battery of questions. Funny, those questions have become a lot less daunting now that I'm able to see that things exist other than myself. Anyway, a wise old priest—" the Monsignor paused and chuckled. "I have to laugh because the wise *old* priest was about my age at the time. Nonetheless, this wise priest and I were having a very similar conversation, and he asked me to hold out my hand so he could show me what he called the fountainhead of faith. The genesis of it all.

"Now, my eyesight had been fully lost to me about two years before, so I vividly remember wondering what he could place in my hand in response to such a vast mystery. We were sitting together, Rodger, much like the two of us now." The Monsignor shifted in his seat. "So," the Monsignor said, "give me your hand and I'll show you what he showed me."

Rodger looked at the gentle man. A day's stubble peppering his chin. Donut flecks caught there. His thin gray hair tufting different directions. And for the first time since this journey began, Rodger truly questioned what he was doing. His stomach knotted.

As though reading his mind, the Monsignor said, "Son, there's nothing here to fear."

Rodger held his hand out across the car seat and alternated between watching the road and watching the Monsignor.

"Be attentive to the road, Rodger," the Monsignor assured him. "Remember I was blind when sitting in your spot receiving my catechism on faith. Relax. Your hand is as hard as a closed book."

Rodger took a breath and nodded. "I hear you Monsignor. It's just this is … ah …"

"A little weird," the Monsignor finished. "I know. I've been there."

Rodger's hand relaxed as it rested palm up in the Monsignor's. He was surprised by the sureness of the hand supporting his.

"Now, the fountainhead of faith, is knowing where beauty is." The Monsignor traced a circle in Rodgers palm as he spoke. "It's not here," he said while finishing the circle. "It's here," and he touched the center of the circle.

"One more time?" Rodger asked, thinking there had to be more to it.

Again the Monsignor traced a larger circle in his palm. "Don't look here, but here," and pressed the circle's center.

"I'm getting some fuzzy reception, Monsignor."

The Monsignor released his hand. "Thought brings clarity, my boy."

Rodger was surprised. "You're not going to tell me more?"

"Tell you? Where's the value in that? Instruction comes in your finding the answer. Things didn't become clear for me for months. But speed isn't my forte."

Rodger looked at his palm and felt a lingering touch in the center. "Can I ask some questions, like animal, mineral, vegetable? Or yes-no, or get some hints?"

"By all means. Faith is a discussion."

"'Faith is a discussion' … 'faith is everything.' It's too cosmic for my neighborhood." Rodger shook his head and smiled. "I'm a solid-ground type. Sol-id ground."

"Then I best not tell you how simple faith is."

Rodger groaned. "Oh, no."

The Monsignor continued. "Simple, not to be confused with easy. Because like we said, easy doesn't get invited to substantial conversation. But whenever a question of faith arises, you can simply use the palm of your hand and one finger to know you've got it."

"So are you saying faith is in my hand."

"No, that's not it."

Rodger mulled. "Let me ask you this, is hope the same as faith?"

"Wow," the Monsignor said. "You've leaped right to the solid ground you were in search of."

"I have to disagree with you on that. Hope is a slippery slope."

"Ah," Monsignor Kief said thoughtfully. "Interesting. Interesting way of putting it. I could compose a guest sermon on that topic. The slippery slope of hope. Very catchy, Rodger. But no."

"No what?"

"Hope is not a slippery slope. Hope is the bite in an otherwise slippery slope. Hope, not too get too distracted in rhyme here, hope is the rope on a slippery slope. Ha! I'm quite pleased with us!" The Monsignor let out a snort.

"So my hand is the faith that takes the rope …" Rodger said, knowing that the explanation of faith couldn't be so trite.

"Nice thought, but that's not it. No, faith is what's inside the outside. It's that simple. It's what alerts you to the rope, and it's what lifts your hand to grasp it. I must tell you, though, I am learning as I go, and I'm always tweaking my definition. Like I said, faith is a discussion. But, since you are a self-professed bottom-line guy, faith is as I drew on your palm."

They drove in silence, catching their mental breath, as it were.

Monsignor Kief's voice was melodious. "When my sight ebbed away I asked myself, 'what is it that God wants me to see that I can't?' I thought of John 20:29, Blessed are those who have not seen and yet have believed. That kind of faith comes from somewhere, just as my faith in the dwindling light comes from somewhere. There are large burdens put on your reserve of faith, and smaller ones. And through this, faith gets durable. I have a friend, a parishioner back home, who has her faith tested every time she receives the Eucharist. Without fail, she gets the hiccups after receiving the host. Why, she asks me? Why this burden? Your guess is as good as mine. For years she tried to interpret this happenstance, but God speaks in unusual and partial ways. Remember my question to myself, 'what is it that God wants me to see that I can't see by remaining on the outside?' Find the answer in your hand. The beauty is on the inside. Get past the exterior doubt, Rodger. Doubt can either be a destination, or a departure point. Make it your departure point. Saying things like, 'I feel like we're getting close,' launched this entire discussion and it is making your faith real and more durable."

Rodger blew some air into his cheeks and then let it pop out. "My head is spinning, Frank."

"Enough for now. You'll find equilibrium, sure as an Iowa barn." The Monsignor smiled warmly.

Rodger witnessed the peace in the man's face. And then, in the center palm of his own hand, there was the faintest tingle.

In HomeSky's dream she was warm and cared for. She was good and bright. There were flowers in the grassy south pasture as numerous as carefree thoughts.

In HomeSky's dream she observed herself. Past self? Future self? With fascination she watched this lean, strong woman with dark hair braided by wind stride peacefully across the open field. Bees pollinated at flower tops. In front of her, a young boy skipped on his toes, hair dancing in the light, his weight shifting from side to side. With each skip, a sliver of light was freed from below his shoe bottom. The precious amount of light was almost imperceptible, yet he was momentarily airborne, unpinned from our earth.

Then the sky filled with clouds, and the clouds ripped apart, releasing a billowing blackness. In HomeSky's dream the boy was now skipping on the river's surface, oblivious to any danger. HomeSky chased and chased and called after him, but her voice fell short. Somehow the boy remained suspended on the water's surface. She shouted a final warning. Hearing her at last, the boy turned and waved, and in that movement he pierced the surface. Under he plunged.

HomeSky was thrown against the seat in front of her as the bus driver locked up the brakes. The scream of tires and the sickening thud of the deer's impact came almost simultaneously. Startled voices filled the passenger cabin as the bus skid-stopped, straddling the centerline of the highway. In front of the bumper, motionless in the middle of the road, lay the body of a full-grown doe.

"Holy Hanna!" the driver exhaled. "Stupid thing ran right into me. Out of nowhere!" HomeSky, shaking dream remnants, her shoulder temporarily numb from crashing into the seatback, gathered her wits. She stood, and strode up the aisle of to the door in front. "Let me out," she told the driver.

"Lady, you gotta be kidding me."

"Please. The door."

"We'll just back up and drive around it …"

"NO!" HomeSky screamed.

The driver, shocked by the combination of recent events, obliged.

HomeSky stepped down onto the road and came around to the front of the idling bus. A beautiful amber-coated doe lay on her side, motionless. The asphalt was hot where HomeSky knelt. She looked at the deer's long, closed eyelashes. Putting her hands on the deer, HomeSky let her eyes also close. She felt a life source. The sun was strong against her eyelids; she knew the sun was for her. Softly, she stroked the belly of the doe.

When HomeSky opened her eyes, the doe's eyes were also open, looking into her own. Seconds passed like minutes. Transfixed, eyes locked, something passed between them. Then the doe's tangled legs unfolded. Her weight wobbled as her hooves moved under her to stand. She angled gingerly to the side of the road, standing against the lush green backdrop of the pine forest.

A group of passengers had gathered inside the bus, gawking in disbelief out of the windshield. HomeSky remained kneeling in the road as the doe swung around to take one last look. Flicking her tail high, the doe bounded into the woods, in the direction opposite the bus.

HomeSky looked down at her fingertips, still warm with the touch of the doe. "She's pregnant," HomeSky whispered. And for the first time in four years, she knew where she was meant to go.

SPRING 1985

LU ANN

Meadow was sitting in the kitchen eating the pancakes and bacon that Pat left for her. She heard him upstairs getting ready for church.

Coming into the kitchen, Pat was working his second arm into the canary yellow sports coat. Meadow almost asked aloud if the color of the coat was intended to divert attention from Pat's rather brutish-looking face.

"Do you think people will notice the stains?" he asked, absorbed, trying to get a look at the back of the coat.

"You mean if the yellow doesn't blind them first?"

Pat took two beats, and frowned. "What? It's not so bad. You know, for springtime." Pat pointed out a stain. "But your father got some mud and blood on it. I can't seem to get it out. I used half a bottle of Shout. Waited for a while like the bottle says before washing it."

"You put a sports coat in the washing machine?"

"Yeah, but not the dryer. It's already too small. I put it on the line to wind dry."

Meadow looked away. "One thing. He's no father to me."

Pat tried to catch up. "I don't follow."

"You said my father messed up your coat. He's no father to me."

"Oh. Got ya."

Meadow switched topics. "By the way, I think Ms. Rainy Day Chili from the freezer called." Meadow took a bite of pancakes and watched Pat. "Man, I'm always hungry."

Pat cocked his head. "Miss who?"

"Ms. Rainy Day Chili. Remember last night? The perfect Tupperware bowl from the freezer with the tape that said two servings? I'm pretty sure the woman who went to all that trouble tried calling you while you were showering."

"You mean Lu Ann."

"Didn't catch a name."

"What did you say to her?"

"I said you were in the shower. In hindsight, wrong move on my part. I think she took it wrong. She's kind of the jealous type, am I right?"

"What?" Pat twined his fingers and put his hands on top of his head. Walking to the window over the sink, he muttered something under his breath that sounded very much like for shit sake. "What did she say when you said I was … indisposed?"

"She asked 'who is this?' In a pretty unfriendly tone."

"What did you say?" Pat turned to face her, holding his breath.

"I returned serve."

"What?"

"I said 'who is *this*?' right back." Meadow fiddled with the scrap of bacon on her plate. "Sorry."

"Then what?"

"You're not going to like it." Meadow squinted.

"Then what?"

"She hung up."

"WHAT?"

"Told you you wouldn't like it."

Pat was visibly upset. "She hung up? We've been here discussing your appetite and your ability to read relationships based on Tupperware labeling, and she hung up?" Pat's voice was rising; he saw it in Meadow's eyes. "Sorry. Sorry." He turned his back to her and through gritted teeth said something that sounded like a sex act with a duck. "Okay," he exhaled, smoothing down his sports coat. "Let me get on the phone with Ms. You-Know-Who and see if I can put out this tire fire. Meanwhile, if you're going to be staying here you have to improve your phone etiquette, which means taking down messages. Politely. Agreed?"

"Roger that." Meadow was going to mention it was Lu Ann who hung up on her; what kind of etiquette was that? But she bit her tongue. Pat went into the other room to call.

He came back looking like a guy who'd just been cut from the high school basketball team.

Meadow was drying her plate. "Didn't go so hot?"

"Didn't go, period," Pat said. "She's either not answering, or she already left for church, which I was supposed to call her about but forgot."

Pat poured a cup of coffee and traced his finger around the thick rim, mentally weighing his options. He made for quite a sight with his canary yellow coat and two black eyes.

"Well," he finally said, "you'll have to go to church with me so I can get everything explained."

"I thought we agreed to put church on hold."

"Change of plans. You need to help me get out of the doghouse. Consider it a calling from God."

Meadow looked at Pat. She did owe him for taking her in. "Okay. Can I wear this?" She had on jeans and a sweatshirt. "It covers up Bulge, for now."

"I think God already knows about your baby."

"It's not His judgment I'm talking about."

"Oh, got ya. Sure, you look fine. Jesus welcomed rags and bare feet into His church."

"I think I'll stick with this instead." Meadow smiled wryly, trying to defuse the tension.

Pat did his best to remain upset, but failed. He was beginning to appreciate Meadow's sense of humor.

Lu Ann sat on the back stoop of her house. It was sun-drenched here and warm and shielded to where her hair wouldn't be undone by the wind. The sky was as clear as hindsight and the wind was coming with purpose.

"I'm old," she said with finality to herself. Her back was sore. Feet hurt. Shoulder ached. Waitressing full time since turning 18 takes a toll. The body dreams of long white beaches and warm oil rubbed into your shoulders by capable hands. "Dream on, lady," she said.

She tried not to hear the phone ringing behind her in the kitchen. Lu Ann was wearing her new teal church dress. She had unfolded the Sunday newspaper and sat on it to think a spell. She didn't like who she was becoming: a jealous woman. She knew things with Pat were going to take time. They had discussed that, on more than a few occasions.

They stayed clear of the L word, as Lu Ann referred to it. But certainly they were more than friends. Pat spent most every weekend at Lu Ann's, but that was as far as they took it, or, more accurately, as far as he took it. They had never spent a night together in the farmhouse, and that gnawed at Lu Ann. But she was a grin-and-bear-it gal. She understood, best she could, that it was the house Pat had built for HomeSky. She knew he had waited for her there. But after months, and then a year, and then another year of waiting, it was obvious HomeSky wasn't coming back. She recognized this as Pat's grieving period, and honored it. She left things unsaid.

SPRING 1985

They became very close. At first, just good friends. They both had lost the first love of their lives. The common empty place inside, they didn't have to explain or apologize for.

After HomeSky had been gone almost three years, the barriers were lowered. Particularly, on one of those idyllic holiday season nights. Large, seesawing snowflakes dropped out of the darkness and came inside on the eyelashes and coat collars of the merry guests at the Christmas party at the Baudette Legion Hall. Decorations twinkled from every direction, mingling with lights and spruce boughs and holly and nutcrackers. The tree in the corner of the bar was tinseled and winking green and red. A three-piece band of townies in Santa hats played. It was dancing and laughing all around.

There was a punch bowl. With more in it, it turned out, than just punch. And there was mistletoe. Pat didn't have any punch—he'd been sober for over six years, but he did partake of the mistletoe. Lu Ann was dolled up in her prettiest dress, the heat of the bodies in the dancehall had put her cheeks in high color, perspiration fastened a perfect wisp of bangs to her forehead, and after one too many trips to the punch bowl, she found herself with Pat under the mistletoe for an extended stay. Lu Ann was too tipsy to drive so Pat took her home. When they arrived at her front door, there was no need for music or tinsel sparkling in each other's eyes. Or, for that matter, mistletoe.

They spent the weekend at Lu Ann's, shoveling snow that had no intention of stopping. Nor did they. They had crossed a threshold.

A bit of awkwardness followed in the ensuing few weeks, but they talked through it. Spoke about not rushing ahead too fast, but not backing up entirely either. They found their way to this place where they were now. They trusted each other. They had deep, deep feelings for one another, but were careful. Especially, Pat was careful. Which Lu Ann knew ran counter to his nature. She chose not to dwell on that.

But now, Lu Ann wondered, *who is this woman who picks up the phone and says Pat's showering? Why hadn't he called like he said he would to make plans for Mass? What about this brawl he's had and said so little about? Why did he insist on going home to "mend alone"?*

Lu Ann went inside and scrambled herself an egg. Only one. Such was her way. She scooped out the last of the egg from the shell with her fingertip, just like her grandmother had. One piece of unbuttered wheat toast. She wanted to devour the entire loaf. She wanted to gorge on cookies and chips and ice cream. Instead, she put a half a stick of gum in her mouth, breathed into her hand to check her breath and ignored the ringing of the phone a second time. Church was in a half hour. What to do? She carefully tied an apron over her dress, found an SOS pad and nearly scrubbed through the stovetop getting after a few difficult spots of grease.

SPRING 1985

11:05

For some it was awe. For others, fear. When HomeSky reentered the bus after crouching with the struck deer, the passengers parted. She asked the driver where the next stop was. He stared at her. Mumbled something about Rochester, 30 miles ahead. She asked if she could get off there. Yes, the driver quickly responded.

Sheriff Harris found what he was looking for at the rectory. He now had his answer to whether or not Monsignor Kief had been taken from his home against his will. The evidence: a toothbrush. Or in this case, the lack thereof.

The Sheriff had concluded if the Monsignor's toothbrush was missing, it was prudent and reasonable to assume that the Monsignor himself had packed it before leaving the rectory on his own volition. If on the other hand, the toothbrush was still in the medicine cabinet, then a hasty exit and foul play were a near certainty.

So when the Sheriff returned to the rectory, and, with the assistance of a nearly catatonic housekeeper, discovered the toothbrush missing, he eliminated the possibility of kidnapping. The absence of the toothbrush, the housekeeper insisted, was impossible. For the Monsignor to find his things, she said in a climbing voice, they were always placed quite exactly. To now have an empty space here—at which time she pointed at the bare right side of the first shelf of the medicine cabinet—just could not be. She as much as hollered her judgment at the Sheriff, as though somehow he was responsible for the toothbrush's disappearance.

For more than one reason, he couldn't get out of that tiny bathroom fast enough. This case now had a clue pointed in a different direction. And there was no keeping the Sheriff from following it.

In the two hours since, the Sheriff had been speeding south toward the Twin Cities, on the same highway where the Monsignor's personal items had been found. He had come to two conclusions, both jotted on a square of paper in the front pocket of his uniform shirt, behind the red licorice. One: the Monsignor had set out freely toward some destination where this road led. Two: the Monsignor's housekeeper should be institutionalized.

Hanna held Singer's hand who held Cory's hand. The made a V as they came along the sidewalk, Singer leading the way, toward the sun-coated stairs that led into church.

Few people in the parish knew Hanna and Cory, but all recognized them as they found a seat. The parishioners nudged each other and flicked their eyes in the direction of Duluth's celebrity couple. Some were less discreet; they pointed at the news anchor and the local hero as they found a spot up by the piano. Singer's smile was broad as the ivory keys.

Bangs blew over her eyes as Meadow waited for Pat to back his green '66 Toronado out of the barn. Except for an occasional special trip to Baudette, Pat usually kept his pride and joy washed, waxed and covered in the barn, opting to drive the pickup instead.

SPRING 1985

Meadow assessed that the car was more than sufficiently cool as it reversed into the sun of the farmyard. She couldn't help laugh when she saw the vanity license plate: SAY14U.

As they headed south, driving the five miles that separated the farm from the Rez church, they spent most of the time talking about Meadow's least favorite subject: herself. Pat was deft at steering a conversation. They settled in on Meadow's passion for swimming. It could be traced back to a single provenance, at age nine, when the elders circled the bank of Porcupine Bay, holding out traditional morning-star blankets to wrap the participants of the fall swimming initiation. As this tribe of Ojibwe had done throughout their history here, children stripped down and braved the icy November water, seeing which young warrior could cross the bay the fastest, and who would be chased back by cold. Rarely did girls compete. As the nine-year-old boys stripped to their underwear, so too did Meadow, also leaving on her t-shirt. Meadow was not only the first to cross the pond, she was the only child to make the return trip.

The reliving of that day made Meadow long for water. Pat asked about her high school swim team, specifically how she was faring in competition. She looked away as she told him how this year she'd won state in the 200 freestyle and 100 backstroke.

"Good to know," Pat said as they pulled down the gravel road to the Rez church. "Because I'm big time up a creek. No paddle."

Rodger was thinking, *that's the longest Monsignor Kief has gone this entire trip without talking.* "Everything all right, Frank?" he asked.

"Yep. All good. Just saying my Sunday thank yous."

"While you're at it, throw in one that the bus is running late."

"How are we for time?"

Rodger looked at his watch. "It's almost 11 now. And we just passed a sign that said Rochester 10 miles."

"And the bus is supposed to picking up more passengers there at 11?"

"Uh-huh. Hopefully they'll be delayed. Otherwise we'll have to catch them at the next stop down the line." Rodger looked at the palm of his hand, thinking about their earlier discussion about faith. The car pushed down the highway, straight into a stiff headwind. *Figures*, Rodger thought, going heavier on the accelerator.

The blind Monsignor responded to the increased speed. "Have faith, Rodger. Have faith."

A narrow center aisle divided the two sections of polished wooden pews in the small Rez church. As usual, the back rows were filling first. Lu Ann had slid into their regular spot near the front on the right. This side of church was referred to as Mary's side because a statue of the Blessed Virgin stood up front, aligned with the right row of pews. A statue of St. Joseph stood at the front left, making it Joseph's side. Pat came in the back entrance, quickly smoothing his hair as the last of the candles were lit. Father Dan and the altar boys were in the entryway preparing for the entrance song. There was no hiding the look on the priest's face upon seeing Pat's broken nose. Pat whispered that it looked worse than it felt, shook the priest's extended hand, and told him he'd explain after Mass. He quickly handled introductions between Meadow and Father Dan. Lu Ann craned her head. Seeing them brought a rash of color to her cheeks. *Who is she?* Lu Ann studied Meadow as Pat waved and began making his way up the center aisle with the self-conscious teenager trailing behind. Lu Ann observed that the Native American girl became more stunning with each closing step. *She couldn't be half his age!* Lu Ann's face went from hot to cold as Meadow looked up from the threadbare, carpeted floor to return her stare. Lu Ann slid over and across the pew, not so much as an invitation for them to sit next to her, but more as an escape attempt.

Sheriff Harris pulled into Moeller's service station just off the freeway exit. It sat across the road from a newly constructed megachain gas station, one that sold pizza slices and designer coffee instead of windshield wipers and hose clamps. The Sheriff sneered. Gas stations should have a bell that rings when you pull up to the pump; they should be able to patch a flat in under 30 minutes; they should have a fan belt to get you home. He knew these newfangled "convenience" stations were burying the true service stations alive, and it left a lousy taste in his mouth. Or maybe that was the licorice. He tossed the half piece in the trash as he grabbed a long-handled windshield squeegee and cleaned his glass. The pump handle stuck out of the rear panel of his cruiser and he reviewed the details of the Monsignor's disappearance.

The missing person's alert he'd sent to the Minneapolis and St. Paul Police Departments was routed to the usual places—airport, prison, hospitals, train and bus stations—and surprisingly, they got an immediate hit. A supervisor from the Greyhound bus station confirmed he'd seen a man matching Monsignor Kief's description, and that he was traveling with a sighted man, in his late 30s or early 40s. They were last seen looking for a woman who had bought a ticket earlier that day. It was further reported that the elderly blind man seemed to be cooperating with his kidnapper and they were headed for a bus stop south of the Twin Cities in Rochester, in an attempt to rendezvous with the woman. Sheriff Harris was curtly given this news when he was finally put through to the detective in charge of the case. Sheriff Harris told the detective to hold his horses, that there was likely a different explanation in light of the Monsignor's missing toothbrush. The detective scoffed. He said he was a busy man with no time for theories involving dental hygiene. He told the Sheriff to stick to finding lost dogs and busting locals without a fishing license. This was "big league," was his exact quote.

Sheriff Harris went into the gas station to pay for fuel and to get the distance to Rochester. He didn't like one bit the direction this case was sliding. He was dealing with an overzealous city cop who was envisioning citation ceremonies carried on national news.

On his way to back the cruiser, the Sheriff made a small detour to the air hose on the side of the service station. As a manner of habit, he got down on his haunches, dropped his eyeline to the tarmac, scanning the pavement in front of him. He saw nothing but road grit, a discarded gum wrapper, and cracks in the cement. He looked harder, his eyes patrolling every inch. Then, five feet to his right, bingo. He found one. It was so crushed he almost missed it. Standing with a groan, he walked over and picked up the flattened valve cap, left behind when someone put air in a tire. He turned the smashed plastic cap in his fingers, walking back to his cruiser. At the passenger side door, he stood, his mind drifting elsewhere. When he regained focus, he pulled open the car door and reached into the glove box. Under his citation pad there was an old scratched Sucrets tin. He popped open the lid where inside, there were years of abandoned valve caps, maybe 40 in all. Flattened, cracked, some perfect. The left-behind. He gave them a light shake, creating an open spot. He placed the new one, closed the lid, and tapped it twice with the artificial finger. His watch read 11:00.

Mass in Duluth opened to a chorus of singing, as Hanna held the hymnal for both Singer and Cory. Not that Singer could read the words, nor did he seem to need to. He had the refrain down by the second return, and somehow the rest of the verse just seemed to be there for him. Neither Cory or Hanna were born singers, but they gave it the old congregational try. The Duluth faithful around them, especially the grandmothers, were pleased as punch with Singer, standing tall on the prayer kneeler, decked out with his clip-on necktie. But as his voice lifted and spread, the cuteness was quickly traded for a cautious reverence.

Reg deposited himself on his usual stool and pounded the bar with his fist like he was planting a flag on a mountain summit. The Grain Belt beer sign read 11:00. He said to all who weren't listening that it was noon somewhere. A double brandy seven would hit the spot, he announced. When his drink arrived he told the bartender to bring him a bowl of cheese popcorn and four quarters. He snapped his fingers and held out a buck. The bartender lifted his middle finger to Reg, and then used it and his thumb to take the dollar.

With quarters in one hand, cane in the other, Reg made his way to the jukebox. Like a washed up ballplayer stepping up to home plate, he was showered with insults from the bar about his inability to play music that didn't royally suck. He turned to the crowd, kissed the quarter, held it high for the group to witness, and then pantomimed depositing it in the crack of his butt.

Rodger and Monsignor Kief had no sooner stepped out of the car before hearing the upshifting of the bus as it accelerated away, down the frontage road. The parking lot of gas station that doubled as a Greyhound stop was deserted. Monsignor Kief asked if he heard what he thought he heard and Rodger said if you didn't laugh you'd have to cry. They just missed her.

As they turned to get back in the car, a quiet voice from behind them said, "Monsignor Kief?"

Pat genuflected before sliding into the pew; Meadow lagged behind. She hated the gauntlet of eyes one had to endure to sit up front. The bells in the church tower were ringing and the organ music had begun, accompanied by a choir of three off-key nuns in the balcony. Brilliant sunlight glorified the stained glass windows. In the pew, for every inch Pat scooched toward Lu Ann, she nullified by sliding away from him. He'd scooch, she'd scooch. Him, her. Him, her. It was like a bizarre mating ritual for birds of the tropic. Pat in his canary yellow sports coat. Lu Ann in her electric teal dress. As they moved left to right along the pew, Meadow, along with the rest of the congregation, gaped in fascination.

The notes came out of Singer, resplendent, unhalting, pitch-perfect. He had slipped out of his seat during the hymn, now facing the front of the church, near the body of the piano where he could feel the music go into him. As *How Great Thou Art* climbed to its crescendo, he held his arms aloft, his right hand clasped as if holding something lost. His soul sang out in a voice strong and sure. Each delicate note rose above the din just loudly enough that when other voices heard it, they fell silent. One by one, row by row, pew by pew, like concentric rings spreading across a pond, the congregation silenced. The church was rapt. Singer's pure voice remained. Until.

HomeSky let her paper bag drop to the tarmac. The Monsignor turned and held out his arms to her voice. "HomeSky," he said with certainty. She entered his embrace as four police cars roared into the gas station with their sirens silenced and lights flashing. Rodger froze in front of the scream of skidding tires. Car doors flew open and officers sprang out, weapons drawn, safeties off.

Reg slotted his four quarters into the jukebox very deliberately, one by one by one by one, to make sure there was a mechanical reckoning for each piece of silver. He pushed his first selection, a heartbreaking Roy Orbison ballad. The machine registered no response. He jammed the buttons again. Again, nothing. He'd been cheated. He brought his fists down on the machine, not once but twice and a third time. What was his had been taken.

In Duluth, as Singer's final note rang out, he turned to face the silent congregation.

At the Rez church, Pat reached for Lu Ann's shoulder just as the side door yanked open to a howling wind, extinguishing every candle on the altar and beyond.

In Rochester, a scrum of officers shoved Rodger and HomeSky face-down on the asphalt, tightening handcuffs around their wrists.

At the Mutineer's Jug, Reg cursed, bringing his full body weight against the jukebox, causing it to spark-pop and short out.

Just then, all the lights in Baudette went black.

SPRING 1985

COMING HOME

Thank God for Sheriff Harris.

That was Monsignor Kief's quiet devotion as the tangle of misinformation and overzealous police work was undone at their headquarters in St. Paul. As luck would have it, the Sheriff arrived at the police department not five minutes after the squad cars had returned. The officers had left Rochester fully believing they were transporting an elderly kidnapping victim and two perps. But it's an hour's drive to St. Paul. The more the officers heard from the apprehended in the back seat, the more things began to reek.

At headquarters, in separate interrogation rooms, officers asked HomeSky and Rodger their motives for the kidnapping. In a third room, the lead detective was beginning to sweat rings through his shirt as the Monsignor explained how he came to be at the gas station in Rochester, and the role of the different players there. He was understandably very upset. Forgiving. But very upset.

When the detective was interrupted that a sheriff from Baudette was here to see him, he had no other choice but excuse himself and go into a fourth room where he humbly presented the morning's misunderstanding.

The Sheriff was less prone to forgiveness. This was the same arrogant city boy who had humiliated him over the phone a few hours ago. Sheriff Harris paced the room, filling it not only with his size, but, despite his best intentions, with a cavalcade of expletives knit together in inspired and uncommon sequences. He made it clear to the detective that smaller offenses were known to knock captains down to horse duty at the rear of parades. He folded his arms across his large chest and stared at the detective. He put both hands on the table between them, and in a level voice spoke of lawsuits so large the city of St. Paul would be without capital improvements for the next millennium. He finished with his coup de grace. He asked the detective if he could check his fishing license because that's all small town cops were good for. The detective was willing to agree to any terms that Sheriff Harris offered as long as he could get this mess swept under the nearest available rug.

The Sheriff could have continued to use the detective as a footstool but the sport went out of it. So like a big kid with a little guy in a headlock, he released. He told the detective to escort his group to the bathrooms because of the long drive ahead. Meanwhile he used his phone to call his deputy back in Baudette so the town could stand down from the kidnapping alert. Relief would be followed by woebegone; how they thrived on the carcass of rumor.

He informed the detective that he would pull around back. The Monsignor, HomeSky and Rodger were to be discreetly ushered out the back door only after each of them was given a full apology by the geniuses making the arrests, with the detective being the first in line. Were there any questions? the Sheriff asked. The detective said there were not.

When the Sheriff strode out of the police station, his urge to smoke, for the first time since he and Pat had laid money on his quitting, was indeed sated by the piece of red licorice that he drew from his right front pocket, halved, tapped on his forefinger and placed in his mouth, dragging from it deeply. He looked every bit the conquering hero, undiminished by the limp section of red licorice curling from his upper lip.

They said their goodbyes in the shadows of the back parking lot of the police station. Rodger's car was retrieved from the impound lot and brought around. He shared a stiffly polite embrace with HomeSky, but when he stepped back from an enthusiastic hug with Monsignor Kief, Rodger asked if they could have a word in private. Rodger said a few things before taking out his wallet, removing the cash inside, and pressing it into the Monsignor's hand. The Monsignor tried to decline, but on the matter, Rodger was firm. Then Rodger promised to write; after all, a letter was the linchpin of this grand odyssey. The Monsignor told him how delighted he would be to correspond. And even more so, his housekeeper, who loved to serve as intermediary, reading any and all juicy details aloud. It was better than her soap operas.

With that, HomeSky and Monsignor Kief got into the back seat of the Sheriff's cruiser. The doors shut with an efficient "thunk thunk." It was an unusually emotional moment for Rodger, watching them disappear into the vehicle, this rare mix of authority and spirituality and loneliness. The left blinker switched on, and the cruiser turned out of sight.

The vehicle was quiet except for the occasional low rattle coming over the police radio. Everyone was emptied emotionally. About 20 minutes out of the Twin Cities, Monsignor Kief started to laugh. A chortle at first, quiet, to himself. But it quickly blossomed. That got the Sheriff snickering, which escalated to a series of nose-snorts, which was the tipping point for HomeSky, who hadn't laughed since she didn't know when. The outburst was brief as a summer downpour, but it softened the space between them. Then, upon the gentle snoring of Monsignor Kief, all breathing regulated.

When the good Lord was handing out the art of small talk, it's safe to say that Thurgood Harris was seriously AWOL. The Sheriff despised the idea of circumnavigating a subject. True to form, he kicked the door down and strode in.

"You must be nervous as hell coming back to town." He turned the country western station down a half click.

HomeSky could do nothing but smile wryly. "I see you haven't lost your way with words, Sheriff."

"I mean the way you went out. That's arson you know."

"I guess."

"On a private residence not a federal offense, but a felony."

"Shall we proceed straight to my cell?" HomeSky looked out the window at nothing.

"The hell," the Sheriff said. "I mighta done the same thing myself in your shoes."

They paused. Each waited for the other. The Monsignor stirred, but snored on.

"Pat rebuilt it, you know."

HomeSky stiffened. "What?"

"Pat rebuilt it."

"The farmhouse?"

"Yep. Did one hell of a job. Turns out he's quite the carpenter."

"The farmhouse is there?" HomeSky's mouth went dry. "On my land?"

"Same footprint. Looks just like the old one, only less crooked. And he added a cupola."

HomeSky's processing was a few sentences behind.

"A cupola?" she said. HomeSky remembered telling Pat that she always wished the farmhouse had a cupola. Windows on all sides. The fields there in all four directions. HomeSky put her head down. She squeezed he eyes shut, forbidding the sting of tears.

She took a catching breath. "How is Pat?"

"Oh hell, rock solid. Except when I left, it hurt to look at him. He got his nose busted by some drunk off the Rez yesterday." The

Sheriff pulled out a piece of black licorice, tossed one half out the window, and stuck the other between his lips. "Trying to quit smoking," he explained.

"Why would anyone from the Rez assault Pat? He's the priest there."

"Good night, you have been gone awhile. Pat hung up the vestments years ago. Let's see …" the Sheriff pinched the licorice out of his mouth, exhaling, "must have been just after you disappeared. How long's that go back?"

"So if he's not the Rez priest, what's he doing there? And why would that get him punched?"

"Actually he got it right on his front steps, or your front steps, I should say. There at the farmhouse. Sucker punched on his way out the door to Duluth to see Cory graduate college. From what I gathered, Pat is counseling the assailant's daughter on the Rez. Pat has an office there at the community center. He's some sort of headshrinker. And he still runs a shift up at the plant. That's Pat. Busy as ever despite being out of the priest business."

"But why punch him?"

"Because the guy's a shithead drunk," the Sheriff said emphatically. "How do I know? You tell me. You know that Rez well enough not to live there. Give me why."

A picture flashed in HomeSky's mind with such impact she flinched. She was in front of the bus with the doe. Her hands on the deer's belly. The life force. The doe's eyes opening. "The girl that Pat is counseling, is she pregnant?"

The Sheriff didn't see that question coming. The investigator in him was aroused. "He never said anything to that effect. What makes you ask?"

Again HomeSky sidestepped his question. "And you say Pat is staying at the farmhouse?"

"Yep. He's been keeping it. For you, I guess."

"I need to talk to him about that girl. But I don't know."

"Don't know about what?"

HomeSky looked out the window. How can there be so much sun out there, she wondered. Next to her Monsignor Kief stirred.

"Don't know about what, HomeSky?" the Sheriff urged louder.

"The farmhouse. Seeing it," she whispered.

"I was having the most wonderful dream about ice cream," Monsignor Kief said groggily. "Pistachio mint. Soft, and easy to scoop as air. All you could eat on toppings." The Monsignor straightened and stretched his arms until his hands hit the roof. "Sorry. Just resting my eyelids. Did I miss anything?"

The Sheriff spoke up. "We were just catching up. I told HomeSky about Pat and the farmhouse."

"I see," the Monsignor said. He reached across the back seat and found HomeSky's hand. He tried not to be alarmed by its coldness. "My dear, this must all come as quite a shock."

"I need to talk to Pat about the girl he's counseling. But I can't stay at the farmhouse." HomeSky's voice bordered on desperation. "I can't. It's important."

Monsignor Kief didn't completely understand what was so important and what she couldn't do, but rather than trifle, he thought fast. Moving closer he squeezed her hand. "I have just the idea." He was sure. "You'll come stay with me, for a time. My third-floor guestroom is the most welcoming place." His voice was melodic. "The aromas this time of year now that the windows are lifted open, mmm. And to hear it, the breeze playing with the new leaves in the maples. And you're the first to know of the rain, so close to the roof. And for me, one level below, the music of a friend on the floorboards, a concert!" He paused. "Do you think you could put up with an old roommate like me with his snoring and practical jokes?"

"I think I could somehow manage," she said with a slight smile to her voice.

"Promise not to hide my favorite ice cream spoon?"

"I'm not sure I can promise that," she said.

SPRING 1985

"Perfect," the Monsignor said, clapping his hands together to finalize the arrangement. "But first, we have something to do." Monsignor Kief strung out the pause for dramatic effect. "We need to go ... shopping."

"What the hey?" Sheriff Harris craned his head to the backseat. "Shopping?" He seemed to linger over every letter in the word. "I'd rather chew aluminum foil."

"Tough," Monsignor Kief said. "My house guest needs a few things before we return to the high society of Baudette, Minnesota, USA. Did we pass St. Cloud while I was dreaming of ice cream socials?"

The Sheriff grumbled they hadn't.

"Ex-ce-llent," the Monsignor said. "I have a dear old friend who manages Herberger's downtown there. She will welcome us with a brass band. You'll love her, HomeSky. She's a peach." HomeSky didn't protest, but Sheriff Harris more than made up for her silence. Nonetheless, they were going shopping.

When they stepped out of the cruiser at the downtown department store, the Sheriff chided himself for not noticing sooner the motivation for the shopping trip. HomeSky's coat, stained and worn. Zipper broken. The tattered cuff of her pants. Her shoes, scuffed raw and streaked, with one lace knotted where it had broken. But as disappointed as he was with the failure of his observational powers, he was doubly mystified how a blind priest knew they needed to go shopping in the first place.

It was the kind of gorgeous spring day that made car windows descend. Cory and Hanna decided they would drive a little longer. Singer was asleep in his booster in the back seat, the breeze through the truck keeping him cool. They were transitioning out of naps, but the day had been full of adventure and mystery—for everyone. If he didn't get at least 60 minutes now, things would unravel fast, on cue, right about dinnertime.

They were off schedule to be sure. But what are schedules when there are tractor rides to take, and a giant tractor tube to inflate, and a super-loud air compressor to turn on and off, and glue to squeeze on a patch, and even getting to be a rope dog, pulling hard when tying the giant inner tube down in the truck bed. PLUS having ice cream made right on the farm while sitting on the lowered tailgate of the truck. No wonder Singer was lights out.

Cory stifled a yawn. "He's cute when he sleeps. Just like his mother."

"Thank you." Hanna looked over at Cory, watching, as his face grew speculative.

"But," he added, "I think he sleep-drools a little less than Mom." The front of Singer's shirt was soaked where his chin had dropped.

Hanna slapped Cory's leg. "Be nice."

Cory took her hand and held it.

She almost said out loud how surprised she was.

"What do you make of what happened at church?" Cory asked.

Hanna shook her head. "Bizarre. I've always known he was musical. But lately," she paused, "pretty unfathomable. What do you think?"

Cory cocked the rearview mirror to check on Singer. "I know people always think their child is special, but I'm pretty sure Singer is off the charts."

Hanna shook her head. "I don't know if I want off the charts. Not sure I'm up to that."

Cory's eyebrows went up. "Well my dear, I don't think the decision is up to you. You saw him today. So did everyone else. The boy has music coming out of his pores, and it's not Row, Row, Row Your Boat."

Hanna nodded. "Like at the party yesterday. Latin? C'mon, where does a boy who isn't even four learn to sing Latin?"

"His mother is awfully bright?"

"Seriously Cory," Hanna insisted.

"Could he have picked it up at daycare?"

SPRING 1985

"I wouldn't think so ... maybe. The only music I've ever heard at Ms. Kortuem's is polka. But I'll ask. Maybe she's a closet hymn singer."

Cory watched the road, thinking. "Did you see how his singing affected Monsignor Kief? It really got to him, and nothing gets to him."

Hanna let go of Cory's hand and rubbed hers together slowly like she was putting on lotion—something she did when thinking. "I realize this is more than you bargained for."

Cory frowned. "What do you mean?"

"A child. Church. Tractor tires. Latin. All of this."

"It's not so much."

"Don't do that. Please." Hanna crossed her arms. "Don't make little of it because you're doing it. It reduces you. I hate that."

Silence filled in between them. Hanna continued, quieter. "You're 24, Cory. There are a lot of other things you could be doing."

"Are you breaking up with me?" Cory asked, only half joking.

"I just want you to know that this is getting to a point ..." Hanna looked at him intently. "Not only with me, but with Singer. He's starting to count on you. And me too. So if this really is 'not so much' for you, I need to know. I'll understand, but I need to know."

Cory nodded quietly. He wished he knew what to say. He wished he could make the right promise at the right moment. He wished he trusted the idea of future.

Then there was the humming of Singer. Cory looked in the rearview mirror. The boy's eyes watched him. Like he was awaiting an answer, too.

When they pulled up to Hanna's house, Cory gave Singer a piggyback ride in. Hanna was quiet. She went in the kitchen to get Singer a snack and start dinner. Cory sent Singer in to wash his hands and help.

At the window, Cory looked out on the remains of the day. The shadows had moved out from under the trees and were bent east. Cory thought about time, and timing, and days stretching into what? Into futures? Was he ready for this? He was never one to shirk responsibility, nor was he the first volunteer. He let things play out. First moves were for rookies.

Singer's plants sat on the windowsill garden. Cory smiled, thinking how children believe so fully in the certainty of tomorrow and in the kindness of time. What greater proof than putting a seed into a cup of dirt and watering it where the sun shines.

The green shoots pushed out of the black earth, reaching into the air. The last of the six plants was the lollipop plant with its bare white paper stick inching out of the dirt. Cory removed it. Taking a wrapped cherry Tootsie Roll Pop from his pocket, he sunk the bottom end of the stick deep enough into the soil so it would remain standing. Cory stood back for a look.

"Hey Singer," he called over his shoulder. "You got to see this."

Just as the Rez church was divided into a Mary side and a Joseph side, the parishioners were split over the significance of all of their candles being blown out. No one could precisely say how many were extinguished, because the votives lit for personal petitions and intercessory prayers were also out. What Sister Margaret Mary Anne could say for sure was that relighting them reminded her of the card game concentration; she had shut her eyes, and from memory, brought a long wooden match to the wicks she recalled being previously lit. In the end, the number generally accepted was 48.

How could 48 candles *just* be blown out by a single gust of wind? asked the Mary side. It was surely a sign from God.

The Josephs had a different explanation. The back door could have been propped open due to the unseasonably warm spring air. Then, with the way the wind was blowing, a sort of pressure vacuum built up, the side door flew completely open, allowing the wind to rush through. Don't make too much out of a spring wind gusts, they admonished.

Mass did, however, resume after the candle incident, and when the service finished, Pat was able to put the mystery of the "shower" phone call to rest by introducing Lu Ann and Meadow. They talked briefly in the parking lot. Meadow kicked at the gravel and provided one-word answers. When he and Meadow had first met in his office, Pat had promised to keep her pregnancy confidential unless it involved matters of her health or that of her child. When and with whom Meadow discussed her pregnancy was her choice. She was 18. Pat remembered being that age himself. Nothing drove him away faster than a virtual stranger telling him what to do. What he did tell Lu Ann was that Meadow's living situation was unsafe and it was her father who assaulted him in the yard. The Rez police were notified, and because the attack happened off-Rez, Sheriff Harris was in the loop as well. Meadow would stay at the farmhouse until things settled down. As long as she needed, Pat added.

Lu Ann suggested they continue their chat at her diner. She and Pat had a tradition of splitting a Sunday caramel roll after Mass. Lu Ann didn't work Sundays, but she couldn't help but look in on things. They agreed to meet there, despite Meadow's hangdog body language.

The diner was bustling thanks to extra foot traffic coming in with sunshine on their shoulders. "Thanks, Mary Alice," Lu Ann said as her longest-tenured waitress set side plates in front of each of them in the booth.

Mary Alice leaned into the table and whispered hoarsely. "Don't look now but there's outstanding diner hair at the far end of the counter." She tipped her head to the right to indicate where a customer was sitting. They glanced over where a farmer had removed his seed cap to eat. His gray hair stood dangerously precipiced, lurching to the left.

"Don't mean to be unChristian-like, but watch out. That could avalanche at any moment."

The waitress put her hand over her mouth to stifle her baritone laugh.

"Number three looks low on coffee," Lu Ann told her.

Mary Alice's eyes didn't budge. "You're off the clock, missy." Mary Alice gave her the schoolteacher finger wag. "Be a good customer or I'll toss you out on your ear." She winked at Pat and headed over to three with the pot of coffee.

Pat and Lu Ann sat on one side of the booth, each with a warm half of a frosted caramel roll on their plates. Meadow was across from them backed into the corner with an English muffin with cream cheese, peanut butter and a Coke. Lu Ann switched plates with Pat.

"That one has more frosting. I gain weight just looking at it." She took a sip of coffee, sampling it before swallowing. "I don't know if we've ever served soda with an English muffin made the way you're having it," Lu Ann said, trying to draw out Meadow with small talk. It had the opposite effect as Meadow retreated further into her hooded sweatshirt.

Pat was somewhere else. "Strange thing about those candles at church." He chewed his lip.

"Did anything like that ever happen when you were pastor?" Lu Ann asked.

He took a swab of frosting off the caramel roll with his finger.

"No. Don't know what to make of it. Although the side door does have a bad latch. If you pull hard it pops open." Pat rallied around this new possible explanation by sitting up straighter. But it was short lived. "I don't think that was it."

"What do you think, Meadow?" Lu Ann asked.

"About what?" She was thinking about ordering a grapefruit for Bulge.

"About all those candles at church getting blown out."

Meadow pulled the cuffs of her sleeves down lower on her hands. Lu Ann was going to say something about getting cream cheese on them, but caught herself. "Pretty major," she said.

Pat asked what she meant.

"I don't buy the door latch argument. I'm not sure of some huge message, but I think it meant something."

Pat looked at Meadow. "Give me a possibility."

"You're the expert on that stuff."

"Not necessarily. In your opinion, what could it mean?"

Meadow looked from Pat to Lu Ann. They were looking at her weird, like she might possess some secret.

"Can I get a grapefruit, do you think? And a water."

"Sure, hon," Lu Ann said. "I'll just go tell Mary Alice. It'll be quicker." She shot out of the booth with purpose.

Meadow spoke quietly now that Lu Ann was gone. "Maybe God doesn't want a pregnant teenager sitting in the front of His church."

Pat recoiled as if slapped. "Meadow. No. That's impossible."

"I thought you said you didn't know what the meaning was."

"Meadow. God welcomes all to his church."

She fiddled with her silverware, looking there. "You sure about that?"

"Absolutely."

Now she looked at him with force. "What about gays? What about women priests?"

Pat matched her intensity. "God welcomes all." He tapped the table with his finger. "The *Church* has a shorter guest list."

Lu Ann returned, out of breath. She slid across the vinyl booth, close to Pat. "Everybody is hungry and grumpy today. Grapefruit and water coming right up, dear." She looked from Meadow to Pat. "What are you saying about church?"

"Oh, just that God and church are not interchangeable words."

"Wow," Lu Ann said, biting into her caramel roll. "Calories never tasted sweeter. What do you mean not interchangeable?"

"My opinion, the Church is a man-made organization, and therefore, forgivably but inexorably flawed. God on the other hand is God. Beyond human error, pettiness and prejudice."

Meadow engaged. "So you're a big fan of human beings."

"Love 'em. But as Monsignor Kief says, 'every gem has its flaws.'"

"So you love my old man?"

"I do. Not so much the punch in the face part, but yes."

Meadow picked at her food. "There's no waiting in line in his fan club."

Lu Ann decided to perk things up. "How about I come over later and Meadow and I make three-cheese lasagna with Italian sausage for dinner?"

Pat's eyes widened. Pat could eat lasagna for breakfast. He could eat lasagna after finishing a full meal. Pat could be ill and the smell of lasagna would make the back of his mouth tingle while he crawled to the table.

"Great," Pat said, slurring slightly.

"To save some time I'll put it together at my house and bring it over because it's about 40-40-20." Lu Ann was thinking out loud.

"How's that?" Pat said.

"Forty minutes covered in the oven, 40 minutes uncovered, 20 minutes cooling."

Pat was looking at Lu Ann, but he wasn't hearing much. He was already tasting the melted cheese and red sauce.

"I could pick up Radio Voice and bring him out, too," she said.

Pat said nothing

"Hellooo?" Lu Ann teased.

Pat snapped out of it. "Sorry. You lost me at uncovered."

"I thought I'd pick up Radio Voice on my way out."

"Perfect." Pat said.

"Radio Voice?" Meadow asked.

Lu Ann had a bite of her caramel roll in her mouth so Pat jumped in. "He's a boy—actually a man—I work with at the plant who has Down syndrome. He comes out to Sunday dinner at the farm once a month or so."

"But I don't get the name Radio Voice," Meadow said.

Pat smiled, thinking about his answer. "He has this transistor radio that he carries in his pocket. It has to be, what, 30 years old?" Pat looked at Lu Ann.

"At least. He's had it since he was a kid."

"You mean a Walkman?" Meadow asked.

"No. From before that. Just a simple radio with an earpiece that plugs in the side, not headphones like you have. He loves it. Keeps him company. If he's been listening to the weather or something, he has an uncanny knack of repeating it back in this deep baritone voice like you hear the radio announcers use. Almost like it's recorded. Everyone at work calls him Radio Voice; they have since before I started there. Most don't even know his real name."

Meadow's brow furrowed slightly. "And he's okay with being called that?"

"He loves it," Pat said. "It's his thing."

"That's cool," Meadow said quietly to herself.

Meadow's grapefruit came and she ate it quietly. Sticky carameled fingertips were licked. Everyone looked at one another in the slightly awkward way you do when you've run out of food to eat and things to talk about. "Well," they all said at about the same time.

"Yep." Lu Ann concurred.

"I got the tip," Pat said. When he and Lu Ann ate together, the meal was on the house. But when Pat ate alone, he insisted on paying full freight—something that bothered Lu Ann, but not enough to bring up.

"Thanks," Meadow said. "For the food and all." She finished her water. "This is a pretty cool place. It's cool that you own it."

"I'll have to tell you about that later, while we're getting dinner ready. I wasn't much older than you when I bought it. Can you believe I was actually close to your age once?" Lu Ann winked.

Meadow noticed for the first time how pretty Lu Ann was. There was something about her, especially her eyes. They were young and happy and bright. "Okay," she said.

"Good thing we'll have some baking time," Lu Ann continued enthusiastically. "My story has more layers than my lasagna."

THE FARMHOUSE

Aromas ferried Radio Voice into the kitchen. Tomato sauce. Ricotta cheese. Italian sausage. Onion. Basil. Garlic. Lu Ann had put aside a small cache of buttered French bread before wrapping the dinner loaf in aluminum foil. She called these sneaker pieces, used to hold off the appetites of those lured in.

Radio Voice had left his cribbage game with Pat. Again. He bounded opportunistically into the kitchen. "Any more sneaker pieces? Just a half?"

Lu Ann told him he'd cleaned her out. "Tell Pat that there's five minutes left in your game. Shoo now."

Radio Voice just had to peek under the aluminum foil at the dish of cooling lasagna. He hugged his stomach and squinted his almond-shaped eyes shut. "Mmmmmmmmm."

All of this was foreign to Meadow—it had a light-headedness to it—beginning with the sense of place. She was learning Pat's

SPRING 1985

kitchen, what cupboards held what, what surprises awaited behind each drawer pull. But beyond the keeping-place of whisks or salt and pepper shakers, she discovered that dinner aromas didn't have to fight with stale beer or farting contests. And that shouting and cursing and slaps on the back of the head didn't have to accompany a meal. Meadow tuned into the quiet, waded into it, really. This was the quiet of a house together, yet for the moment, divided. From an adjacent room, the occasional muffled shout or burst of laughter. From the side pantry, the click of a closing door. From behind her, the refrigerator and the oven opening and closing, but absent the rattling slam of a door or the shrill of an unclean hinge. Here was a quiet that wasn't replaced with Lu Ann's humming, but rather, the quiet was framed within it. And the footfalls overhead. This was part of Meadow's new quiet. Her life up to now was limited to a single-story house. The pad of feet on the joists above continued to cause her look to the ceiling.

Vegetables were washed and lettuce tossed. Plates and flatware were brought to the table in sets of four. Between peeks at the lasagna, Lu Ann told Meadow her story. As the story went on, it worsened before getting better. Meadow noticed Lu Ann's lack of emotion when she spoke. Like the unfolding of a cloth, corner by corner, revealing a bauble within; like an heirloom, small, fragile, but belonging to another time, or so it seemed to Meadow, to another person.

Lu Ann was in love and pregnant and in high school—relatable subject matter for Meadow, other than the in love part. It was her high school biology teacher, Lu Ann said, with a hint of irony. But he was less than five years her senior, so they began to plan a future. Until her father. That's how Lu Ann put it: "Until my father." The teacher was beaten and run off and Lu Ann raised her twins alone, a boy and girl whom she dearly loves but who have made lives away from what they call the goldfish bowl of a small town. Lou and Anne, she named them. She said that what the names lacked in imagination they made up for in simplicity—as simplicity quickly abandons a teenaged mother. Lu Ann left home, started waitressing at the local diner, found an apartment and raised them, essentially, on the laps of her customers, most of whom had long-lost feelings awakened by the soft press of her baby's cheek against theirs. Four years later, at 21, she became the proprietor of the diner, and made it her namesake in neon over the front door. So the moral of the story, Lu Ann told Meadow, is to be careful to enjoy it, through all the difficulties. Because crazy as it sounds, life seems to go faster than the time it takes to make lasagna. She smiled at that notion, and so too did Meadow. But Meadow remained silent. Despite their similar predicaments and shared hardships, she only nodded. Trust, for some, takes longer than lasagna.

Inside the car was quiet. It was just past 8:30 in the evening when the Sheriff's cruiser reached the Baudette city limits. Despite the dulling weariness of highway hour after highway hour, postures straightened, backs came forward off car seats, eyes were rubbed. Anticipation.

May days burst with life and are stubborn to end, but when they do depart, it is no small act. A brilliant golden light fanned out for miles on the horizon, finding the distant small town of Baudette as it rose out of the hard ground of northern Minnesota. The angular shapes of the town's buildings were cut out of the skyline with threads of yellow light, scoring their edges and curves. How many others had returned here to be touched by some version of this scene? How many soldiers coming back from wars? How many young lovers coming to town to dance? How many prodigals lured to the veneer of the big city had returned to this forever embrace? A small town's imperfections are forgiven in sunset light. You love it with everything that aches inside you.

They'd been driving six hours, not including the shopping spree. In the store, Monsignor Kief left HomeSky in the capable hands of his dear friend, Bea Frank, who locked arms with her and they whisked away like sisters with their mother's credit card—which was partially accurate; they had Monsignor Kief's American Express card.

SPRING 1985

Somehow Monsignor Kief had prevailed to get Sheriff Harris into the store, and then found it equally difficult to get him out. The Sheriff discovered an impressive inventory of over-sized items, and frankly he shopped only as frequently as holes appeared in his wardrobe. After the Sheriff found his things, they went down one floor to the shoe department. The Monsignor had inexplicably lost one shoe from the extra pair he had packed in his suitcase. To his delight, he found a new pair that was equally comfortable right out of the box.

Undoubtedly, this esteemed fellowship of shoppers must have caught the eye of passing St. Clouders as they paraded out of the store. The Sheriff, his badge winking sunlight as he lumbered in front, two Herberger's shopping bags in each hand, flanked by HomeSky with three, and Monsignor Kief, tapping his red-tipped cane, bringing up the rear. They filled much of the available trunk space in the Sheriff's cruiser with the colorful green bags.

"Does Baudette look the same?" Monsignor Kief asked HomeSky as the highway led them to town.

"That's exactly what I was thinking," HomeSky said. He couldn't tell from her voice if that was a good thing.

The Monsignor continued. "You said you wanted to speak with Pat about something. Would you like to do it in the morning, after you've had time to rest?"

HomeSky's answer surprised even herself. "No. If it's not too much to ask, Sheriff."

"Nah. I'm happy to swing by the farm. I have to show Pat his time is running out on my smoking bet. One more week and he owes me 50 bucks."

"I'm sure you have much to talk about," the Monsignor said.

HomeSky's voice strengthened. "Yes, and no." She paused. "It's more about the young woman he's counseling. I have a feeling she may be in trouble. There may be a child ..." HomeSky didn't know how to articulate her hunch.

The Sheriff interrupted. "That's the second time you brought up the pregnant thing. Based on what evidence?"

"No evidence," HomeSky said.

What then? the Sheriff wanted to know.

"I don't think you'll deem it admissible," HomeSky said.

"Try me."

"Based on a dream."

The Sheriff exhaled loudly enough to express his opinion.

"Good enough," the Monsignor said, casting his vote. "Let's go see Pat."

Honestly, the Monsignor wasn't the least bit concerned about what brought HomeSky back. What he knew was this reunion was healing for both her and Pat. Be it the singing of songs in Latin or hitchhiking in the dark or dreams on a bus, these were not the essence of the story. A journey in faith that arrives at healing was, and is, the story. The Monsignor knew this to be true throughout humankind's existence. The details change in time's retelling, but the ending is ever faithful.

Monsignor Kief took HomeSky's hand. It was pleasantly warm. "Are you anxious?" he quietly asked.

She squeezed his hand. "Not so much anymore."

"Well I'm tingling like a school bell," the Monsignor said joyfully.

The Sheriff stiffly craned his head around to address the back seat. "Probably just your legs fell asleep. Been a hell of a drive."

It's the same driveway, HomeSky thought. *The same sunset. The same treeline and ridge and fencelines squaring the fields. But the farmhouse isn't the same.*

Maybe her time away changed it. Or did the original have an irretrievable authenticity? There's no fooling someone who has loved greatly and lost. Not that anyone was trying to fool anyone.

The Sheriff felt a responsibility to say something—nobody else was. The car sat in the sideyard of the farm, stone silent. "Here we

SPRING 1985

are," was the best he could muster, The words clanked around his cruiser.

"What do you think?" Monsignior Kief asked.

HomeSky struggled to find words, yet she felt for everyone around her as they tried to make this easier. "Let's go in," she said.

Meadow insisted on doing the dishes as Pat and Radio Voice and Lu Ann played a card game called 31 in the living room. Actually she didn't know how to play cards of any kind. Never had the opportunity. The dishes spared her embarrassment.

She was just beginning to rinse, when from the window over the sink she saw the Sheriff's cruiser slowly pull into the driveway. "Son of a bitch," she said, jolted. "And I believed him." She smiled cynically to herself, shaking her head. "We believed him, Bulge." She dropped the sponge in the sink and moved athletically out of the kitchen, quietly up the stairs and began to quickly stuff her things in her backpack.

"Trust is for fools," she said to Bulge, feeling tears. She clamped down, refusing to acknowledge how this treason affected her. "Shoulda, shoulda, shoulda—SHIT! Shoulda seen it coming." She wiped her nose roughly on her sweatshirt sleeve. It was too warm for her jean jacket. Hurriedly, she tried to jam it in her overstuffed backpack. It wouldn't go. Her hands shook. Tears obscured her vision. Nothing worked. Meadow flung the coat to the floor. She grabbed her guitar case and slipped down the steps and out the back door just as the front doorbell rang.

"Who could that be?" Lu Ann asked out loud.

Pat had a bad feeling that he knew, but the last time the guy didn't use the doorbell. "You and Radio Voice go in the kitchen with Meadow and stay there until I come get you." The tautness of Pat's tone frightened Radio Voice.

"What's wrong?" he asked Pat.

Pat managed a smile. "Nothing. Just go into the kitchen and get a snack with Lu Ann."

"But we already had dessert," Radio Voice said.

"Pat, who is it?" Lu Ann asked, getting up from her hand of cards.

"It might be my friend from yesterday morning." Pat lightly touched his nose.

Lu Ann's eyes widened.

"Why would we have a snack if we already had dessert?" Radio Voice wanted to know.

Lu Ann took him by the hand. "It's your lucky day. It's two-dessert Sunday."

"Wowee," he said, pulling Lu Ann into the kitchen.

Pat tried to think. He knew Roy Lee FastHorse had a shotgun the last time they met. The Sheriff warned him about that, but Pat chose to ignore it. Now what? He had an old aluminum softball bat in the front closet, which he retrieved, for what purpose he wasn't sure. Pat walked with the bat to the front window and looked out. The Sheriff's cruiser was there, and standing in front of it was Monsignor Kief and … who? Pat looked at the woman.

Pat jumped as the doorbell rang for a second time.

"HomeSky?" Pat said under his breath. "My God." Pat raced to open the door, finding himself face to face with the Sheriff, who was startled not only by the speed of the door's swing, but by the sight of Pat, who had forgotten he was carrying a bat.

"Expecting company?" The Sheriff glanced at the bat.

"Oh, shit … shoot I mean." Pat stuck the bat out of sight around the corner of the entryway. "You have HomeSky with you?" He looked out past the Sheriff. "Is everything okay?" Pat was talking to the Sheriff, but watching HomeSky next to the cruiser.

"Everything's fine. Kinda crazy, but fine. She said she wanted to talk to the FastHorse girl. About some dream. Indian stuff, I guess." He waved a dismissive hand.

None of this was making sense to Pat. He walked past the Sheriff, who was beginning to mention their wager. With every step he took toward her, he saw more of the HomeSky he remembered. His chest tightened. "HomeSky, hello," he said as he approached. "Hello Monsignor."

Pat and HomeSky stood facing one another.

She scanned his face. "You look like you ended up on the wrong side of a swinging door." HomeSky smiled faintly.

"Yeah, I do. I guess. You've cut your hair."

HomeSky looked down. "Monsignor, do you mind if I talk with Pat for a minute?" She touched his arm.

"Why of course not. Sheriff!" the Monsignor called out. "If you'd be so kind, I need to go to the little priest's room. Long drive."

To have been as close as HomeSky and Pat were, and then to have been abruptly separated by nearly four years, made these first moments together almost unbearable. They took a few steps away from the house, facing the fields. When Pat and HomeSky did look at each other, it was careful, hesitant. This left them uncomfortably redirecting sightlines to the distant trees or to the dirt they stood on.

How to begin? Where to begin? Pat stole a longer look at HomeSky. Her change was startling. The short hair, peppered with gray. She appeared somehow smaller. And the body weariness. Pat started over again. "How are you?"

HomeSky deflected. "I should be asking that of you. What happened?"

Pat chuckled to himself. "There's a pretty big question, but I'll start on the small end. I got punched by a father of a young woman I counsel on the Rez. It was … wow, only yesterday morning? I can't believe it but, yeah, yesterday. Seems like forever ago." Pat looked at HomeSky. He recognized that furrow in her brow that she had when thinking. "That's a lot of stuff coming at you at once," he said.

HomeSky looked at him. "No, no. Sheriff Harris told me of some of it. So you're counseling on the Rez?"

"I am. Mostly teens. A few others. It's pretty loose that way."

"And you've left the priesthood?"

"Yes. Not long after you left."

"And the house." She turned to face it. "You've rebuilt it." HomeSky's eyes slowly panned across the beautiful farmhouse, but all she saw was fire. She grit her teeth.

"I've been keeping it for you. For when you came back. It's yours."

HomeSky only managed to shake her head no. She brought her hand to her face and rubbed her eyes.

"You've been busy," HomeSky said, leaving it there. Pat heard her voice, but it didn't seem to belong to her. It was deeper. Detached.

"And you?" Pat asked. "How are you? Where have you been?"

HomeSky looked directly at Pat. "We can get to that, but not now. Tell me about the girl you're counseling. Is she okay?"

Pat brightened. "Yes. She's fine. She's here."

"She's staying at the house?" HomeSky asked surprised.

"Yeah," Pat explained. "I hope that's okay. She has an abusive father who—"

"No, it's fine. I just had no idea she was here. Can I see her?"

Pat remembered that Sheriff Harris said something about a dream. "Sure." Pat hesitated, not knowing if he should ask more. "Of course."

"She's pregnant, isn't she?" HomeSky asked.

The astonished look on Pat's face cued HomeSky.

"There was a dream. It brought me back here. I need to talk to the girl. What is her name?"

"Meadow. Meadow FastHorse," he said. Now it was Pat who was trying to sort out everything suddenly coming at him. *She had come back for Meadow?*

"How old is she?" HomeSky asked.

"Eighteen. Great kid. Funny, in a way."

It pained HomeSky to see Pat like this. Not the broken nose nor the black eyes, but settling for this disfigured moment. HomeSky recognized that this wasn't the homecoming he had dreampt of when he rebuilt this house. But she could offer nothing. Pat's homecoming was constructed on countless hours of oversimplification, on square feet of lumber, over pounds of screws, on the frames of windows and doors and paint colors that match. Life isn't so cooperative.

Pat went to rub his face, forgetting about his nose. A jolt cut through him causing his eyes to tear. He took a breath, "Some things are beyond us," he said, finding some clarity in all that was happening around him. "You need to meet Meadow."

They turned toward the house and Lu Ann and Radio Voice and Sheriff Harris were on the porch, waiting. HomeSky recognized her old friends, but didn't know how to approach. Praise be for Radio Voice. The moment he saw HomeSky, he bounded down the steps with his arms open three feet wide in front of him. Lu Ann, on the other hand, was considerably less excited.

As they said their hellos near the porch, Monsignor Kief tapped his way out the front door, onto the porch deck. "You have a homecoming and leave a blind man to find his way? That's either callous, or the makings of next month's guest sermon." The Monsignor lifted a hand, palm up, leaving it for the group to decide.

"Frank. Sorry," Pat said, leading everyone up the steps. "I thought you and Meadow were talking."

"No," the Monsignor said. "I didn't hear anyone inside."

Pat walked into the house while the others tried to decide whether to stay out or go in. "Meadow?" Pat called out. He called again from the half-landing of the stairs.

"Weird." He smiled tightly. He went into the kitchen, to the sink where the dishes were done. The warm water still stood in the sink with the sponge floating on top. As Pat turned to look elsewhere, his line of sight went out the window. Centered perfectly in the window frame was the Sheriff's cruiser. "Oh, shit," he said loudly enough for Lu Ann to hear, as she came into the house.

"What is it?" she asked.

"Just a minute," Pat said, touching her arm before he bounded up the steps, two at a time, to the guest room. "Meadow …?" he said quietly, rapping on the door as he entered. The bedroom was empty, except for her jean jacket sprawled on the floor. No backpack. No guitar case. No Meadow.

He scooped up the jacket and came down the steps quickly. By this time everyone was wondering what had happened. They looked at the jacket under his arm.

"Where'd she go?" Lu Ann asked, dumbfounded. "She was here a second ago."

Pat exhaled. "I think she bolted."

HomeSky took a step forward. She was sure she hadn't heard him correctly. "She's where?"

"I think she was doing the dishes and saw the Sheriff's vehicle out the window and misread what was going on. I don't know. Maybe she thought …" Pat couldn't finish.

The Sheriff filled in. "She thought you turned her in. And the big bad sheriff was here to toss her into juvy hall."

"Or worse." Pat looked down at Meadow's jacket. "She thought you were taking her back home."

SPRING 1985

FINDING MEADOW

The group stood in the farmhouse living room. Dusk had swept in. Quietly, they looked across the room at the dark rectangles of windows. The contrast between the brightly lit interior room and the empty blackness outside made Meadow seem very far away.

"Lu Ann and I recognize her the best," Pat said, "so we should split up." He looked at Lu Ann for confirmation. She nodded, trying not to focus on the alternative meaning of split up. "Sheriff, how about you, Lu Ann and Monsignor Kief go in your car. You head south to town."

The Sheriff reflexively tapped his front shirt pocket. He often had a cigarette when thinking. The licorice was a disappointment. "Sounds feasible. What's your plan?"

"I'll take HomeSky and Radio Voice in my truck and we'll go north to the Rez. Maybe she's headed to the community center or to a friend's. Let's give it an hour. If neither of us has found her, you go to the rectory and I'll come back here and call you. In an hour, who knows; she might come back once she sees your vehicle is gone."

The Sheriff stood with a groan. "Let's get it pointed down the road, people." The group got up to leave. The quiet in the room had a chill to it.

"C'mon guys," Pat said, cheerleading. "We'll find her." The group headed for the door. Pat caught the Sheriff's attention. "Can I ask you one more thing?"

The Sheriff stepped to the rear and waited with Pat, who sorted through his keys. On second thought, he decided not to lock the door. "Thurgood," he said to the Sheriff, "if you see her, I think it'd be best if you just stopped the car and let Lu Ann out so she can talk to her and explain the misunderstanding. No offense, but, ah, you cast a big shadow and she doesn't know you. She's confused, and probably feels betrayed." Pat wasn't sure how the Sheriff would cotton to advice.

He squinted down at Pat before he let him off with a little nod. "You'd make a half decent deputy." He took out a piece of licorice, cut it with his front teeth, flipped one half off the porch and smoked the other. "No good at wagers, though." He inhaled deeply in front of Pat before walking to his cruiser.

Pat, Radio Voice and HomeSky were sandwiched in the cab of the pickup. Pat said he'd keep watch on the left shoulder of the road while the other two focused on the right.

Radio Voice was equal parts excited and unnerved to be a part of all this. "Is it hard to drive at night?" he asked, looking out at the spray of headlights in the darkness.

"No. You get used to it." Pat assured him.

"Do you want to go to sleep?"

"Uh-uh. Driving keeps you very alert."

"Not everybody," Radio Voice informed him. "I heard a story on the radio where a truck driver fell asleep and crashed into a river."

Radio Voice nodded his head vigorously, to emphasize that it had indeed happened.

"Where are you living these days, Radio Voice?" HomeSky asked, diverting.

He sat up straighter. "I have my *own* apartment."

"Really?" she said. "All by yourself?"

"Yes. An efficiency. You can only have one in there. Those are the rules."

"I know. That's what I had, too." She and Pat traded a glance. "In St. Paul."

"Wow. That's really far away," Radio Voice said, impressed. "I can't go that far on my bike."

"You have a bike, too?" HomeSky asked.

"Yeah. Groveland."

"Groveland is the name of your bike?"

"Yep." Radio Voice laughed. "Cory named it. He gave it to me. It has three wheels, but it's big. Not like a trike. We put a high flag on it and reflectors and a bell to make it safe."

Pat found a speed that let them watch for Meadow, but still cover highway. He and HomeSky scanned ahead, quickly checking the intersections of side roads as they passed. It was straining, searching through the black; the truck's old highbeams didn't throw much light roadside.

"We're coming up on the Rez," HomeSky said. A shiver shot through her. She never liked this place. Doubly so at night.

Pat looked over at her. "We'll start at the rec center. The gym is open till 10."

The community center was a well-lit red brick building that was beautiful in its straight lines and plain solidity. When they checked the indoor basketball court, a few teenagers looked up. What they saw in Pat, HomeSky and Radio Voice had to make for a peculiar picture.

Pat waved and got a head lift in return. "Sup, Mr. Pat."

HomeSky and Radio Voice waited as he went across the court to talk to the group.

"They haven't seen her," Pat said after returning from the teens. What he didn't say was one of them heard that Meadow had taken off from home and that her dad was cruising the Rez with a case of beer looking for her.

They quickly searched the grounds at the community center, accomplishing nothing more than flushing a pair of young smokers from the playground area.

Not more than a half hour earlier, Meadow was walking down the side of the same highway that Pat drove in on. She was heading for the Rez with her thumb out. She didn't know where she was going, she just knew she was going. She'd figure it out. The hell with shithead adults.

Five miles away, Roy Lee FastHorse pulled into the community center, scraping another car as he parked. Nobody was around, so he backed out and left his car on the other side of the lot.

"Ungrateful bitch," he said, finishing a can of beer. He tossed the empty in the back seat and climbed out to check the gym.

On the highway, Meadow could hear a car coming. She decided to turn and face it as she hitchhiked. Walking and thumbing wasn't working; maybe this would get someone to stop. The car was accelerating at her fast, then it quickly slowed. She looked into the blinding lights. When the car reached her, teenagers from both sides stuck their heads out the windows and whooped causing her to jump. Laughter, music and tail lights disappeared into the night.

Soon after, another car was coming, but Meadow decided she'd had enough. She would just walk. The highbeams of the car found her. She could feel the car's presence. Meadow picked up the pace, her guitar case banging off her leg as the car slowed, and slowed further, and then pulled beside her, gravel popping beneath the tires. Meadow stared straight ahead, taking long strides, her path now fully illuminated by the headlights. She heard the driver's window going down.

SPRING 1985

"Everything okay?" a voice asked. It was a kind voice, the voice of an older woman.

Meadow squinted at the driver. She didn't recognize her. "Yeah. I'm good." She stopped walking, catching her breath as she looked ahead into the darkness.

"Can I give you a ride someplace? Not the greatest time to be out for a walk." The elderly woman laughed to herself quietly.

Meadow looked at her again. Still, there was nothing familiar, but her voice had a warm informality. "I guess so. Sure. Should I stick my guitar in back?"

"That's where I'd put it," the woman said, gently chuckling again.

When Meadow got in the front seat, the dome light gave her a moment to see what she was in for. The driver looked harmless enough. Grandma-ish. She was wearing a mustard-colored blouse, embroidered with the words Bonaducci's Grocery. A number of star-shaped pins sat above her nametag, which had Rose engraved in it. Meadow pulled the passenger door shut.

As the woman steered the car back on the road, she looked at Meadow. "I know it says Rose, but it's Rosaline." The driver straightened her nametag. "My manager says they charge by the letter when they make 'em, so he said just put Rose on it. Keep it short and sweet cause he didn't know if I'd be quitting on him and didn't want to be out too much for the nametag. That was six years ago." They drove in silence. "This is where you're supposed to tell me *your* name," she said with a smile.

"Oh. Meadow."

"Meadow. That's pretty." Again, a pause. "Do you have a surname, Meadow? Or just Meadow?" There was a lilt of teasing merriment in the woman's voice whenever she spoke.

"FastHorse," Meadow said. "I'm embarrassed to say."

The elderly driver didn't comment. "FastHorse? I may have known a FastHorse way, way back when the Great Spirit first made the lakes and the hills and I was in high school." She giggled. "What was her name?" The woman frowned. "FastHorse? Oh well. My mind is a steel trap. Just been left out in the rain too long." She reached across the driver's seat and patted Meadow on the leg. "Where can I take you, Meadow?"

Meadow had been thinking about this very question since the car first pulled over. Where should she go? The community center would be the first place they'd look. She could stay with her friend Kristi, but they'd had a huge fight. *Where would they not look?* she wondered. *Where?*

Meadow's eyes widened. From out of nowhere, she had her answer.

Pat's truck idled on the side of the road. They had been looking in vain for 45 minutes and Pat could feel time and Meadow slipping away. He'd driven the dark roads around Meadow's house, but as he suspected, she hadn't gone there. He had maybe five more minutes before they had to get back to the farmhouse and call Sheriff Harris at the rectory. *Maybe the others had found her.* Optimism raised its hand momentarily. He had a feeling, though, they hadn't.

"Sorry. I'm running out of ideas," Pat said to HomeSky and Radio Voice.

"It's hard." HomeSky said, responding to the frustration in his voice. "It's so dark. Like finding the proverbial needle …"

"I know," was all Pat could manage.

"What's a proverbial needle?" Radio Voice wanted to know.

Pat kept thinking while HomeSky explained the expression. *Where hadn't he thought of?* Pat rubbed his brow. *Where would he go if he were Meadow?*

"But she'd never be in a haystack," Radio Voice said to HomeSky. "It's not safe there. She'd go to the safest place."

Pat was pulled from his thoughts by what Radio Voice had said. "What did you say?"

Radio Voice looked at him confidently. "She'd go to the safest place."

Pat's face relaxed. A large smile towed its way across. "That's it!"

SPRING 1985

He reached over and hugged Radio Voice. "You're brilliant. Brilliant, brilliant, brilliant! I know where the safest place is." Pat ground the stick shift into gear and let the gravel fly. Down the road they went, light cutting though the solid night.

Meadow set her guitar case down next to the side door of the church. There was no overhead light, but she easily made out the door. The nighttime air was too cool for crickets. Meadow's eyes could adjust to the darkness, but the silence was another thing.

"It's creepy quiet, Bulge," she whispered. Meadow cleared her throat, trying to add volume and confidence to her words. "I'm glad I have you to talk to. If this doesn't work we're shit out of luck."

Rosaline from the grocery store had dropped Meadow off near the well-lit front entrance of the church rectory. Meadow insisted she'd be fine and told her she'd gone far enough out of her way. When the car was swallowed up by night, Meadow made her way not to the rectory door as promised, but across the lot to the side door of the church.

"Well Bulge, Pat said this door has a bad latch. A big yank and it'll open right up. Supposedly that's how that wind got in today." It was comforting for Meadow to have someone to talk to. "You count to three, Bulge, and I'll pull this sucker open." Meadow waited three beats and pulled hard. The door banged as it came forward in the frame, but wasn't going any further. She pulled again. Locked. "Son … of … a …" she substituted an angry yank for the next word and the door unexpectedly flew open, sending her backward off her feet into the grass. In front of her, the door yawned fully open, but began to slowly reverse. "No, no, no, NO!" Meadow, scrambling to her feet, stretched for the door. Her fingertips just brushed the steel handle as the door swung shut.

"No," she whispered. Meadow went limp, her hands falling to her knees, her head hung. She took a shaky breath. She looked at the closed door. "I didn't hear a click, did you, Bulge?" Meadow took a step, gently reached for the handle and applied only the slightest backward pressure. And the door came to her.

Right here, Pat thought. He stood at the side door of the church and looked at his watch. He was supposed to have called Sheriff Harris five minutes ago. But this was the kind of day that rewrote schedules. HomeSky and Radio Voice walked behind him along the narrow sidewalk.

Here I am. Here is HomeSky. Here is my church. He wouldn't have believed this nexus possible, but here they were. He could imagine no ending to this day more well-suited than right here, right now.

"Is that the door you said?" Radio Voice asked, pointing.

"Sure is," Pat confirmed.

"The lock is broke?" Radio Voice continued.

"The latch, it doesn't hold too well." Pat got a good grip on the metal handle and set his feet. "Stand back a little." He arched his back and with one strong pop, the door came open.

The nave of the church was black and shapeless. "The light switch is around the corner. Hold on just a sec." Something caught Pat's eye from across the sanctuary. A flicker from the candle bay in the petitional area. He thought it strange. The sisters put the candles out every night as a safety precaution. Pat flipped on the lights.

"Hello?" he said. "Meadow?" His voice sounded foreign, almost unfriendly, echoing in the empty space.

HomeSky and Radio Voice walked in quietly and stood near the sanctuary.

"Meadow, it's Pat."

Meadow crouched with her back to the pew, sitting on the kneeler trying to make herself tiny. She winced at the sight of her guitar out of the case on the floor over by the candles she had lit for companionship while she played a song.

Pat called out. "Meadow, if you're here, I want you to know it's not what you think. That sheriff's car had nothing to do with you. Remember my friend I was telling you about? HomeSky. Well, Sheriff Harris was bringing her home. That's all, I promise. She's here with me now." Pat looked at HomeSky.

"Boozhoo, Meadow," HomeSky said. Her hello lifted and opened up like music in the church.

When the greeting reached Meadow, Bulge gave her such a kick she audibly gasped. Meadow repositioned herself, both hands on her belly. Bulge kicked again, equally hard. "Okay," Meadow said standing up. "Okay."

The four stood apart, but every breathing second brought them closer. Meadow, in her oversized swim team sweatshirt, bangs falling across her face, arms limp at her sides. She appeared small and young and unsure among the rows and rows of empty pews. She pushed her hair aside. Her gaze never left HomeSky. She drew a breath, her heart slowed, her body shedding some armor. "Boozhoo, HomeSky" she said.

Under the lights of the sanctuary the two women watched one another until they shared a faint smile. Something about it said they knew this day would come.

Arrangements were made that night, and in the ensuing days. Everyone was tentative with outcomes—everyone except for Monsignor Kief, who dealt with each conclusion as if foregone. He couldn't have been surer had he walked this ground before, lived this story, and now arranged the parts according to a blueprint. He was undistracted by appearances, by past indiscretions, by what couldn't be, by cultural absolutes. He was in love with the now of this story, its caretaker and shepherd. Why were letters kept in sock drawers and rosaries found in the weeds? What about the reemergence of dreams and buses halted by deer that rose again? How do blessed candles blow cold and how is it that church doors are installed with defective locks? The Monsignor clearly saw what was obscured to the sighted: these events weren't to be puzzled out; they were fire and rain and sun. They were new life. For better and for worse, winds will blow. And rather than howling into them, he met them with the only words that have ever made a difference.

So be it.

SINGER

He was filled with music like a pail fills with rainwater.
Freely. Agape. Beyond containment.
As such, the boy sang out. His song rising, overflowing, exalted.
And so it was he gave life to all he touched.

BOOK Two

SUMMER 1985

All respect starts with self.

PART ONE

July

PIANO

Knuckleheads, the whole lot of them.

Not that their intentions weren't well placed. Or, for that matter, their backs, their quads, their obliques and every other straining muscle group. But the piano was plain stuck. Sheriff Harris was sure it would go through. Cory gave it no chance in hell. Pat said you never know until you try, thus casting the majority vote. And try they did to get the Sheriff's piano out his front door. The verdict, resounding. The piano was beached. The only solution was in reverse: back through the front door and exit out the back door, its original point of entry those many years ago. None of these men were comfortable in retreat. But sometimes inevitability is as obvious as a piano wedged in a doorframe.

They called the experts, who were due shortly. Costs double on weekends, said Hal Johnson, the patriarch of Hal Johnson & Sons moving. It was a small price to pay to get the instrument out of the house with none of these men perishing. Not that they would go by heart attack nor other natural causes. No, each had considered homicide, more than once, during the unsuccessful process of trying to exorcise the piano from the house.

A rented U-Haul box truck was standing by, doors propped open, packing blankets and tie-downs laid out on the grassy boulevard. The grand plan was to be on the road by nine and take the piano to Hanna's, where Singer was destined for an early birthday present.

They sat on the front steps, gathering their wind and more so, their pride. The baby grand rested on its side, poking out at them. July's morning air was thick and sticky and unmoving.

"You're overdressed," Pat said to the Sheriff, whose sweatshirt was living up to its namesake, wrung wet around the neck, under the arms and in the back. He had new matching sweatpants, too.

"I avoid underdressed. Not a pretty sight."

"When will the Johnson cavalry be here?" the Sheriff wanted to know.

"Hal said he'd round the boys up after breakfast and be on his way." Pat pulled a Kleenex off his bleeding finger to see if it had stopped.

The Sheriff scratched his neck. "They're calling for rain."

The men looked up at the sky, and couldn't agree on what they saw there, either.

"Doesn't look like much," Pat said.

"Something's coming. I feel it in my knee," Cory commented.

"That's probably the lower register of the piano you feel," the Sheriff said.

They could use the rain. The wind was kicking up; a fine layer of grit dusted every outdoor surface.

Across the street a door opened and a woman came out with two leashed schnauzers at her heel. The Sheriff snapped out of the indolent lean he'd taken up on the front step railing. If Pat wasn't mistaken, the Sheriff also drew in his stomach.

"Yoohoo, Thurgood." The middle-aged woman moved both leashes to her left hand, pulling the front door closed behind her, then waggling her fingers at the Sheriff. She wore matching red sweatpants, tank top and tee.

The Sheriff took a few strides down his walkway. "Hello, Ms. Duncan," he said, clumsily half-waving.

From across the street the woman gave a sharp command for the dogs to sit, followed by a snap upward on the leashes. "It's Kitty, Thurgood. We've been through this."

"Yes ma'am ... Kitty. Nice day to get Hansel and Gretel out." The dogs remained in statuesque sits.

"We figured if we got out, it might bring the rain. You know how those things go: wash your car ... plan a picnic ... have your hair done, here comes the rain."

"True enough," the Sheriff said, wishing something breezy and spontaneous would come to mind.

Kitty studied the situation from across the street. "Looks like you fellas have found yourself between a rock and a hard place." She directed a wave at Pat and Cory, the beards of the schnauzers following the path of her hand. "Hello gentlemen!"

"Hello Kitty," Pat said loudly, making sure the Sheriff heard him as well as the neighbor across the street. "Why don't you come over and say hi?"

"Yeah," Cory added. "It would be our pleasure, Kitty." He spoke like they were old friends.

The Sheriff turned and gave them a knock-it-off frown; the two of them sat grinning mischievously on the front step.

"Oh, what friendly boys!" Kitty said back across the street. "I'd take you up on your kind offer but Hansel and Gretel need to get to the park should this weather take a turn."

"A rain check then," the Sheriff blurted, quite pleased that his brain found functionality.

"Oh, Thurgood," Kitty teased. "A rain check. Yes. How clever." Her fingers played air piano. "Toodles!" With that Kitty released the dogs, their short stubby tails switching into high gear as they moved down the sidewalk at a pace that was just short of a jog.

Pat looked at Cory, eyes sparkling. "Oh, Thurgood, how clever."

Cory piled on. "Yoo Hoo, rain check." They cracked each other up.

"Sophomores," the Sheriff grumbled under his breath, trying not to smile. He had to turn away to maintain his poker face.

"Who's Kitty?" Pat asked.

"Yeah," Cory added. "It isn't every day you meet a dog-loving Kitty."

"Give it a rest, boys. She's not my type."

"What type is she?" Cory asked.

The Sheriff looked down the street at the blur of red with two slack leashes, dogs in perfect heel. "Young and attractive."

"Give yourself some credit," Pat said, getting up to stretch. "Ohh," he complained, working on a hamstring. "She seems to have a crush on you. What's her story?"

"Moved in a few months ago, after the widow Reedson packed up. Last year's winter blew her to Florida for good."

"Kitty is single then?" Pat raised an eyebrow.

"Far as I can tell," the Sheriff said. "Her and the dogs."

Cory stretched out his left shoulder. "Hansel and Gretel? Really?"

The Sheriff shrugged. "If nothing else it's simple to remember."

Just then the Johnson & Sons moving truck pulled up. The father and the two eldest sons hopped out of the cab, came around and rolled up the back door. The five other sons got off two couches strapped down in the back. They jumped out onto the street, sequenced like D-Day paratroopers.

"It ain't legal for passengers to ride that way, Hal," the Sheriff said. "Consider this a warning."

"Only in emergency situations, Sheriff. You guys sounded desperate, and by the looks of it, there's no time to waste yakkin.'"

The boys awaited their orders. Pat walked over and shook Hal's iron vise hand. "How can we help?" Pat asked.

"Hey-ya, Pat. Just keep your distance and watch good breeding in action." He slapped Pat on the back to infer that no offense was meant. Then Hal Johnson went to work. Or, more accurately, his boys did, as Hal was equal parts father, choreographer and lion tamer. His sons had that baby grand surrounded, strapped, lifted, moved, blanketed and secured in Pat's rental trailer in the time it took most people to pull on socks and shoes.

"That'll be $175," Hal said, clicking his pen and handing the top copy of the invoice to the Sheriff. "Don't suppose you have cash?"

"Do I look like a drug dealer?" the Sheriff snapped. Hal was going to comment on the baggy sweatpants and sweatshirt but let it drop. The Sheriff went in for his checkbook, inspecting the doorway trim as he passed through. The boys passed around a tin of chewing tobacco, spitting wordlessly on the boulevard. Cory walked up to the one who went by the name Skinny because he wasn't. He used to play hockey with Joseph.

"Skinny, right?" Cory said.

The mover said yeah.

"We met back when you played hockey. With Joseph. When you came down for the tournament. I'm Cory Bradford."

"Yeah, I know. Didn't think you'd recognize me." Skinny put out his hand.

Cory shook it. "I remember that shot of yours from the point. Right D. First line."

Skinny grinned, as one of his brothers gave him a playful shove. "Hell yes. How'd you remember that?"

"That was a great game," Cory said. "I think if there would have been four periods, you'd a had us."

Skinny spat a stream of brown juice. "We still get together for a few beers and talk about it. Me and the guys. That was the best team I've ever been on." Skinny's face dropped, "'Course we miss Joseph."

Cory looked at Skinny, his big round face, two-day growth, his bottom lip loaded with chew. "Everybody misses him." Cory slapped him on the shoulder. "But he wouldn't want us moping around, you know?"

"Hell no," Skinny said. And just that quick he was all grins.

You need about five hours to get from Baudette to Hanna's house in Duluth. Just tip the steering wheel southeast and take a crooked line down. Pat was driving the U-Haul with the Sheriff riding shotgun. Cory had left his cabin in the dark to come to Baudette. Now he was going the other way, following the truck, watching the left brake light wink on and off with every bump.

The plan called for Hanna and Singer to be out of the house. They'd go to the library and the playground for a few hours. Theoretically, the piano could be moved in and set up during that time. Cory wasn't so sure anymore. Pianos grow larger when you go to move them.

The Sheriff looked over at Pat, who was biting his fingernails. "I thought you gave those up?" he said.

"Huh," Pat said, blinking out of his far-away stare.

"Chewin' up your fingers."

"Ah, crap," Pat said, quickly dropping his hand from his mouth. Then he held it up to the light coming through the windshield. He shook his head contritely, looking at the irritated skin around the nubs.

"So what's bugging you?" the Sheriff asked. "Other than losing our bet."

Pat frowned, and let out a long breath. "You're the counselor now?"

"I've got a few hours to kill."

"Nice bedside manner." Pat paused. "I don't know. I've worked my way into knots."

The Sheriff knew enough about the human condition to shut up and listen.

Pat filled in. "I've hardly had 20 sentences with HomeSky, except a little talk about the weather at Monsignor's Sunday dinners. It's been—and don't you repeat this to Lu Ann—a little ... awkward."

"A little?" the Sheriff said, slapping the dashboard hard enough to make Pat jump. "Ha! You could use the Monsignor's electric carving set to cut the tension." The Sheriff shifted in his seat and looked intently at Pat. "I get that HomeSky is reacclimating, and everyone is walking gingerly around Meadow and all, but hell, even Lu Ann is acting weird. And she's one tough cookie, that gal. Let me tell you, it's more than a little awkward. Not that it's my business."

"You're right. I started to talk about it with Monsignor Kief last Sunday. I showed up an hour early to dinner, while HomeSky was still at work. Asked him his thoughts on how everyone seemed."

The Sheriff shifted again, finding it impossible to get comfortable with the shoulder harness seatbelt. "What'd he say? He notice it?"

"Oh yeah. Said it's going to take time. Then he said something else, kinda off-handed. The more I've thought about it since, the more I think maybe he's on to something."

"Yeah?" the Sheriff said impatiently.

"He says everybody's waiting."

The Sheriff bore down, thinking. "What the hell's that mean?"

"With Meadow, it's the adoption. For HomeSky, it's waiting to return, or not to return, to the farmhouse. And for Lu Ann, he says, she's waiting for me to decide where I'm going."

The Sheriff wasn't sure he was connecting the dots. "Where you're going?"

Pat looked at him. "I built the farmhouse for HomeSky—for us, really. I have a relationship with Lu Ann that's getting pretty serious. So where am I going, meaning where am I going with that ... choice, I guess."

The Sheriff's hand went up to the chest of his sweatshirt, where his cigarettes were typically pocketed. He grumbled at the reflexivity of the act—how thinking triggered the urge. He'd fix that. The Sheriff lifted and snapped the red rubber band on his right wrist. It was his attempt to attach a negative association with the craving. "So we know what all them are waiting for," the Sheriff said. "What are you waiting for?"

A dissatisfied smile came to the corner of Pat's mouth. "As always, Thurgood, you've kicked down the door to the matter." Pat tapped the top of the steering wheel with his bandaged index finger. "When I counsel kids, I tell them they have to say things out loud. Make it real. So they can't pretend it's not there anymore." Pat raised his eyebrows in recognition. "I've been afraid to say it. I'm waiting for HomeSky," he said. "Have been for years."

SUMMER 1985

MEADOW

Meadow stood barefoot in a bright splash of kitchen sunlight, surrounded by the eggshell-white walls of the farmhouse. The floor was cool. A touch of breeze slipped through the nearby window screens, and with the front door open to the latched screen door, the room was filled with stereophonic notes of songbirds. Meadow stretched her arms above her head, long and slow, turning 360 degrees, taking in the entire kitchen.

She smiled thinking about a Pat-ism, as she called it. "Bulge," she said, "Pat says farm kitchens are made for summer mornings and I guess I know why." Meadow's glance carried out the south- and east-facing windows where sunlight and pasture eddies flooded in. "What did we do to deserve this?" She stretched on her tiptoes. "When is someone going to step in and say, joke's over. Get your butt home?" Her arms came down, her hand on her growing belly. "You, young man, are too big to hide anymore." She looked at her midsection. "Maybe I'll rename you McKinley."

It was 8:30 on Saturday and she was due to work at nine. Waitressing at Lu Ann's was going better than she'd expected. First off, Lu Ann insisted that Meadow sleep in and start a little later than the other girls. Meadow knew that would cause resentment, but she was wrong. The waitresses were giddy with the idea of a new life coming to the diner. Lu Ann also tried to keep Meadow away from the heavier trays and full bus bins, but Meadow was flat-out stronger than anyone at the restaurant, including Tim who cooked and typically bussed most of the full tubs. Meadow reminded Lu Ann that she must've handled such jobs just fine when she was her age and pregnant, and it probably led to a healthier delivery. She also offered to arm wrestle Tim to prove she was up to it. No one was happier than Tim when Lu Ann said that wouldn't be necessary. In all, Lu Ann agreed not to be overly protective, but remained so nonetheless.

Noticing the time, Meadow quickly swept up her toast crumbs and took them out the back door. The golden-winged warblers knew to look for them on the back steps. She locked up the back, grabbed her apron off the kitchen chair and headed out the front, locking the door behind her. This act caused her skin to prickle, her throat to tighten. It was the unshakable memory of turning around and finding her old man there, reeking, unshaven, reaching for her. She physically shook at the apparition in the shadows as she hurried away from the thunk of the deadbolt. Pat had recently increased the security of both front and back doors.

Roy Lee FastHorse had pursued his daughter to the farm. He would watch with binoculars and find the opportune time to materialize. When Pat was out running. When Meadow was on her way to swim practice. When she walked the fenceline lost in the simple geometry of bean rows sprouting from the black earth.

The first time, he grabbed her arm and ordered her home. She refused, using language she'd learned from him. Okay, he said sarcastically, releasing her. Maybe one day, you might just disappear. Happens all the time in big open country like this. Just poof. You're gone.

SUMMER 1985

They called Sheriff Harris. Meadow's father was persistent, but not particularly hard to fool. The Sheriff had driven into the farmyard and parked around back in the dark of the morning. Pat drove off to work as usual. And when Roy Lee showed up on the farm porch with his half-cocked smile and his deer-hunting knife in his belt, Sheriff Harris got up from the kitchen table to greet him. Typically he didn't carry a sidearm, but that day he had made an exception.

The Sheriff gave Roy Lee an ultimatum, and a temporary restraining order. You're in my jurisdiction, not on the Rez, he had told him as he stepped closer. He stuck the piece of paper into his chest and held him with his eyes. Your options are: be in court in 10 days, meet with the judge and get slapped with a permanent restraining order, violation of which will cost you a year in jail and $10,000. And, the Sheriff had reminded him, that adventure starts in *my* jail. Or stay away. Far away. Leave Meadow to her life. She's a legal adult. She knows where to find you if that's her wish. What she does is her business alone and it's against the law to harass, threaten or stalk her. If he stayed away, the Sheriff would erase the court date from the judge's docket. Be smart, the Sheriff had said. For the first time in your life, be smart. Now get off the property before you have an accident.

And Roy Lee had stayed away in the weeks since. But you're never completely alone when you've had someone like that in your life. So it was as Meadow walked quickly across the farmyard to the barn to go to work. For that short stretch, there was no sun on her hair and there were no birds singing. Only the cold tension of what might be waiting in the shadow.

Pat had given her the keys to the '66 Toronado, which she had said was too generous and could not accept. But Pat insisted. It was a cool car, no doubt. But the custom license plate that she used to laugh at, SAY14U, now took on new meaning. When she looked at it as she hopped into the driver's seat and locked the door, she thought, *I hope you do, Pat. Maybe say two.*

The Saturday lunch rush at Lu Ann's was waning and the staff was beginning to settle into the quiet. Lu Ann brought Meadow a glass of milk to go with her peanut butter and cream cheese on English muffin.

"Sit now," she commanded. They both took up places at the Formica-topped table across from one another. "Is HomeSky coming for lunch today?"

Meadow nodded as she sipped her milk. "Yep," she said with a hint of a milk mustache. Suddenly, Lu Ann saw Meadow as so young and simple and easy to love. She wanted to take her up in her arms. She wanted to know the smell of her hair. She wanted to be the parent she'd never had. But this ache inside, she did her best to conceal. She knew the danger of pushing Meadow away with affection. And equally, Lu Ann was protecting herself. It was becoming apparent that Meadow had a different, stronger bond forming with HomeSky. About this, she prayed on Sundays. *Help me to be accepting and gracious.* Lu Ann knew jealousy was among the most corrosive sins.

So too, she knew that Pat had become different in the seven weeks since HomeSky returned. The two had seen little of each other—HomeSky hadn't even been out to the farmhouse since the night of her return—but Pat had become preoccupied. For someone as outgoing as Pat to turn introspective, this had Lu Ann up at night punching pillows and flopping in bed. And more often than not lately, with no one next to her to disturb.

"You okay?" Meadow asked.

Lu Ann blinked. "Me? Heck yeah. Fine. Just a smidge tired. Forgot about the Walleye Day Parade planning committee coming in. Got a little blindsided." Lu Ann sat up straight. "More importantly, how are you? How was your checkup?"

Meadow smiled, an all-too-rare event. "All's good. Over the halfway point now."

"Still on track for November 14?" Lu Ann asked.

"Locked and loaded, as Dr. Cold Hands likes to say."

SUMMER 1985

Lu Ann almost choked on her oyster cracker. "Meadow! Really?"

"He creeps me out. But there's nothing I can do. Go underwater and hold your breath."

Lu Ann took a sip of her diet soda. "He's not so bad. Sure, he's been around a while …"

Meadow pushed her silverware around. "Whatever. He never really says anything except for weird little phrases like locked and loaded and let's see what's happening under the hood. I think he disapproves, to tell the truth."

Lu Ann patted Meadow's hand. "Could be hormones. Could be you're a touch paranoid."

"Yeah," she replied. "Could be I'm a touch Indian and a touch pregnant."

Lu Ann let that sink in. She thought back to the looks she got at as teen, pregnant.

"Do you want me to go with you next time? I'll be happy to."

"Nah. It's not that bad. Cindy's a cool nurse," Meadow said. "Thanks though." What Meadow didn't mention was that she had already asked HomeSky to go with her.

HOMESKY

HomeSky only had 45 minutes for lunch. She craved the physical movement of walking to Lu Ann's more than the promise of food. Standing at a cash register and ringing groceries puts your feet in cement, and your body follows.

But HomeSky harbored no complaints. Being a cashier at Bonaducci's Grocery offered her about the perfect amount of social interaction. Most customers kept things pretty transactional. A little back and forth on the weather, the high school sports struggles, the escalating price of strawberries. Some didn't recognize her at first, but word quickly spread that Joseph's mother was back. In they came. Those with empty pantries, but also those with too much time on their hands. She was a spectacle. *What does loss look like on that level?*

HomeSky had worked at the grocery store over a month now, and as such, received her silver star-shaped pin and an extra five minutes added to her breaks. The silver one-month pin was meant to be worn above her nametag until the gold annual pin took its place. The first owner, Sebastiano Bonaducci, was a military man, and believed in decorating the rank-and-file. His tradition was honored by the following generations of sons who ran the corner grocery. The best HomeSky could do was keep her pin in her pants pocket. The idea of removing the press-grip backing from the little star and pinning it to her blouse was inconsistent with her self-view. When the owner asked about the pin's whereabouts, she said the backing had fallen off and was lost. He was always happy to find her a new one.

So when HomeSky reached into her pocket for the folded letter, it was the unbacked pin that pricked her finger. She flinched, standing at the mailbox, a few blocks from Lu Ann's, watching a droplet of blood rise on her fingertip. *A drop on a fingertip* she thought. There and then, she reconsidered her measure of pain in this world. She challenged herself, for the first time, to view her grief on a greater relative scale. It was devastating, her loss. She had buried her two greatest reasons for living. *Is there something beyond my pain? What if we are shown a larger perspective to help us cope?*

She saw herself there, on the sun-painted sidewalk in front of the blue mailbox. There was the blacktopped stretch of Main Street pointing to Lu Ann's. The town divided by a river; the vast surrounding forests; the hard angles that cut Minnesota's borders; the United States; the continent of North America. Her view rose higher and higher and still higher until she saw the marble-shaped beauty of Earth and its small place in the boundless universe. Why this idea came to her made no more sense than why an unbacked pin came to be in her pocket. But there it was. HomeSky wiped away the single droplet of blood, and let such thoughts rest for now.

She took the letter from her pocket and made sure everything about the address was legible. It was stamped and ready to go to Mick back in St. Paul. It had been seven weeks since they parted at the bus station and she knew he would be concerned. HomeSky kept herself to a single page, letting Mick know mostly where she was, rather than how she was. She added a bit about Monsignor Kief, the comfort of staying with him, and how he was fascinated, if not obsessed, by Mick's happiness triangle and resolved to unlock the mystery of the three Fs. The Monsignor was sure, HomeSky had written, that one of the words was Faith.

As the mouth of the mailbox swung shut and the envelope thunked into the hard emptiness inside, HomeSky closed her eyes and asked for a sign. *What am I to do? Where am I to go?* She opened her eyes to the street. There was nothing there of particular circumstance. Except that she felt hungry, which for her was unusual.

Outside Lu Ann's diner, HomeSky caught her reflection in the large window that ran along the sidewalk. She realized that she had reached a point where she didn't know how she appeared to others. For so long she didn't care. Now she was met by the reflection of a virtual stranger, with mid-length hair that you'd call neither long nor short. Her drawn cheeks and eyes set in dark shadow put years on her. The mustard-colored uniform shirt opened at the collar, her chest withdrawn, her shoulders square and thin. *Is this the woman I saw in the bus station glass? It seems yes, it seems no. Who are you now?* How long she remained there, she didn't know. Meadow's rap on the window from inside, and subsequent small wave, got her moving.

"Sorry," HomeSky said, slipping into the booth across from Meadow. "Not only am I late, but I'm window gawking on top of it."

Meadow signaled that her mouth was full. "No problem," she said, before taking a drink of water. "I would have waited to eat but Bulge has zero patience."

HomeSky's eyes twinkled just so. "We're going to have to find a more appropriate name for the child, don't you think?"

"Yeah, I know. That's what everyone's saying. But I'm completely locked up."

SUMMER 1985

"It'll come to you."

"It better pretty quick. I'd at least like a few on the list that feel good."

"Maybe with adoption you're better leaving it to the new parents," HomeSky offered. "Any news to report?"

Meadow's face went slack. She shook her head. "Not really. Pat's trying to be optimistic but he's talking to the adoption agency who's talking to lawyers who say they wouldn't touch this with a 10-foot pole. Too much federal regulation crap. From what I get there's this thing called the Indian Child Welfare Act that makes placing an adoption off-Rez almost …" Meadow didn't finish. Her eyes moistened. "You have to give every relative due diligence—whatever exactly that is—which could take over a year. Then if you do go off-Rez, it's supposed to be a tribal placement. I know it's not healthy to get freaked out but I just want to find someone who will love my kid and raise him how he deserves to be raised away from all the bullshit."

HomeSky considered telling her there's no such place, but that would do little good. "Is there anyone on the Rez who could work?"

Meadow wiped her eyes and looked at HomeSky with frightening fierceness. "Are you serious? You wouldn't live there. Your family moved off, right?"

HomeSky nodded, holding the strength of Meadow's eyes.

Meadow looked down at her food, which had lost its appeal. "I don't mean to bite you. Mad, happy. Cold, hot. Hungry, nauseous. It's a blast being pregnant."

HomeSky looked at the beautiful young woman. "You're doing great. Okay?" She waited for Meadow to look back at her.

"Okay," Meadow said. "If you say so."

It was Lu Ann's practice to bake two trays of fresh chocolate chip cookies every day. 12:45 sharp. Call it her way of giving her regular lunch crowd a warm reminder of why they came in today and why they should return tomorrow. This act fell somewhere in between shrewd business and down-home hospitality.

When the hot trays came out of the oven, she let the cookies set a moment so the spatula wouldn't make a mess of them. Lu Ann peeked out at the tables. Everything seemed under control. Her eyes fell upon Meadow and HomeSky. Their body language spoke of the close nature of their conversation. She ducked back in the kitchen feeling like an eavesdropper.

This is not me, she thought. *I can't be angry with Meadow for being drawn to HomeSky. I can't be angry with HomeSky for returning home. I can't be angry with Pat for …* She stopped there. She was angry. Or frustrated. Or maybe hurt was the word. Lu Ann had a difficult time putting her finger on the knot of emotion she carried.

Picking up the spatula, she began putting the cookies on a large bakery plate to bring to the register. This always got a line queued up, checks at the ready. The cookies would go fast despite Lu Ann's strictly enforced one-per-customer limit. Near the back of the baking tray, the edges of two cookies had fused together as they stretched under the oven's heat. She put them aside on a smaller plate for Meadow and HomeSky. But before she brought them out to their table, she used the spatula to break them apart.

SUMMER 1985

REG

Reg detested hot weather. Great as it was for business—blistering Julys are a boon for air conditioning repair work—the heat did things to his skin he didn't understand. And so when he scratched impatiently at his t-shirt, it caused a violent flinch that nearly sent him off his ladder. The rash-festered skin under his armpit was raw and tender as an open wound.

Reg was 10 feet off the ground outside the Mutineer's Jug working on a wall-mounted air conditioning unit. The red brick facade was blasted in late-morning sun. His head pounded. Sweat stung his squinted eyes. *What kind of dumb bastard would be idiot enough to cut a hole in brick and stick an AC in it?*

The old air conditioner had gone kaput, or so it seemed. This morning, when the bartender opened at 10, he cranked the dial to ON and … nothing. He went down and checked the fuse box; everything was good. Went back up, unplugged and plugged it in.

Still nothing. Looked like the streak of heat had been too much for the old beast. So he called Reg, who'd got it running a few times before. Woke him. Told him to get his pruny ass in his van and get down here for a look. They're calling for 90s, the bartender told Reg. I need that air conditioner.

When Reg arrived, two floor fans were oscillating back and forth, blowing the Budweiser table tents over. Nonetheless, the bar was heating up like a Dutch oven. Reg said he'd have a look, but it would cost double. Saturday rates. The bartender told him he was lucky to make rates any day of the week, but was in no position to negotiate. Seventy dollars an hour plus parts plus beer while he worked. It's hotter out there than shit on a turtle's back, Reg had said as he approached the bar for his first ice-cold down payment.

Reg came down off the ladder, taking his cane from the lower rung where it hung. "I'm too damn old for ladders," he grumbled, draining his Budweiser. In his other hand he held a part from the air conditioner: a coil switch. Two wires came out of its front like antennae on an alien beetle. He shuffled back into the shade of the bar.

"Got to go back to my shop and look for a part," he told the bartender. "I'd say it's a coin-toss either way if I have a replacement. Good thing for you I tear the old ones down for parts. Maybe it'll be your lucky day."

The bartender looked at the coil switch, then at Reg. "That thing's uglier that you."

"You wouldn't be saying so if it got the old beast working. Give me a roadie."

The bartender could hardly stand it. He wrung the top off a Bud. "Get your ass in gear. You're on the clock."

Reg took a long, leisurely pull off the bottle and dabbed his mouth with a bar napkin. "Don't I know it." He showed him his yellowed teeth.

Reg pulled up in front of his shop—which was little more than his dilapidated double garage with a faded Beware of the Dog sign glued in the center of each door. He poked the button on the garage-door opener. The right door staggered up, revealing a cluttered space crammed with air conditioners and refrigerators and furnaces both old and new. It was a world of rusty and shiny metal, precariously stacked cardboard boxes—some yet unopened—and machine parts everywhere. A narrow walkway, just wide enough for a person to slip through sideways, snaked deeper and deeper into the hulking stacks, some piled over six feet high. In the center of the garage sat a wooden workbench, chipped and dinged, with a vise on one end and a drill press on the other. Parts were scattered everywhere in no discernible fashion: on the tabletop, the floor, on shelving, on top of stacks of cardboard boxes. It was rank with the smell of grease and mildew and rot.

Reg shuffled sideways though the scrap, making his way around a few turns before reaching the workbench. Overhead, the utility light from the garage door cast weakly through the yellowed plastic hood. Reg wasn't searching for something; he knew exactly where he was going. At the workbench, he pulled open the single drawer. Inside there was a snub-nosed .25 caliber pistol. He pushed it aside and pulled out a bottle of gun cleaning solvent. With a shop rag around his finger, he dipped into the wide-mouth bottle. Then he went to work on the coil switch. Carefully, Reg scrubbed the sides spotless, then the top and bottom. When he finished, he smiled to himself, holding the part up to a thin ribbon of overhead light, squinting. "Good as new." He licked his dry lips, turning the coil switch back and forth in his hand. He clipped the ends of the wire and re-stripped them to reveal the shiny stranded copper. Reg wasn't much for humming, but as he slipped back toward the daylight, through the dilapidated maze, humming he was. Hell, happiness is relative.

Reg's work van was a cream-colored 1970 Ford Econoline. Rusted. Dented. With paint dulled and spider-cracked from years of weather. But it was a good vehicle for his line of work. Not that he did much of it.

SINGER

The letters stuck to the van's back doors read HANDYMAN. Rather than paint, Reg had opted for the rectangular reflective letters commonly used on rural mailboxes. They were affixed one next to the other. Hardly straight. The H started a good two inches higher than the final N. Beneath the word HANDYMAN was his phone number. The van had two swing-out doors. On one: AIR CONDITIONING. On the other: FURNASE. Over the years, a few intrepid customers told Reg that he had the spelling of furnace wrong. It's supposed to be a C, they told him, good-naturedly. Reg told them he didn't give a flying F. Or a flying C. Or a flying A. My job is to fix 'em, not spell 'em.

Beyond those mentioned on his van, other odd jobs, Reg mostly botched. He installed roof gutter in such a way that water ran away from the downspout. His screen work was slack and shoddy. When painting, he never scraped off enough old paint to get to the good wood, and his "primer" came from the liquor store. Usually the inadequacies of his work didn't fully expose themselves right away. By the time they did, Reg was nowhere near the mess. Being burdened with too much repeat business wasn't something Reg had to worry about.

Reg swung his van in front of the Mutineer's Jug, squealing the front passenger tire on the curb. He climbed out, reached across the seat for his cane before flicking his cigarette butt over the hood into the street. Tapping his pocket, Reg made sure the part was there.

"You may be in luck," he told the bartender when he got inside.

"Where the hell'd you go, Minneapolis?"

"Miss me?" Reg smirked. "I'll take a Bud."

"Like hell you will. Why *might* I be in luck?"

Reg spread his arms open, as though addressing a crowd. "Is that any was to speak to the man who might save your sweaty ass from getting even sweatier?" He took the coil switch from his pocket and gingerly set it on the bar, watching the bartender closely. He loved what was coming next.

"Hmm," the bartender scrunched up his eyebrows and lips, picking up the part. "Looks like the other one."

"Yeah, but looks can be deceiving." Reg grinned.

He examined it further. "What's the difference?"

"Other than it's new?"

"Hell, I can see it's new," the bartender said. "How come you're not sure I'm in luck and it'll work for sure?"

"It came off a smaller unit," Reg lied. "The beast might be pulling too many amps for that coil to handle. Only one way to know. I'll take that Bud."

The bartender grit his teeth, slid open the stainless steel cooler top and got him a cold beer. "It better work," he said, putting the beer bottle down firmly on the polished bar. He set the coil switch on top of it. "This heat is testing my patience."

"We'll know soon enough, Mr. Patience." Reg took the part and the beer and went out. He got his tool belt from the back of the van, checking inside the leather pouch to make sure he had everything he needed in there. At the ladder, he hung his cane, and climbed. Quickly he had the coil switch reconnected. He screwed the control panel back on and was done. Almost.

He stood on the sun-baked sidewalk and snuck a look both ways. Reg pulled a folding step stool out of the back of the van. Then, moving with unusual quickness, he made his way to the back of the brick building, off the alley.

The step stool shrieked as he opened the legs. Reg's heart quickened as he climbed to reach the exterior fuse box. Reg doubted the bartender even knew this box existed. He unscrewed the lid just as he had done the night before when he took out the good time-delayed fuse and replaced it with a burned-out one. That was why the air conditioner wouldn't run this morning. Quickly, he switched out the bad fuse with the good, and screwed the lid back on. He made sure to keep the bad time-delay fuse. This trick had worked like a charm on businesses and homeowners alike. When Reg needed work, he fabricated it.

Back inside, Reg put his empty on the bar. His T-shirt was rung with sweat. "Damn ladder work is going to kill me."

"Well, d'you fix it?" The bartender's concern didn't extend beyond the air conditioner.

"Flip the switch and see for yourself. Unless you want me to charge you for another hour," Reg told him.

The bartender made his way out from behind the bar. At the wall-mounted air conditioner he looked tentatively at Reg.

"Go ahead. It won't bite. I don't think."

"Asshole," the bartender muttered. He turned the knob and the beast shook, rattled to life, and settled into a deep hum. "It's blowin' cold," the bartender said, smiling enough to show his chipped front tooth. He raised his hand to feel it. "Damn if it ain't blowing cold! Can I put it on high?"

"Let it run 10 minutes," Reg told him with authority. "Make sure that new switch is up to it. Then put her on high."

"I'll be damned," the bartender said, coming back to the bar with a bounce to his step. "You're not all shit for brains." He slapped Reg on the back a little harder than he needed to. "Let me get you something stronger than a beer."

Reg looked at the air conditioner and laughed. "Damn. This is turning into a regular lovefest."

SUMMER 1985

SINGER

Sunlight tangled in Singer's curls as they shone golden around his head. He bounced down the front steps of his house singing the words "picnic, picnic," a dinosaur lunch box swinging in his hand. Hanna stood back and breathed it in. Tears suddenly were in her eyes; she was struck by how uncharacteristic this was. Then she shrugged, smiling just noticeably, and left it behind in the gathering pile of mixed emotions that surrounded her of late. She was grateful not to be at work, not to be thinking about work, caring only about her Singer.

Hanna, carrying a small cooler, joined her son. "Picnic, picnic, life can be a picnic." They held hands. "Pack the pickles, pack the buns, leave the fuss, it's time for fun ... SQUEEZE!" And they squeezed each other's hands, Singer's favorite part.

"Don't squeeze too hard," Hanna bluffed. "You'll hurt your mother."

Singer rolled his eyes at her. "Mooom," he said to her like it was beyond absurd that a child could ever do any such thing to his mother.

Their plan was to walk the mile to the county library. Singer was a proud card-carrying member, a card he kept in his big-boy wallet along with the two dollars he got for pinning Cory in wrestling. Adjacent to the library was a new multi-colored playground that would captivate Singer for a good hour. In between, they would have their picnic on the grass—a perfect afternoon for it. Cory asked that they be out of the house by 2:00, and so they were. If all went right, the piano would be moved in and ready to surprise Singer when they returned home.

Walking in Duluth is great when you're going downhill, the direction they were headed. The return trip was the opposite story. Although either way was equally fun for Singer because coming home he'd typically get a horsey ride. Cory liked the extra leg workout. Hanna not so much.

They zagged their way down the hill, Singer skipping ahead, kicking a stone back and forth between his feet, trying to keep it on the sidewalk. Hanna wondered if he did it because it was fun, or because Cory had told him to work on foot coordination. She frowned at the idea when Cory had first brought it up. Hanna said that for a boy not even four, foot coordination meant not tripping over your own shoes. Cory looked at her in a lingering way. Maybe so, for most boys, Cory had replied.

Of course, Hanna wanted to think of her child as special, *did* think of her child as special, but in what regard? She liked athletics—got her start in journalism covering sports. She was drawn to the discipline and the focus of an athlete, the health benefits, but she could care less if sports were for Singer. She told Cory it's just about finding an avenue of success. That's all any of us are looking for. Cory was looking at her when she said this, but Hanna sensed he wasn't hearing her. I just want him to have his shot, he had said. Not everybody gets their shot.

SUMMER 1985

They passed the stately Victorians on the hill and Singer's head was down, his face intent. Keeping that rock off the grass was his focus.

"Singer," Hanna said for a second time, a little louder now. He stopped, looked at his mother. "I want to show you something." She caught up to him. "See that big house on the hill? That mansion?" She said this with dramatic inflection, pointing at a turn-of-the-century Queen Anne Victorian. The house had an elaborate roofline with turrets, a second story tower with projecting bay windows, and a third-story walkout balcony, lavished in decorative trim. "It's called Shipwreck Mansion."

"Wow," Singer said, transfixed.

Hanna knelt on the grassy boulevard next to him, putting her arm around his waist. At 26, her beauty was quite possibly at its apex. Her hair was parted just off center and pulled back in a ponytail. A few auburn bangs hung across her forehead, but the sunglasses on top of her head kept most of her hair off her face. Her skin was tan now from the July sun, and her nose only slightly freckled. Her news director "despised" freckles and made sure they were buried under foundation in the summer months. Freckles scuttle credibility, he'd say.

Hanna continued. "A long time ago, almost 100 years, a man owned this house." Singer snuggled into to his mother. He loved stories. "He was a lonely shipping man because all he did was work, work, work."

"Why?" Singer asked.

"No one knew for sure. But he became very rich. He had the largest fleet of steamer ships on Lake Superior. He could see them from the high tower on his house. See the tower?"

Singer looked at the house, his large brown eyes brightening. "Right there," he said, pointing a perfectly chubby index finger at it.

"All day long, the shipping man stood in the tower room and watched his steamer ships leave for far-off places like Chicago and New York and even across the Atlantic Ocean. Every time a ship left, he carved a notch in the floor with a knife to remind himself of his many lucrative business deals."

Singer could hardly believe it. "With a real knife?"

Hanna nodded. "He had everything he wanted, but one thing. Can you guess what it was?"

"A truck?" Singer tried.

"No. He had everything but love."

"Why didn't anyone love him?" Singer's forehead creased.

"Well, he didn't make friends. All he cared about was making money." Hanna and her news team had done a story on this house when it was being restored. It was bought in disrepair, returned it to its original splendor, and converted into one of Duluth's finest Bed and Breakfasts.

"Then one day, the rich shipping man traveled on business to New York, where he fell in love with the beautiful daughter of one of his customers. He was 30 years old and thought it was time to be married."

"Thirty!" Singer said. "That's old."

Hanna suppressed a smile. "For sure. Well, the two of them fell in love and planned a big wedding back in the mansion …"

It was at this point in the story that Hanna stopped, realizing her situation. How idiotic, she thought. The story of Shipwreck Mansion has a terrible ending. She edited on the fly. "The shipping man and his new bride had a beautiful wedding, everyone from town was invited, they made friends of the whole town, were very generous with their wealth, and lived happily ever after up in the tower watching their ships steam off to distant lands."

"Will you and Cory have a big wedding? Will everyone in town come?"

Now she'd done it. What started as an attempt to take a boy's eyes off the ground and get him to absorb the simple marvels around him had turned into a revised life-and-death story, ending with a question Hanna herself struggled with daily. Singer waited, a smile perched on his face. Hanna was disappointed as her journalistic instinct for interviewing took over. "Would you like that?" She answered a question with a question.

"Yeah. It would be the best," Singer beamed.

"We'll see," she said. With that reversal she had successfully reduced Singer's question to the level of *will I get dessert after lunch?* She felt lousy, but she had no answer for his question.

In the library, they read a half-dozen books. Singer's dagger elbow kept Hanna from completely nodding off on the pillowed, wall-length couch. They saved the reading of the Clifford books for later, checking them out to be stacked next to Singer's big-boy bed.

On the library playground, Singer's appetite eventually won over everything, including the steep slide with the attached spiral slide pole. He came over to Hanna and momentarily rested his hot head in her lap. Very little about this boy's physicality was delicate, save the ringlet curls that now adhered to his forehead and temples. Hanna put her fingertips to them, but the moment gave way to Singer's declaration that he was so starving that his stomach might turn inside out.

Sitting on the shaded grass, they ate beneath the apple trees. The trees were a landscaping decision the city planners regretted some years after their planting. They bore fruit, or more accurately, bore objects that begged to be hurled at the library's brick façade by neighborhood teenagers. Singer hummed, chewing his PB & J, which he declared was better with the crust cut off, sliced in triangles, and then triangled again. He sang a tune to himself that Hanna didn't recognize.

"What are you singing?"

"I don't know. A song."

"Where do your songs come from?"

Singer shrugged, looking up into the branches of the trees. "They just come. Someone sings them to me and I sing them out loud." The boy looked over at his mother and smiled.

"What do you mean someone sings them to you?"

"I just hear them."

"You mean on the radio?"

"Yeah."

This allowed Hanna a deep breath.

"And I hear them other times too." Singer raised his eyebrows innocently. Before Hanna could ask the next question Singer said, "Mom, who's John Denver?"

"He's a singer, and a songwriter."

"Oh." Singer said. That was good enough for him. He noticed some jelly had made it to the grass. He flicked at it with his finger.

"Why do you ask about John Denver?"

"I don't know. I heard him on the radio."

"When?"

"Going to the grocery store once."

Hanna had to think. "You mean last week?"

"Maybe. Is he happy or sad?"

"Why do you ask that, honey?"

"Because his voice sounds both."

Hanna reached over and wrapped her boy up in her arms. "You are a goofy one, you know that?"

Singer giggled as they wrestled.

"Super duper double goofy," Hanna said, squeezing him some more.

"I hope he's happy." Singer said. Then he wrested free from her grip and ran back to the slide.

"One, two, three, LIFT!" Pat groaned as they raised the body of the piano up from the resting position on the last step of Hanna's stoop. They shuffled like a giant six-legged bug through her front door.

"Keep 'er going if you can, boys," the Sheriff encouraged through clenched teeth. "Al … most … there!" He exhaled, crimson-faced. "Christ in a Corvette, that thing has cement in it." The body of the piano rested on two folded moving blankets that they had placed on the hardwood floor. The Sheriff and Pat remained bent over, hands on knees. Cory went back out to the truck for the legs and then the piano bench. They were running behind. Hanna and Singer were due back any minute and he wanted the piano in place so the surprise would be perfect.

Quickly they reattached the legs. It took everything they had, but moments later the piano stood in the living room, right off the stairway leading to the second floor. For Singer, the piano would be the first thing he'd see every morning when he bounded down from his bedroom.

"What a way for him to start his day," Cory said.

"What a way for *us* to start the day" Pat quipped, out of breath.

They turned to see what Sheriff Harris had to add, but he was standing across the room, staring out the window.

"Sheriff …?" Cory said, his voice lined with concern.

"Just keeping guard," he said, raising his hand. "Don't want Hanna and Singer to walk in on us and spoil the surprise." The Sheriff kept his back to the room.

Cory looked over at Pat and shrugged. Pat spoke up. "He's one lucky boy to have such treasure. That piano's been with you a long time, huh?"

"Since I was 10," the Sheriff said. "A lot of water under the bridge since then."

Cory hadn't thought to ask about the piano's history when the Sheriff brought up giving it to Singer. Instead his thoughts raced to the practical: *how will we get it here?*

The Sheriff turned from the window and faced his friends. "It's the right thing, the piano being here. It can do so much good." The Sheriff looked at Cory. "A piano is a safe place for a boy. Always there when he comes home. It's a good thing, a solid thing when all around you is changing." The Sheriff nodded, confirming his thought. "We better retire to the backyard, boys," he said nonchalantly. "Hanna and Singer are making their way up the street."

Surprise was something Cory typically didn't much care for—a two-sided beast. He left the back door open to the screen door, and sat on the stoop so he could hear Hanna and Singer come in the front.

"You run up and put your books away in your bedroom," Hanna called out.

"'Kay, Mom." Singer's legs took him as far as the stairway where he felt the presence more than he saw it. The piano called out. Books didn't tumble out of his arms in shock. He set the pile neatly on the hardwood floor and walked over to the piano with a beautiful smile creasing his lips. He put up the key box and took in his first glimpse of smooth white ivory keys. Such comfort, such peace, such abiding company.

Hanna was pulled into the room by her child's silence. She watched him standing before the piano. Singer reached with a tiny index finger and depressed a single key and it sang out into the room and that one note had the capacity to fill the house and the next and those all around.

"Mom!" Singer shouted. "You won't believe this!"

"I see," she said quietly so as not to startle him. There was no start. Only impenetrable joy.

"Where'd it come from?"

Hanna smiled.

"Is it ours?" Singer came to her and looked up with eyes bright. "Ours to keep?"

"I think so," she said. "An early birthday present."

"Wow," Singer said, looking back at the piano to make sure it was still there.

"I think you have some friends in the backyard to say thank you to."

"Cory?" Singer asked.

"Maybe," she answered coyly.

"And Sheriff Harris?"

She frowned. "How did—?" But Hanna's question was cut short. They boy had already begun to run toward the backdoor.

"It's the best present in the world!" Singer said, finding Cory on the stoop. He leapt into his arms with enough force to push Cory back.

"What do you think of that, huh?" Cory said. "Pretty cool."

Singer's arms squeezed his neck so hard Cory had to adjust the boy. But he squirmed down, jumped off the stoop to the ground and ran to the Sheriff and hugged him around the waist. "Thank you for bringing me your piano."

The Sheriff got stiffly down to one knee. "And how did you know it was mine to give?"

Singer looked at him like it was the silliest question. "You told me about your piano. You used to play it with your wife who went up to heaven. You told me I could play it someday." Singer nodded at him.

"I didn't think you'd remember all that," the Sheriff said.

Singer just smiled until the Sheriff smiled back.

"Will you show me a song?" he asked, taking his hand.

Singer's touch released the Sheriff of all thoughts that his artificial fingers were something to be hidden. "You got it, maestro." The Sheriff got stiffly back to his feet.

"Hey, you look funny without your Sheriff clothes," Singer confided, as they walked hand in hand toward the house. And then, "Did you bring your licorice?"

SATURDAY NIGHT

HomeSky was carried by a light smile as she clocked out at Bonaducci's. She welcomed the thought of tonight, of what Monsignor Kief called their "blockbuster Saturday night."

The housekeeper was given Saturdays off, and although neither of them said so out loud, the two of them savored an evening alone. HomeSky would sneak a small bag of groceries through the back door, filled with something impermissible on the weekly hot-dish-and-casserole menu. They'd tune in Garrison Keillor and prep the meal with the radio turned up loud enough to wake the dead. After the meal was patiently cooked and consumed, they'd light candles and spray air freshener to cover the dinner's subversively aromatic tracks.

Tonight would be steak tortillas, featuring from-scratch corn tortillas. HomeSky recalled she had a stash of chili powder and cumin hidden behind the spice rack, but she did need to get cornmeal and raspberry double-fudge chocolate ice cream as she left work. Such was the beauty, and the bane, of grocery store employment. All the food you could imagine was right there waiting for you.

These past few months were what HomeSky needed; she knew so without making mention of it. To be with Monsignor Kief. To move forward, unrushed, at the halting pace of an unsighted man. To bump along in her darkness, beside him.

She was staying in the third-floor rectory guest room, finding herself a little less apprehensive each week. She'd quit drinking, so grateful that alcohol no longer called her and took her away. She wasn't exactly happy sober, but more importantly, she was no longer sad sober.

The Monsignor had turned over the keys to the rectory and the Cadillac. She came and went without expectation or explanation. This arrangement was perfect, but temporary; she grasped that.

"Hello?" HomeSky said coming through the screen door in the rectory's back way. The door slapped shut.

"Did you remember the ice cream?" the Monsignor practically shouted as he turned into the kitchen.

"Oh … ice cream," HomeSky said dejected. "I could run back for it."

The Monsignor slumped. "No, no," he said, poorly disguising his disappointment. "We'll manage fine."

"Just joking," HomeSky said meekly, feeling badly. "Raspberry double-fudge chocolate."

"Raspberry?" Pause. "Double-fudge?" Pause. "Chocolate?" The Monsignor broke the flavor into sub-parts because if said all together, he might very well have fainted. "Alleluia. That more than compensates for the jolt you delivered to my poor aging heart. But you had me!" Monsignor Kief smiled enthusiastically; he savored practical jokes as much as ice cream. "You should have kept me on the line. Played me like a violin. If it were me, I wouldn't have come clean till midway through dinner."

"You're much more accomplished than I."

"Ah, yes. It does pay to apprentice under a master." Monsignor Kief's hand found the counter, sliding along it until bumping into HomeSky's arm. He let his hand rest there. "Good to you see you feeling up to tricking an old priest. But aren't you the least bit ashamed?"

"You were quite clear," HomeSky said. "House rules. First on the list: practical jokes."

The Monsignor nodded and smiled. "Guilty, I confess. I do have an impressive record in that regard. Did I ever tell you when I first met Pat, how I didn't let on that I was blind until he pressed me to drive him somewhere? Had him for better than 15 minutes. Virtuoso performance."

HomeSky grew wistful. "I do remember. Pat had loaned me his car. After RiverHeart's accident."

"Goodness, you're right," the Monsignor's tone tautened. "Forgive me for not recalling the circumstances. That's a long time now."

"Twelve years this October," HomeSky said flatly.

"How life leaves us such adaptations."

HomeSky pulled back from the Monsignor's hand and tightly folded her arms. "For the worse, I'm sorry to say."

"Now, HomeSky, please. This life we're given is not easy … it would be utterly unsatisfying if it were. And you, brave woman, have had more than a fair share of trials. But as impossible as it is, you must never let go of the idea of hope."

"Hope seems far away."

"Okay. But as long as you can see it. Funny thought, from a blind man, yes?" Monsignor Kief bowed his head. "I didn't see hope very sharply when sighted. Ironically, I see it far better now. Hope is the beginning of goodness; it's goodness in its youth."

"Monsignor, I'm well past my youth. If you could see what the others see, in front of you is less a brave woman than a sinful one."

"Please, who you are can't be seen on the outside."

"I'm not sure there's much to admire inside, either."

Monsignor Kief frowned. "HomeSky, all respect starts with self. Never forget that."

HomeSky offered no response.

The Monsignor continued, stronger now. "Listen to me. I too know loss, and have gratefully been transformed by it. You, dear HomeSky, are new today. You *are* in your youth. You are not the you of old. Not of 12 years past, or 3 years past, or of yesterday. You are now. As am I. God offers the miracle of transformation—in every breath."

HomeSky tried to absorb this before shaking her head. "God is punishing me," she said to the floorboards.

"Absolutely He isn't. He loves you more than RiverHeart, or Joseph, or Pat or I ever have, and that is no small measure. I'm afraid it is you who is punishing you."

"That could be," she whispered.

"God is sad for that. So He gives you a new breath."

"If only it were that simple," HomeSky said. "Just breathe. If I could separate from the things I've done."

"And what is it you think you've done?" the Monsignor prodded.

HomeSky paused, and then leapt. "I angered Him. For that He took Joseph."

"Are you referring to your relationship with Pat?"

"With *Father* Pat," she corrected. And then shaking her head in disbelief, "With Father Pat."

"HomeSky, will you kneel with me? Where are you? Take my hands, please. Kneel with me." The Monsignor put his hands out to her.

"I can't."

The Monsignor knelt on the hard linoleum kitchen floor. "Please HomeSky." He held his hands up, his fingers spread apart.

"It isn't right," she said.

"What could be more right? Why do you think we are here right now? Do you know the unfeasibility of our coming together? There could be no other explanation."

HomeSky hesitated before taking his hands. "Are you sure?" Her hands shook as tears streaked down her face.

"It's time you spoke to God." The Monsignor said this so clearly, so inevitably. "This is why I left in the night and came for you."

HomeSky knelt across from the 71-year-old priest, her hands in his, her shoulders shaking. Tears came faster. "HomeSky, it's a miracle I found you. I'm here to help reconvene your conversation with God."

"How do you know?"

"I know. I was told in a song." The Monsignor smiled, "And there must be something that you know, that you haven't told me, about why you are here in my kitchen rather than at the destination stamped on your bus ticket. What were you told on that bus that kept you from leaving us?"

HomeSky took a catching breath. She looked off. "Our bus was en route when it struck a doe. The deer lay in front of the bus, dead, we all thought. I went to her, to put my hands on her. When I did, the deer's eyes blinked open. There was a connection. I know. Crazy, right? The doe stood, and ran back to the woods. I felt a life there. The doe was pregnant."

The Monsignor squeezed HomeSky's hands. "How did you interpret it?"

"A baby was coming. I was to come back."

"So you know your prayer, HomeSky. You do! Start the conversation. Say it out loud."

HomeSky shut her eyes. Her grip on the elderly priest's hands softened. "You've called me home, Great Spirit," she said. "How can I help Meadow? How can I help her baby? What is my place in all of this? I'm listening. I'm here."

The Monsignor smiled fully. "Beautiful. A perfect start. Just look at us here on God's floor, in this wonderful kitchen, on this

Saturday night, as the ice cream melts. What could be better than to have a purpose, and to have ice cream?" He squeezed her hands.

HomeSky didn't know what to say. She expected a moment like this would be treated more reverently.

"Relish it, HomeSky," the Monsignor said, offering her a wise secret. "Rejoice with gusto."

"And with ice cream?" she said timidly.

"Especially with ice cream."

They held each other then, rocking, for some time, until the floor won out over the knees. The Spirit had reentered HomeSky. Her sunken shoulders spread. Her chin was tipped up. Her lungs could find a full unhalting breath.

HomeSky was again new.

HANNA

They sat on the couch. What a forgotten pleasure that can be. The house was cool and finally quiet. Pat and the Sheriff were headed back for Baudette. Singer had endlessly played the scale on the piano, as the Sheriff had taught him, singing along with each note. Finally, a few wrong keystrokes, mixed with exhaustion, and the declaration that his hands were the wrong size for his piano, sent Singer stomping away from the bench.

But as storms will, this too passed. Now they found the simple act of being on an old soft couch particularly gratifying. Cory's knee ached from a day of over-exertion. Singer napped, his head in Hanna's lap. She reached her hand across and massaged Cory's shoulders. He looked at her. She was beautiful there, young and strong and so capable with her son's curls laid out in her lap. Cory smiled, a careful dimpled smile that she saw too rarely.

"What are you grinning about?" she whispered so as not to disturb Singer.

Cory shook his head and let his eyes close. He had driven from his cabin to Baudette to fetch the piano, then here to Duluth to set it up, all since before dawn. "You should have seen our Three Stooges' act with the piano this morning. We had it stuck in the Sheriff's doorway. It was like the whole town drove down his street just to see." Cory laughed.

"He must have been mortified," Hanna said.

"Yep. Never underestimate a piano. That's my new motto. I think I'm going to put it on a t-shirt."

"What did you do?"

"The Sheriff called some movers from town and they showed us how it was done. Or undone, really. A bunch of boys and their dad. Strong as bulls."

"How did you get it in here?" Hanna asked.

"Got lucky. Your doorway is bigger. Plus they loaned us some moving straps. The Sheriff said if we'd had those all along we could have done it all ourselves."

A crease of concern came to Hanna's brow. "How's your knee?"

"Good as new," Cory said. "Not sure about the rest of me."

"You should stay here tonight instead of going back to the cabin."

"I know. But there are a few things I need to look over before my meeting with the department head Monday. Need to brush up on my pre-algebra. Even my geometry is fuzzy."

"What will you have to cover? There's not like a test or anything?"

Cory opened his eyes and sat forward. Hanna was sorry she asked the question because she could see he was done relaxing. "No, nothing like that. I think he wants to make sure I'm solid on my subjects. He may want to talk to me about my teaching philosophy, which at this point is hypothetical, right? Maybe we'll go over curriculum stuff or what classes I'm assigned to. I know they have to shuffle things around with me coming in. He told me when I interviewed I'd get one group of seniors who are failing math. Need to get their scores up to graduate. That's what you get. The first-year treatment. Like how the freshmen had to carry the hockey bags to the bus."

Cory grew quiet. Hanna could tell he was thinking about his playing days, reliving some part of it. There was something to the way he pressed his lips together and squinted, looking off at a distant memory.

Since there was no good time for it, Hanna broached a subject she'd been avoiding. She took a deep breath. "I have some news of meetings and interviews myself." She waited for Cory to come back to her.

He blinked. "I'm sorry?"

"Oh, I was saying I have a meeting. Or I guess you could call it kinda an interview. Coming up. Well sort of."

Cory looked at her, puzzled. Hanna was rarely nervous enough to put so many verbal hedges into one disjointed thought. Journalism taught her concision.

Singer shifted on Hanna's lap, his little fingers pantomiming a piano scale. She turned to face Cory. "Do you remember that station owner in Philadelphia who I've talked about a few times?"

"You mean the media mogul stalker?"

"He's not a stalker."

"Isn't this the guy who flew to Duluth, drove to your station and blocked your parking spot so he could offer you a job?"

"Well not exactly blocked. I wasn't returning his calls," Hanna tried to lighten things.

"Yeah. Little extreme."

"He liked the plane crash piece I did. A lot. He's a self-proclaimed over-passionate broadcast executive. His credentials are impressive, and he likes my work."

"Maybe he admires more than your journalism," Cory knew it was the wrong thing to say halfway before finishing.

Hanna frowned. "C'mon. Give me a little more credit than that."

"I'm sorry. But he was extreme. If I remember right, there were a lot of phone calls coming in back then. Only his ended up in a scene at the station." Cory thought a moment. "You get phone calls all the time, right?"

"Some. But this guy's passionate ... or persistent ... or both. He calls every month. Calls me Hanna of the Midwest. Says he'd like to fly me out. Says Philadelphia, then New York, then Dianne Sawyer's chair."

Cory finally nodded. For as bright as he was, it took him a while to grasp what she was telling him. "You're going out there, aren't you?" He tried his best not to make that sound like an accusation.

"I don't know. I've always told him no. But last week I said I'd think about it."

He looked at her with her hair pulled back, her features so fine and photogenic. "Brains and looks." Cory smiled at her. "No mystery why the man's persistent." He paused. "I think you should check it out."

Hanna's expression was somewhere between surprise and hurt. "You *want* me to go?"

Cory reached around Singer and took Hanna's hand. "You deserve to know what's out there, so you can make a decision based on facts. That's journalism, if I understand it correctly."

"I guess so. But what about him?" Her hand brushed back Singer's curls.

"I'll take him. He's been talking about a bachelor's week at the cabin. Or maybe we'll go up and visit Stu and Darlene. They'd love to have us up."

"I've never been away from him overnight." She exhaled. "But I don't know, maybe it would do us good somehow."

"You'll always wonder otherwise. Did I make the right decision, using only scraps of maybes and what ifs. That can be haunting. Go, Hanna. Find out what this really is. It's almost like doing a story on yourself."

Hanna let go of Cory's hand. Her whisper raised an octave. "I don't want to do a story on myself. Shit, I don't know what I want.

I mean, this is what I want." Her hand swept outwardly to include the quiet room, her sleeping child, Cory. She took back Cory's hand. "This is what I want, but I just don't know. It's pissing me off."

Cory nodded. "It's okay not to know, Hanna. You're 26. You're really good at your job, and you happen to be better-than-average looking, which doesn't hurt in a business full of ugly news. You have a boy who's about to turn four, who is almost incomprehensible. And you've got me, who is …" At his point Cory laughed quietly and shook his head. "I've already used the word incomprehensible so I'll defer description of Cory Bradford for the moment."

Hanna straightened, her eyes implored. "But that's a big part of the question. Right? Do I have you? Really?" Hanna looked at Cory, holding her breath for an answer.

He shook his head. "I don't know. I guess that's part of what you need to find out."

SUMMER 1985

LU ANN

Saturday evenings arrive gently to a small town's Main Street, laying it down cool and slow and empty. As the light fades, there is a parting touch that makes for the stuff of beautiful, battered old love songs.

Lu Ann stepped out the front door of her diner and crossed her arms. Heat dissipated out of the building's brick as she leaned against it. *How can a girl be lost in the only town she's ever known?* Her thoughts thrashed in the gold-spun surroundings. Pat would be coming by after his AA meeting for a closing piece of pie and coffee, if they made good time back from Duluth. He had called from Hanna's to say the piano was a big hit, but sounded even further away. We should talk, he said. Those words stuck like a raspberry seed in Lu Ann's teeth. He said, no, the Sheriff wouldn't be joining them, as was customary on Saturdays. Typically they played three-handed cribbage, or had a circuitous argument about the state of the country as they rolled clean silverware into napkins for tomorrow's start of business.

Tonight something was coming, she could feel it.

Her eyes narrowed, looking down Main Street, her deep crow's feet testifying to much joy and pain. The sun had tucked behind the buildings giving the road an inky darkness. Nothing moved beyond the breeze.

Damn if she didn't feel wronged by HomeSky's return. Damn! This thought stomped around, defiant and angry. But the rebound emotion was sadness; saddened by herself, her selfishness. HomeSky had every right to return to her home. But why did it have to be a home rebuilt by the hands of the man Lu Ann loved?

A breeze picked up and dropped a bang down across her eyebrow. "Criminee." Lu Ann kicked a stone that hopped across the empty street. She knew what she was getting into as her friendship with Pat developed into something more. He was upfront about his emptiness when HomeSky left. Their friendship, and eventual relationship, was built on mutual emptiness. But emptiness creates a vacuum that must be filled by something of substance. Lu Ann hoped they could provide for one another. And they had—they were. But now this.

Lu Ann looked down the street at the lone stoplight. *Two wrongs don't make a right, but three lefts do.* This would be the hand-lettered sign she'd make for the back of the cash register, her mini-billboard for social commentary. But what had caused her to think of these words? Was she wronged? Or contemplating the wronging of another? She was relieved to ponder no further, for here came a sight for sore eyes. Radio Voice, high on his three-wheel bike, pedaled down the middle of empty Main Street. He lifted her heart. He slalomed around invisible obstacles, overdressed for the temperature, wearing jeans and a long-sleeved Vikings football sweatshirt. He squeezed his hand brake and came to a fast stop right in front of the diner.

"Did you know I was coming?" he asked, out of breath, wiping the sweat from his furrowed brow.

SUMMER 1985

Lu Ann said she did.

"Right now?" Radio Voice asked, still perplexed by Lu Ann standing curbside.

"I had a feeling you were coming right this instant," she said.

"For real?"

Lu Ann improvised. "For real deal Mr. Bicycle Automobile."

Oh, how Radio Voice laughed at her rhyme. Without restraint; so in the moment. Lu Ann was struck by the sparkling joy in his eyes. "You are a good teacher, you know that?"

"I'm no teacher. Custodial engineer." He proudly nodded.

"Hey, what's with that sweatshirt you're wearing?" Lu Ann asked. "I thought you were a Packers fan, not a Vikings fan."

Radio Voice looked at what he was wearing. "Oh." Then he pointed to the Vikings emblem. "Look."

"I know," Lu Ann said. "What's up with you wearing that?"

He pointed again. "No. Look! Paint." He pointed to other paint splatters. "It's my painting shirt, but I forgot I was wearing it. I don't wear it for good because the Vikings stink. They lost four Super Bowls. 23-7, Kansas City Chiefs. 24-7, Miami Dolphins. 16-6, Pittsburgh Steelers. 32-14, Oakland Raiders. The Vikings make me cry."

"Me too," Lu Ann said. "What do you say we have some pie?"

"Yes please! In a minute." Radio Voice almost fell over his heavy bike as he rolled it up on the sidewalk. Cory had found it at a farm auction. Radio Voice was fast to point out what Cory had said: it wasn't a trike because trikes are little. This was a full-sized three-wheeler that they named Groveland. They had painted it red, attached lots of cool reflectors, put handgrip streamers on the monkey bar handlebars, and a basket in the back with two mini American flags that flapped when he went fast, but he couldn't look back and watch them flap because he did that once and hit a light pole. Radio Voice rode Groveland to work except for winter days when the snow was too deep. Groveland was stolen once, but the Sheriff retrieved it from the cemetery after Marybelle Turcott reported it was desecrating her husband's plot. Since the theft, wherever he rode, Radio Voice carried a chain and padlock in the basket, and a key on a string around his neck.

"Be right in. Have to lock up Groveland safe." Lu Ann was going to tell him not to bother, but you just didn't know these days. Baudette was changing, in many ways not for the better. Or maybe it was just her mood.

"Can I have thirds?" Radio Voice asked with two bites of his second slice of apple pie still on his plate.

"We want to save some for Pat, right?" Lu Ann asked.

"You can make another," Radio Voice said craftily.

"Not that fast I can't. He should be here in an hour."

"And Sheriff Harris too." Radio Voice polished the plate clean.

"No Sheriff Harris tonight," she told him.

Radio Voice stopped chasing a crumb around his plate. "Huh? Why? He always comes for Saturday closing time pie and coffee."

Lu Ann wondered what to tell him. "Well, Pat and I are going to have a quiet talk when he gets here."

"Can I too?"

"Hon, that wouldn't make it very quiet, would it?"

Radio Voice dropped to a whisper. "I promise not to be louder than this."

Lu Ann smiled and gave him a squeeze. "No, silly. I mean we are going to talk about some private stuff."

"But if it's private, you don't talk about it, I thought."

Lu Ann considered getting him a third piece of pie. "Father Pat and I have some things to work out."

"You just called him Father Pat," Radio Voice covered his mouth as he laughed.

Lu Ann sat stunned. "No. Really? I did?"

Radio Voice smiled wide and nodded vigorously. "He's not a Father anymore. Just Pat. He and God are still best friends, but he doesn't work for Him like he used to."

"That's right," Lu Ann said. "I guessed it just slipped." Flummoxed, she looked off, past the tables and the booths, out the plate glass window. *Father Pat? Where on earth …? Either it's been a very long day, or I'm moving backward. Or both.*

ROY LEE

Roy Lee FastHorse sat in the back seat of his car with his shirt off and a warm can of Pabst balanced on the ledge of his beer gut. He watched it bob up and down with the rise and fall of his breathing. It was hypnotic, looking down the dark silver opening in the can. The lids of his lifeless eyes would droop, come to closing—then snap open. He'd catch the can before it fell to the floorboard, take a swallow, and put it back on its fleshy shelf, where the process repeated itself.

The back seat is where Roy Lee slept off last night's jag. It didn't end until the sun was about to rise, so he pulled off the road. What particular road, he couldn't have been less sure, but he hurtled down a logging trail far enough not to be spotted if the Rez police patrolled by. Chances were slim, but getting dragged into detox sucked.

SUMMER 1985

The heat shook him awake sometime the following afternoon. His neck felt like an ice pick was left in it. His skin was gluey. Stumbling stiffly out of the car, Roy Lee pissed, had a smoke, climbed in the back and checked the inventory. Nine lousy beers. Five smokes. One joint. "Hardly enough to make me hungry," he said, "but maybe enough to make me shit." He patted the remains of his torn cardboard 24-pack companion.

He napped through the late afternoon, and as sunset approached he started feeling the thrum of life return.

Roy Lee finished the last can and flung it out the window. "Dead fucker," he said. Exactly what he was referring to wasn't clear because his mind was racing. *Cops. Wife. Lying friends. Debt. No phone service. Broken fishing rod. Meadow.* That's where his thoughts hit the brakes.

A look came across his face like an epiphany. "She needs to be taught some respect." Roy Lee looked at the eagle tattoo on his right forearm. When he clenched his fist the wings lifted under muscle, but not like they did 15 years ago when few dared to disagree with him. "Respect." His smile was as foul as his breath.

He climbed awkwardly out of the back seat and pulled on his shirt. The logging road buzzed with descending mosquitoes. He popped open the trunk and lifted the old stained blanket and smiled for the second time of the day. Admiringly, he lifted the 12-gauge pump-action shotgun, its weight feeling good in his hands. On the open edge of the trunk he sat, resting the gun across his lap. Evening had come. He pumped open the chamber but there was no shell inside. There was an old Folgers coffee can in the trunk. He pried off the lid and scrounged out the four magnum shells it held. He loaded the weapon. "Four ought to do it," he said, raising his eyebrows.

A grey squirrel chattered in a nearby tree, unaware of Roy Lee's presence. The squirrel scurried across a branch and down the trunk about halfway ... and froze. Something strange was in the road. Something that wasn't there other days when he scratched for acorns or found a fresh pinecone to seed or chased his sister to the creek for a drink. RUN! The alarm was sent through the little creature's body just as the explosion came. The squirrel was blown clear off the tree.

Roy Lee FastHorse laughed, lowering the shotgun stock from his cheek. "Flying squirrel," he said, ejecting the spent shell with a quick, efficient pump. "I guess three shells will have to do."

SUMMER 1985

MEADOW

She stepped out of the shower and stood inspecting her body in the mirror. "Bulge, who is this strange woman carrying you? I have never seen her before in my life." Meadow slid her hands up her belly, under her swelling breasts. "You make me look like I got a boob job." She turned profile to profile. "And what have you done with my waistline? I'm a cantaloupe with legs."

She stepped over the towel and came closer to the mirror; her hair combed tightly back. "Could my nose really be getting wider? Would you do that to me?" She turned her head, looking closely. "Don't blame me for having you adopted. This is how you treat me and you're not even born yet?" Her skin goosebumped as it air-dried. She looked down and caressed her belly. She whispered, "No, really. No hard feelings, 'kay?"

Six months into her pregnancy, Meadow's physical changes were coming faster and more noticeably. Her feet hurt more than she could ever remember and her back was stiff by the day's end. But despite the aches, Meadow wanted to slow the process. She was sleeping poorly and the heat made her crabby, but somehow, she was enjoying it—or perhaps treasuring it; that word had occurred to her of late. Of course, life was very different, what with living at the farmhouse and working at the diner. Days had quiet in them, where the Rez shouted at her that she sucked: shouted in rusted outbuildings, shouted in mattresses in front yards, shouted in dogs on chains. Every broken window and rotting road kill and torn open bag of garbage called her ditch litter. But now, to have this long gentleness. *Would it end when Bulge went to some other woman? Who will be my child's mother? Who will I become?* She wanted to know, and she didn't.

"Young lady, getting adopted isn't supposed to be as easy as getting pregnant," a starchy agent from the Bureau of Indian Affairs had told a frustrated Meadow two months ago. She and Pat had been in the BIA offices for a third time, and still her casework had hardly moved. Meadow held her tongue. Pat had told her over and over about the power that this office wielded. He said their best chance was if they took pity on her and trusted him, so best behavior, please. Ever since the Indian Child Welfare Act, the courts had become extremely strict about keeping native adoptions within the family, or a least within the tribe. Only after due diligence proved those options put the baby at risk would they consider off-reservation adoptions. Meadow remained politely resolute. Her child would not be thrown to the wolves. Her family was lazy, broken and addicted. When Meadow spoke like this, Pat, too, found that he had to monitor his response. Years of working on the Rez had shown him there was good there. But for now, his focus was on Meadow, not defending the work he was doing.

He helped build Meadow's case by providing the tribal arbitration committee with documents signed by the county sheriff's office and the district court showing that Meadow's mother was unfit. And her father's long list of run-ins with the legal system, most recently his citation for the assault on Pat and court-issued

SUMMER 1985

restraining order from Meadow, struck him from the list of potential adoptive parents. Next they had to show why aunts and cousins and even other tribal members were poor candidates. It's going to be a fight, Pat had told Meadow. But we'll just keep showing up at their offices doing what you know in your heart is right for this baby. We won't back down.

Meadow tried to disperse the anxiety as she dressed in shorts and a light blouse. She was about to head downstairs, remembering that the red light on the answering machine had been blinking when she came in from work. Before she left the room, her guitar in the corner caught her attention and offered some diversion.

She sat with it on the end of the bed and felt the cool lacquered wood on her legs as she tweaked the tuning. Pocketed in her jeans, which hung on the hook on the backside of the closet door, was a folded piece of paper. She spread it out on the bed, and with a pen behind her ear, picked up where she'd left off on her latest song. The title had been crossed out and replaced with: I am again now.

No looking back
no runaway glance
scared and pissed off
here's my chance

I spun too long
down your drain
held by nothing
I walk on pain

I am
again
now

I'm
here
some
how

I WON'T
not Ever

*be back
forever*

*I am
again
NOW*

*You slammed doors
I opened windows
here is sun
there is shadow*

*Be out of the way
What's past is dead
free at last
the future ahead*

*I am
again
now*

Meadow strummed and quietly hummed, making notations along the song's margins about chord changes. She crossed out, stretched and shrunk words, listening for lyrical.

*I am
again
now*

*I'm
here
some
how*

*I WON'T
not Ever*

*Be back
forever*

SUMMER 1985

I am
again
NOW

I am
again
now

I am
again
now

Meadow let the last note ring out. It was a pretty, sweet note, but she heard something behind it. Discordant. A noise. A door? A floorboard squeak? She wasn't alone in the house. She set her guitar down quietly, wondering if Pat had gotten back early from his trip to Duluth.

SHERIFF AND PAT

"Probably not the brightest idea to speed with an officer of the law in your vehicle," the Sheriff said.

Pat was cruising down the highway in another world. "Huh? Oh, crap." He let up on the accelerator.

"A few miles per hour we'll give you, but you were 15 over." The Sheriff's hand went to the spot on his chest that typically pocketed his cigarettes. Then, correcting the reflexive act, he smartly snapped the red rubber band on his wrist.

"Ouch," Pat said for him. "Is that really helpful, or necessary? I liked the licorice remedy better."

"Left 'em home on the counter," the Sheriff said. "Plus, I've added a second layer of behavior modification."

Pat laughed. "Say. Such glossy language. But that's not behavior modification, it's corporal punishment. Illegal in most jurisdictions."

"You just don't want to lose a bet—for a *second* time." The two of them had gone double down that the Sheriff couldn't extend his no-smoking streak to three months.

Pat checked his speed. "I guess all's fair in love, war and quitting cigarettes."

The Sheriff nodded and looked out the window. They were maybe an hour from Baudette and he knew Pat was pushing it because he wanted to get back for his 8:00 AA meeting. "You were no stranger to tobacco yourself, if I remember right," he said.

Pat agreed.

"Do you miss it?"

"Only when I go hunting. Which, by the way, we need to do this year. I haven't shot a duck in far too long."

"Hell," the Sheriff grumbled. "No birds left. Duck hunting is going the way the buffalo went for the Indians."

"What about back behind Rodeen's place? That slough we used to hit?"

The Sheriff smiled to himself in memory. "Might be a few locals we could pop there on opener. Maybe. I'll talk to Darryl. He's a good man. Plus he still owes me from the night I drove his kid home from the homecoming kegger."

Pat went back to the other world he was thinking about. Namely, Lu Ann. He had run it over in his head a thousand times and all he could come up with was, *we need to take a break.* It sounded so high school, but it was true. Or at least he needed a break. But did that sound too much like we need to break up? That wasn't what he was saying ... or was it? Shit! He just didn't—

"Second warning," the Sheriff said crisply.

Pat looked down at the speedometer: 81 miles per hour.

"Want me to drive?" As much as the Sheriff didn't want to, he thought it might be for the best.

"Nah. I got it. We're only what, 40 miles out?"

"Something like that." The Sheriff checked his watch. "It's only 7:15. Isn't your meeting at eight?"

"Yeah," Pat said. "But I promised this new gal at group that I'd bring her a book, and it's at the farm. I was thinking of swinging by on the way into town."

"Can't you get it to her another time?"

"I could, but I already forgot twice and it's something we talked about and I don't want her to think it's unimportant. You know?"

The Sheriff nodded half-heartedly. "I still think we'll make it even with the stop. Plus they know how to start a meeting without you, right?"

"I know," Pat said. "I've never been late in over six years. It's a respect thing."

Roy Lee sat up on the road that overlooked the farmhouse. He tossed his binoculars back on the front seat. All clear. The car clock read 7:55.

Meadow's car was in the farmyard. No sign of Pat's vehicle, or that meddling asshole of a sheriff. Roy Lee had done his homework over the past month. He knew Pat would be at his stupid AA meeting by this time. The fool was like clockwork on Saturday nights.

He turned over the ignition and rolled onto the gravel road, headed toward his daughter. She was a whore like her mother. Ran out on him like her mother. Pregnant as a teenager like her mother. What party had she been at? How many joined in? It was time to set a few things right.

Roy Lee didn't shut the car door all the way as he slipped the gun out of the back seat. The porch was well-built; only the third stair tread made a sound under his weight. The front door was left open to the screen door. Sloppy. He had expected to cut a screen and go through a window. The screen door slipped, banged little as it shut. Roy Lee heard a guitar stop playing. She's upstairs.

"Pat?" Meadow called out as she came down the stairs. "Hello? Ah, shit," she said to herself for leaving the front door open. When she went to close it, the sight of him nearly made her faint.

Roy Lee stepped out of the den and put away his buck knife. Meadow noticed that the blinking light on the answering machine was no longer blinking. "Roy Lee smiled and made a cutting gesture with his hands. "Oops. No more dial tone."

"Get the hell out of here. Now! Pat's around back and you're going to be in a world of hurt just like last time."

Roy Lee had a terrifying flat stare. "I don't think so." Meadow saw the shotgun leaning against the desk. "I'm Pat and I'm an alcoholic," he mimicked. "We know where he is so FUCK THAT!" Roy Lee's voice exploded, his eyes flashing as he pounced. Meadow screamed and ran. But he got her by the back of her hair and yanked violently. Her feet shot out from under her. She slammed, back first, on the floor, driving the air from her lungs just as her head struck the hardwood. She couldn't breathe. Screams merely squeaked out.

Roy Lee showed his rotten smile. "Did you really think it was going to be that easy?"

"That's FastHorse's car," Pat said in alarm as he turned in the long driveway.

"Son of a bitch," the Sheriff said gravely. "Stop." The Sheriff put a hand up in front of him, trying to process all the thoughts that were simultaneously firing. "Okay," he turned to Pat unbuckling his seatbelt. "This is serious."

Pat interrupted. "But he's got a restraining order."

The Sheriff ignored that. "It doesn't look like he plans to be here long because he pulled up in plain view. We gotta move fast. Do you have any kind of weapon?"

"In the car?" Pat said, his voice rising in incredulousness.

The Sheriff's firm monotone remained. "This man is armed and dangerous. You've witnessed that already. We need a gun. A pipe.

Anything. Is there something in the barn? A baseball bat? Anything?"

"A baseball bat?"

The Sheriff's voice climbed an octave. "Pat, think! Anything that could function as a weapon."

His eyes sparked. "There's a spade. In the barn. Long-handled. Heavy-duty."

"Good. Okay. I'll get out quietly by the front door, by the car, there." The Sheriff pointed, a drop of perspiration sliding down his temple. "Drive quickly to the barn. Get the shovel and run as fast as you can to the back door." Again the Sheriff pointed, eyes fixed on Pat. Pat nodded to his instructions. "When I see you get around back, I'm going to count to five-one thousand and go in the front loud and proud. I'll distract him. You need to enter quietly in back, sneak up behind him and take him out."

"What do you mean take him out?"

The Sheriff's eyes went to stone. He reached over and took one of Pat's shoulders and squeezed hard. "I mean take him out."

Roy Lee stood over Meadow. Her eyes had rolled back when her head struck the floor. They fluttered open. Wide, frightened open. She squirmed and kicked for a breath. Her bare feet pushed on the floor, her body sliding away from him, squeaking on the hardwood. "Look at you. Little squeaking mouse. Not so disrespectful anymore. Right? RIGHT?!" Meadow nodded "Your mom was pregnant when I met her, and she thinks she can just fucking disappear. But you have nowhere to disappear to, little mouse."

The Sheriff slid out of Pat's car and pushed the passenger door so it latched quietly. He signaled Pat to go. As the Sheriff ducked behind the hood of FastHorse's car, he touched the grill. Still warm. Pat lurched to a stop at the barn, throwing the car into park. He pushed open his door but couldn't get out. Paralyzed by fear. GO! he ordered himself. He couldn't get out. Then he realized he was still buckled in. He released the seatbelt and sprinted into the barn. The spade hung there, in its spot. The heavy metal blade and long wooden handle were weightless as Pat made eye contact with the Sheriff as he crouch-ran toward the back of the farmhouse. The Sheriff held up five fingers to start the five-one thousand count.

The Sheriff stayed low as he went up the porch steps. "One-one thousand. Two-one thousand …"

Pat's hand shook as he reached for handle on the screen door in back. "Our Father who art in heaven …" The door was unlatched. He stepped in the empty kitchen and from the front room he heard, "Sheriff's Department! You're under arrest!" Pat's heart leapt. Meadow's scream was followed instantly by the explosive report of a gun. "Thy kingdom come, thy will be done…" Pat gripped the spade with both hands and ran noiselessly through the kitchen down the hall to find Meadow lying on the floor.

Roy Lee yelled, "Ha! Flying squirrel!" and followed the shotgun blast out the front door onto the porch steps. Sheriff Harris had fallen backward down the steps, splayed on the grass, bleeding. Roy Lee ejected the empty shell and pumped in a new one. He stood above him, one foot on the porch deck, the other on the top step. "This'll teach you to mess with Indian business." He shouldered the shogun, bringing his cheek to the stock. Sheriff Harris's eyes grew wide at the sight. The sight, that is, of Pat coming out the door, lifting the shovel over his head, and with every bit of adrenaline God put in him upon creation, bringing the shovel blade down on Roy Lee's head.

LU ANN

By 9:30, Lu Ann wondered. By 10:00, she was angry. By 10:15 she was frightened. She had poured the last cup of coffee and turned the closed sign facing out. The lights remained on as she sat at the counter, not knowing what to think.

Picking up the phone, she again called the farmhouse, but got that same fast-paced busy signal. Weird. She hung up and went into the kitchen to see about the butter inventory when she heard the brass bell over the door tinker.

"Well it's about—" was all she got out as she came out of the kitchen. Pat stood just inside the doorway. His shirt was covered in blood. His hands hung at his side, motionless, like the rest of him.

"You're bleeding," she said, running to him. "Let me get you a towel." She took him by the arms. "For God's sake, what happened?"

"Let's sit. I need to sit." Pat said in an exhausted voice. "I'm not bleeding."

"Like hell you're not." She quickly ushered him to a stool at the counter.

"It's the Sheriff's." Tears welled. His face was dirt-streaked. He looked down at his blood-soaked shirt. "It's his."

"What?" she said. "The Sheriff? Were you in an accident? Are you hurt?"

Pat shook his head no. "Sit down. Here." He took her hand. "Sit next to me."

Pat told her the story, reminding her that FastHorse was the man who had broken his nose two months back. He said they had stopped by the farmhouse to get a book before coming in for his meeting. That's when they found his car parked in the yard. He had come for Meadow, Pat told her. He had a shotgun. Pat had difficulty going from there. His voice choked. "The Sheriff went in front and I went around back." He swallowed uncomfortably. "Can you please get me a glass of water?" He continued when Lu Ann returned. "I couldn't see what happened, but the Sheriff confronted FastHorse in the entryway as I came in through the kitchen in back. I had a shovel."

"A shovel?"

"A weapon," he told her. "We were in my car, remember. We had no weapon."

"Oh dear Lord."

"The plan was he would distract him and I'd sneak up and … hit him."

Lu Ann covered her mouth. "What about Meadow?"

"He had thrown her to the floor. She was in shock and couldn't say much. I'm not sure how seriously she or the baby are hurt. When the Sheriff saw FastHorse with the gun he backed out the way he'd come in, pulling the door shut in front of him. It took the brunt of the shotgun blast. Made a hole you can't believe. Saved his life."

"Oh thank God! He's okay?"

"They airlifted him to Duluth. I just spoke with the nurse who said he's in serious but stable condition. He's lost a lot of blood. A lot of blood." Pat shook his head. "I called Hanna but Cory had already gone back to the cabin. She said she'd check first thing in the morning to see if he could have visitors."

"And Meadow?" Lu Ann cringed, bracing for the answer.

"She went by ambulance to Trinity here. They'll keep her overnight for observation. We can see her tomorrow. She's sore, but mostly worried about the baby. Apparently he threw her hard onto the floor. They're going to do an ultrasound as soon as they can find the doctor on call. So I ran over here."

"That son of a bitch. What was he doing there? Kidnapping her?"

"I don't know. Meadow said he acted crazy. Probably drugs. Booze. Both."

Lu Ann stood and held Pat. "What's going on? How can all this be happening in our little town?"

Pat looked at her, dumbfounded. "What if I hadn't gone back for that book?" He was wiped out, almost beyond mobility.

Lu Ann pulled him back into her arms as he sat on the counter stool. She rocked him. Pat closed his eyes, but kept seeing it over and over.

Then it occurred to Lu Ann. "Honey," she hesitated, "what happened to Meadow's father?"

Pat pushed away and shook his head. "I think I may have killed him."

SUMMER 1985

CORY

The pickup pulled down the rugged, pine-lined road in the decaying light. It was a driveway, per se. When it rained hard, it was more like a duck pond. By late summer, it became an overgrown frog waterpark. In the fall, a safe cut-through for the deer going to the lake to water. To know a road like this is to know something that will always make you happy pulling in and melancholy pulling out.

Cory flipped off his lights. The truck rolled to a stop in front of the cabin. A sight for sore eyes: the epic sky above the crooked shingled roofline. The last trace of peach colored the underside of cloud wisps. The pine treetops arrowing into a sky gone plum. Bats circled for mosquitoes. The wind had retired.

"Nice to see ya, cabin," Cory said as he stepped away from the truck and stretched his legs, then back. He'd need to ice the knee tonight. "What did you do today?" he said to the log façade. "Take my advice. Don't sign up for piano-mover duty." Cory reached into his pocket and found a silver dollar. With the bats above dive-bombing for insects, Cory flipped the coin into the air, catching it with the opposite hand. Back and forth, over and over, it soothed him. Finally, just flecks of light were caught on the coin somersaulting through the blackness. He spat in the long grass that needed cutting. Tomorrow, Cory thought. He'd put aside much of the day to get prepped for his meeting with the department head. He promised himself, no work tonight. Just get his stacks in order so he could get after it first thing. Cory like things in order, despite his distrust that they'd remain that way.

Inside, he put his textbooks and notebooks on the kitchen table. It was a long wooden table, warped in the center. Above it hung a light fixture made with a ring of deer antlers around a single bulb. Singer loved that. The cabin held treasures. Old kerosene lamps that you could light when the power went out. An old Victrola that you hand cranked, with 45 records thick as pancakes. He was looking forward to having Singer out to the cabin for a couple nights, just the boys. Maybe they'd start here before driving up to Lake of the Woods to stay with Stu and Darlene. The more Cory thought about that option the more he liked it. He flipped to the back of one of the notebooks, found an empty page and wrote a quick note.

Hello you two,

Hope the fish are jumping into your boats and Stu is doing all the dishes. Things here are good. Not a lot has happened since I saw you at graduation. I have a meeting coming up with my future boss, the head of the math department. Plus I'm going to help coach the summer hockey camp at the Duluth arena for a few weeks in August, which will be a good way for me to get a look at the incoming freshmen and sophomores I'll be coaching on the JV team. But in the meantime, Singer and I were wondering if we could come pay you a visit. Hanna has some out-of-town work coming up later this month. I thought we might spend some time here at my cabin, and, if it works, some time up on the lake with you—if the resort isn't full and you're not too busy. Stu could teach Singer the finer art of mouse trapping (longest tail wins, right?) and maybe put him on his knee and get out his shoebox of pictures and fill him with tall tales. I don't mean to impose, and I know it's your busy season, so if it doesn't work out this time, we'll find another. I'm sure Singer would be happy here with s'mores and Jiffy Pop around the fire ring. Let me know ... call or write. Hope you two are well.

Cory always had trouble closing a letter. He didn't feel comfortable with Love, Cory. In fact, he'd always wondered how people could so freely toss that word on the bottom of a page or a card. Love is perhaps the most significant statement a person could make. Other endings: All the best, Yours truly, Regards, they all seemed equally wrong for other reasons. He sat over the page, tapping his pen, at a loss. He read over the content, putting in a comma here and there. When no appropriate finish came to mind he simply ended it, Cory. Folded, the letter went in an envelope, which he addressed and stamped.

Walking out to the mailbox before moonrise is tricky business, so Cory took it slow. He looked up through the silhouetted canopy of trees at a sky fast filling with stars. They twinkled on the boughs like distant Christmas lights. A shooter ripped overhead so fast, he questioned whether he saw it. Cory thought of Hanna. What should he wish for? Success in her upcoming trip to Philadelphia? Or did he wish Hanna would come back knowing her home was here? Cory stood at the rusted silver mailbox and wished he knew.

The metal flag squeaked, dialed upward, to signal the postman to stop for the letter. Cory yawned as he pulled open the mailbox door, dropped the envelope inside, and pushed it shut. Cory frowned just as he turned to walk away. He opened the mailbox again, his fingers reaching under his letter. Had he caught a glimpse of another envelope there as he dropped his in, or was the light playing tricks? Sure enough, there was a letter, or something. The envelope was tan, larger than standard size. He held it out into the night, but there wasn't enough light to read the return address. It had some heft. Cory received very little mail here, besides a few bills. "A mystery," he joked to himself.

Once inside, it took a moment for his eyes to adjust. The return address was from Charlie Callahan, Shara's father. Shara was a girl he had known since high school, and would exchange an occasional letter with. He had written her when he first moved out to the cabin.

The envelope was larger, Cory came to know, because it held another envelope inside, addressed to Cory, but unstamped. He recognized the handwriting as Shara's. Also inside the envelope was a newspaper clipping and a handwritten note from Mr. Callahan.

Cory unfolded the clipping and was struck by its photograph. Standing, he leaned on the table, then slowly, sat. It was a picture of him, in the winter of his senior year of high school, on an outdoor ice skating rink pushing Shara. The caption read: *Cory Bradford pushes his paralyzed friend, Shara Callahan, for an hour every Sunday around his neighborhood rink.* She was seated in the skating chair he had made for her, smiling big and wide. Why send me this? he wondered.

He read the note written by Shara's father.

Dear Cory,

If I knew a better way to say this I would, but I have terrible news. It's with a heavy heart I tell you our Shara has passed away. July seventh was her last day with us on this earth. Cory, I'm very sad to say she took her own life. Her mother and I are devastated.

You always meant so much to her. She treasured your friendship and loved seeing you, and getting your letters and phone calls. We found this letter that she left for you. I'd be lying if I said I didn't start to open it 100 different times, and because I didn't, it caused many harsh words between Shara's mother and me. We don't know why she would do such a thing. She gave us no indication. We're lost in this tragedy. But I honor the private nature of enduring friendship, above my needs and those of my wife, so I'm sending you her note, unopened. If it is appropriate, please contact us after reading it. Maybe there is something in it that can remove some of the [here a word was scratched out] confusion from our grief.

I'm very sorry, Cory, to bring you this news. We don't intend for this to be your burden. She was our greatest gift. I don't know where we'll go from here, but we both wish you well, and thank you for all you have meant to Shara through the years. My phone number is 651-699-0619.

Take care of yourself,

Charlie Callahan

Cory's exhale shuddered. He sat, as reality began to twist in his gut. Slowly the truth had him. "Are you really *that* surprised?" he dug into himself. Then his fist flashed down on the table, a hammer blow. "NO!" he shouted. "NO! NO! NO! DAMMIT!" His fist pounding down with each word. He closed his eyes. "Shit." His clenched fist throbbed, but his pulse pounding through it gave him a focus point. Waiting for each pulse beat, he calmed. Finally he rested his head in the crook of his arm that lay on the table. "Oh hell, Shara."

He looked at Shara's unopened white envelope. Cory pushed his chair back and took a step away from it, with his name written so neatly in cursive. Finally, he reached for the envelope, tracing the letters of his name pressed into the paper. "Shara, I don't want this."

He picked up the newspaper clipping again, looking at the picture, the two of them not so long ago. "Why didn't you call me?"

Then, in self-recrimination, "Why didn't *you* go see her?" He'd meant to, planned to, wanted to. But didn't make time.

In the early hours he would push Shara around the open ice, frozen Sunday mornings, strengthening his hockey legs, but more than that. Cory had made the chair for her the first Christmas after her skiing accident. Mr. Callahan would drive her to the park, manage to get her wheelchair down the steps to the large general rink just off the warming house. Cory would lift her into her skating chair, tuck a blanket around her, and they would have an hour or so before anyone else came out on the ice. Shara would pull off her wool hat and feel again the wind through her hair.

"I won't believe this, Shara." Cory put the envelope to his nose. It smelled like her. His temper flashed. "What kind of shitty thing did you do to her, God?" Cory wanted to swing at something. Break something. Fight for her. "A shitty THING!" he screamed, feeling it claw at the back of his throat. Cory raised his hands over his head about to bring his fists down on the table with everything in him, but the envelope in one hand and the clipping in the other stopped him. He set them down carefully, so as not to wrinkle them.

It passed like a black storm. He closed his eyes. The anger leaked out. "You had your chance, Cory Bradford. You didn't do shit."

Cory walked away from the table and sat down in the middle of the pine-plank living room floor. He went limp. "Dead?" he whispered.

He pushed himself up and returned to the table. Over and over, he smoothed out her envelope with his fingertips. Finally, then, he opened it and slid out the two pages.

My darling Cory Boy,

How sad I am. Summer is here and the running voices of laughing children are bounding in my window. That was me. Chasing friends across those same lawns not many summers ago. Now, in my four-wheeled throne of silver pity, it makes

SUMMER 1985

me wonder why I do it. Why get up? I go nowhere but back to memories. I'm afraid I've worn out the path.

Remember in high school when you used to run me down the hall between classes—the looks on the faces of the kids? Ha! Part fear that they were going to get run over, part amazement that it was you pushing me, part holy shit she's going to fly out of the chair on the next turn. And you'd say, Look out! Bathroom break! Bathroom break! The teachers didn't dare ask if it were so. I loved that look, and I don't think I ever told you why. I got so sick of the pathetic-pity look, or the don't-look look, so to see fear-amazement-holy shit in their eyes, that made me different. Just for a second. Damn, it was so worth it. They were paralyzed. I was flying. You know? I know that's not nice, and I'm sorry, but I loved it, while it lasted.

When we were skating, remember how we talked about the silent scream? We'd say, kinda joking, "The silent scream continues!" I'm sure you do because you dubbed it that. When you said it, I got it. Exactly. You heard mine, and you came to my rescue, my jock in shining armor. Well my love; my silent scream is coming to an end. Sorry. Can't do it anymore.

What I need to say to you is it's time for yours to end, too. I saw a look on your face in the picture you sent me of you and Hanna and that darling Singer. I cherish that picture now, but at first I was totally jealous. It took me a while, but that's Shara. That boy, Cory, he's your miracle. He and Hanna are here to take you fast down the hallway. No kidding.

I love you Cory, more than you've given me permission to. I'm deeply sorry for the pain this letter brings. Keep the picture of you and me skating—keep it near always. Please tell my parents there's no fault to be found, especially their own. Sometimes life doesn't work out. I have finally forgiven God. Now I hope He can forgive me. I hope you all can.

Until we skate again. Love forever,

Shara.

Cory laid his head in his hands and took a long breath. He felt behind his ear for the stone braided in his hair. He slowly shook his head. There were no tears. Only silence waited for him.

In Duluth, Singer sat up in bed and began to cry.

PART TWO

August

HOSPITAL

In the four weeks since the farmhouse shooting, life had either raced by at surreal speed, or inched along at the infuriating pace of a straightened coat hanger wedged down a leg cast on a sticky August day. It depended on your particular situation.

For Sheriff Harris, it was the latter. He stood uncomfortably in his hospital room. His damn leg itched beneath the ankle-to-groin cast. He was determined to put an end to that.

"Jeepers crumbs!" the nurse said, horrified. "What on earth?" She stood, hands on her hips, mouth agape, in the doorway of Sheriff Harris's hospital room. "What are you doing?"

The Sheriff was out of bed, balanced on his good leg with his other propped up on a chair. He had a straightened hanger halfway down the cast.

"Cleaning my gun," he bellowed. "What's it look like."

"Looks like, once again, you're not listening to doctor's orders.

You are not to be out of that bed except for therapy and to use the bathroom. We still need that stool sample, by the way."

"I'll get working on that. Meantime, some privacy?"

"As soon as you surrender that hanger. That thing has infection written all over it."

"Hell that." He pulled the wire out of the cast and handed it to her. She waited. "Will there be anything else?" he said.

"Yes, you have a visitor. I suggest you get back in bed. The view from here leaves little to the imagination."

The Sheriff smoothed his hospital gown down in back. "You should be so lucky," he muttered, hopping best he could back to the bed.

"Careful of your stitches," the nurse said, a bit softer now. She saw how the Sheriff winced when his hand brushed against his stomach.

"10-4." When she was out of sight he fell back against the pillow stack. That little bit had exhausted him. "Crap," he said.

He had come a long way since being rushed to the ER for surgery. He was a mess. Vascular bleeding in his left leg. Perforated small intestine, which required an exploratory laparotomy to run the intestine and sew up multiple holes. Wood splinters from the door were carried in with the shot pellets, penetrating the spleen, causing abdominal bleeding, but with time and antibiotics, that would heal. And the broken leg. When the shotgun blast had partially exited through the door, the shot struck his side, spun him off the porch, dropping him on his left leg. The tibia and fibula snapped like matchsticks, piercing the skin. The Sheriff spent his first two weeks of recovery in Duluth before being transferred to the hospital in Baudette.

"Knock, knock," Pat said as he came in the room. "How's the orneriest patient in Trinity Hospital history?"

"Ah," the Sheriff shifted, trying to get comfortable. "They've seen worse."

"Not to hear it from the nurse I talked to coming in. They put you in a new room, huh? Got it to yourself looks like."

"Yep. I guess the guy on the other side there just went home." Then the Sheriff clarified. "I mean home, that way home," the Sheriff thumbed out the door. "Not home, up there home." He thumbed to the ceiling. "Hopefully, I'll be next. Going stir crazy. Like being in prison for a crime I didn't commit."

Pat sat down in a chair that was occupied by a two-foot-tall stuffed black dog with a dainty pink tongue sticking out of his mouth and a matching pink ribbon around its neck. "Don't you already have one of these on your bed at home?" Pat teased, setting it on the ground.

"Cut me some slack. Stick that thing in the closet, why don't ya."

"Oh, it would just get whimpery. Plus you'll want to snuggle when it gets all dark out."

The Sheriff's eyes narrowed.

"Hey, not bad. Clint Eastwood, right?" Pat pointed at the Sheriff. "Let me guess, *Dirty Harry*." Pat thought that was pretty funny. The Sheriff squinted on. "C'mon," Pat said, "you could at least smile at my material. Just trying to cheer you up."

"What next? Twist balloon animals?"

"Jeez, you're meaner than a wet hornet. You sore today?"

"Nah. I apologize. Just this damn cast is itching to beat hell and I'm tired of dinner in a tube. On the good side, lost over 35 pounds. Call it the shotgun diet." He managed a smile.

Pat grimaced.

"So what's the gossip back home? No, wait. First tell me what the pies were at Lu Ann's this week. Go slow. Gimme every flaky detail." The Sheriff closed his eyes in anticipation. He waited. Waited. Then opened his eyes.

In a repentant voice, Pat said he hadn't been there this week.

"Patrick O'Rourke," the Sheriff boomed. "I thought we discussed this."

"I know. We did." Pat shook his head and tipped over the stuffed dog with his foot. "I'm stuck."

The Sheriff was unexpectedly sympathetic. "Okay, I get it. It's complicated. But Lu Ann is a fine woman and she deserves to know your feelings. Or your feelings toward HomeSky."

"I've been over it and over it in my head," Pat said.

The Sheriff waited until Pat made eye contact. "Thinking about the ground won't turn the soil."

Pat shook his head. "I got overwhelmed."

"You're not still worried about FastHorse, are you?" The Sheriff's back left the pillows he was resting on. "As my dearly departed Amanda used to say, he's soap scum without the soap."

"He could be in a coma the rest of his life." Pat was distraught. "I put him there."

"Yes. And I'm grateful to you." The Sheriff's eyes flashed. "And so's Meadow. He was in the act of kidnapping her. Get it? Or even worse. And who knows what could have happened to her unborn child. Plus you know where his shotgun was pointed when you hit him." The Sheriff nodded.

Pat rubbed his neck. "I know he's a troubled person. But my job is to counsel people with problems, not hit them with a shovel."

"Pat. Believe me. You did your job. You saved a life. Maybe lives. And as hard as it is, there are consequences to that. In a way, now you know what it's like to be a cop."

Pat listened without agreeing or disagreeing.

"Now, enough. It's time you put all that aside for the moment and go have the talk you were headed for before all this stuff happened first." The Sheriff frowned. "Did that make sense?"

"I'm afraid it did." Pat nodded. "I'll be back in Baudette tonight. Lu Ann and I will talk. We'll talk." Pat tried to sound sure.

"You want to take that stuffed monstrosity?" the Sheriff asked, trying to adjust the mood.

"Yeah, what's up with that?"

"Kitty," the Sheriff said. "My neighbor."

SUMMER 1985

"You're blushing," Pat laughed.

"The hell," the Sheriff went to nip it in the bud. "Just warm in here."

"She's taken a shine to you, hasn't she?"

The Sheriff tried not to smile, but was losing the battle. "Don't ask me what goes on in the heads of women. She's been up here a few times to visit. Nice company. She sure is a planner."

"How do you mean?" Pat asked

"For one, that stuffed dog … she says she wants to buy me a puppy." The Sheriff looked at Pat with an expression that said this is more than I'm ready for. "I had told her a while back how Deputy had passed, and it had been a few years, and how I like dogs. Damn if it didn't bring her to tears."

"Was it sad? Remind me again."

"Heck of a dog," the Sheriff said to himself. "Deputy was going on 12 so he was pretty bent and crooked. But there was still some hunt left in 'em. He'd taken his usual sideways route down the back steps to go do his business when a rabbit tracked across the lawn right in front of us headed for the side of the house. Deputy looked back at me like 'the audacity!' I looked back at him and said 'that's outright disrespectful' and he looked at me like 'can I go make it right?' and I gave him the hand signal and damned if that dog didn't find a gear I thought was long gone. He raced around the side of the house, tearing up grass, ready to take the cotton out of that rabbit's backside. They disappeared out of sight. I stood there and enjoyed the sunshine for a time. A couple minutes passed. I half expected Deputy to come around with that rabbit in his jaws, but more than likely, I thought, he'd come limping back and we'd see to breakfast. But no Deputy. So I went around the side of the house and there he was, dead where he lay. His heart just went out. Stranger yet, that rabbit was sitting there, not a foot off Deputy's nose, looking at him like he knew what happened." The Sheriff shook his head and let out a long breath. "When I came along, the rabbit made a run for it. Mysterious world we occupy."

"Amen to that," Pat said. "Now Kitty, that's the woman across the street with the two little dogs, right?"

"That's her. Hansel and Gretel. Like her kids."

"So she doesn't have children?"

"Nope. Divorced a husband that never wanted 'em. She always did and finally they came to sword points. She up and left."

Pat raised his eyebrows. "Decisive woman. Why come to Baudette?"

"She's got a sister over in Grand Rapids she's trying to mend fences with. She figured this was close enough for now."

"So d'you think you'll do it?"

The Sheriff paused and frowned. "That could mean more things than I care to sort through."

Pat clarified. "The puppy. Do you think you'll get one?"

"She's got her heart set on it. Says it's for the best. According to her, a dog gets a person up and out of the house, participating with the world. Says it will keep me from rebounding back into the hospital. She calls it extended physical therapy."

"How are you healing?"

"They sewed up a slew of little holes in my intestines. Let everything rest the last few weeks while they fed me an IV. They want to make sure everything's holdin' steady. You spring a leak down there and the infection can finish you."

"What about all the BB shot?"

"They got what they could, left behind what was too much trouble. They say going after some does more harm than good. Muscle and tissue will grow over. With the shot I have inside me, plus the metal rods in my leg, I'll rattle like maracas coming down the street."

Pat winced.

"I'll be fine. The biggest thing is to make sure the intestine's doing its thing. Day before last they unhooked the IV. Now I'm taking real food, so they call it. Christ, it's pablum. Applesauce. Pureed squash with a little rice. Half a banana. May as well not have teeth. They're asking for a stool sample, but the show won't go on."

"Oh," was all Pat could manage.

"Everything quiet in town, then? No major lawlessness?"

Pat smiled thinking about it. "I ran into your deputy the other day. He said he was called out to the Art Barn on County B, you know the one that sells antiques and such?"

The Sheriff nodded.

"Somebody came by with a can of paint and hand lettered a perfect F in front of the word Art so now the Art Barn is famous for customers with indigestion. I guess business doubled once word got out."

"I better get back quick before the desperados strike again," the Sheriff deadpanned.

"Too late. A couple nights later the Coverdales—you know, the family across from Mount Olivet church with the plastic yard deer? Someone snuck in late Saturday night and rearranged those deer with the bucks mounting the does. I guess the Franks were out of town, because both the eight and ten o'clock mass prayed for the souls of the delinquents."

"Well," the Sheriff said in a tone that suggested wrapping things up, "I guess I better get busy with lunch. Pudding and warm water. Plus nine-grain toast. Want to stay?"

"Maybe next time," Pat said. "But by the sounds of it, next time might be back at home."

"I do hope so," the Sheriff perked up. "I think this is the room they assign before patients are RoR."

Pat shrugged. "RoR?"

"Released on your own recognizance. As for you, you got your marching orders."

"I do indeed," Pat said, trying to look sure. "Life isn't easy, is it?"

The Sheriff tried not to think about the itch under his leg cast. "Not the last time I checked."

THE FARM

It had been a summer blessed with rain and sunshine in abundant shares. The land lay in a lovely lush, becoming more emerald by the day. When a car turned up the gravel road to the farmhouse, walls of corn on either side swallowed it. The alfalfa and hay had been through a second cutting and it looked like a third harvest might come early enough so as not to battle late season dandelions or killing frosts.

Meadow had come out of the hospital, in her words, more lucky than hurt. The ultrasound showed the baby was fine, but the doctor worried about a concussion after seeing the contusion on the back of her head. They kept her a second day, but she showed none of the nausea or lethargy, so she came home to the farm. And that's how it felt: home.

It was more than gratitude that walked from the barn to the farmhouse with her, past the grass where the Sheriff had fallen, past the front door that had been replaced, down the hallway where she had been ripped to the floor. It was more than relief that her child was healthy and growing and putting a pronounced waddle in her once effortless stride. She was changed. She was no longer scared. Not because her old man was in a coma and showing no sign of improvement. But more, she'd seen life at its most foul and heinous, and survived. It hardened something in her, beyond resolve. What she had to fight for had come fully realized.

Pat tried to keep Meadow off the tractor for a week or so, just to be safe. Ha. Ever since he'd shown her how to start the old John Deere, how to pull the New Holland haybine to cut the fields, she'd fallen in love with the rhythm of harvest. Back and forth, up the fields and down again, cutting the hay, then pulling the rakes, and lastly, when the grass was dry, pulling the crotchety old round bailer. After the attack, she'd accepted the coddling and the reduced hours at Lu Ann's without complaint, but wouldn't hear of leaving the steel saddle of the tractor seat. With Pat's seed cap pulled low, an old extra-large white t-shirt ruffling in the wind, running straight swaths through the field—gopher mounds be damned—she bounced under the sun canopy, sometimes until the tractor ran out of diesel. It was her thinking place. She was testing the feasibility of a few different plans.

HomeSky had come out to stay with her on afternoons when Meadow wasn't working and Pat was at the plant. It was a gentle transition for HomeSky, back to the ground she once loved and made her home. They'd walk the land. HomeSky would point out the yellow foxtail and sow thistle and how the meadowlarks were bringing grasshoppers to the nest to feed a second brood. The farmhouse was rebuilt, different now when the light traced the roofline with the jutting cupola. Nonetheless, HomeSky felt familiarity taking her back, like a prodigal.

In these same weeks since Meadow's return from the hospital, HomeSky and Pat had found that having this enigmatic, soon-to-be mother to watch out for had eased them back into each other's company. Conversations centered on Meadow's needs, not their own. It was a quiet mending, allowing them to politely bump into each other in the kitchen, or shyly brush past each other in the doorway, as they had years ago—a forever length of time ago. The impossible distance between them was closing. They had come from far off and met at Meadow.

"What do you think for dinner?" Meadow asked.

HomeSky stood at the refrigerator with a challenged smirk on her face. "Hmmm," she said. "Doesn't seem as though Pat is much of a shopper."

"He is, I hate to say, lousy. There are five unopened rolls of aluminum foil in the cupboard, and enough three-packs of paper towels in the back pantry to clean up after horses."

HomeSky opened the freezer. "Did you see all the bacon in here?" She giggled.

"Seven or something," Meadow offered.

"Five, six, and under the ice cream makes seven. I don't get it?"

Meadow laughed. "He told me every time he shops he thinks we're out of bacon and paper towels, so he stocks up."

HomeSky shook her head. "I'm not even going to try to analyze that."

Meadow saw the opening and went for it. "You know him pretty good, don't you?"

HomeSky turned to her. "Knew him … very well … once. A lifetime ago. Before I ran out. Not one of my finer moments."

"If you don't want to talk about it that's okay."

"If you don't talk about it, it owns you," HomeSky said. She folded her hands at her waist. "After my husband died, Pat and I became friends. He was Father Pat back then. You know that, I imagine."

"Yeah. I remember him at the Rez church. We'd come over from school before Christmas and help decorate the pews and stuff."

"We became more than friends. Pat was struggling with his calling, thinking of leaving the priesthood. I didn't want to be the reason he left. I thought God would never forgive me."

SUMMER 1985

Meadow looked at HomeSky. "Hard place to be."

"I didn't know whether to trust my feelings. They felt right and good. It felt like there was a future there." HomeSky looked away. "Then my son Joseph was killed. An accident. A car … it was nighttime … he was out running with Cory when he was … hit." HomeSky thought about how ugly the word hit is. The word just hung there, refusing to leave the kitchen. "Do you know Cory Bradford?"

"I know of him, I don't know him." Meadow's voice grew solemn. "I've heard your story. I'm very sorry. It's strange to know a story from it being told around, and then hear it from you. It's different now."

"What makes it different?"

Meadow thought. "It's real now, not a story. With real people and real pain. In a way, it's like what happened out here to me. For most people, that's just a story to gossip about."

"Yes, it's real. You've learned a lot for only 18." HomeSky looked at the young woman. She wanted to hold Meadow, feel her heart, but was afraid to.

"I'm sorry. I didn't mean to make the conversation about me."

HomeSky came across the kitchen floor and put her arms around Meadow. Meadow was strong and stiff, unsure of how to reciprocate. "That's the point, my dear. The conversation isn't yours to direct. Something Monsignor Kief helped me understand. Joseph's dying wasn't about me. Pat leaving the priesthood wasn't about me. Your father's troubles aren't about you. If your heart is good, then all cannot be bad."

Meadow took a step back. "You sound like a songwriter." She took a deep breath and her face tightened. "I've been thinking a lot lately, since the deal with my old man. I wonder if you will help me." She paused. "It's hard to ask."

"I'm happy to help," HomeSky said. "It's why I'm here."

"I mean help me with the adoption," Meadow said.

"Yes." HomeSky said, nodding. "I'll be with you every step of the way."

"No," Meadow said, her eyes flashing. "I mean, help me with the adoption as in," Meadow swallowed, "adopt my baby."

HomeSky's eyes grew large. She stood in suspended animation, like waiting for a sneeze. "Oh," she finally said.

"I don't know how to translate that," Meadow said defensively. "Maybe it's a bad—"

HomeSky took a step toward Meadow and put her hands on her shoulders. "No, no. It's just you've had more time with this question in your head than I have with it in my ears."

Meadow nodded.

HomeSky began to smile. It built slowly and grew until she fully grasped the heft of the moment. She nodded. "Tell me your plan."

Meadow was buoyed by the enthusiasm in HomeSky's voice. "Okay." She took HomeSky by the hand and led her to a chair at the kitchen table. "But it involves Pat, too." Meadow looked at HomeSky in a manner that said, *are you sure you're ready for this?*

SUMMER 1985

HANNA

Am I a rotten mom? Hanna plopped down on Singer's big boy bed in near tears. The little red tugboat t-shirt is what got her. How could she leave anything so tiny in pursuit of a career? She inhaled the shirt and then held it on her lap.

She had been putting out the clothes that Singer would need for the week with Cory at Lake of the Woods. Singer couldn't have been more excited. A week with fish big enough to push boats with their noses and thunderstorms of cookies; Cory had been putting Singer to sleep for weeks with Stu whoppers.

Do I even want this if they offer it to me? The station owner had been spinning some pretty good stories of his own. How Hanna could have Philadelphia wrapped around her little finger in a year, and then it's just a simple, but deftly handled, step to Manhattan to the big stage. Limos, a Midtown loft a block off the park, private school for her little one. Somehow he always managed to leave

Cory out of the fairy tale, and frankly Hanna didn't feel obligated to insert him.

Cory had always been careful with his feelings, the only exception being Singer. He had moved closer to Hanna lately, but Shara's suicide backed him up, left him more silent than not, with a too-frequent furrow creasing his forehead. He didn't talk about the wake and funeral much, other than to say he was completely unprepared when asked to speak at the wake. Cory's gift of a memory didn't fail him as he pulled out wonderful heirlooms from Shara's past, some that even her parents had forgotten or were unaware of. The hours upon hours they'd spent on the ice, Cory pushing her in the skating chair, provided him with anecdotes and nicknames and family vacation spots—even the name of a childhood turtle.

He had told Hanna about the letter Shara had left before her suicide, but said nothing of its content. Hanna wasn't sure she wanted to know; she found the notion disturbing and, honestly, unfair to Cory. She had never met Shara, other than pulling the newspaper article out of the archives as background when she did a piece on Cory back when she covered Badger hockey at the University of Wisconsin. It became part of the Cory Bradford legend, pushing a paralyzed girl around the rink to get in shape for the high school state hockey tournament. Hanna had to admit it, though; she too had a hand in furthering that legend. Part of her job was to turn people into stories. She wasn't particularly proud of that.

Hanna stood up from the bed and steadied herself. She expelled her doubts and found the courage that made her an intense competitor and a noteworthy professional. *It's only six days. Singer and Cory will have a great time. And I'll see what the job really has to offer. Ignorance is bliss, if and only if you wish to remain ignorant.*

Cory was up early. His knee was stiff from all the skating and shooting he'd just finished at the weeklong summer hockey camp. He'd gotten a good look at many of the underclassmen he'd be coaching. Good skaters, many of them. No doubt, the game was getting bigger and faster than when Cory was in high school. And there was a strong, spirited incoming goalie; a little undersized, but not in the heart department. Can't win hockey games without tenacity between the pipes.

The plan was to get his things together and drive over to pick up Singer for their big guy trip to Lake of the Woods. Sore knee or no sore knee, Cory went through his morning balance ritual that had him putting on his socks while standing. He balanced on one foot, pulling a sock onto the other. If at anytime he lost his balance, and the foot touched the ground, he'd remove any progress he'd made and start over. Cory was big on balance, just not always where it mattered.

The front window of the cabin summoned him. Cory poured his first cup of coffee and made his way over. Morning was working its magic. At the screen door, Cory laid his hand on the frame, thinking about Hanna.

Up the grassy slope of the east-facing bank, the dawning sun crept. Silently, the sweep of light advanced across the overturned aluminum boat, brushing the rope swing hanging from the giant white pine, crawling under the clothesline strung between tree trunks, until it touched the logs of Cory's cabin like a mother's reach for her sleeping child.

The crows had left their roosts and lit in the spread of pines that lined the lakeshore, their raucous caws launched back and forth across the distance. A heron had had enough of the crow's shrill. Rising in heavy wing beats from his spot by the lily pads, he made his way to quieter hunting grounds, muttering a protest as his body lengthened like an arrow in flight.

How could anyone wish to leave this place? Outwardly, Cory had fully supported Hanna's decision to see about the job in Philadelphia, but his deeper thoughts he characteristically left unsaid. *A million and a half people on a cement conveyor belt, trying to push past the person in front on them on the turnpike, preoccupied with halfwitted thoughts of a tiny yard away from the pollution and car alarms. For what?* He momentarily took the other side of the argument. *Maybe one person's crows are another person's car alarms.* He didn't buy it. *Perhaps for an adult, but what's the trade-off for a child?*

Cory brushed these thoughts aside, recognizing that they were parochial. Many things fall into an open mind, or so it was written on a poster in the classroom he had cleaned out earlier that month. After his meeting with the department head, Cory was shown his homeroom, number 115. He was struck speechless by the moment. The tenured supervisor patted him on the back and left Cory alone to acquaint himself with the room and arrange it as he pleased. The walls were filled with things left by the outgoing teacher, a man who had spent 30 years at the high school. Among them, the poster. In the end, Cory had an industrial-size garbage bag filled with remnants of his predecessor. But the poster remained on the wall. And now, sitting among the morning sounds, he had cause to think about the heron that was driven from his tranquil spot and of the words about an open mind.

Cory stepped outside and turned over his cup. The coffee grounds, along with the last sip, fell on the wild ferns that grew tall around the foundation. The cabin came with an old percolating pot, which was stored hanging by its handle on a shank nail over the stove. The steel filter didn't keep all the grounds contained, which led to a chewy cup of coffee, but that was part of its indelible signature. Or inedible signature.

Cory washed the cup and left it upside down on the drying rack. Shara was there, suddenly in his mind. In her letter she had asked that he keep the picture of them from the newspaper article. He had bought a frame, hanging it on the wall next to a small antique needlepoint of a cabin that said Home Sweet Home. The needlepoint was a keepsake from a time distant, yet still right behind him. Cory took a half step back, his focus moving back and forth between the needlepoint and the framed black and white newspaper picture. Loneliness entered through the open windows.

SUMMER 1985

So talented. So observant. Cory had always wondered what it was he was running from. And there it was, right in front of him, hanging on the wall.

Singer's morning was spent with his nose glued to the front window. He looked out at the slant of road. Nothing. It was as though Duluth had been abandoned. He reported every two minutes, no cars. Cory wasn't here yet. Cory still wasn't here. Hanna had packed his things and hers. She deliberated over her wardrobe. What was too casual, too formal, too sexy, too conservative? Two or three times the suitcase was closed, only to be reopened, re-laid out on the bed, reconsidered, repacked.

"He's here!" Singer sprung off the couch, landed effortlessly on the floor and ran to the front door. No sooner was he there than he ran back to the couch to get his fishing cap: a sun-faded Rapala baseball hat that Cory had dug out of the back closet of the cabin.

"I'm ready," Singer announced, pulling up the brim of his hat up so he could see Cory. The hat had been readjusted to its smallest fitting, but was still too big.

"Hey, tenderfoot," Cory said, picking Singer up and holding him to the sky. "We need to get you a pin for that cap." He lifted him higher yet. "Look how big you're getting."

"I'm ready," Singer squealed.

"I heard that. Jump in back." Singer swung around Cory's neck for a piggyback ride into the house. "Where's your mother?"

"I'm here." Hanna stood in the half shadow of the living room with her suitcase in one hand and Singer's in the other. Her auburn hair was pulled up. The line of her neck and shoulders pronounced by the thin-strapped summer dress, with its simple ribbon tie around the waist, the hem falling just above her knees. The look on her face was pained, like you'd see in a Rockwell painting. She looked like a mother at a train station seeing her boy off to war.

Cory went down on one knee. "Jump off, gum drop. Play us a song, hey." Cory went over and hugged Hanna who smelled of powder and lavender. "How do you do, world traveler?"

Cory felt a tremble go through Hanna. Then she hardened herself, speaking into his shoulder. "I didn't think it'd be this hard."

Cory held her tighter.

"I feel like I'm leaving him, somehow. And you." She took a deep breath. "I'm sorry if I've been acting like a spaz lately." Hanna pushed back and looked at Cory. His hair curled in the August humidity; t-shirt from some hockey camp tight across his chest; sport shorts showing off his tanned, muscled legs. He gave her a dimpled smile. From behind them came the notes of Hot Cross Buns off the piano. Cory kissed her softly. "It is hard, but it'll be okay. I guess it's part of growing up. For us all."

Hanna looked at Cory. How could she want anything else? Why wasn't she going with them to the lake? She wanted to stop everything right there and now. Then she saw the stone braided into the hair behind Cory's ear. "Do you still think about Joseph?" she asked out of nowhere. Her fingers brushed his cool ear as she touched the stone.

"Every day," he said, as though expecting the question. They looked at each other.

"I am rea-dy, I am rea-dy, I am rea-dy," Singer sang a little tune, finding an ascending note on the piano to accompany each syllable.

Cory moved to safer conversational ground. "You look great. You're going to knock their socks off."

Hanna smoothed her dress and managed a smile. They both watched Singer kneeling on the piano bench, humming now along with each note. He couldn't have had a sweeter look on his face even with a piece of hard candy in his mouth.

SUMMER 1985

LU ANN'S

Pat stirred a splash of milk into his coffee, finding it symbolic of how he felt. His head swirled with convoluted thoughts and incomplete tasks. He'd left a man in a coma, near death. He was desperately trying to help an 18-year-old unknot legal red tape so the right adoptive family could be found. He had a girlfriend who was getting impatient at the stalled progress of their relationship. And a woman he'd once loved—still loved?—had reappeared, putting an ache in his chest like he'd broken a rib.

A quick prayer later, Pat opened his eyes and felt better. Then, borrowing from Meadow's practice of keeping an unfinished song in her back pocket, he unfolded his latest project. In front of him he smoothed out a sketch of the loft he was thinking about building in the barn. Or maybe he wouldn't. Well, none of this had been discussed or finalized—it may never get off the ground—but Pat had gotten excited about building a living space in the upper reaches of the barn. It would clear room in the house for HomeSky to move in and help Meadow with her last trimester. The two of them were getting closer by the day, like sisters, like mother and daughter, like best friends: Pat hadn't settled on the appropriate comparison.

The diner was quiet. Pat had dropped in after the breakfast rush so he could have a talk with Lu Ann. She had taken advantage of the lull to walk up to the bank, and had just missed him. He sat with his coffee and the drawing, careful to have the sketch put away when she got back. Somehow he got immersed in the dimensions of the knee walls and Lu Ann's voice broke his concentration.

"What a nice surprise." Lu Ann kissed his rough cheek. "You smell good, like apples—what's that?" Her tone was bubbly as she sat down across the table.

Pat's hand went down on the paper like he'd been caught cheating by a grammar school teacher.

"What is it?" she repeated in an altogether different tone. They both looked at the drawing.

Pat folded his paper. "I hadn't meant for you to see it," he admitted.

Lu Ann's brow creased. "What are you building?" she asked, more carefully than she thought should be necessary.

"I need to talk about something with you," Pat started.

"Is it FastHorse?" Lu Ann asked. She knew Meadow's dad's situation weighed heavily on Pat. He had said countless times how he struggled with the violence he had inflicted, regardless of how it might be justified. "Has he died?"

"No. No," Pat said, waving a hand. "I went and visited him in the hospital a few days back. No change."

"What is it, honey?" Lu Ann reached across the table for Pat's hand. "You don't look good. Are you sick?"

Pat took Lu Ann's other hand. "Oh, Lu Ann," he sighed. "I don't feel very good, but I think it's because of a decision I feel I need to make."

SUMMER 1985

Lu Ann swallowed hard. "Decision?"

"I've thought and thought about this …"

"Are you here to break up with me?"

"I wouldn't choose to put it like that."

"You are, aren't you?" Lu Ann pulled her hands back.

Pat's voice stayed low, but tightened. "No, I am not here to break up with you. I'm here to talk about taking a break … from each other. Taking some time."

Lu Ann voice rose. "Taking a break? That's something you do at work. Is that what this relationship has become for you?"

"Shhh," Pat said. "Please—"

"Don't shush me in my restaurant!" The two customers joined the waitstaff in staring at Pat and Lu Ann.

Pat tried to slow things down. "Maybe we should discuss this later. After work."

Lu Ann would hear nothing of it. The vein rose in the side of her neck; the one that declared she was angry. "Tell me what you came here to say! What is this?" She grabbed Pat's sketch.

Pat's head went down, his voice barely audible. "I'm thinking of building a loft in the barn. Staying there for a while."

Lu Ann was flabbergasted. "The barn? I thought you were moving to town? We found you an apartment."

"Lu Ann," Pat looked up at her, "you found the apartment. I'm not ready to move to town."

Lu Ann's voice snapped. "You're not ready to commit to me, is what you mean."

"That's right," Pat said level and firm. "Not at this moment."

"What?" Lu Ann said, tears welling.

"I'm not ready. I'm sorry. There's Meadow and the baby."

"We could adopt the baby." Lu Ann was showing all her cards now. "The baby could live with us," her tone pleaded.

Pat reached for her hands. "Oh, Lu Ann—"

She recoiled. "Oh no you don't." Her voice was taut. "Don't you ever oh Lu Ann me." Her eyes bore in. "I have made it in this life for 39 years without others, or certainly without their pity. That will not change now!" Her hand slapped down on the table. She grit her teeth so hard her jaw twitched.

"Lu Ann, please understand that I love you. I just don't know in what capacity."

Lu Ann looked at Pat like he was speaking another language. "Don't. No psychobabble doublespeak. Let's be honest. Who you really love is HomeSky."

Now it was said. It lay there between them, bare, ready to be dealt with.

"I can't talk to you about HomeSky, about my confused feelings, because you'd deem it more of the same psycho-babble."

Lu Ann lowered her voice to where it didn't sound like it was coming from her. "She comes back here, and does this to me? To us?" The fight was going out of her.

Pat wished he could reach her. "Was it ever unclear that I had feelings for HomeSky? Did I ever misrepresent that?"

"Pat, you never talked about *that*."

He looked at Lu Ann. "We," he paused, "we never talked about that. Right? We chose not to."

"Okay. Right. I guess so." Lu Ann slumped. She pushed the sketch back across the table to Pat. "Why would you bring this in here?" She looked up at him with tears running down her face.

Pat shook his head, ashamed. "If I had a nickel for every dumb mistake I've made, maybe I could buy some common sense."

Lu Ann sat up ramrod-straight and blew her nose in a napkin from the dispenser. "I think you're right." She stood. "We should take a break. Maybe I'm just one of your dumb mistakes."

Pat reached for her. "Lu Ann, no. That's not fair. Don't go like that."

She stepped back. "Break's over. Time to get back to work."

SUMMER 1985

REG

Reg was so hung over he had to remove his shirt to defecate. Quickly his perspiration dried leaving him clammy and chilled. He sat on the toilet and stared at the dripping sink faucet. His sallow skin was blotched with rashes and small ulcers. To look at him was to see mostly ribs, shoulder bones, a sunken breastplate, except for the beach ball he carried in front, owing to his diet of alcohol, frozen fish sticks and chocolate-covered Mini Donuts. In his opinion, fruit was a name you called someone who was compassionate, and vegetable was what happens to old people when you stick them in a nursing home. Longevity, he decided, wasn't something he'd concern himself with.

GOOD MORNING, REGINALD. READY TO GO TO WORK? The voice of Kemp came echoing out from behind the shower curtain. ARE YOU READY TO LISTEN TO ME AND DO EXACTLY WHAT I SAY YOU HOMOFAGGOT!

Reg cowered. He looked down at his toenails, whimpering.
WHAT?

"Yes, sir," Reg corrected.

THAT'S MORE LIKE IT SHIT FOR BRAINS. YOU'RE CUTE SITTING THERE. REMINDS ME OF OLD TIMES.

Reg covered himself, shivering.

IT'S TIME FOR A PLAN. A MAN'S PLAN.

"I know. I know. I'm working on it."

THAT'S WHAT YOU ALWAYS SAY. YOU GET UP IN THE MORNING SAYING IT'S TIME TO DO SOMETHING AND THE SAME SHIT HAPPENS EVERY DAY WHICH IS NOTHING.

"These things take time. You know that. You're the master of that." Reg managed a little laugh.

Kemp's voice exploded. YOU THINK THIS IS FUNNY! YOU THINK I'M NOT SERIOUS?

"No, sir. That's not what—"

SHUT UP! I HAD ENOUGH!

Reg lurched forward on the toilet and grabbed his ankles. He knew he was going to get hit. His eyes squeezed shut. The smells of perspiration and grass and gasoline and tobacco and oil and a rotting dead mouse were there. He heard the ping ping ping of the first raindrops striking aluminum. Blazing. Trapped. Kemp.

He sat curled like that for five minutes. His stiff back spasmed on the verge of cramping. He opened his eyes and sat up to silence. His breathing regulated. He stood stiffly from the toilet and reached for his cane, which hung on the sink. Coast was clear. He hobbled to the shower and braced himself to pull back the curtain.

"Don't you worry," Reg said aloud, as friendly as he could. "He's going to get his. We're on the same page with this. Right?"

The bathroom was silent except for the dripping faucet behind Reg. He reached for the shower curtain with his cane. As he pushed it open, the curtain rings dragged like fingernails. A waft of cold mildew reached out for him. At the feet of the wrinkled, broken man, the shower tub stood empty.

Reg held his trembling hand out in front of him, checking its steadiness. His stomach rolled, but he held the bile down. For now. "Fuckers," he said, wiping his mouth with the back of his hand. Then reaching for the cold water tap, "Fuckers, the all of 'em."

ADOPTION

Meadow set down her glass of cranberry juice. Her throat was dry, due more to nervousness than to the long stretch of talking. "So, what do you think?" her eyes bright with hope. She had just finished outlining her adoption plan to HomeSky.

"I don't know," HomeSky smiled. "I wasn't planning on being a new mother again at age 45. And if I say yes, we don't know if the Bureau of Indian Affairs would approve, right?"

Meadow looked certain. "They've told Pat and me over and over to try to find a family within the tribe. My mistake was thinking that was impossible because it meant the Rez. But if this is his home and you're his Ojibwe mom, we're within tribal law. It's solid, I'm pretty sure."

"But I'm not exactly a family," HomeSky said. "I'd be a single mother. With, unfortunately, an unstable history. Remember what

SUMMER 1985

happened to the first house that was right where we're sitting."

Meadow was undeterred. "Compared to what they see on the Rez? Are you kidding me? You're a model citizen with a ... I don't know ... who got careless. No disrespect."

HomeSky tapped her finger on her lip, thinking. "Okay, let's say you're right and they overlook my past. Have they said anything about single-parent homes versus two parents?"

"Yeah," Meadow's enthusiasm wavered. "Two is better. But one isn't unheard of."

HomeSky folded her hands and looked across the table at Meadow. "What about mixed-race couples? What if, say, Pat and I married?"

Meadow nearly spat out her last sip of cranberry juice. "What?"

HomeSky held up one hand. "Hypothetically. I'm just asking. Do you know anything about mixed couples?"

"As long as you're Ojibwe, that's all that matters. But are you saying Pat and you are—?"

"No." HomeSky was firm. "I'm not saying Pat and I are anything. I'm just getting a lay of the land."

"Gotcha."

HomeSky looked at Meadow across the kitchen table. It suddenly became so familiar. The walls around her. The earth sounds in both ears coming in on pasture breezes. An intimate conversation about hopes and dreams and future. She thought all this had perished. Gone with Joseph. All trace of good and plans and wonderment. Love reentered her heart through an 18-year-old-mother-to-be. She hadn't realized it until Meadow began to blur across from her. A tear slid down the side of her nose.

"Are you okay?" Meadow asked, standing up.

"These are sweet tears, not salty," HomeSky said. "I'm happy, dear one."

Meadow stood there not sure what to do next. Then, something inside her gave. She took a step. They held one another. Good was present. Ancient, timeless good.

When Pat pulled up they were on the porch swing. HomeSky was knitting something and Meadow was strumming her guitar with a light blanket over her legs. The evening had turned cool under the touch of soft rain. He waved as he came out of the car, looking at the two of them. *What is it?* he thought. *What is it that looks so familiar?*

"Boozhoo," Pat said.

They looked and smiled. "Boozhoo."

"I hope I'm not interrupting," Pat said waiting at the bottom step of the porch. They both looked up again from what they were doing. Then they looked at each other and giggled.

HomeSky set aside her knitting. "Nothing too exciting happening here." The women looked at each other again.

"Hard to interrupt nothing," Meadow added. The both found that funny as well.

Pat raised his eyebrows, a man left out on a joke. "Okay …?"

"Pat," HomeSky calmly said, "this home is as much or more yours than it is ours. You can't be interrupting."

Pat came up the steps and leaned on the porch post, folding his arms. "You guys seem pretty content sitting there."

"Mm-hm," they said. Meadow strummed her guitar. HomeSky worked her needles.

"I was thinking about a run and then getting a shower," Pat said.

HomeSky looked up and smiled. "We'll talk about dinner when you're done." She went back to her knitting.

Pat crossed the porch and went into the house. *Strange.* It was like a comfortable routine had stepped into their space. He shrugged his shoulders and went upstairs to get into his running gear.

It was a perfect jogging temperature, but the gnats were doing their best to ruin things. Running, Pat still carried the anxiety of the morning conversation with Lu Ann on him. He'd expected a difficult talk, but nothing could have prepared him for how things went. Of course having the loft sketch in front of him was boneheaded, even for Pat. Although it did get things out and said. He knew that was the first hard step to finding a healthy definition of their relationship. But honestly, he felt himself moving toward HomeSky and Meadow and the peace that had taken up residence on that summer porch. What had transpired between the women he didn't know, but there was harmony.

Pat stopped dead in his tracks. Doing so, he almost lost his footing on the loose gravel in the road's shoulder. "That's it!" he said aloud. He knew now what it was, what there was in the scene, uniting the women on the porch.

It was like Joseph was there, and what was new was old.

At dinner, HomeSky and Meadow asked Pat about his workday. He began with the mundane particulars of managing the plant but then seized the opportunity to take up a more important thread.

"During morning break, I did step out of the plant for about an hour. Went down to see Lu Ann for coffee. To have a talk, I guess you'd say."

The women looked up from their plates.

"We talked about—well more so I talked about—building this." Pat pulled the sketch out of his back pocket. "Learned my filing system from you," he said nodding at Meadow. Pat flattened the drawing onto the kitchen table and turned it facing the women.

"What is it?" Meadow was the first to ask. Pat watched HomeSky whose dark eyes were intently scanning the paper.

Pat spoke haltingly. "It's a rough plan for a loft. For up in the barn rafters. That I might build." HomeSky looked on quietly. Meadow, not so much. "You mean like for living there?" she asked directly.

Pat watched HomeSky and shrugged. "I was thinking about it. But not before talking to HomeSky, and you, Meadow."

They remained listening.

"It's just, I thought it would be nice to have HomeSky back here in her house. Now I know you like it with Monsignor Kief," Pat nodded at HomeSky, "but I guess that can't last forever. And since Meadow might need some more help preparing for the baby, my thought was I get out of the way a little bit. I had talked about getting an apartment in town, went so far as look at a few, well, Lu Ann had found a few listings, but I honestly am a little spoiled by all the space here. I've grown pretty fond of it. Then last week I was in the barn working on the bailer that's been acting up—"

"The one I hit a rock with," Meadow offered sheepishly.

"And as I slid out from under the axle, on my back, staring up at the sunlight coming in the haying door, it hits me. I mean literally." Pat waited.

"Okay," HomeSky said, with a faint smile. "What hits you?"

"Bird poop. From up in the rafters."

"Ewww" the women said, wrinkling their noses.

"Hits me dead center, right on the heart." Pat touched his chest. "I kid you not."

"You're making that up." Meadow smiled. "Did it really?"

Pat looked at HomeSky and nodded. "I'll show you."

HomeSky winced a bit. "You mean you didn't wash it out?"

"I thought it was pretty cool so I took off the shirt and hung it in the barn."

"Really?" HomeSky said looking at Meadow.

"Super gross," Meadow finished.

Pat continued, feeling some excitement around the table. "So for the last week, I've been doing some sketching and measuring, and I think I could build a pretty decent loft up there, at least until the baby comes and we find the right home for him and things settle down again." Pat smiled. "Every plan starts rough, right?"

Pat was greeted by silence, not the reaction he was looking for.

HomeSky spoke up. "Well, speaking of plans in their early stages, Meadow and I have a plan to share, too. Rough, or not, as it may be. Meadow would you like to start?"

Meadow looked on apprehensively. "You go."

HomeSky nodded. "Meadow and I were talking about the adoption … and all the resistance you're getting from trying to place the child off-Rez."

Pat jumped in. "We're not giving up." He reached across and took Meadow's hand. "Where there's a will there's a way."

HomeSky continued. "Well there might be a way right here," she said softly. The words hung there, before they began to settle.

"Here?" Pat asked.

HomeSky reached for Meadow's other hand. "Meadow has asked if I would be willing to adopt her child." The words *adopt her child* came out like they were sung. HomeSky smiled and squeezed Meadow's hand. "I've told her I'd be honored." HomeSky blinked back a tear and smiled.

Pat, who had been studying the Indian Child Welfare Act, and who had been back and forth with the tribe on the adoption issue for months, was mentally ticking through the possible objections. Meadow and HomeSky watched for his reaction.

"My Father who art in heaven, I think it just might work." Pat lit up.

"Really truly?" Meadow asked, gripping his hand more than tightly enough.

"I think it REALLY TRULY will work." He took HomeSky's hand, lifting his, as they made a ring around the edge of the kitchen table. "Praise God the Great Spirit."

Energy hummed through them, between them, uniting them. They looked at each other and broke out in laughter. Let it be known that healing does have a sound, and that sound filled the kitchen.

SHERIFF AND KITTY

The Sheriff was rolled by wheelchair toward the front doors of the hospital. He had his oversized stuffed dog on his lap along with his crutches.

"This is humiliating," he said for the third time. "It's not like I'm paralyzed."

"Hospital policy will be followed, to the letter." The floor nurse lifted her chin a tad higher. "Our discharge protocol is quite clear. You of all people should respect adherence to rules."

"I'll remind you of that the next time I see you a few miles over the posted speed limit." The Sheriff laid the dog sideways hoping to minimize its presence.

"I don't speed," the nurse said with a pinch of self-congratulation.

"Obviously," mumbled the Sheriff. He looked at his watch. "Step on it. I have a train to catch."

SUMMER 1985

Pat pulled his car around to the hospital entrance. He brought the Toronado because it was easier to get into than the pickup. When the Sheriff was rolled out of the front doors, Pat pulled over, leaning across the seat to speak out the open car window. "Shouldn't that thing be on a leash?" Pat pointed at the stuffed dog. It was the Sheriff who growled.

"Christ in a carwash it's good to be free." After five minutes of driving, the Sheriff was finally capable of speech. He put his hands behind his neck and stretched. They cruised down Main Street. "As you know I'm not much for automobile travel, but you can take your sweet ol' time." He rolled his window down the rest of the way.

"That was a long visit you had."

"Thirty-one days and seven hours."

Pat whistled.

"And 37 pounds."

Pat looked over at the Sheriff. "You're going to have to shop in the juniors department."

The Sheriff smiled. "Will have to have my uniform tailored. Don't know what to do with the trousers." He tapped his cast.

"How long will they keep that plaster on you?"

"This one comes off end of the week. Then I get a knee-high one with a rubber thing-a-ma-bob on the heel so I can walk."

"Maybe we put a spur on it. You know, to toughen you up some when you stroll down Main Street. A cowboy hat might be a nice touch, too."

The Sheriff shifted in his seat. "Not even your weak attempt at humor can spoil my mood. Freedom is worth fighting for." He put his arm out the window, letting his hand momentarily surf through the oncoming air. "What's got you in such a comedic mood anyway?"

Pat pulled up to the town's only stoplight. "That thing's programmed to go red when my car is within 50 feet, by the way." He looked at the Sheriff. "I've got some news."

"You're going back to the hospital to have a funny bone transplant."

"No."

"You're thinking of growing a mustache."

"No."

"HomeSky is moving back into the farmhouse."

Pat's mouth dropped open. "How'd you know?"

"It's green."

"What?"

The Sheriff pointed at the stoplight.

"Oh." Pat pulled away. "But how did you know?"

"Law officer intuition."

"Really?"

"Um, no. Meadow told me."

"Meadow? How? She visited you in the hospital?" Pat was incredulous.

"Yeah," the Sheriff said as if slighted. "Am I that hard of a person to visit with?"

Pat looked at the Sheriff as if that question was way too easy to answer.

"Okay. I'm a little difficult. But it got to where I really looked forward to her visits."

"Visits? Plural?"

The Sheriff smiled smugly.

"She never said a thing to me about it." Pat shook his head. "Huh. Impressive."

"She is an impressive girl. Or gal. Or woman, I guess."

"What did you two talk about, if you don't mind me asking?"

The Sheriff left his elbow out the window and leaned back to take in the sun and the breeze. "I do mind. Although you would be well advised to close your door at night." The Sheriff raised his eyebrows. "Snoring louder than a ripsaw, from what I hear."

SUMMER 1985

"Baloney." Pat said. "You're full of it." They drove on. "Really?"

When they pulled up to the Sheriff's house all conversation about Pat's sleeping habits was forgotten.

"Ho-ly buckets," Pat said, awestruck.

"What in the name of Abraham Lincoln's mother?" said the Sheriff.

Pat added, "Have you ever seen so many balloons?"

"What's that hanging in my tree?"

"Looks like pink crepe paper," Pat said.

The Sheriff's house and front lawn were decorated for the homecoming of all homecomings. Out the front door marched Kitty.

"Is that the woman from across the street?" Pat asked.

"Um, yep," said the Sheriff.

"She has a key to your house?" Pat raised his eyebrows. "You move pretty quick for a guy in a cast."

"Ah shut up." The Sheriff looked at Kitty, who was waving. "She knows I hide the spare in the drain spout. She just watched after things while I was laid up. Watered the plants."

"You have plants?"

"I do now." The Sheriff puffed out his cheeks. "What in hell's doorbell is that in her arms?"

Pat scratched his head. "Looks like a …" Kitty waved broadly enough to dock a cruise ship.

The Sheriff interrupted, "That better not be …"

They looked at each other. "A puppy," they said in unison.

"Daddy's home!" Kitty squealed, waving the puppy's paw.

"Oh crap," the Sheriff groaned.

"Looks like you have a family," Pat said, slapping the Sheriff on the back.

The Sheriff let out a weak laugh. "Don't suppose you could drop me back at the hospital," he said, only half kidding.

Pat came around the front of the car and helped the Sheriff out. "One small step for man, one—"

Speaking very quietly, the Sheriff smiled through gritted teeth. "One more wisecrack and I'm going to introduce you to my crutch." He stood and waved. "Hello, Kitty," he said, forcing a smile. "What do we have here?"

She came a few steps down the front walkway before the puppy started to piddle. "Oopsie do. Look who's a little too excited," she said, holding the black ball of fur to the side as it discharged like a squirt gun. The pup was all tail and paws. She set him on the walkway. "Go see Daddy." The puppy, confused, looked back at Kitty who was gesturing toward the car. "Go on!"

Pat stepped aside so there was a straight shot down the walkway to the boulevard where the Sheriff stood, speechless, crutches under him. The puppy's eyes locked on his target. His tail went into overdrive. He seemed to understand now what all the excitement was about. He scrambled down the cement path straight to the Sheriff like long-lost pals.

"Would you look at that," Kitty said, clapping her hands together gratefully, a tad misty-eyed.

The pup didn't miss a beat. He ran directly to the Sheriff and pulled the red sock off the toe of his cast. Then he dashed across the front yard shaking his head, growling, tripping over the sock. Kitty chased close behind, letting the puppy—and the whole neighborhood—know that he was very naughty.

Inside the house, things had settled down considerably. The pup slept under the dining room table, curled up with his red sock as Kitty handed out seconds of cake to the Sheriff and Pat.

"Well, Thurgood," she said to the Sheriff, "how does it feel to be home?"

"Good. A little … different."

"No cake for you?" Pat said to Kitty as she set down the serving knife.

SUMMER 1985

"Cake and lemonade turn girls into old maids," she sang quietly. Then to the Sheriff, "It's traumatic to reacclimate after being away for a spell." She patted his hand. One of my magazines calls it "Reentry Syndrome."

Pat coughed, choking on his cake. "Wrong tube," he said, swallowing.

"Well, no," the Sheriff clarified, "I meant different with all the signs and balloons around the yard, and a puppy in the front room."

Kitty perked up. "A puppy is just what the doctor ordered. Animals keep us young, it's a well researched fact." She smoothed her party dress.

"Don't know about that," the Sheriff said, trying his best to remain tactful.

"They do indeed. I remember clipping out an article sure as I'm sitting here. I'll see if I can put my finger on it."

Pat jumped in. "I know many respected psychologists write that the companionship of an animal is both anti-aging and an antidepressant." He and Kitty nodded their heads, like a team.

The Sheriff kicked Pat under the table with his cast. "I don't know. It's just caring for an animal is a full-time job. Being an officer of the law calls for some pretty uncertain hours."

"Oh piffle sticks," Kitty disagreed. "We'll meet here on weekdays for lunch and a walkabout. My Hansel and Gretel will adore the company. The walking will help in your recuperation. Not to mention keep those pounds you shed off for good."

The Sheriff sat up a bit straighter. "You noticed? I did drop a few."

"A few?" Kitty waved her hand through the air. "Get out. Your clothes are hanging on you like a drying rack. I'll have to get after some alterations. I can't think a Sheriff can be seen around town in an ill-fitting uniform."

"I agree," Pat said with a mouthful of cake.

"You can do that?" the Sheriff said, ignoring Pat's color commentary.

"According to Seamstress magazine, clothes-making and alterations are a lost art in these disposable times." Kitty shook her head in disapproval.

"A lost art," Pat agreed. "But not on this block. If you're as good with a needle and thread as you are with a baking spatula, we will have one of the sharpest-dressed sheriffs in the lower 48."

"Well thank you, Patrick." Kitty blushed.

The Sheriff could see he was outnumbered. He looked at the snoozing pup. "Well then, guess we'll need to be getting him a name. It is a him, if I sized him up correctly."

"He is indeed," Kitty replied, delighted in the progress they were making. "I have a short list of names here that come recommended—"

The Sheriff held up his hand. "Oh, no. That won't be necessary. The naming of a pet is a unilateral act. To invite collaboration into the process is the equivalent of a dog chasing after his own tail. When the dog is ready, he finds the right moment to communicate to his master what his lifelong name should be. This, I believe, is called the Dog-Master Privilege. I may have read that in a hunting magazine."

Kitty looked on suspiciously.

"Isn't that right, Pat?" the Sheriff said.

Pat braced himself for another kick under the table. "That sounds vaguely familiar," he said nodding. "Maybe I have heard of such a thing."

The Sheriff gave the dog a little push with his foot. "Would ya look at that? He's waking up. Maybe he's ready to tell me something." The pup yawned wide, all pink tongue and milk teeth. The Sheriff coaxed him out from under the table with a scrap of chocolate cake.

"Here boy," he said, scooping him up. He brought the pup's face close to his, just beyond licking rage. The pup's tail whipped as he licked the air. "What's your name?" the Sheriff asked slowly. And then again, monotone, almost hypnotically, "What's. Your. Name?"

They stared at each other, nose-to-nose, as Kitty and Pat looked on, ready for some sort of an event.

The Sheriff set the pup down. He looked up at his master, bright-eyed, then flopped his rubber-like body onto the carpet and proceeded to lick himself.

"Oh my," Kitty said, looking away.

"Eureka!" the Sheriff said. "That's it. From this point forward he shall be known as Private."

MONUMENT BAY

"Do you know what an island is?" Cory looked into the tilted rear-view mirror, finding Singer buckled in the child seat in the truck's crew cab. They had left the blacktop and were now 45 minutes from the marina, running gravel, as they say in these parts. A single powerline stretched from pole to pole off the right side of the road, bringing electricity to an area that for generations had relied on ice packed in sawdust sheds for summertime refrigeration.

"Hmmm," Singer thought earnestly. "I know!" He burst with excitement. "An island is a place with coconut trees. I read about them in *Curious George*."

Cory laughed. "See. Reading makes you smart."

Singer nodded. "That's why we brought books for our trip."

"Right," Cory said. "Except the island we're going to has different trees than coconut trees."

That stumped Singer. "How come?"

"Well, islands are different. Some, for example, have pine trees. Some are just sand islands—"

"Oh, sand islands sound good. Let's go there."

"Someday," Cory said. "With your mom."

"How 'bout when we get back, or next week?"

"No, not quite that soon, bud. But sometime. Do you know what all islands have, no matter if they have trees on them or sand or coconuts?"

"Monkeys?" Singer guessed.

"No. Want to guess again?"

"Um, nice people?"

"That is a fantastic guess. But some islands are deserted, which means they have no people at all on them."

Singer was in the back seat thinking hard.

"Do you want me to tell you?" Cory offered.

"Okay. My brain is kinda tired."

"We've been driving a long time. How about some road rations?"

"Yes please!"

"Jerky or crackers or fruit roll-up?"

"Crackers!"

Cory reached into a shoebox on the passenger seat. Hanna had packed it with treats. He pulled out a single-serve crackers-and-cheese pack. Opening it was an adventure. "Here you be," he said, handing it back. Cory slid the top back on the box, looking at the pink paper hearts Hanna had glued to it. One said Singer, the other, Cory.

"Thank you."

"Good manners, Singer. You are most welcome."

Cory drove on, thoughts pulled to Hanna in a strange city with her slick East Coast mover and shaker showing her the sights. A jealous pang tapped him.

"What about the things all islands have?" Singer asked through a mouthful of crackers.

"Oh yeah," Cory said. "All islands are surrounded by water. All around. So to get to ours we have to go by boat."

"Cool," Singer said enthusiastically. "The car, too?"

"No. It's not that big of a boat. We'll park the car and leave it at a place not too far ahead called a marina."

Singer became upset. "But what about all my stuff?"

"Oh, don't worry about that, pal. We'll take it all on the boat with us. Like treasure on a ship."

"Yea, treasure!" Singer went back to his crackers.

"Yep. So all the cabins at the resort are on the island. And Stu and Darlene's house, too. And where we eat our meals is on the island. And once we get there we can walk to all of those places. Including the Trading Post, where you can buy candy bars and fishing lures and even a slingshot. The Trading Post has the cool stuff."

"Wow," Singer said. "It's going to be fun."

"It's one of the best places on earth," Cory said, contemplatively.

"You sounded funny when you said that."

"That's 'cause I was thinking about when I came here, my first time, as a boy."

"Tell me. Tell me," Singer asked.

"Oh, not now. We're almost there. Pretty soon you'll see the big lake. Let's look for it."

Singer persisted. "Will you tell me another time? I want to hear the story."

"I will," Cory said.

"Promise sure and true?"

"Sure and true," Cory told him.

The gravel road was rutted and spotted with puddles from a recent rain. It was hardly more than one lane, causing drivers to pull over for a vehicle coming from the other direction, especially if that vehicle was pulling a boat. Walls of pines ushered them ahead, tacking through miles of national forest to Lake of the Woods. What steadfast it required to cut this road, to give access to a place, a sanctuary of water, where for more than a century, the natives traveled only by foot and canoe.

At the Northwest Angle Marina, Cory and Singer walked hand-in-hand along the side dock that led to the office. They had been to the end of the pier and looked out at the miles upon miles of water. Singer said it reminded him of his lake but Cory told him it wasn't as big as Lake Superior. That made Singer proud.

The inlet marina was set in from the big water, quiet and protected, but the wind still found Singer's curls and fooled with them. Cory breathed it in, beautiful. The smell of fresh sunshine on wet wood, as gulls circled, begging over the continuous slapping of waves off the jetties. He knelt down and pointed the direction to Monument Bay Resort, 30 minutes by boat. Stu and Darlene had told Cory to go to the marina office and radio the resort when they got there. They would send a boat to pick them up.

"Hey-ya," the grizzled man said from behind the counter. He was whittling a walking stick out of diamond willow, carving a muskie for a grip. The marina office smelled of old bait and coffee that had been on the burner too long.

"Hi," Singer said before Cory could. "We're here."

The man smiled, a tooth or so short. "So you are." He examined Singer. "And I betcha I know your name."

"Bet no you don't," Singer shot back.

"Hmmm," the man said, scraping his fingers across his unshaven chin. "This ain't going to be easy, I can tell."

Singer giggled with delight.

His voice grew soft and secretive. "I know. I'll ask my magic bear."

Singer's eyes grew wide.

The man reached for the pegboard behind him where stuffed black bears the size of coffee mugs hung. He brought one down and asked the bear, "Tell me, what's this lad's name?" He held the stuffed animal out in Singer's direction. "Get a little closer here, so he can have a good look at you. Bears don't have the best eyesight but they sure can smell."

Singer looked up at Cory who nodded it would be okay. Singer took a small step forward, focused on the stuffed bear.

"A bear can tell a lot about a person just by looking and smelling," the grizzled man said. "Can tell he's scared, or not. Can tell he's friend or enemy. Bears are very perceptive." The man looked at the bear. "Well. I've talked you up plenty. Do your thing. Can you tell me the boy's name?" The man made the bear's head nod yes. "He can!" he said to Singer like he, too, was surprised. "Okay. Let's hear it." He put the bear's muzzle to his ear. "What's that?" he said. "Nah. That can't be right. It doesn't even sound like a boy's name."

Singer interrupted, excited. "My name's not like usual. It's a nickname, but everyone calls me it."

"Well maybe he's right after all." He set the bear on the counter. "Nice to meet you, Singer."

Singer smiled big as can be. He grabbed Cory's hand. "It worked. Did you see? The magic bear knew me."

Cory lifted Singer up and set him on the counter. "That is one magic bear," he said.

"And the bear told me you must be Cory," the man said. "Good to meet you." He reached out his hand. "Or, I should say, good to meet you again." The man looked at Cory, a smile in his eyes as they shook.

The man's hand was as hard as driftwood. Cory hung onto it a moment, before releasing. He looked at his weathered face, a face that had survived many seasons on the big lake.

"Don't remember me, do you?" the man half-chuckled.

Cory studied his face, his eyes, going back in time. "Looks like I'll have to ask for some assistance." He picked up the magic bear.

Now it was the man's turn to be caught off guard.

SUMMER 1985

"Can you tell me this man's name?" he asked the bear. Cory waited. Then he pressed down on the bear's head, nodding yes. "You can?" Cory said, quite impressed. "Well I don't think so. It's been a very long time since we've seen each other. Since I was just a boy."

The man's face grew serious. Singer watched, rapt.

Cory brought the bear to his ear, but remained focused on the night-dark eyes of the grizzled man. "You sure?" Cory said. "That doesn't sound like a given name either." Magic bear nodded again. "Okay then." Cory put his hand out to shake. "Good to see you again, Dancer." Cory smiled. "You were one of the guides who helped me find the outboard motor lost in the accident."

Dancer took Cory's hand enthusiastically. "Well slap me on the butt and call me a newborn," he said. "Never thought you'd remember long these years."

"Couldn't have done it without magic bear," Cory nodded, setting it on the counter.

"That there's for the boy." Dancer said, handing the bear to Singer.

Singer pressed the soft little bear to his cheek.

"What do you say to Dancer?" Cory said.

"Ah, no need," Dancer said. "He's already said it right there."

They looked at the little boy, hugging his new friend. The room was filled with gratitude beyond speaking.

"That the last of it?" Stu asked Cory as he came up the pier with Singer's dump truck backpack and a present Hanna had wrapped for Darlene and Stu.

"That's it," Cory said. "You'd think we were crossing the Atlantic to start a new life."

"Well, I imagine Hanna had a hand in it." Stu pulled the brim of his cap down against the wind. "Sure as thunderstorms in August you can tell the difference between the sexes in the bags they pack. When Darlene and I came for the day to your ceremony, heck, she had enough clothes laid out on the bed for three husbands." Stu waved a hand through the air before switching subjects. "No trouble finding the marina? I radioed ahead and told them to be looking for two tenderfoots going by the names Cory and Singer."

"Nope. Not a hitch," Cory said.

"When was the last time you were up for a visit?"

"Let's see," Cory said. "The year we rebuilt the resort docks, remember?"

"Golly, that sure is right," Stu smiled at the thought. "How long does that make it?"

"Well, I stayed out two years of college after Joseph," Cory hesitated. "Came up that first summer, so that's three years." He squinted out at the symphony of blue water rolling in front of him. "Doesn't seem that long, does it?"

They stepped into Stu's Boston Whaler. "No, it sure don't. I wish I could slow it down."

"I see the old girl's still running." Cory slapped the boat's gunwale. Singer sat at the steering wheel with his bear.

"Gonna outlive me," Stu said. "You got the ropes?"

"Yep," Cory said, not forgetting the duties of a first mate. He went for the ties on the bow and stern.

"Darlene really wanted to come too, but we've got six full cabins and supper coming on," Stu said. "She's especially looking forward to seeing you, tenderfoot," Stu said, picking Singer up.

"Hey," Singer squealed. "That's what Cory calls me."

"That's because that's what I used to call him. Are you ready to captain this vessel?" Stu turned over the ignition. The old Johnson motor coughed, caught and roared to life. "Lifejackets?" Stu said, scanning the boys. "Check." Stu spun his baseball cap backward, shifting Singer a little higher at the wheel. "Let's run her home."

Cory reached behind his ear, found the cool comfort of the stone braided there. It was good to be back.

SUMMER 1985

"Darlene!" Singer said with his arms as wide open as they'd go. He ran in choppy little steps down the sunny dock toward her. Darlene's exterior was as tough as they came, but the little boy turned her inside out. She got down to a knee, the lake breeze pushing back her shock of wiry white hair. Joy came to her like the wind.

"Oh my," she laughed, wrapping Singer in her arms. "You nearly bowled me over you're getting so big. And just a few short months since we saw you last."

"You smell good." Singer said. "Like bacon."

Darlene wore a tan flannel shirt that the years had made soft as cashmere. She'd worked right through to holes in the elbows, which she cut and tailored into short sleeves. "This shirt here is about as old as me. There are a lot of breakfasts you can smell in it. Now, let's have a look at you. You know, something's changed since I saw you last." Darlene stood up stiffly, rocked a bit as the rollers ran under the floating dock sections.

Singer hunched up his shoulders.

"Something's definitely different," she said, examining him, her hand on her chin, tapping her cheek with her finger. "Wait. How old are you now?"

"Four," Singer announced proudly.

"Well that's it. You must have had a birthday. Let me guess ... it was last week."

Singer nodded and smiled.

"Hmmm. I wonder if we have a belated birthday present for you up at the lodge?"

"Let's see," Singer said, grabbing her hand.

"Okay. But I need to say hello to Cory first. And let's each get something to carry up from the boat. Everyone has to do their part, right?"

"I'll get my backpack. And my bear."

"You have a bear?" Darlene filled her face with astonishment. "How will I ever feed the both of you?"

"A magic bear. I got him back at the boat place where Stu picked us up."

Cory stood in front of her on the pier, backlit in golden afternoon sunshine. Darlene's heart swelled. It didn't matter how many times she'd seen him here—as an adult now, or as a college student, or as a growing teenager—when a hard afternoon light angled off the lake onto this dock, that forever made Cory 13 years old. Standing in defiant silhouette. Alone. Frightened. Resolute. With his jaw set against fate and its ill-begotten winds. He was as he was before, and they hesitated in recognition of this, before moving toward each other, advancing years in every forward step, until they had passed through the old into the now. They hugged each other like they could hug no other. There is peace to be had if you're fortunate enough to persevere and forgive and reach again.

"I'm so glad you came," Darlene said quietly into Cory's shoulder.

"Me too," Cory said. "It's good to be here."

And as they separated, Darlene knew he meant it. She had always worried that he would never want to come back here, or be able to, that her home would be a place he'd banish from his heart, even if he couldn't from his mind. She would understand, yes, but understanding makes the weight no less to carry. But as with nearly everything this boy had done in the past, he surprised her. He found a way back, again. Tentatively, willingly, and eventually, lovingly. For this she said a quick word of thanks.

Shep, the dockhand, mechanic, fish-cleaner and all-around handyman, drove the four-wheeler down from the lodge to the dock. He pulled a small transport trailer for the gear that rattled like the cavalry galloping downhill. When they first met, Shep didn't much like Cory, what with the attention Darlene and Stu lavished. But an island has a way of running people into each other. The trails are only so wide and the destinations limited. Over the years they grew accustomed to one another, found a few things to talk about, even went so far as to fish together now and again when Shep could spare the time.

SUMMER 1985

As the whitecaps hammered away at the dock, he came stomping bull-legged down the pier, focused on the task of getting the bags loaded on the trailer. "I'll take that one," he said, gesturing to the large duffle bag Cory had slung over his shoulder.

Cory knew better than to disagree. "Hello Shep," he said, handing over the bag.

"Hello to you, little beaver," he said, using the name he'd given Cory long back.

Cory reached for a ducktaped cardboard box on the boat seat. "You'll want to take this too," he said, giving Shep a knowing smile before turning back for the rest of their things. Cory had packed a carton of Camel cigarettes, two good paperbacks and a bottle of Jim Beam in the box. S-H-E-P was handlettered on the top in marker. Some provisions are hard to come by on an island.

"Thank ye," Shep said, a sparkle coming to his eyes.

"Put 'em in Grouse?" Shep asked Stu.

Stu looked at Cory. "We have Grouse open if that's good by you. Pretty quiet there, you'll remember." Grouse was the name of a small cabin on the rocks high above the water. Stunning view, set back a distance from the lodge, making it quieter there when the fishermen came whistling in for dawn pancakes before hitting the water.

"That'd be great," Cory said, taking Singer by the hand.

"No," Singer pulled his hand away, shouldering his backpack. "I'm going with Darlene." Darlene had two sleeping bags, but arranged them under one arm and caught Singer's hand with the other.

"What's Grouse?" Cory heard Singer ask, just as the wind caught his words and swept them away.

Stu had re-sided Grouse in cedar plank and painted it Adirondack red with clean white trim to match the nine cabins of the resort. Despite its age—Grouse was one of the first cabins built back in the early 1950's—it was perfectly maintained. There wasn't a hole in a screen or a door that wouldn't properly close. Not that all the lines were straight; in fact that was hardly the case. Stu and Darlene just came from an era where you took pride in trim paint that wasn't peeling and spring-drawn screen doors that shut with a solid bang-BA-bam.

Grouse had one small bedroom with a bunk bed built into the wall and a double bed taking up nearly all of the remaining floor space. The front room faced the lake, with a large bay window filling most of the view. A small eating table stood off the window with a deck of cards under the salt and pepper shakers.

The space was finished in knotty-pine paneling and modestly furnished with a cast iron pot belly stove, a wood bin, two gold-colored recliners separated by an end table stacked high with fishing and hunting magazines, and a working kitchen space with cupboards over either side of the sink. A small window above the kitchen sink faced inland toward the lodge. For guests who didn't sign up for the resort's meal plan, the stovetop of an old Tappan gas oven reliably fried walleye fillets. The bathroom had a shower the size of a phone booth. A painting of a buck leaping over a deadfall offered the perfect outdoorsy touch.

Cory tossed his duffle and Singer's suitcase on the beds. Rather than going directly up the path to the lodge, he circled around the cabin, past the small deck out front, to the burnt-colored rock outcropping overlooking the lake. An American flag snapped on the flagpole, letting all boaters know which side of the border they were on. In the distance he saw the channel buoys that tracked out, becoming pinpoints in the blue vastness.

For a moment, a rowboat was there, a boy pulling with all that his young legs and back would give, against the heartless waves, a tarp up front, over the boy's father, one corner rended by the wind. Cory looked at a single aspen branch; its perfect heart-shaped leaves shimmering. He focused on his breathing, sealing his lips to allow the breath to expand fully. His eyes closed, he felt the sun on his face. *Me, myself and I.* Cory internalized the mantra of his youth. But faces flashed, there in front of his closed eyes. Cory said their names aloud, mixing them with the wind sifting through the

SUMMER 1985

branches. "Singer. Hanna. Pat. HomeSky. Darlene. Stu. Sheriff. Monsignor Kief. Shara. Joseph." He sensed the pieces coming together, grafting a whole. Far from complete, but there was possibility—great possibility—shallow-rooted in cautious optimism. For the first time in his 24 years, Cory glimpsed something stronger and larger than his solitary trinity. He took another full breath, as big as he could get, and then sipped in a final last bit. When he opened his eyes to exhale, the boy in the rowboat in the distance was gone. The blue water had been wiped clean.

PHILADELPHIA

The moment just after the jet wheels touched down on the tarmac, Hanna carefully awaited her next thought. What would her reaction be?

It wasn't anxiety that greeted her. Instead, excitement.

She walked up the aisle to deplane, drawing the eye of more than a few businessmen, wedding banded and otherwise. Her confidence multiplied with each step as she looked them back. They glanced down, pretending to be busy with some task. She was on the verge of a departure point, in more ways than one.

The station owner, Thomas Dickerson, said there would be a driver waiting for her as she came around to the baggage area. A stout mustachioed chauffer holding a Hanna Donnovan sign was second in the queue as the passengers hurried past. Hanna approached him.

"Ms. Donnovan?" he said

SUMMER 1985

She smiled. "Hello. Please, call me Hanna."

"I would very much like to, Ms. Donnovan. But company protocol precludes me from such informality. Please, this way." And he was off. Hanna hustled behind him.

As they approached the baggage carousels, the driver turned to her. "Your bags will be coming in on number four. I trust your flight went well?"

"Perfect," Hanna said, cheerfully. "What does protocol say I should call you?"

"I'm Kevin, ma'am," the driver said, bowing slightly, keeping a curtain of professionalism between them.

"A pleasure to meet you, Kevin," Hanna said brightly, putting her hand out. He took it lightly. "I hope you don't mind questions," Hanna said. "I tend to ask a ton of questions." She smiled, playfully. "Ferociously curious. Beware."

"However I can be of service," the driver said. Hanna was pretty sure she saw a hint of a smile at the corners of Kevin's eyes.

"So my mom tossed the bum out, and raised the four of us herself." Kevin had been talking for 15 minutes straight, as their stretch limousine powered toward downtown Philadelphia. Hanna had cracked Kevin's teflon exterior before the first bag ever made it in the trunk. As he drove, he would turn his head sideways toward her, what he called chauffer eye contact. "I grew up just a few miles west of here. All drugs and gangs now. Pretty tough even back then, but at least it was neighborhood—and family."

"How did you get interested in driving professionally?"

Kevin perked up. "It's probably not the narrative you'd expect. Most people don't aspire to a career in driving, as much as end up there. Ironically, I have my father to thank for it."

"Sounds interesting," Hanna primed.

"When my mother tossed him out, she threw the car keys at him, too. 'I get the house, you get the highway,' she told him. He took the deal. So growing up, we had no car. I could never really get beyond the brownstones of the neighborhood. All this road out here became like forbidden fruit.

"For Mom, it was a necessity, building a safe place and staying as close to that as possible. Of course I didn't understand it at the time. I was a kid. I longed for what I couldn't see.

"I worked very hard, our whole family did. I've had some sort of paying job since I was 10. Saved my money like an old widow, contributed my part to the family fund, but kept adding a little bit on the side every week. Had a hiding place. You'd be surprised how hard work adds up if you keep it in a cigar box in the basement. Taught me a great life lesson."

"I'm sure it did," Hanna agreed. "Let me guess. You fell in love with a car."

Kevin nodded. "You are a good journalist. But you're not 100 percent right. On my sixteenth birthday, my neighbor took the day off work and drove me out to the DMV for the road test. I remember that day as vividly as yesterday. I got in the car and didn't even know how to start the thing. It was my first time behind the wheel. Let's just say I got the car started but didn't get much farther than that. The examiner scoring my test felt bad for me. Must have been because I was soaking the interior of his car with tears the size of nickels," Kevin looked back at Hanna and laughed, but she could only manage a sad face.

"That's terrible," she said.

"Don't despair, Ms. Donnovan. Good fortune will step out of the shadows faster than a tear can dry. The man scoring my test happened to be the manager of the driving center. He made me a proposition. If I would come after school and do odd jobs, clean the toilets, mop the floor, empty the trash—that kind of stuff—he would take me out on the driving course and teach me to drive before he locked up at the gates at six. It took me three bus transfers to get out there, but what an adventure. I loved it. And you know what? I never missed a day of work. Every day for a month."

Kevin paused dramatically. They had ducked into the bright

lights of downtown Philly, but Hanna had hardly noticed. "And ..." she said impatiently.

"Guess what I got on my score when I took that test one month later?"

"Did your friend do the scoring?"

"Fair question, but no. He said he had a conflict of interest so he fed me to Mrs. Festerling. The woman hadn't smiled in her entire adult life."

Hanna considered. "You got a 99 percent because it wasn't in Mrs. Festerling's constitution to give anyone a perfect score."

"You are a perceptive one, if I can be so bold to say, Ms. Donnovan. But I did get 100 percent. The first and last such score that Mrs. Festerling ever gave. She said I drove like it was my calling. And you know what, I believed her."

"So that's how you got here," Hanna said, putting a bow on the story.

Kevin glanced back. "But Ms. Donnovan, you of all people should know a story never finishes so neatly. There's more, but here we are." The limousine turned smoothly into the hotel's drive-up, stopping in front of the massive glass doors with gleaming brass handles. "The Ambassador. I assure you, you will be well taken care of here."

No sooner had Kevin said so than the limousine door opened. "Good evening, ma'am," the doorman said with a full white smile. "Welcome to the Ambassador."

"Wait a second," Hanna said more brusquely than she intended. She leaned forward, resting her arms on the front seat. "You mean you're going to leave me hanging here, at this climactic note of the story?"

The doorman's smile disappeared as he considered his next move. Kevin turned in his seat and looked at Hanna. She certainly was beautiful, like all of the prospects Mr. Dickerson flew in. But this one was different. "Oh," he said, "you're not through with me quite so easily, Ms. Donnovan. I'll be your driver for the week. I'll be back, in fact," Kevin consulted his watch, "in 90 short minutes to take you to dinner. Your reservation is for 10 but I'll be here at 9:45. I trust that gives you sufficient time?"

Hanna's eyes narrowed. "Make it 9:30. We'll drive around the block if we have to until I get the rest of the story."

"As you wish. Nine-thirty then."

"It's a date," she said. "Nice to *really* meet you, Kevin," she said, offering him her hand.

He took it and gave it a squeeze. "The pleasure is all mine."

Hanna would have kicked herself with both feet were she able. "Why didn't I ask Kevin about the dinner reservation? Formal? Casual? Professional? Hip?" She looked at herself in her slip in the mirror. "Hell. I don't do hip." She scrunched up her lip.

She decided on professional. Hanna had met Thomas Dickerson on two other occasions. Once at the Midwest Journalism Award show when she was being recognized for the piece she did on Cory's small-engine plane rescue. And a second time when he came, unannounced, to her station in Duluth and followed her out to the parking lot after the six p.m. newscast to offer her a job, repeatedly—on what turned out to be the coldest day of the winter. To say the least, Thomas Dickerson didn't have confidence issues. He was a third-generation media mogul who made news in addition to selling it. He was known for having a very good eye for talent, having undeniable sway with the networks, and for opening a lot of doors for female anchors, including, typically, the door to his bedroom.

When Hanna came through the hotel lobby at 9:30, Kevin was there to greet her. "Good evening, Ms. Donnovan. If I may say, you look particularly stunning tonight."

"Hi Kevin," she said like she was greeting her brother. "How about we take a walk around the block and you get back to that story we started. You left off just after you impressed Mrs. Festerling beyond any prior experience and were about to—"

SUMMER 1985

"Excuse me, Ms. Donnovan. But Mr. Dickerson is waiting for you. We should be going." Much of the prior conversational manner of his speech had been starched and pressed out.

"Oh," Hanna said, stopping for a moment. She took a deep breath. "Time to get into what Cory calls 'game mode.'" She waited for Kevin to inquire as to who Cory was, but he too appeared to be in game mode. Hanna caught up with him at the door. "Okay. You're momentarily off the hook. Until drop off. Then prepare for a merciless interrogation."

Hanna glanced up to find Thomas Dickerson leaning against the door of the limousine looking like something out of an advertising photo shoot.

"Who is it you'll be interrogating?" Thomas said, pushing away from the car.

"He's here?" she said to Kevin. "You're here?" she said to Thomas. "I thought we were meeting at 10. At the restaurant, I mean. I was only kidding about the interrogation thingy." Hanna was flustered and began to blush.

Thomas brought his hand out from behind his back and presented her a single red rose. "Welcome, finally, to the City of Brotherly Love, Hanna Donnovan. God, I love the sound of that name. I've never seen you flustered before. You're one of the few television journalists who actually gets prettier when she blushes." He looked at her like he was studying a painting. "Amazing."

"Well thank you for inviting me, Mr. Dickerson." Hanna regained her composure. "I only blush for babies born in traffic jams, orphan twins meeting for the first time as grandmothers and dinner meetings that begin early." She smiled.

"Splendid recovery. An invaluable skill for broadcast news. Please, call me Thomas."

As it turned out, dinner was more like a movie than real life. The best table. A choreography of waitstaff whisking in this and dancing out that. The chef coming out to greet them, as well as cooking off the menu, preparing courses suggested by Thomas. All of it left

Hanna slightly lightheaded. That, and the frequency with which the head waiter was topping off her glass with champagne.

Thomas was much as Hanna remembered. Forty-something. Gray-black hair combed back with pomade. Good looking, in a fine-featured soap opera way. Athletically fit from a testosterone-rich diet of adventure hobbies. Polite. Witty. And even more confident here on his home field. Hanna tried to stop herself, but she kept imagining that Thomas had stepped out of one of the ad pages of her magazines.

"What are you thinking about?" Thomas said, returning her stare.

Hanna blinked. "I'm sorry. Was I staring?"

"Now it's my turn to blush," he said.

Hanna wouldn't give him one that easy. "Come on, Thomas. You haven't blushed since the second grade."

Thomas let out a fork-dropping laugh. "God, that's what I love about you. That Midwest honesty thing. It's intoxicating when mixed with beauty." Thomas paused. "For the record, it was the first grade. I blushed when I got caught holding hands with Pamela Riley during the Pledge of Allegiance."

Hanna started to laugh but a yawn came out instead. "Excuse me. I guess it's been a long day."

"I'm sorry," Thomas said. "You must be tired. We'll have our nightcap in the car. I just have one more question I'm dying to ask, but it can wait for our ride to the hotel."

What Hanna learned to hate about limousines, in her limited experience called today, was deciding where to sit. Luxury beckoned from all directions. There were beautiful long leather seats along each side, and a spacious back seat area. "I'm not quite sure where to sit," she confessed as Thomas slipped in after her.

"Let's go to the back. It's more comfortable there."

Hanna considered a bit of commentary about the relativity of comfort, but decided to keep it to herself.

SUMMER 1985

The limousine took the long way back to the hotel. Along the Delaware River, through a few of the older, more well-to-do neighborhoods like Society Hill. Hanna noticed the sound-proof glass between Kevin and the passenger area had been raised, giving her a tweak of sadness. She found no comfort in social stratification.

"What can I offer you?" Thomas asked, a bit open-ended. "We have a full bar at your disposal."

"Oh, just water for me," Hanna said. "I'm not much of a drinker."

"Are you sure I couldn't offer you something? I have a 60-year-old cognac that sips like honey from the bees of royalty."

"Thank you, no. Water would be perfect."

After they both got settled with their drinks, Thomas set the limo lights down to what could be best described as candlelight, scooted a little closer and put his hand on Hanna's knee. She all but froze. "As you know, Hanna, you have the job anchoring my Channel 3 newscast if you want it. The desk is there, ready and waiting. I've studied hours of your tape, and am quite confident in what I'm getting. But," he hesitated, a slight smile coming to his lips, "there is one thing I've wanted to ask you since we met, for the second time, in that godforsaken frozen food locker I believe you call Duluth, Minnesota." Thomas removed his hand from Hanna's knee as casually as he had placed it there.

She braced herself, looking at him in the soft-cast light. "Ask away," she said with nary a waver to give away her apprehension.

"What's the difference between a serviceable anchor woman and the anchor woman I go home and tune into religiously?"

"Hoi," Hanna exhaled a bit clumsily. "That wasn't the question I was expecting." She smiled. Thomas simply looked back at her, awaiting an answer.

Hanna sat up straighter in the seat. The slackness left her shoulders, and the tiredness in her eyes vanished. "But an excellent question," she said, stalling just long enough to let her thoughts locate and load the answer. Hanna often thought her mind was like the large bank of tape players housed in the production bay of the engineering room. It would shuttle through hours of material, dependably cuing up the right answer. That's why Hanna was so good at what she did. "I think of it like this: A good anchor delivers the news, professionally. A *great* anchor is someone you trust to tell you a story." She paused for emphasis. "Telling you a story," she repeated. "Accurate, yes. Compelling, certainly. Moving … there's the key. She can't be a robot under an inch of makeup. She's a respected friend." Hanna sat back in her seat and tapped her legs, pleased with her answer.

Thomas looked at her. "I quite appreciate your brevity. You'd be amazed how many times I've asked very good anchors that same question, and have needed multiple commercial breaks before getting a complete answer." Hanna smiled and started to say thank you. "But," Thomas held up his finger, "isn't there supposed to be a professional distance between you and your audience so that you can gain their respect? Especially for a woman broadcast journalist? And a beautiful one at that?"

Hanna raised her eyebrows. "No," she said directly. This time it was she who patted Thomas on the knee. "Absolutely, no," she repeated with a second pat. "Distance is the enemy. It's about connection. You want to be invited back into their living rooms."

"Candor and conviction. Check and checkmate." Thomas nodded to himself as though all hopes for Hanna Donnovan had been fully realized. "Tomorrow morning I've asked Kevin to get you at nine sharp. I'll have a few people waiting for you at the station. They'll take you around, show you how we stay afloat in the raging river of news that is Philadelphia. Unfortunately, I've been called out of town unexpectedly for meetings in Boston. But I'll reach you either at the station or at your hotel to check in on your day. How many days is it that we can expect the pleasure of your company?"

Hanna had been anticipating this question since the night began, but hadn't decided how she'd answer. She arranged for the week off, and Cory and Singer were going to be gone five days, so she didn't have to rush back. "I'm pretty flexible," Hanna said. Then she remembered it's always best to underpromise. "Two or three days."

Thomas smiled, sat back and took a sip of cognac. "A lot can happen in two or three days," he said.

BAUDETTE

It could be a lonely time of day, although Lu Ann didn't typically feel this way. She walked to the diner at 5:30 a.m. to prep for the 6:00 open. The old newspaper van rattled through the intersection just a block in advance of her, so she didn't get to exchange a wave with Harold. As her footfalls boomeranged off the facades of the closed merchants on Main Street, they echoed back, singular, almost like a slap across the face. When she pushed her key in the lock of the diner, it was remindful of her solitary place in this world. And when she threw on the diner lights, the emptiness presented a message. She started to take the chairs down from atop the tables, but with only two on the floor, facing each other, for better or for worse, in sickness and in health, she turned away from the task, went to a counter stool and cried quietly into her hands.

Three days had passed since she and Pat had talked—or argued, as she remembered it. Food had lost most of its appeal. She had been hurt to the point where she didn't pick up her feet and move around the restaurant like she was known to do. More than a few customers asked if she wasn't feeling well. A touch of something is what she told them. Lu Ann had finally called Monsignor Kief, who would be coming around about 10:00, a time when the diner would catch its breath before the lunch rush. A talk with him was the only thought she seemed to agree with.

At just a few minutes before 10, the familiar tap tap of Monsignor Kief's walking cane touched the glass of her front window, heralding his eminent arrival. It was the Monsignor's equivalent of a friendly horn beep. Stepping into Lu Ann's under the ting-aling of the brass bell, his nose swung upward. "Sourdough pancakes? What a surprise. Please tell me this ravenous town hasn't dispatched with the entire batch." The high-pitched joy in his voice seemed to sweep the dark from the dining room's corners. His hand traced along the halfwall of coat hooks just inside the door. The third one had his name under it. He removed his coffee mug and hung his cap. "Well?" he said. "Who's here with enough space left in their mouths to say hello?"

"Hello Monsignor," a few voices went out. He recognized them and exchanged good mornings using their names. Lu Ann was always struck by the Monsignor's ability to identify people by voice only. He was a study in the adaptability of human beings: a subject, Lu Ann recognized, on which she needed an accelerated course.

They found a quiet booth in back. Lu Ann insisted on bringing out a plate of sourdough cakes with bacon and Hash Browns O'Brien. His eating, she said, would force her to talk and him to listen.

Lu Ann went through what seemed to her like the emotional four seasons, beginning with her and Pat's dormant feelings for one another, to their first bursting forward, to their slower maturation, to what now felt like a cessation. Monsignor Kief had to be coached on a regular basis to pick up his fork and please eat. He didn't interrupt.

When she finished, he gently pushed his plate aside and took her hands. "God told me something once in His inimitable way. I forget exactly where I was stuck in life, but I was sure stuck. Then these words came to me like rain in the morning. 'Love doesn't end, it changes.' Okay, I thought. I'll give that thought a trial run. I took the words with me that day, walked with them, sat with them, saying them over and over to myself like a rosary. And by midday, I kid you not, lightning could not have struck me more profoundly. Love does not end, it changes. Praise be, I said to myself. Those words have stretched across my life experiences, the good and the bad, with such comfort, fit and durability."

The Monsignor let go of Lu Ann's hands and placed them fingertips down on the tabletop. "When times are hard, as I know they now are, you need to close your eyes and feel the space in front of you. Your life. Feel it there." The Monsignor gently started her fingertips moving across the table. "Let your fingers trace the contours, the differing degrees of smooth and rough. Truly shut out the limitations of sight, shut out the noise, feel the imperfections in what you thought to be smooth, or the smooth in what you thought to be imperfect, the ups and downs, the surprises you didn't expect to encounter. God is not going to take everything out of the way. There are obstacles to navigate, and there are edges to fall from. But if you and Pat started with love, and I know you did, then your love is not ending, but changing. Feel it just as you feel the table in front of you. Make peace with the obstacles just as Pat and HomeSky have had to make peace with theirs, as have I, as has Wes over there in losing his wife and two brothers and who wouldn't complain no matter how cold life has left his coffee. Life is gaining and losing. We want things to stay the same, but life is a volatile force. So my dear, close your eyes when you need to during these next few weeks or months, wherever you are, take a moment. Close your eyes and you'll find life there in front of you. Know that among good people like yourselves, love changes. And changes back. And changes yet again. But it doesn't end. It's that enduring."

SUMMER 1985

Lu Ann opened her eyes. "If you could see me right now," she said, "you'd see me with a smile on my face. The first in days." She looked at the beautiful, gentle Monsignor Kief.

"I can see you, lovely one," he said. "Better than you think."

Pat was in his sanctuary. The lumberyard was empty except for the aroma of new wood and the solid KA-THUNK as he flopped aside a board in order to grasp and lift and sight his eye down the one that was true.

He tossed another length into the keeper pile in the back of his pickup. God, it felt good to be out in the morning air before the heat awakened; that was the small prayer Pat whispered. He had taken the week off from the plant to work on the barn loft. He hadn't been out a week straight in over two years, so he was told by Dot in the front office. If Dot said so, count it as fact.

Pat found himself whistling all week. Actually, it was HomeSky who pointed it out. Her saying so had heightened his awareness, making the companionship of his own whistling bittersweet. Obviously, he was happy with what was happening at the farm. But there was a dull throb that wouldn't leave him. How was Lu Ann, he wondered?

Work, especially carpentry work, is a wonderful tonic. Here where the pieces fit, where accomplishment is measured, cut and nailed in a permanence you don't often find in life's random dynamic. It's solid, progressive. You can run your hand along it. It's a transformation played out in days rather than years.

Pat's load bounced and shifted in the pickup bed as he swung into the farmyard. *Got to fill that thing,* he thought, looking into his sideview mirror as he drove over the washout area off the edge of the gravel driveway. To Pat's reckoning, this would be his last load of framing lumber.

The morning sunlight laid up on the first step of the farmhouse, telling him it was about 8:00. Meadow might still be asleep; she was working ten to three at Lu Ann's these days. HomeSky usually disappeared mornings for a long walk.

"Hello," Pat heard from behind him.

"Hey, there," he said, surprised. "I figured you'd be out walking."

HomeSky approached, directly, as though she'd been waiting for his return. "Why has God given me this back again after taking it all away?" She looked like she hadn't slept much last night. Before Pat could recover from the question, HomeSky took another step forward. "I'm sorry to pounce." She held her hands out as if to slow things down. "It's an unfair question, and I don't expect an answer." Pat did his best not to look overwhelmed. HomeSky was about to say something more but stopped.

Meadow was stirred from her sleep by the sound of Pat's old pickup humping into the sideyard. She lay in bed for a moment, heard the engine diesel and cough as it was shut off. There were low voices talking. Throwing off her light bedcover, she went to her bedroom window and looked out. Below her in the farmyard, Pat and HomeSky stood an arm's length apart. Meadow contemplated the distance. She'd noticed in the months since HomeSky's return that the two of them had not come much closer than this. Now the distance between them, she could see from her vantage point, even as close as they stood, was a river, was a cliff, was a mountain, was an ocean. Such risk lay in the crossing. Meadow recognized that each saw the peril, as though they had stood there before. She nudged them with her thoughts. She looked out to the cropland beyond, and summoned the Great Spirit. Resting her hands on her swelling belly, she asked for the river to dry, for the ground to heave, for the mountain to be swallowed, for the winds to blow them together. *Take the space separating them and put it between rocks, between branches, between clouds.*

The heat of the morning brought the day's first breeze. It came strong and purposeful, setting the leaves to motion. From the porch overhang, the wind chimes bumped. The first timid morning notes sang out. Pat stepped to HomeSky, and HomeSky to Pat.

And the distance between them went to the clouds.

SUMMER 1985

The Sheriff's leg rested on the footstool at the end of the recliner. His pup wasn't sure what he liked to chew on better, the Sheriff's toes poking out of the end of the cast, or the rubber heel jutting below.

"Private!" bellowed the Sheriff. The puppy's head snapped to attention. "Sit!" he commanded sharply. The pup's little butt plopped to the floor. "Wait!" he commanded. Private did as he was told, a fuzzy black statue with only his tail moving. The Sheriff stood stiffly from his chair. Private's eyes moved, tracking the Sheriff's hand as it went toward the front pockets of his uniform shirt. His fingers dipped into the top right pocket where he kept a small snack bag of bacon-and-sausage flavored puppy treats. In the left, he kept liver-and-cheese flavor. The Sheriff leaned over with the treat. "Waaait." Private trembled like he was about to launch. "Waaait … good wait!" The Sheriff bathed the wriggling pup in strokes and scratches as the pup devoured the treat. "Very good."

Kitty came out of the Sheriff's kitchen with a single tuna fish sandwich and a carrot, neatly quartered, on a plate. "I thought you were going to sit for a while," she said. "You've been pushing that leg pretty hard."

"Ahh," the Sheriff deflected. "Can't help but play with the little guy. Won't let me sit still even if I had the notion to." He scooped up Private, who squirmed to face the Sheriff and delivered some bacon-and-sausage affection to his cheek. "Goofy little guy." He set him back on the floor. "You're going to be too big to do that with pretty soon here."

"If you hold this," Kitty said, handing him his plate, "and sit down, I'll bring the TV tray. Do you need to wash your hands?" she asked hopefully.

"Na. There's more bacteria in a bathroom sink than in a dog's mouth."

Kitty frowned. "A pleasant thought right before lunch."

"I could haul myself into the kitchen," the Sheriff offered.

"No, no. Let's eat in here," Kitty said. "We've got such a nice breeze."

The Sheriff's first week of half-days back on the job was going well, but it left him more tired than he'd anticipated. His reduced schedule had him at work from eight to 12:30, after which he'd come home for lunch.

The first day back he thought it was an awful nice surprise for Kitty to be waiting for him with a sandwich, which she ran across the street. Day two, she was waiting on his steps. Yesterday, she helped herself to the spare key and let herself in. After lunch they would walk the dogs and she'd ask about his day. There might come a knock on his door in the early evening as well. It wasn't that he didn't appreciate all Kitty was doing for him, but wasn't accustomed to so much company. In most cases, the Sheriff was as delicate with a person's feelings as a hacksaw, but with Kitty he worried about saying the wrong thing.

"Gosh darn good sandwich. Don't suppose there's another."

"Well thank you, Thurgood. But no, I made just the one. A slimmer Sheriff Harris is a more vigorous Sheriff Harris."

"Any chips or anything? You know, kinda like a side?"

"There is another carrot. Shall I cut it up?"

The Sheriff was beginning to think that Private's liver-and-cheese treats smelled better and better. "No. Thank you nonetheless."

The Sheriff thought maybe he could tear into a bag of pretzels under the cloak of doing up the dishes. "I think I'll clean up my plate then," he said, beginning to rise.

"Nonsense," Kitty insisted. "You stay off your feet a few minutes more. I'll get that and then we can circle the block a few times with the boys."

The Sheriff looked over at Private whose tummy was rising and falling as he slept on his back, one leg stuck up in the air like he ached to answer a question in grammar school. A nap with a Western on the TV, that sounded pretty good right now. Kitty came over and took the plate with one carrot bite left uneaten. "One left," she half-sang.

"It has something funny looking on the end." The Sheriff scrunched up his nose.

Kitty took it off the plate. "Now that won't hurt you one bit," she said, handing it to him.

Outside, walking their dogs, the tops of the Sheriff's ears were burning and it wasn't because of the 80-degree afternoon sun. *If someone drives by and sees me looking like this I might as well turn my gun on myself.*

"You sure are quiet," Kitty said. What are you over there thinking about?

"Not a whole lot," the Sheriff fibbed. "Just getting adjusted to this new outfit of mine."

Kitty had done some shopping. She went to the Duluth Mall, which offered infinitely more choices than anything you could find in town. "You can hardly find color in our newspaper," she liked to say about the lack of styles offered in Baudette. In Duluth, she hit the jackpot. Matching exercise outfits in a hue that the Sheriff thought best described as bike reflector red. The outfits came with long and short pants, featuring a double pinstripe up the sides, and a zippered sweat top with white accents and the words Prime Time sewn across the back.

The Sheriff tried to "forget" his sweat top on the kitchen chair before they went out in public, but Kitty was so excited to see it on him. The top was bad, but the biggest betrayal to his image were the shiny red shorts. The Sheriff didn't do shorts. Shorts were for heavyset little boys with large rainbow-spiral suckers. He told her that his legs were so pasty that you couldn't tell which one the cast was on, but that complaint got no audience. You look athletic, she said. He told her she was close. The word was pathetic.

Hansel and Gretel cantered out in front of Kitty on a double leash, noses high in the air. "You seem uncomfortable. Are your shorts too snug?" Kitty inquired. "They're so cute."

That cut like a dagger. The Sheriff stopped abruptly, and when Private ran out of slack in the leash, he was yanked off his feet.

"Kitty," the Sheriff cleared his throat. "Let me start by saying I do appreciate all you're doing for me. The sandwiches, the extra grocery shopping, the tidying up around my place, the new plants, even the help with my wardrobe. But I can't be seen out in public like this."

"Whatever do you mean?" A pained look transformed her face.

The Sheriff surveyed his outfit. "I look like a deranged tomato. If I saw me on the street I'd call for back-up before approaching."

Kitty's chin started to quiver.

"It's not like I don't enjoy the company, 'cause I do. It's just I've kinda been, how do I put it?" The Sheriff thought for a second. "A belt buckle without a belt, for a long time." Private scampered over and gave the Sheriff a little bark. Either he wanted to get going, or he was offering advice. "I've grown accustomed to my own space."

Kitty bore down, keeping her emotions at bay. "I see," she said. "Well I didn't mean to be invasive. I'll take the workout suit back; I believe I filed the receipt. And I won't be intruding on your space in the future."

"Now, Kitty. No one said nothing about intruding."

"Good day, Sheriff Harris," Kitty said. "Hansel. Gretel," she commanded. The miniature schnauzers sprang to their feet from the sitting position. "Heel!" The dogs, head and tails held high, swung past the Sheriff and caught up to their master who was walking in the opposite direction.

"Kitty, if you'd let me pull this cast out of my mouth and explain. Things don't always come out. Exactly. Right. Kitty?"

"Home!" she commanded to Hansel and Gretel as they strode away.

The Sheriff's arms fell limply to his sides. Private looked at him like, *do something!* "Shitfire," the Sheriff said under his breath. Private let out a single high-pitched yip! in Kitty's direction. Hansel looked back, receiving a sharp correction on his rhinestone collar for the treason.

Private ambled over and sat next to the Sheriff's cast. The Sheriff unzipped the left side pocket of his sweat top and pulled out a liver-and-cheese biscuit. "We ain't going be able to slap a patch on that blown tire and call it new." He flipped the treat to his pup. The biscuit bounced off Private's head, and he chased it down. "Next time I open my mouth," he said to Private, "come over and take a hunk out of my big toe, will ya?" He nudged Private with his cast.

A car turned onto the quiet tree-lined street, slowing as it approached the Sheriff. "Come on," the Sheriff said to Private, who was splayed out, crunching away on the treat. "Standing in the middle of the sidewalk draws more attention than walking. Get now," he pulled Private to his feet.

The car pulled over and the window came down. "Not possible," the Sheriff groaned to Private. The driver was Cam Williams, the head football coach of the high school team.

Cam liked to talk so much he did so in his sleep. "Well hey-ya Sheriff," he said. "When I first saw you standing there I thought someone moved the stop sign."

The Sheriff quickly pulled off his red sweat top and slung it over his shoulder. "Hey Coach. Sure is a warm one." The Sheriff was desperate to divert the conversation.

"You look like you're getting ready to try out for football this year. Practice starts next week." The coach considered that pretty funny material.

The Sheriff grit his teeth and tried to sound conversational. "Just trying to get the leg back in shape. And the pup needs to burn some energy."

The coach started giggling before he even got the next words out. "Sure could use a center. Half my front line graduated last year. Whadaya say?" The coach's head was out of the window and he slapped the side of the car door he was laughing so hard.

The Sheriff started walking. "Good luck with that."

"Although you look pretty fast in that get-up. Maybe you'd make a better fullback."

The Sheriff stopped and gave the coach a look that could cut steel. "Coach, I advise you to move that car before I cite you for obstructing traffic."

"Don't be sore," the coach said. "We're just having some fun."

The Sheriff jerked a thumb in the other direction indicating it was time for the fun to get moving.

As he pulled away, the coach couldn't help himself. "Not sure where you'd keep a citation book in those little shorts of yours." The Sheriff could still hear him laughing a block and a half away.

"Let's saddle up and move out," the Sheriff said to Private. "No stopping for business on the way home. You're going to have to hold it." The pup bounced to his feet and returned the Sheriff's look of resolve. They made their way down the tranquil neighborhood sidewalk. The high canopies of elms and walnut trees put out long ribbons of shade. The Sheriff's uneven walking-cast gait was further accentuated because he'd picked up the pace. Private scampered ahead on a taut leash, trying his puppy best to ignore butterflies and the endless smells wafting off tree trunks. At the corner of every street they crossed, the Sheriff would command Private to sit as they checked in both directions for cars. Then the Sheriff would make the sign of the cross, and they'd step off the curb. It was a long five blocks home.

SUMMER 1985

HANNA

What a whirlwind the last two and a half days had been. Hanna sat down carefully in the champagne yellow leather office chair, mindful of the massive desk in front of her. Over 200 years old, the mahogany desk originally stood in Independence Hall and was used in the writing of the United States Constitution. Hanna set her hands on the unvarnished wood, smiling in disbelief.

Night had somehow arrived. When you're in the newsroom, where lights are everywhere, you tend to lose track of the daylight hour. Yes, you're busy watching the clock, more specifically, the hands as they move toward the top of the hour, but the actual time of day doesn't register. It's all about the minutes and seconds until you're on.

Hanna reclined in the chair, looking through the glass wall in front of her, taking in the Philadelphia skyline. These were the same glass walls where the famous 24-karat gold-leaf letters, DBN, short for Dickerson Broadcasting Network, ran up the side of the skyscraper. Each letter was 14-feet tall, and reportedly insured for a million dollars. DBN headquarters took up the twenty-third, twenty-forth and twenty-fifth floors. The newsroom and broadcasting facilities were on floors one through three.

Hanna rapped lightly on the desk just to be sure it was real. How incredible was this: to be on the twenty-fifth floor, looking out at the cityscape through the letter D—and her, an anchorwoman from a mere hayseed-sized television market. She adjusted her sitting posture as if delivering the nightly news lead-in to camera number one. Her hands, resting lightly on the desk in front of her, shuffled invisible papers. "News anchorwoman Hanna Donnovan, 26, from Duluth, Minnesota, found dead today in DBN headquarters. Cause of death, police say, shock."

Thomas Dickerson had instructed his assistant to have Hanna wait in his office for his phone call. He was flying back from Boston tonight and wanted to see her. Among other things, he was anxious to talk about the last two days she had at the station.

Hanna swiveled around in the chair to scan the wall behind her, which was covered in framed photographs of Thomas shaking hands, having drinks, playing golf, or backslapping with a jaw-dropping assortment of industry big-shots, movie stars, national dignitaries and local celebrities. There he was with Presidents Carter and Reagan, and Prime Minister Thatcher; industry icons such as Dan Rather, Dianne Sawyer, Bill Paley and Roone Arledge; entertainment stars including Johnny Carson, Clint Eastwood, Bruce Springsteen and Elton John; and local celebs like singers Patti LaBelle and Chubby Checker, Phillies legends Steve Carlton and Mike Schmidt, not to mention billionaire business tycoon Senator John Heinz III. She studied one picture in particular where he was standing at center ice in a Flyers hockey jersey pulled over his dress shirt, with the two-time Stanley Cup winning Broad Street Bullies. *Who is this guy?* she found herself wondering.

SUMMER 1985

The phone on the desk rang, giving her such a start that it almost fulfilled her mock news lead-in from moments before. The second ring, less shocking, bounced off the walls of the empty office. Should she pick up? What if it wasn't for her?

"Thomas Dickerson's office," Hanna said into the sleek phone.

"Well, it appears you've taken over Philly 3 News. How do you like your new digs?"

"Thomas?" Hanna said into the receiver. "It's amazing."

"How is Philadelphia's next big thing doing this fine night? I hope you're not too tired for dinner. I'm ravenous."

"I have to do the 11," she said.

"Talented. Pretty. And conscientious. What do they put in the water in the Midwest?" Thomas laughed. "No. You officially have the rest of the night off. My colleagues tell me you've earned it."

Hanna's voice sparkled with excitement. "People have been great. I've been meeting all the reporters, working with editors, reviewing treatments with producers, writing lead-ins, helping with some news writing—"

"Ho there. Deep breath," Thomas said. "Save some for dinner. I want to hear all about it."

"One-one thousand exhale," Hanna said, using her on-air mental exercise for slowing down when reading copy.

Thomas chuckled. "I'm pleased it's going well. The staff is extremely impressed, as I knew they would be. I apologize for skipping out on you, but I'm very close to expanding our network into Boston. I'll save that for dinner, too. How about 10 o'clock? Can you tell Kevin, or shall I?"

"I'm happy to. Ten is great. Kevin has spoiled me rotten. I walk out the door, he's there to drive me wherever."

"Get used to it," Thomas said. "Out here, when you sit at the big desk, you've got the world at your hem."

Hanna smiled. It was a dream. Out beyond the glass office walls, the beguiling lights of the city winked. It wasn't what you'd call beautiful, like the night stars of Duluth; more so, it was breathtaking, like hanging at the top of a rollercoaster.

"You still there?" Thomas' voice asked. Hanna looked at the handset, forgetting she was still holding it.

"Oh, yes," she said. "Got lost in the lights up here. The view is like nothing I've seen before."

"Just remember to tell Kevin 10 sharp." Thomas paused. "Hanna, I'm excited to see you."

Hanna felt a warm rush—a blush—unexpectedly race through her. "Me too," she said.

Kevin was parked in front of the news station, behind the wheel, doing a crossword puzzle under the dome light. He didn't see her coming as she opened the limousine door herself.

"Hey there," she said, poking her head in.

Kevin quickly put the crossword aside. "Goodness. My apologies, Ms. Donnovan, for not attending to that door." He turned around more fully. "I'm afraid I'm in desperate need of your help. Once again."

"It's going to cost you a detour to the coffee shop." She slid in and shut the door.

"Deal. Eight across: four-letter word for cautious."

"Any letters?"

"Third letter r."

"Wary," Hanna said.

Kevin nodded slowly. "Goodnight, I believe you have it." He penned it in. "Fabulous! Are we quickly back to the Ambassador then, after the coffee? I didn't expect you until *after* the 11."

"Change in plan," Hanna said, checking the time. "I talked with Thomas and it appears I have the rest of the night off. He's made a dinner reservation for just over an hour from now. You're to call him."

"Certainly ..." Kevin was a bit flummoxed. "I hadn't heard from Mr. Dickerson." He started the limo.

SUMMER 1985

"He asked if I would relay the message. Probably testing me."

Kevin pulled smoothly away from the curb. "Not in the least," he said. "Not to talk out of school, but earlier Mr. Dickerson mentioned all reports on you from the station are glowing."

Hanna sat back, as much thinking aloud as talking to Kevin. "Everyone's been so nice. Almost too nice. Everything seems so ... perfect."

Kevin left her to her thoughts until Hanna spoke up. "Kevin, can I ask you something?" Her tone was pensive.

"By all means."

"It gets back to what you said about talking out of school, or as I call it, off the record."

"I see," Kevin said.

"I mean, we've talked a lot. You've shared a ton, from way back ... the perfect 100 on your driver's test, the crappy job at the used car lot that got you your first car to drive cross-country to the Pacific." Hanna's thoughts coalesced as she spoke "And you know what? You did that, chanced all that, to see if the block you grew up on was too small to hold you for life. Right?" Hanna didn't wait for an answer. "And then you came back because it wasn't too small." Hanna let that thought settle. "Now here I sit feeling the same way, wondering the same thing, like we're kindred spirits. I don't know if my block back home is big enough. It's sad one minute and exhilarating the next."

Kevin stole an occasional glance at Hanna in the rear-view mirror as she looked out the window at the lights of downtown Philadelphia.

"I haven't told you I have a son," Hanna said. "Why haven't I told you that?"

"You've been quite busy, both with work here and putting up with my stories," Kevin said. "What's his name?"

"Paul," Hanna said. "But we all call him Singer. Everywhere he goes he brings music."

"Oh, that does sound nice. How old is the lad?"

"Just had his fourth birthday. It's gone so fast."

Kevin could see a crease in Hanna's brow as she thought.

"So, off the record," she continued. "I wonder if I can ask you why everyone has been so nice to me and if I'm just one of many Ms. So-and-sos that you escort around in this limousine at the whim of Thomas Dickerson?"

The car didn't so much drive through the sparse evening traffic as glide. There was a silky soundlessness inside, as though nothing from the real world could touch you here. Kevin didn't answer right away.

"You're not one of many, Hanna," Kevin said, using just her first name for the first time since they met. "That I assure you." They pulled up at a red light. Halfway down the next block Hanna could see the marquee of the Ambassador Hotel. Kevin continued. "I think you know I need this job and like this job and try to adhere to the few rules Mr. Dickerson has assigned me."

Hanna sat forward and rested her hand on Kevin's shoulder. "I'm sorry to put you on the spot. It was wrong of me to ask." Hanna kept her hand there, and then gave him an pat. "Everything will work out," she said brightly.

They pulled into the arcing drive, under the marquee. "I've forgotten your coffee," Kevin said suddenly. "What on earth has gotten into me?" He got out and opened Hanna's door.

She looked up at him. "That's okay." Hanna stepped out, taking his hand. "I hope I haven't spoiled our friendship. I don't really have anyone to talk to here."

"No, please," Kevin said uncomfortably. "I'm flattered to be counted as a friend."

"Ten o'clock then," Hanna said, shaking his hand, putting on her best newscaster's smile. "I've got some work to do," she joked, looking at her outfit.

"Ten sharp," Kevin replied.

Hanna turned toward the glass doors of the hotel. The doorman saw her coming, his white-gloved hand reaching for the brass handle.

SUMMER 1985

"Hanna," Kevin said, suddenly behind her.

She turned, startled. "Kevin?"

"There is something you need to know," he said.

By the tone of his voice, Hanna knew it wasn't that she had left her briefcase in the back seat.

LAKE OF THE WOODS

Singer was running out of steam. Who wouldn't be? It was a day of making chipmunk traps, helping to carve a walking stick, swimming at Sandy Beach, looking for bear tracks, picking blackberries, finding a rock that looked just like a baked potato, going for wheelbarrow rides as Stu and Cory split wood, using a real biffy, catching a walleye on a leech, finding cloud animals in the sky and learning how to pyramid kindling to start a fire. Not to mention the practical jokes he and Stu pulled.

Stu was in his element. Had been all day. Starting first thing after the breakfast dishes were done and the fishermen had gone out for the morning. Darlene had just finished drying the big pans. All that was left to do was to pull out the chairs to sweep under the long tables in the dining area. Stu and Singer had gone off on the pretense of stacking firewood, but really, they had only ducked around the corner of the dining room.

Pinched between Singer's fingers was one end of virtually invisible monofilament fishing line. The other end was tied to a fuzzy old wool sock that they had placed on one of the chair seats across the room. As Darlene approached the table with her broom, Singer's little hand, with Stu's on top for guidance, pulled the sock off the chair, triggering a shriek in Darlene that Cory heard all they way over at his cabin. Stu and Singer did their level best not to giggle too loudly as they twitched that sock across the pine plank floor with Darlene giving chase, broom cocked over her head. She got the sock with the second swing, and almost got Stu two swings later as he and Singer and made a run for it. What a day!

Things were mostly quiet now. The fishermen had been fed a late dinner—overfed, to know the truth—and had groaned back to cabins, belts loosened a few notches. Bourbon and a few hands of poker would cap off their perfect day.

Cory took Singer back to their cabin to brush teeth and put on pajamas. One last story back by the lodge fireplace was promised, but just one. Then lights out. They had another big day on deck for tomorrow.

The fire in the massive stone hearth of the lodge had burned down, the red glowing logs occasionally popping and cracking to punctuate Stu's velvety voice. He was regaling Singer with tales of a heat wave they had on the island when he was a kid. Darlene was knitting Singer a red cap with four green frogs ringing the trim. Cory sat in a high-backed wooden rocker while Singer, humming to himself, curled up on his lap.

"It got so hot up here that summer," Stu said in a low voice, "the first thing that happened is the bottom of the thermometer began to inflate like a red balloon, getting bigger and bigger and bigger until the whole thing just lifted off its nail and floated into the sky."

Singer's heavy eyes widened. "Like the balloon that got away at my birthday party?" he asked in a quiet voice. Cory adjusted the boy on his lap.

"Just the same, I'll bet," Stu told him. "Then guess what happened to all the leaves on the trees?"

Singer shrugged.

"They cooked into potato chips. You could just pick them off the branch and eat them. Crunch!" Stu pantomimed enjoying one.

"Wooow," Singer said.

"But best of all, right along three o'clock, there in the heat of the day, I'd spot a few honey bees and walk behind 'em with my hand out like this." Stu showed him how. "And they'd be buzzing along through the air until they POPPED! just like popcorn and landed right in the palm of my hand. And since they were honey bees, guess what they tasted like?"

Singer was too entranced to imagine.

"Caramel corn!"

"Can we try that?" Singer begged.

"We'll see," Stu told him. "Don't think it's going to get *that* hot tomorrow."

"Never know," Singer said, ever the optimist.

"No you sure don't, and that's a good policy to have." Stu winked at the boy.

Cory rubbed Singer's shoulders. "You know what we have to catch now, bud?"

"Hmm?" Singer said, now in the mood for adventure.

"Some Zs. Do you know what catching some Zs means?"

Singer shook his head no.

"It's an expression that means going to sleep. They call it catching Zs."

"I don't get it," Singer screwed his body backward to give Cory a confused look.

"Let's talk about it tomorrow." Cory picked Singer off his lap and set him on the ground. "What do you have to say to Darlene and Stu?"

Singer wobbled on sea legs over to Darlene sitting in her chair. She set aside her knitting for a big hug. "Goodnight. Love you," Singer said in her arms.

"Goodnight, my dear," she said, wishing that Singer's soft cheek could stay pressed to hers just a little longer.

Singer made his way over to Stu. "Thanks for my favorite day ever." Stu bent forward in his chair and Singer wrapped his little arms around Stu's sun-beat neck.

"Mine too, tenderfoot." Stu's hands spread across the soft fabric of Singer's pajama top, so large they covered his entire back.

Cory and Singer stood on the deck on the lakeside of the cabin. A silver path swayed loosely across the water under the rise of a full moon. "It's fun peeing off the deck," Singer said.

"Just don't tell your mother."

"Why can't we do it at home?"

"It's not how they do it in the city."

"Can I do it at your cabin?"

"Heck yeah. Thou shalt pee outdoors at cabins. It's the eleventh commandment. Okay, time for bed."

"What's a commandment?"

"Quit stalling. Bedtime."

"Do I have to?"

"Yes, it's late. Big day tomorrow."

"Do I have to wear my top PJ? I'm hot."

Cory was getting tired. He took off his baseball cap and rubbed his hair. "Okay, you can take it off. Let's put it under your pillow in case it cools down later."

There was almost no breeze. A mugginess intoned rain was on its way.

"Story?" Singer asked.

"You knucklehead," Cory smiled. "Stu already told you four stories."

"Letters and scratch?"

"Okay, but a fast one."

Singer climbed in bed, his stuffed magic bear waiting for him on the pillow. He gave him a hug and pulled him under the sheet. Cory lay next to Singer, pulling the sheet back so he could scratch the boy's back.

"I'm erasing the blackboard," Cory said to Singer as he scratched. "Okay, what's this?" Cory traced the letter G on Singer's back.

"C?" Singer said into the darkness.

"Try again," Cory's fingertip repeated the big sweeping G on Singer's skin.

"Oh, G!" Singer said.

"Right. How about this?"

"K!" Singer said, excited to get it right.

"Okay last one. A hard one." As Cory traced the letter he felt himself getting a little sleepy.

"B?" Singer said.

"Try again," Cory retraced, his finger on Singer's small back.

"R!" Singer guessed.

"Correct. As in, R you asleep yet?"

"Not yet," Singer giggled.

Cory sat up, careful not to hit his head on the upper bunk above. There was no sneaking off the old steel-spring single mattress. "Goodnight," he kissed the boy's cheek.

"What about prayers?" Singer asked.

"Oh, yeah. Say a quick thank you to God for everything He gives you."

"Can we do it together?"

"Sure, but I'm not laying back down because I'll fall to sleep and sleep and sleep for a month straight."

"Why don't you do it?" Singer asked hopefully.

"You start the prayer," Cory said. "Then I'll go next."

"Thank you God for Cory."

"Thank you God for Singer."

"Thank you God for Stu."

SUMMER 1985

"Thank you God for Darlene."

"Thank you God for magic bear."

"Aren't you forgetting someone?" Cory asked. "Someone who loves you very much but isn't here right now?

"Oh," Singer said. "Thank you God for Mom."

Before Cory got up to leave, he snuck his baseball cap under Singer's pillow. Hide-the-cap was one of their games. When Cory had "sleepovers" at Hanna's, he would stick his hat somewhere in Singer's bed. Usually, he would hide it when he came in to check on a sleeping Singer. The treasure hunt would commence in the morning. "All right. Good night, buddy. I love you more than 500 barrels of caramel corn." Cory stood to leave.

"I love you more than a zillion red balloons."

"'Night."

"'Night."

"Cory?" Singer said as Cory was closing the bedroom door. "Will you leave it open a little?"

"Sure, bud. I'll be back in a jif. Just going to say goodnight to Darlene and Stu. Get some shut-eye."

"Yep," Singer said, rolling onto his side.

Cory looked through the crack in the door, the light slipstreaming in, rimming the delicate curve of Singer's back. "Thank you God for little beams of light," he whispered. He listened closely as Singer hummed himself toward sleep, wondering if his little hand would slide under the pillow and find the hidden cap.

Cory carefully opened and shut the screen door as he stepped out. The bright moon showed him the two deck steps he needed to descend. Then it was a short worn path to the rock outcropping overlooking the lake.

The stars cast a net above him. *They haven't moved,* he thought. *The same stars I looked at 12 years ago. How can someone be so alone looking at them one time and so connected another? How does a view show no change when life has changed entirely?* Cory didn't typically engage in such roundabouts. He preferred firmness, discipline and equations that come with concrete answers that circumstance can't influence. He spat on a rock without looking away from the stars. A bank of clouds was moving in from the west, snuffing them out from the edge in. He thought about his island out there, Boom Island, and what was lost there. He thought about positive influences standing in random places. He though about the unbreakable breaking, and wondered why he'd been spared.

Walking back to the lodge, Cory saw muted yellow light filling the windows. His first guess was Stu had put another log on the fire and was staying up, having a pipe. Darlene preferred he didn't smoke in front of Singer.

The aroma of wood smoke loitered in the heavy air. As Cory approached the building, the full moon was positioned in the sky as if to appear perfectly balanced atop the lodge's chimney. It was quite a sight, smoke curling through the orb, fascinating yet eerie. *Is Hanna looking at that same moon?* A cloud wiped in front, taking it from view; it was as though the moon had fallen down the chimney.

Cory came quietly into the main room. "I saw the lights on. Expected to find Stu," he told Darlene.

"Nope. Singer plumb did him in. I sent him to bed before he swallowed himself yawning." Darlene observed the knitting on her lap. "I'm going to have to be a night owl to finish before you leave. I wish we had more time."

Cory sat down in the same rocker he had earlier. "We still have all tomorrow."

"I guess you guys are missing home," Darlene said.

"Yes and no." Cory stood again. "Are those toothpicks where you always kept them?"

"Yep. Left pantry. Top shelf."

"We miss Hanna, of course," Cory said as he made his way toward the kitchen. "Hard for Singer not to talk to Mom all these days."

SUMMER 1985

"I'm sure," Darlene said, a bit disturbed. "It's difficult at times with no phone here, but the radio usually gets everything we need done. Of course there's always the marina phone if you want to take a ride over."

Cory returned, working the toothpick in a trouble spot. "Nah. We're good. It's nice to be somewhere where everywhere you look there are no telephone lines." Cory hovered, not sure, it seemed, whether to sit or to go.

"Have a seat," Darlene nodded. "Stu says rain tonight, likely a gully-washer. Hopefully it will blow on through and tomorrow will be sunny."

Cory yawned. "Excuse me," he said. "Singer did the both of us in." He sat in the rocker.

Darlene turned to Cory. "He is some kind of wonderful, that boy. You do a great job with him."

A smile dimpled Cory's cheek. "He amazes me." Cory looked at Darlene like there was something else he wanted to say, but didn't.

They watched the fire burn down. "How have you been doing?" Darlene asked quietly over the clicking of her knitting needles. "We've hardly had time to talk, you and I."

Cory evaded. "You're not going to get that hat done with questions like that." A log shifted and fell. Cory got up and used the fireplace tongs to put it back. He adjusted the logs, fire flickering back to life from beneath them. He paused at the hearth. "Do you remember my friend Shara, from down in St. Paul?"

Darlene had to think a moment. "The girl who is paralyzed?"

"Yeah," Cory said. "She passed away earlier this summer." Cory put another small log on the fire and sat back down in the rocker.

"Oh, so young," Darlene said. Her nature was not to nose into others' business but Darlene sensed Cory had a reason for broaching the subject. "How did she die?"

Cory rubbed his eyebrow. "Suicide." The word sat there like rock in the room.

"Good heavens," Darlene said. "Had you seen much of her of late? She was a high school friend, wasn't she?"

"I'm afraid I hadn't been a very good friend in the past years. She was down in the Cities, so I didn't see her much. Thanksgiving or Christmas when I'd see my mom and sisters. She was the girl I made the skating chair for, if you remember."

"I do," Darlene said. "I remember your picture in the paper. Gosh, I'm so sorry."

"She left a letter for me before she died." Cory looked over at Darlene. He chewed the inside of his mouth. "I really haven't talked to anyone about it. Not even Shara's dad or Hanna."

"I see," Darlene said.

"I just kind of read the letter. Over and over."

"Can you tell me about it?"

"There's one part in there that I've been thinking about a lot, especially up here." The rocker that Cory sat in was hand-built by a local craftsman. It was native pine, stripped and varnished, finished with crisscrossed leather straps for a seat. Cory's hands slid up and down the smooth knots in the armrests. "I used to push—or more like run—Shara down the hallway in high school once in a while just so we could see the panicked looks on the kids' faces. I think it released her from her wheelchair in a way. Well, in the letter, Shara told me that Singer and Hanna are my release. That she thinks they're here to take me fast down the hallway." Cory's brow furrowed. "She only wrote a page and a half. Why would she say that? I mean it had to be important, right?"

"Cory," Darlene said. "Don't take this the wrong way, but would you say you're happy?"

Cory frowned a bit. "Relatively," he said.

Darlene set her knitting down. "Cory," she said energetically, "happiness is not a relative thing. You are, or you aren't."

Cory thought about that. "I'm careful about assumptions of happiness."

"You're going to have to translate that, honey."

"I don't see it as an entitlement."

"Why on earth not?"

Cory cocked his head. "The law of averages says for every happy person there must be an unhappy one."

"That's a bunch of malarkey, Cory. The law of God says we all start happy. It's His gift to us."

"Could be," Cory said calmly. He wasn't looking for an argument.

Darlene tapped a finger on the armrest of her chair. "Let me put it to you another way," she said. "If you were going to tell me about a happy Cory Bradford, if you could change your story in any way, what would it be?"

"A happy Cory Bradford?"

"Yep."

"Hmmm. Well, I'm 24, like now, but physically at my peak. No bad knee. I'm playing in the NHL. I don't care what team. I'm scoring goals like I used to. I want to feel like I felt after a great game."

"So," Darlene said, "if I could make it that you could trade the current Cory Bradford sitting here with me with the Cory Bradford you just described, no bad knee, no Monument Bay Resort, no Darlene, no Stu, no Hanna, no Singer, would you make the trade?"

"You could arrange that?" Cory's eyebrow raised.

Darlene smiled. "Let's say I could."

They looked at one another. For a change, Cory didn't look away first. "No."

Darlene's smile broadened. "Then I would say you are as you should be: happy. With all the bruises and scars and questions that go along with happiness to give it some meaning and some contrast."

Cory smiled back at Darlene. "You're sure about that?" he said lightly.

"Sure as I'm sitting here right next to you," she said. "Your friend Shara was right. Hanna and Singer are your wings."

Cory nodded.

"When Stu and I visited for your graduation, we were worried about you, to be honest. We came back here and talked about it long into the night. You seemed so … unsettled. Always somewhere else. Like you're getting today checked off the list so you can move on to tomorrow where the real living could start happening. Sound familiar?"

"Yeah, maybe."

Darlene leaned in. "Cory, I don't know much but I know this. Life is a miracle, not a job. Don't be one of those people who discovers that too late."

"I get that." Cory's voice caught. "I'm trying."

"I see that, dear. Stu and I, we both see that. It's great. These few days we had with you, to see you with Singer, ah hell, it's enough to make an old lady cry."

"It's that home cooking of yours." Then Cory decided not to sidestep. "No. I know what you mean. I feel like I've been running for a long, long time. Getting by. Not really trusting anything good that was happening, like it was going to be taken away so stay ahead of it. Beat it at its own game. But with Hanna and Singer, things are different, and it's taken me a few days to put a word to what it is. It's permanent. That's a new one for me. I don't remember permanence, even as a little boy. Isn't that weird?"

"No, it's not weird," Darlene insisted. "You're brave to talk about it. Sometimes our dear Lord tests us in ways that seem absent of love." Darlene looked off, mentally revisiting some great tribulation of her own.

Cory spoke up. "So I told you where Hanna is, right? In Philadelphia interviewing for a job. Well not exactly interviewing. There's a big shot out there who wants her to relocate and be the anchor there. So she's checking it out. He says she's too big for her pond." Cory thought for a moment. "I guess she's trying to decide what makes her happy."

"What will you do if she says she wants to go?" Darlene had cut right to it.

"You know, I didn't know till right now." Cory reached above his head with both arms and stretched. "I'd ask her if I could come with." He folded his hands on top of his head and gave Darlene a relaxed smile.

"Ha!" Darlene clapped her hands together. "There you go. That's the right answer."

"Hmm. Funny to hear me say that out loud. Thanks for the talk." Cory took a deep breath. "I'm glad I saw the light on." He came over and gave Darlene a hug. "I'd say you were knitting more than a hat tonight."

Darlene held on strong. "I want you to know I thank God every night for bringing you to me, regardless of why. You are the boy Stewart and I were never able to have."

Cory swallowed hard. "Thanks. It means a lot to hear that. Well, don't stay up too late now, okay?"

"Don't you worry," Darlene said as Cory took a step back. "I'm going to sleep great. As long as I can get Stu onto his quiet side."

"Good night then," Cory said, a half-moon dimple in his cheek.

"Good night to you," she said.

Outside, the aroma of smoke from the fire was strong in the damp air. There was no wind, just low pressure from the incoming storm pushing down. Clouds had closed in, stealing the stars.

Exhausted from the conversation, and the day, Cory quietly went to his cabin. He smiled a little, kicking a rock, keeping it in front of him until it was lost to the darkness. He planned to read, but first he'd check on Singer. He loved looking at his sleeping face.

Cory frowned. The bedroom door was swung open more than the crack he'd left it. As he opened the door fully, the light swung across Singer's bottom bunk. The sheet was pulled back and his bed was empty. Cory stepped farther into the bedroom, checking his bed, and the top bunk. They too were empty.

"Buddy?" Cory whispered. He quickly scanned the room. His eyes hadn't adjusted. Off balance. Nothing made sense. He flipped on the overhead light, trying to stay calm. Nothing in the small closet. Nothing under the beds. His movements were getting faster. "Singer?" he said trying to sound less scared than he was. Walking quickly back in the front room, he searched. Empty chair. Empty dinner table. Nothing by the refrigerator. He went directly to the bathroom, where he had left the light on in case Singer needed to use it. Nothing. The broom closet. Nothing. Perspiration burned on his skin. His breaths were shallow and quick. He spun around, taking in a 360-degree look at the empty cabin.

Singer was gone.

SUMMER 1985

MUTINEER'S JUG

The full moon left them thirsty. And payday had them strutting taller through the front door of the Mutineer's Jug. The creeps, the cheats, the antisocial, the louts, the sick and the vulgar. Every bar in Baudette drew a different type of clientele. The Jug got the backwash.

Reg occupied his usual center barstool, his back to the jukebox, at the spot nearest it. A stack of quarters waited next to his coaster. His music was drawing the same accolades it always received.

"Hey asshole, play something from this century," somebody had shouted at him when he came back from loading his songs. "Go home and strangle the swan," said another.

The past had never been kind to Reg, but songs like this gave him a faint confabulation that maybe once, a long time ago, life had had sweetness. Shelley Fabares was singing "Johnny Angel." In the queue were songs each from Loretta Lynn, Patsy Cline and

Tammy Wynette. The Delphic voice of the wronged and the lovesick would have their day.

"Make it a Crown Royal and RC Cola." Reg pushed his empty Bud bottle at the bartender. "I'm bored of beer."

"My, my," the bartender said. "Moving up in the world. Fancy shirt, too." Reg had shaved and put on one of his good shirts from Night & Day. Reg's plan was beginning to coalesce. He was in a mood to celebrate.

Reg was on a roll. He had already gone off on, in no particular order, sniveling religious hypocrites, rich city pricks, drug-dealing welfare niggers and spineless Democrat homos. He raised his glass. "To the good life." The cubes tinkled the edges. "Whatever that might be." The first sip, he let hang in his mouth, nipping at his inner cheek as he moved it from side to side. He let it linger till all the coolness faded. Swallowing, Reg went into the drink with his finger for an ice cube to chew.

Lenny Furr staggered in just then. Not a pretty person, Lenny. You'd think he'd fit in perfectly at the Jug, but Lenny was in a different league. Comparatively, this was a bar full of boy scouts. Lenny was in-grown. Lenny was festering. Lenny was necrotic. No one had seen him in town since they could remember. He mostly kept to his overrun farm. Years ago, kids on the playground would jump rope and sing a song about Lenny Furr's farm.

Lenny Furr
it's for sure
likes the boys
more than girls

Farms in June
whistles a tune
plants the corpses
under the moon

Lenny's eyes were bleary and pink-riddled, the skin beneath them dark-stained, creating the illusion they'd been deep-sunk by someone's thumb. Rocking to a halt, he looked up. The place went silent. He scanned a jagged line across the bar, leaving Reg cold as his eyes swept by. Lenny's glance came back to Reg for a moment, but he didn't seem to notice. He was looking for someone else, or as it turned out, something else. The bathroom. It had been some time since he'd been in the Jug. Lenny smiled as if recognizing a war buddy when his eyes locked on a sign that read Men. The big man lurched forward and headed for the door as if the bar had tipped in that direction.

A murmur came up from the patrons as soon as Lenny disappeared into the bathroom. Those who didn't know Lenny Furr were quickly getting the condensed biography.

"Who in hell's that?" the bartender asked Reg. Reg looked ill. He pushed off his barstool, slipping and catching himself just before his chin struck the bar. Snatching his cane, Reg moved almost athletically to and out the door.

"Holy shit," said the guy sitting to the left of Reg's full drink. "You'd think he'd seen a ghost." His laugh was cut short by the reappearance of Lenny, who weaved up to the bar and took the one open barstool.

"Now didn't I see my dear friend Reginald Cunningham sitting here just one teensy weensy minute ago?" Lenny's squinted through a tiny distance he put between his oversized thumb and forefinger.

The bartender tossed his bar rag over his shoulder, sizing Lenny up. "He was here," he said flatly. "Now he ain't."

Lenny laughed. "I bet he'll be dearly missed by all," his arm sweeping out into the room. "Have we met, sweetheart?"

The bartender stood up a little straighter.

"Would ya lookie here," Lenny said in a light voice. "My little pal left me a present." He scooped up Reg's drink and killed it in one swallow. Lenny was unshaven. His bulbous nose went in one direction and his disheveled crop of gray hair pushed the other.

"You've had enough." The bartender took one step closer, picking up the empty glass. He and Lenny were about the same height, but

Lenny, who was in his late fifties, had at least 50 pounds on him.

Lenny scratched like an animal at the flaky skin on the back of his neck. "I've had more than enough, sweetheart. I've had what's mine and I've had what's his." Lenny's grin showed his teeth, the color of weak coffee. "And if I was 30 years younger, I'd have what's yours." Lenny closed his eyes and took a deep breath through his nose. "I can almost smell ya."

In a flash, the bartender reached across the bar, grabbed a handful of Lenny's shirt and drew back his fist. Lenny smiled, unimpressed. "Help yourself," he said. "I've been hit a lot harder than you can throw."

The bartender shoved him backward. "Get out!"

Lenny stumbled, but righted himself. He stood for a moment, swaying. Patsy Cline sang. There was no other sound in the bar. He tilted his head back, mouth falling open, and looked at the ceiling in a way that made you want to look there, too. "Sometimes the moon takes you places you oughtn't go," he said. "It leads you to town, but it's gone in the morning when you have to get home." Lenny brought his attention to the bar. There was clarity in his face for a moment. Up went his hand with his index finger raised, wagging in warning. "Don't be fooled." Lenny half-tripped, but settled into place. "Don't be fooled 'cause nothin' never lasts." He looked down at himself and began wiping his shirt down with his big hands. Over and over he wiped. Then he laughed and disappeared out the door.

The bartender lit himself a cigarette and poured a shot. "Fucking full moon. What in hell is that prick's story?" he asked of the guy who was on the barstool next to Reg's.

The patron finished a swallow of beer. "Lenny Furr," he said in a cringing voice. "He was a few years ahead of me and Reg in grade school. Never went past that. He was needed on the farm. Back then, you'd get a farm permit to drive when you were 13. Lenny'd get sent in with the truck for supplies and such. Reg and me was in sixth or seventh grade. Lenny had been out a couple years, but he'd still hang around at school once he got them supplies. Guess he missed it, or something. Supposedly he was friends with the school custodian. A rotten apple by the name of Kemp. Forester Kemp. Everyone said that Kemp and Lenny was more than just friends, if you get my drift."

"Just a second." The bartender finished his shot before moving down the bar to take care of a few customers who were bellyaching about glasses so dry they were dusty. "Okay," he said when he got back. "So what do Lenny and Kemp have to do with Reg?"

The man leaned in and lowered his voice. "Not that I give a flying fig about Reg, but rumors go around a schoolyard like gum wrappers. I don't know what happened, if anything. All I know is me and Reg went to school as kids and he was no worse than the rest of us. His folks didn't have much growing up, so to help with the cost of school, Reg worked some around the grounds. Cut the lawn in the spring, shoveled the walk out front in the winter, helped sweep the lunchroom, odds and ends like that. He got to know Kemp, because as custodian, them were his jobs too. And Lenny was hanging around, like I said.

"What I heard, what we all heard, was one afternoon after school—it was in spring, June is what I remember, right before school was to let out for summer—was when it happened. There was this shed, old metal thing back behind school, kinda by this patch of trees, where the lawnmower and rakes and ladders and such was kept. What was said is that Reg was back there after cutting the lawn. Hot day, so he had his shirt off. Kemp was watching him. Lenny too. They went back there after him and Kemp pulled him in that shed. That's what they say. Lenny started a lawnmower so nobody'd hear. Leaned on the door so Reg couldn't get out. Did lookout. Sick sonsofbitches."

The bartender put out his unsmoked cigarette. "Christ. Did the police get 'em?"

"No they did not."

"What do you mean?" the bartender demanded.

"No charges. Reg's old man decided if they pressed charges, then it happened. If they didn't press charges, then it didn't. You think Baudette's small now? You should have seen it back then. Best not to talk about it. Let it die away."

"That's fucked up," the bartender said.

"Yeah. But like I said, just a rumor. Maybe it never happened. Just like Reg's old man said."

The bartender looked at his shot glass, considered refilling it. He tossed it in the soapy water of the sink. "So I've met Lenny. What ever happened to Kemp?"

"The next school year we had a new custodian."

"And what about Reg?"

"You know how Reg is, right?"

"Yeah. Prize-winning shithead."

"My memory's for crap. But he didn't always used to be that way."

The waitress on the far end of the bar hollered for the third time. She held a trayful of empties in front of her Slippery When Wet t-shirt. "I've got dead soldiers here that need reinforcements." She snapped her gum.

"No goddamn wonder," the bartender mumbled, walking her way.

SUMMER 1985

HANNA

She couldn't believe she was kissing him. Or, more accurately, he was kissing her. Thomas slowly pulled back. He looked quizzically at Hanna. "That's a Switzerland kiss," he said.

Hanna blinked, a little lightheaded. "Switzerland?"

"Decidedly neutral," he said, smiling. Hanna had never seen such white teeth on anyone who wasn't a news anchor.

They were in a back booth at an exclusive Philadelphia seafood restaurant called Beach. Everything was high-key white except for the floor: Venetian tile as blue as the Mediterranean. "It's just a little unexpected," Hanna said. "It could be damaging to your reputation as the city's most eligible bachelor to be seen kissing an unsophisticate from the frozen tundra."

"I'll take my chances," Thomas said. He took a bite of the prawn appetizer.

Hanna smiled. "I can hear the lead-in now." Hanna swept a hand in front of her. "Thomas Dickerson's Serendipity."

Thomas looked bewildered. "I'm brain dead on meetings, travel, as well as this nice '45 Liberation Bordeaux. You lost me."

Hanna discreetly took a peek at her watch. "Do you know the definition of serendipity?" A mischievous glint flashed in her eye.

"I'm sure I do, roughly," Thomas sorted through his response. "Serendipity. Um, a discovery, a fortunate discovery, when looking for something else."

Hanna shook her head no, looking quite beautiful as she did. "Serendipity," she said, "is looking in the haystack for a needle, and finding the farmer's daughter."

"Bravo!" Thomas clapped his hands loud enough to make the waitstaff jump and stride his way. He held up his hand. "Well done, Hanna." He continued with light applause. "The farmer's daughter. I'm sure that would send the ratings in the right direction."

Thomas looked over to the waitstaff and raised his arm. When he did, Hanna peeked at her watch again. It was a minute before eleven. "Will you excuse me," Hanna said sliding out of the booth. "I trust they have indoor plumbing here." She smiled at Thomas, as the waiter gave her a hand out of the booth. "Ladies' room?" she asked.

"All the way through, once past the bar, first door on your right, ma'am."

"Please, call me Hanna," she told him. "Ma'am feels like my mom."

"My pleasure, Hanna." The waiter bowed.

"I'll just be a moment." Hanna smiled at Thomas.

He sunk back in the booth. "What ever will I do?" He placed his hand on his chest. "The separation."

Hanna spun and made her way through the dining room. She was wearing her hair high off her neck. Thomas was happy to see he wasn't the only person in the room, male and female, who watched her exit.

SUMMER 1985

Hanna picked up the pace once she left the private rear section of the restaurant, making her way as quickly as she safely could in high heels. She came through the main dining area and approached the all-turquoise glass bar, lit from within with soft waves of light. Behind the bartender, a mirrored backsplash with glass shelves was stocked to the ceiling with every imaginable bottle of high-end liquor. The bar was empty except for one couple practically sitting in each other's laps, arms twined, feeding each other cherries from their drinks.

"Good evening," the bartender said as Hanna approached.

"Hi." Hanna leaned in unpretentiously. "I have a favor to ask," she said with a twinge of dare.

The bartender raised his eyebrows acknowledging that he was game.

Hanna gestured to the large-screened TV behind him. "Is that one of those wide-screen TVs?"

"Yep," the bartender said. "You're looking at the future."

"Could you turn it on? I've never seen one."

The bartender looked to his left and right. "We're only supposed to put it on for Philly sports nights ... but, for a beautiful customer like yourself, I can make an exception."

Hanna charmed him further with a smile.

"Any requests?" he said picking up the remote.

"How about Channel 11."

"The news?" the bartender shrugged. "Your wish is my command."

It had been less than two hours since Kevin stopped Hanna as she left the limousine on her way into the Ambassador Hotel. As a driver, and an employee, he knew he was overstepping in doing so. Mr. Dickerson had always been generous, and Kevin knew from years of conversations with other drivers that he had it good. Certainly, every driver had his stories. Often, there were some you-won't-believe-this-ones shared, in confidence, between professionals. But Kevin always played it by the book. His motto: The front seat is my business and the back seat is Mr. Dickerson's.

But then Hanna Donnovan dropped into his limousine. She was different. When she asked Kevin about himself, it wasn't just to pass the time between looks in her compact mirror; she genuinely cared. When she told him about Singer and her boyfriend and the pros and cons of her station back home, it was because she was conflicted and needed someone to talk to. In the days they had spent together, a trust had formed. Whereas with Mr. Dickerson's other "projects," as he called them, they mostly got what they deserved. Kevin didn't concern himself.

Hanna, though, had him worried. She was smart enough to make her own decisions, but she deserved to know what was up; if she wasn't from out of town, she *would* know. Everyone at the station, and Kevin, were told to be nice. And it was strongly suggested that there was no need to mention the competition down the street. Specifically, the anchorwoman for Channel 11.

What Kevin had told her was simple. Watch the Channel 11 newscast tonight before going further with any of this.

"Wait till you see the picture quality," the bartender told Hanna. "Amazing." The TV blinked on and walked through the channels before settling on 11. Hanna didn't know whether to sit or stand, so she opted to lean on a bar chair.

The music and the news graphics came streaking in. They flashed the faces of the news team, starting with weather, then sports, and when they got to the face of the anchorwoman, Hanna's hand slipped from the bar chair and she stumbled. "Oh my God," she said.

The bartender gave her a most peculiar look, before looking back up at the screen, then back at her. "That's a pretty cool trick," he said. "Being two places at once."

Hanna stared as the anchorwoman read the lead-in to the night's news. It was as though she were looking at her identical twin sister.

SUMMER 1985

"Thank you," she said halfheartedly, walking away from the bartender. "You can turn it off now."

In the bathroom Hanna swayed, feeling like she was going to be sick. So many scenarios ran through her head. *If Thomas wanted an anchor who looked like me, why didn't he just go down the street and get her instead of halfway across the country? Had he tried to recruit the other anchor and failed? Were they lovers once and she'd left him? Was the likeness just a coincidence?* No, Hanna told her reflection. *This is no coincidence. Now what? Confront Thomas? Dye and cut my hair? Did I ever really want the job? Do I still want the job?* Hanna was close to hyperventilating. She wanted to hold Singer. She exhaled deeply. "Get it together girl," she said to a reflection that looked pale and ill. That gave her an idea.

Hanna weaved back toward Thomas, who waited in their alabaster wrap-around booth. As she went, she purposely clipped a table for two. "Sorry," she said as a wine glass toppled on the white tablecloth.

Thomas stood and went to her. "Hanna?" Her hair had partially fallen across her face. Her mascara was running slightly. He took her elbow. "What's wrong?"

"I don't know," she said as he helped her sit. "I was feeling queasy, so I excused myself. I'm sorry." Then she looked at the appetizer. "Are those prawns?"

"I'm not sure." Thomas summoned the headwaiter. "What's in the appetizer?" he insisted.

"It's a dill and prawn pate, sir."

Hanna covered her mouth. "I'm allergic to shellfish," she lied. "I think I'm going to be sick." Hanna gagged.

Thomas was petrified. He was wearing a two-thousand dollar suit. "I should get you back to the hotel."

"I feel so foolish."

"Please," he said, "don't. I should have inquired."

As one waiter apologized repeatedly, Thomas told another to arrange for his driver to pull around back so they could exit discreetly. By the way the request was expedited, Hanna sensed it wasn't the first time Thomas Dickerson and his female companion left by that exit.

Thomas squeezed her hand. "Will you be all right?"

Hanna gave him, Thomas thought, a peculiar look. "I'll be fine. By tomorrow. It'll pass."

They came down the back steps, Hanna holding her stomach, Thomas at her elbow. Kevin stood by, limousine door open, looking very concerned. As Hanna passed him she glanced up and winked.

The limousine snaked through the city, then followed the Delaware River toward the Ambassador. Hanna asked that the moon roof be opened to the fresh air, keeping the act going. Thomas kept his distance. She looked up, the moon hanging so full and bright in the sky. Resting her head back, Hanna wondered if Cory and Singer were looking at it too.

SUMMER 1985

SINGER

Stu handed out the flashlights. "It's blacker than the bottom of your shoe out there with the storm pushin' in. I was just on the weather radio. It's going to be a humdinger."

Each and every customer in the resort had been rousted, their cabins checked in case Singer had wandered off and somehow ended up in the wrong unit. Now they gathered in the lodge, anxious to help.

There were 17 in all waiting on Stu's instructions. Cory wasn't sure he could stand there another second. His brain screamed. Get busy! Get looking! Get going for chrissakes! Yet he knew the last thing the situation needed was people going off willynilly. Teeth clenched, he looked around the lodge dining room. Voices talking in hushed volumes. Feet shuffling. Strangers trying to put on an encouraging smile. All of this had an eerie familiarity about it.

Stu turned over a plastic red-and-white checked tablecloth and told everyone to gather up. He was working fast. "The island is pear-shaped, like this," Stu said, using a pen to draw on the tablecloth's white underside. "The top here faces north. Everyone got their bearings?" Stu raised his arm and pointed north. The group nodded. "The main docks we all use are here. Docks will be the salt shaker." Stu slapped it down where the stem would come out of the pear.

"We're going to go out in groups of twos so none of us gets lost or turns an ankle on a rock and can't get back. Stay close. Teams should be able to see each other's flashlight or hear each other's voices. We don't need one more lost. Remember, this ain't that big of an island. Go briskly, but carefully. Walk straight. You'll hit water. We'll likely hear each other calling, with the size of things, so let's call out, then hush up to hear if Singer is calling back." Stu took a breath and looked up to be sure everyone was with him. Rugged, attentive faces matched his intensity. "When the rain hits, everybody get back here immediately. It's going to come with authority."

Stu drew a square near the top of the pear. "Here's the lodge. It ain't but 200 yards to the water. I want you two to go here, and you two to go here." Stu drew two parallel lines from the lodge to the waterline. "Clear?" The groups nodded. "You guys will have the fish house on your side of the dock, you others have the boathouse. Check 'em."

"Here's Cory and Singer's cabin to the east. They have a higher elevation here so Cory and I will have come all the way around through the woods to get below, then walk the shoreline."

A man raised his hand. "Can I ask a question?"

"Shoot," Stu told him.

"It's for him," he pointed. "Cory, right?"

Cory stepped forward. "Yeah."

"Does your boy sleepwalk? Has this happened before?"

"No," Cory said. Then he hedged. "Well not that I know of. He lives with his mom and I'm not there all the time. But she'd tell me."

SUMMER 1985

Cory felt he was talking in circles. "I'm not sure, but I'd say no."

"Reason I ask," the man continued, "is my youngest did. Just came on. He was a walker for over a year. Put a bell on his doorknob and battened down the house at night. He outgrew it as suddenly as it started. What I learned is you don't want to startle the boy when you find him. His eyes will be open, he may even say a few words, but he's deep asleep. Just walk him gently back to bed. Or if he's a ways out, carefully carry him. Chances are he won't remember a thing in the morning."

Stu asked everybody if they got that. Then he finished drawing up search routes. Darlene and two others would go to the farthest end of the island. She knew every trail, root and deadfall between the lodge and there. "Listen up, people," Stu concluded crisply. "From what I'm seeing and hearing out there, we got about 15 minutes."

Flashlight beams bounced off in all directions. Thunder rolled above and the name Singer was soon echoing from all corners of the island. Cory and Stu strode for the narrow path that wound around the hump of the island and zig-zagged its way down to the waterline. Stu stuck to the path. Cory walked in, among the pines, staying close enough to occasionally see the remains of Stu's flashlight beam sprinkle through the foliage. The wind had gone slack. Lightning bloomed in the distance. The guttural rumble of thunder soon followed. The calm before the storm.

"Singer!" Cory called through his cupped hands. He stood quiet, perspiring. The air was oppressively sticky. "Stu, you there?" Cory stopped and listened. No response. Louder this time. "Stu!"

"This way." Cory heard Stu's faint voice, but it was hard to track as it bounced around in the trees.

"Give me some flashlight!" Cory shouted. Cory looked in the direction he expected Stu's light to come from. Blackness. Then from off his left shoulder, a flicker of light made it through. "Got ya!" Cory said, walking that way.

Cory hiked a few minutes, wondering why he hadn't gotten to the water yet. "Stu?!" he hollered. There was nothing but the sound of his breath pounding in his head. A trace of wind started to find the treetops, giving the branches a kind of nervousness. "Singer!" Cory shouted, staying on course with the light he'd seen.

Stu stood on a rock the size of a den chair. He could feel the hands of foul weather closing around him. "Shit!" he said, the word sounding like water striking a red-hot skillet. He had hollered for Cory a third time, with nothing but silence coming back. Stu shook his head. At the waterline, he slowly scanned the area with his flashlight beam. How long had it been since he heard Cory call for the flashlight? *Two minutes? Five?* Stu looked up, back over his shoulder, at the lights from Cory's cabin set just in from the rock outcropping. His stomach clenched at the thought. *Had the boy wandered off those rocks?* Stu began to pick his way down the sliver of riprap shoreline for the area directly under the cabin. *If he's fallen, it's better Cory not be here to see.*

By the time Cory finally made water, the wind, finding force, swirled in the treetops. Here was the rushing sound of millions upon millions of leaves in motion as trees bowed to one another whispering, it's coming, it's coming. Cory knew he'd gotten off course. The storm was about to unload.

"Damnit," he whispered through clenched teeth, wondering where he went wrong. Lightning flashed over his left shoulder. Cory dropped his head in disbelief. "Dumb shit," he said, realizing now it wasn't Stu's flashlight that he'd followed in this direction, it was a lightning flash. Cory felt his temper rising. The wind pushed. A large harbinger drop of rain splattered on his shoulder. Just as he was about to really get angry with himself, lightning flashed again.

He saw Singer.

The boy had waded knee deep into the lake in his pajama bottoms. Cory put the flashlight beam on the child. Singer stood with his back to Cory, shirtless, with his hands raised halfway skyward.

Cory quickly waded out. A few more drops of rain spit, striking his face. The wind swung behind them, snarling in the treetops.

SUMMER 1985

The water churned. Cory took one of Singer's hands, which was balled in a little fist. "Hey there, buddy," he said calmly.

Singer looked at him, glassy-eyed. "Hi Cory."

"We should be going," Cory told him. Lightning flashed. "It's going to rain."

"Oh. Okay," Singer said peacefully. He turned to walk with him.

"How 'bout I carry you, 'kay pal?"

"Yeah," Singer said.

Cory scooped Singer into his arms just as he began to hear the rain driving across the big lake. It was coming in a wall.

"Can you hold this?" Singer said, opening his fist. Cory looked through the darkness into Singer's small hand. A perfectly preserved stone arrowhead lay in his palm. There was no the time to talk about it. Cory slid it in his pocket and tried to get under the shelter of the treeline before the rain overtook them.

A howling fury of rain struck. But under the canopy of pines it remained mostly dry, dreamlike, protected, almost pleasant. Thunder boomed overhead and lightning lit up the forest floor. Cory trusted his instinct and strode strongly toward the trail he knew he and Stu had taken. He felt the elevation rise, confident he was on track. He had Singer. Nothing else mattered.

Cory's bottom hand, beneath Singer, held the flashlight, making it impossible to aim the beam with any precision. He managed to keep it roughly tracking along the wet ground in front. Had he passed the trail? Would it be a muddy washout? Doubt crept in but Cory drove it aside. Just then, Singer began to hum. It was startling at first, but quickly all doubt vanished.

"You still sleeping good?" Cory asked.

"Yeah. But it's raining. Can you close the window?" Singer asked.

"Sure, bud. I'll have it closed in a minute. You keep sleeping."

Cory sloshed into the lodge, soaked and empty-handed. Darlene had put a stack of towels on the table and the guys were drying off. Stu stepped out of the scrum, looking at Cory. "Nothing?" he asked.

"No." Cory said, water running down his face. "I found him. He's fine. He's in bed. I closed the door to the cabin, but I need to get back in case he gets up again."

"Oh, thank God," Darlene said. Smiles broke out around the room in a collective sigh. She came over to Cory with a dry towel.

Cory looked at all the faces who were awaiting some sort of explanation. "Want to quickly thank everyone," Cory said lifting his hand. "Everything's fine. He was sleepwalking. Sorry to put you through that."

The rain pounded the lodge roof. The trees outside were illuminated by the electricity in the air. The guys shifted uncomfortably in their wet clothes, assuring Cory it was no problem. Cory rubbed his head with his towel. "Stu when you get dry, can you come by? Just for a minute."

"Yeah, sure."

"Thanks again, everyone," Cory said to the entire room. Then he dropped his head and went out the door into the storm.

In his cabin, Cory double-checked on Singer before he dried off and slipped on a t-shirt and a pair of Wisconsin Badger sweats from his playing days. The temperature had dropped a good 15 degrees. With the windows and doors shut tight against the weather, he sat at the small table by the front window.

In wave after wave the wind came, finishing in bursts that shook the structure. The lakeside pines and hardwoods twisted and rocked. Cory jumped when a wet leaf slapped and clung to the rain-splattered window screen, which was peppered with pine needles and the occasional twig.

In front of him, the arrowhead lay on the table. Cory picked it up, his thumb working across the hand-chipped stone surface. It had been tooled sleek, beautiful, only slightly larger than a quarter, with notched corners. Cory set it down and went back to the bedroom again. Singer was sound asleep. Cory had changed the boy's pajama bottoms and worked his arms gently through the sleeves of his top. The temperature continued to nose-dive. He knelt bedside and looked at the boy's face, illuminated by the light from the adjacent room. What would he do without him? Where would he find the purpose to bother with tomorrow?

Stu rapped quickly on the door before ducking in out of the rain. He wore a yellow hooded slicker. "Mother of pearl is it coming down." He got out of his slicker and hung it over a chair.

Cory slipped out of the bedroom and closed the door. "Better start building an ark," he said quietly.

"You ain't a-kidding." Stu nodded toward the bedroom. "Everything good?"

"Yeah." Cory smiled and shook his head. "Peaceful as can be."

"That is scary stuff," Stu said. "I've never been around sleepwalking."

They sat down at the table. Cory stretched. "I think it's the first time for Singer."

"And the last, let's hope." Stu noticed the arrowhead on the table. He whistled lightly as he picked it up. "That's the real deal." He rubbed the stone. "Jasper. Up here the rock is root beer colored." Turning it over a few times in his hand he told Cory that the Ojibwe took a lot of game with these arrow points 150 years ago. Stu looked up from the arrowhead. "Where'd it come from?"

"You not going to believe me when I tell you." Cory said.

Stu raised his eyebrows. "This sounds good. Let me quick bail out the boat before you do." Stu got up from his chair. Cory didn't understand what he meant until Stu went into the bathroom.

"All that running around, I didn't have time to heed nature." Stu sat back down at the table. "So what's the story?" He picked up the arrowhead again.

"When we got split up," Cory started, "it was because I hooked to the southwest thinking I saw your flashlight when it really was lightning."

"Ah, that explains where you went."

"I came out at the waterline, and as sure as I'm sitting here, there's Singer, not 20 feet in front of me. He'd waded out into the water."

"Good Lord," Stu said.

"I did like the father in the lodge said. Tried not to disturb him. He was asleep, but talking some. Pretty groggy. When I picked him up to carry him back, he told me not to lose this. He opened his hand and there was that arrowhead." Cory looked at Stu in a manner that Stu knew he wasn't fooling.

Stu sat forward in his chair. "Where do you suppose he found it?"

"I don't suppose," Cory said. "Singer told me. Damndest thing." Cory frowned. "He said a deer gave it to him."

"Huh?" Stu said. "He must have really been dreaming."

Cory shrugged. "But that's the easy part to believe."

Stu sat back in his chair and rubbed his whiskers. "Well, let's have the rest of it."

"He said the deer's name was Joseph."

SUMMER 1985

WINDOWS

The thunderclap went off like dynamite, shaking the house. Lu Ann jumped clear off the mattress. She'd been sleeping unusually soundly. That second glass of wine had done the trick.

Her arm darted across the bed for Pat. Just as quickly, she knew he wouldn't be there. The rain, driven sideways, blew in through the floor-length curtains that reeled in front of the windows like trapped apparitions. The window screens cut the rain to a mist, where below, a puddle grew on the floor.

Jumping from bed, Lu Ann put her 105 pounds to work wrestling down the large double-hung windows. By the time she was through with the upstairs and downstairs, her heart was pounding, her nightgown was soaked and she had a headache.

The storm walked in from the southwest, the direction of the bean fields. Pat had rolled open the hay door so he and HomeSky could watch from the barn loft. The space wasn't entirely finished, but the loft was set up pretty slick with a sleeping cot, as well as a sitting area with an old beanbag chair that Pat found at a garage sale. Hanging from the rafter timbers was a trouble light for reading. He had built large high-speed fan boxes into the gambrel roof, with one side pushing and the other pulling air through exhaust screens.

"What a light show," Pat said to HomeSky, who was sitting next to him with her legs dangling out the hay door.

"It's beautiful," she intoned, mesmerized by the scope of the oncoming storm wall. "Will you be safe up here?" Lightning rippled across the horizon as she watched for Pat's reaction.

He smiled. "If I see roofing nails getting backed out of the ceiling boards I'll skedaddle."

"I don't know. You're welcome to come in, you know." They looked at one another. HomeSky picked up his hand from the loft floor. It was calloused and one of his fingers had a half moon of purple under a beaten fingernail. "The loft is wonderful. You do wonderful things with these." She turned over his hand. "I love my house. I don't think I've told you. Especially the cupola." Home-Sky's hair was growing out now, black, streaked with silver; it lay on her shoulders. "How is it you remembered I always wanted one when even I had forgotten?"

Pat squeezed her hand. "Some things just stick." He looked outside as the approaching lightning forked to the ground. "You better make your way in. Meadow doesn't like storms. She'll be happy for the company."

"Guess so." HomeSky stood, groaning a little. "That is one hard floor," she said.

"One hundred percent plush plywood." Pat smiled. On the floor next to him was a bowl with three wedges of watermelon. HomeSky had cut it, fresh from the garden patch that Pat put on the south-facing side of the house in the spring. He lifted the Saran Wrap. "Thanks again for the watermelon. You sure this will make me sleep?" Pat was never a great sleeper, but he was having more trouble than usual of late.

SUMMER 1985

"My Granddaddy gave it to us to put us asleep. Called the seeds sleeping pills."

"Why not," Pat said. "I'll take two and call you in the morning." He stood, feeling the labor of the last week in his back. Pat noticed HomeSky staring off wistfully. "Where did you go to just now?" he asked gently.

HomeSky blinked to attentiveness. "Huh? Oh, I was walking barefoot, a little girl in my Granddaddy's watermelon patch. Such a serene place. I'd go out to pick a melon with him when I was too little to carry one back to the house alone. We'd find one and he'd tap a knuckle against the thick rind and say, How do you think all the sun and rain got inside here? It's a very tough shell. And I'd say I don't know. He told me when the Great Spirit made watermelon, He taught it to let good things in, but gave it a rind to protect itself from the bad. When the Great Spirit tasted watermelon, it was so delicious, He decided to teach people the same wise trick." HomeSky shrugged.

Pat looked at her. "I guess we all can learn something from watermelon."

HomeSky nodded. The tension once between them had been dissipating for weeks. In a single breath, the last of it quietly escaped. They stepped and folded into one another, as the storm deferred a moment longer.

Monsignor Kief, of course, worked well in the dark of night. Quickly, he got the last of the downstairs windows closed and latched against the storm. Such dutiful work, he decided, justified compensation. After little negotiation, he secured for himself three—rather than two—scoops of butter pecan ice cream.

In his high-back leather chair in the great room he listened to the storm rock the house around him. He contemplated faith, and took a moment to thank God for the little things and the big things in his life: namely little bits of toffee and a big roof over his head. He thought about happiness, its elusiveness for many, its simplicity for the few. Mick came to mind. The Monsignor had felt an instant connection with Mick when they met in St. Paul. He knew Mick was more than a kind boss to HomeSky, he was a wonderful soul. What a blessing, his coming into her life when he did.

Mick had given HomeSky a puzzle to solve when she left—his happiness triangle. According to Mick, happiness in life was as easy as three words starting with F. Listening to the drumming rain, Monsignor Kief let words shower through his mind. He knew ice cream didn't start with an F, but fudge did. Faith was one of the Fs, he was sure of it. When HomeSky was staying with Monsignor Kief, she would include his triangle attempts along with her letters to Mick. In return letters, there was usually a P.S. telling the Monsignor to keep trying.

Monsignor Kief's spoon searched the bowl, hoping for some sweet castaway, but no such luck. His bowl sat on his lap. Words made their audition. Freedom. Family. Friends. Fun. Fame. Failure. Felicity.

For some, storms leave them anxious. For Monsignor Kief, he was left reflective, his eyes closed in thought. We all have our moments to come into another person's life. What we do with that chance is what makes us who we are.

What awoke the Sheriff, be it the pane-rattling explosion of overhead thunder or the pup's yelping from his kennel in the mudroom, was hard to discern. Half asleep, the Sheriff sat up, tossed off his bed sheet, and stepped down hard and fast on his walking cast.

"Damn a ham!" he hissed, a white flash jolting through him. Or was that just lightning? he wondered, as another flash lit up the room. He hobbled to the mudroom, careful with his cast around doorframes. "Hey-ya, Private," he soothed. "I got ya boy." The Sheriff unlatched the kennel and Private scampered up his arms like ascending a ship's ramp. He pressed into the Sheriff's nightshirt, trembling, a 10-pound bag of Jell-O. "I know this ain't the weather for it, but we have to make for the weeds." He gathered up the leash and umbrella from the closet. Private was landing plenty of licks despite the Sheriff's best effort to bob and

SUMMER 1985

weave. "Easy, scrapper. Just a storm rolling through. No need to wet the both of us."

Private was trained to do his business in the back yard by the bushes. The Sheriff set him down, holding the umbrella over the two of them. Private looked up submissively at the hulking figure holding the strange object over his head, compounded by the booming thunder. He made no progress in the way of bladder relief.

"Do your business," the Sheriff repeated. Usually this command was followed to the letter. "No time for stage fright." The message seemed to get through. Private got on with it.

"Good business," the Sheriff praised. He scooped up Private, scratching his rain-splattered head.

"Let's get those windows shut up," he said, back inside. "We should thank our lucky stars we didn't get sizzled like sausages out there." The pup followed on the Sheriff's heal, staying close. The howling wind had swung to the north so the Sheriff attended to those windows first. While rolling in the front casements, he looked through the rain, across the street to Kitty's house. The deluge cut visibility, but he could make out a backlit figure in the front room, apparently busy with the same activity. The shadow in the distance seemed to momentarily stop. Had they seen each other through the storm? A pang of sadness knotted in his chest. "You have an oversized mouth to go along with the rest of you," he chided himself. The Sheriff looked down at Private, whose tail twitched upon eye contact. "Boy, next time I open my trap in front of Kitty, you have my full permission to tear off one of these toes." He nudged the pup with his cast. Private scooted closer yet. When the Sheriff looked back across the street, the figure in the window was gone, as if it had never been there.

Radio Voice knew the storm was coming. He had heard multiple reports of its size and impending arrival on his transistor radio, and had repeated them in perfect stentorian voice to the cashier at Mark's Convenience Mart. Radio Voice had purchased six Nut Goodies. Rations. Just in case the storm lasted for days.

Radio Voice loved candy bars. He loved Pat. He loved Singer. He loved his radio. He thought about all that he loved when storms howled outside the window of his little apartment. He even loved his mother and his father. He remembered only the good. All the bad, forgotten. Forgiveness can come easy. Say goodbye to the nightly battles, the shrill voices, the baritone anger roiling from the kitchen, flung off hallway walls into his bedroom. Long forgotten, the young boy, hands clamped over his ears, scrambling from bed to find the radio upon his desk. To climb back under the covers. To dial in a station. To set the volume loud enough to find immunity from the roar. Here was salvation. And from salvation, forgiveness. So it was, when the storm pounded at the walls of the apartment building, Radio Voice rose, in small quick steps, put on the bathroom light, took his radio off the desk, slipped back into his bed, warm, found a station playing music, turned it up, slid it under his pillow, and went blissfully back to sleep.

Meadow was comforted to see HomeSky heading for the house just in front of the rain. From her bedroom window, she watched HomeSky stride across the farmyard, undeterred, her hair and shirt and pants pressed back by the wind. "I'm so glad she's helping us, aren't you, B?" Meadow asked. The B was short for boy, which the ultrasound had confirmed.

The adoption was set. Once HomeSky was issued her Certificate of Degree of Indian Blood by the Bureau of Indian Affairs, everything fell in place. There had been concern about her age, and the fact that HomeSky was unwed, but the blood degree trumped all. Even the occasional mention of the incident with the farmhouse was kept out of the case file. She was Ojibwe. She would not try to wash the child's face white nor rob him of his culture nor defile his heritage. That's what mattered to the council. For years, thousands of Native American children were taken from families, displaced from their tribes, and anglicized. After looking the other way, finally the federal courts stepped in.

So now, after months of worry, Meadow could relax. Her child would have a good home. Off the Rez. And she would remain in his life. The relief was enormous. But why could she not truly relax?

Meadow watched the storm tramp over the cropland. Her hands left the windowsill and went to the swell of her stomach. Something gnawed. Something unfinished. It wasn't concern over her old man. If he were to come out of his coma, he could no longer be a threat to anyone. A home here at the farm was as good as any outcome she could have dreamt for. Was it the uncertainty of her future? Was it HomeSky and Pat and the uncertainty between them? Or was it as simple as the fact that storms frightened her?

They had since she was a little girl not big enough to close the windows, not knowing where her parents were, not expecting them back anytime soon.

"You up there?" HomeSky called from the landing, giving Meadow a start.

"Up here," Meadow said. "Closing windows."

"Okay, hurry down. I'll get the ones down here."

How beautiful those words were to her. Fellowship. As the first heavy drops of rain hit the widow in front of her, Meadow felt tears fill the bottoms of her eyes. She looked across at the horizon, her sightline blurred. Be it rain that altered her view, or tears, it made no difference. Someone waited for her downstairs, closing windows, keeping the storm out.

The Barcalounger was in full recline. Reg's chin had drooped to his chest, his monthly bills spilled out across his stomach and lap. A nasal snore mixed in the room with the last trace of cigarette smoke winding up from the butt that had burned itself out in the astray. On the same end table, a refilled drink went untouched, the melted ice making it rheumy.

Reg's hand hung off the chair. Below, an open cereal box lay on the dirty carpet. Reg kept his bills stuffed in an empty Frosted Flakes box. He paid some of them on time, others not. He liked mail. After a few notices, he'd send the bastards their money.

The hard rain was over, transitioning to a steady roof beat. The windows were pushed closed and a saucepan sat on a kitchen chair under a ceiling leak. The drops came slower now, where earlier they had filled the pan. Under the gathering weight, each drop pulled away from the ceiling, freefalling, striking with enough gravity to send as much water out of the pan as was captured. Splashed water beaded on the vinyl chair cover. Over. And over. And over. Some things caught go uncaptured.

SUMMER 1985

AIRPORT

The airport was more like a mausoleum. Those here at this godforsaken hour looked deceased—stretched out prostrate across multiple chairs, slumped over in seats, propped up by posts, mouths dangling open.

Hanna had come by cab, slipping out of the Ambassador by dark, hoping to standby on a 6:15 a.m. flight. She was no sneak, so this decision, multiplied by the 4:30 a.m. wake-up call, left her with a fuzzy surreal sense of being someone else. Nonetheless, she heard herself give her name to the gate agent so there she was, checked in number one on the standby list.

Home. Such a treasure, that word; Hanna wished to put it in a vault and never again jeopardize its security. How in contrast to the word's sweetness was the bitter vending machine coffee. She was careful not to spill as she took a seat in the gate area, across the aisle from a man with the remains of some variety of muffin on his shirt, reading glasses crooked on his nose, a rooster tail of hair spouting up, snoring. Never before could she remember so completely wishing to be home.

Hanna had left an envelope for Kevin with the hotel desk clerk who would see to it he got it when he arrived later that morning. Her letter was almost two pages long. Hanna wrote of her gratitude for having met him. She called it fate. She said she found comfort that his story of youthful restlessness paralleled hers. She thanked him for the tip about the other anchorwoman. At first it angered her, she wrote, before turning comical. It was an apt reminder of the oftentimes extreme shallowness of her profession. Whether her invitation to join Philly 3 was a ratings ploy or payback or twenty-fifth floor gamesmanship, it didn't really matter. Their resemblance certainly was no coincidence and there was no need to dissect it further. By the same token, she assured Kevin, that wasn't the main reason she decided to turn down the job and return home. Hanna explained that there was something illuminating in the full moon last night—not so much about the character of Thomas Dickerson, but about her character. It was time to embrace who she was. To quit worrying about who she might be. Hanna asked Kevin to give Thomas Dickerson the envelope that accompanied his. She recommended that Kevin say nothing of their friendship, or their conversation concerning the other anchorwoman. She assured Kevin that her note to Mr. Dickerson succinctly thanked him for the opportunity, praised him on his staff and station, but told him her heart was back in, as Thomas like to call it, fly-shit Minnesota where the only thing lower than the Arbitron rating was the windchill.

"Where you headed?" the Muffin Crumbs man across from Hanna asked. He had roused from his catnap and straightened his glasses and hair.

Hanna realized she too must have nodded off. "Oh," she said. "Going home."

"Me too," he said like he really understood what she meant. And then, politely leaning forward, he added in confidence, "You were snoring a little bit just now."

All Hanna could do was laugh.

SUMMER 1985

COOKIES

Morning entered bright and musical through the cream-colored bedroom drapes. Meadow woke up hungry. Big surprise. But rather than heading straight downstairs to stick her head in the refrigerator, she went over to the guitar in the corner of her room. It sat in a stand that was as beautiful as anything Meadow had known. Pat made it when she was in the hospital. He'd gone to the woods to find the right diameter pine branches, which he cut and debarked and finished before wrapping leather straps at the contact points so the guitar wouldn't get scratched. To hold something the right way was what this gift meant to her. No small thing.

The day behind the storm had come in unseasonably cool. Meadow took up her guitar and sat on the edge of her bed in her swim team sweatshirt and stretchy shorts. It's not easy playing when six months pregnant. Your arms need to grow longer. No matter. Meadow was happy.

SINGER

"When a person is happy the music suffers," Meadow said to B. She reached behind the body of guitar and touched her belly. "When you rub happy and songwriting together, there's no spark." She strummed a few pretty chords. "Can you hear that in there, B?"

Opening her notebook, humming, Meadow listened for any inspiration that her muse might grant. *Chocolate.* Meadow stopped playing, ready to give in to the craving. Then a song sat down next to her, took up her hands and played. Thirty minutes later, she had written, scratched out, and rewritten a song. Her first happy song.

9 a.m.

I'm eating cookies at 9 a.m.
I'm eating cookies at 9 a.m.
I'm eating cookies at 9 a.m.
Yes I am
I am
I am

I'm eating cookies at 9 a.m.
I'm eating cookies at 9 a.m.
I'm eating cookies at 9 a.m.
Yes I am
I am
I am

Troubles left me not long ago
I sent them away or let them go
I'm wanted here I've come to know
And that's the start I need

All that black I left behind
Anger and beer and rooms unkind
There's light here yes I've come to find
And that's the start I need

SUMMER 1985

I'm eating cookies at 9 a.m.
I'm eating cookies at 9 a.m.
I'm eating cookies at 9 a.m.
Yes I am
I am
I am

Find your place and run there fast
What happened then is in the past
There's goodness here so make it last
And that's the start I need

You can hide there or make a stand
The good will sing the bad be damned
I've allowed myself to take a hand
And that's the start I need

I'm eating cookies at 9 a.m.
I'm eating cookies at 9 a.m.
I'm eating cookies at 9 a.m.
Yes I am
I am
I am

I'm eating cookies at 9 a.m.
I'm eating cookies at 9 a.m.
I'm eating cookies at 9 a.m.
And that's
the start
I need

She set the guitar in the stand. How many times had it slid and banged onto the floor of her old bedroom?

"To hold something the right way," she whispered. Gratitude mixed with every breath. Meadow pulled back the drapes to the daylight. Below, HomeSky and Pat walked past the barn and followed the fenceline out around the hay field. They didn't touch, but they were closer. Their bodies moved comfortably. The land had taken in the rain. And the sun showed anyone who was looking how beautiful life can be.

SUMMER 1985

STORM BALL

Cory awoke, yanked upright by panic. Singer's bed was empty. Then it registered. It was his bed that stood unslept-in; Cory had decided to squeeze in with Singer for the night. At his side, the boy warmly slept. The old bed frame did everything possible to awaken Singer as Cory eased himself out. The boy hardly stirred.

Walking to the edge of the deck to urinate, Cory scanned the property. Downed branches testified to the energy in last night's storm, but to look at today was to disbelieve in any such occurrence. A blue sky spread high like polished glass above the points of Norway and White pines. A cool kiss of wind blew out of the west. The birds lit and sang and moved in small alert clusters. It felt more like September than August.

"Cory?" Singer's voice came from the cabin.

"Coming, bud" he said, hustling through the screen door.

Singer sat up in bed. He gave the morning his best stretch, little arms reaching straight up ending in fists. Tallow-colored curls swallowed his face. "Is it time for breakfast?"

"Are you hungry?" Cory asked enthusiastically.

"So hungry I could eat three whales, a moose, and 100 blueberries."

"Wow. Did you sleep well?" Cory watched closely for Singer's response.

"Yep," he chimed, nonchalantly. He kicked his feet over the side of the bed and slid to the floor.

"Any dreams?"

"Huh?" Singer said.

Cory helped Singer put on a Duluth Bulldogs sweatshirt. "Did you have any dreams? That you remember?"

"Nope. What are we gonna do today? Can we go lumberjacking?"

"Sit on the bed a minute," Cory said. "Here," he underhanded a balled up pair of socks to Singer, which he dropped. "You have to look them in," Cory instructed. "Try again." Singer caught the socks this time.

"Can you help me?" Singer asked.

"You do socks. I'll help with shoes."

Cory watched Singer, looking for any sign, any recollection of last night's adventure. Pants on, shoes on, Singer was ready to bolt up to the lodge. He knew the way and liked the freedom of taking the trail alone.

"Can I go?" Singer asked, anxiously.

"One minute, bud. Come sit with me." Cory was at the kitchen table. He patted his knee. Singer ran over and jumped up. "Do you remember the rain last night?"

"It rained last night?" Singer said. He shrugged his shoulders.

Cory slid the arrowhead on the kitchen table over to Singer, watching for his reaction.

"Whoa," the boy's eyes widened. "Cool. What is it?"

"It's an arrowhead. The Indians who lived on this island a long, long time ago attached it to the end of an arrow. For hunting."

"Can I feel it?" Singer asked.

"Sure thing. Careful though."

Singer's little hand took up the arrowhead. "How'd they make it?"

"That's stone," Cory said. "They shaped it with a special tool. Feel the little chips on the surface? Then they sharpened the point with a bigger stone." Singer tested the sharpness with his finger. His eyes indicated that it was sharp.

"Where did you get it?" Singer wanted to know.

"Do you know?" Cory asked, playfully.

"Nope." Innocently, Singer shook his head.

Cory hadn't thought things through beyond that question. He was stuck. He didn't want to lie to Singer. He himself could hardly believe where it came from, but certainly he wasn't going to bring that up now. "It's a surprise. I'll tell you later."

"When later?" Singer wanted to know.

"Later with Stu," Cory stalled.

"Why with Stu?"

Cory had to smile. The boy was nothing if not inquisitive, a trait that would serve him well. "Because Stu is the best storyteller, right?"

"Oh. Yeah. Let's eat." Singer slid down off Cory's lap.

"Should we let magic bear enjoy the sunny day?" Cory picked the stuffed animal off the chair. "Maybe we let him look out the window."

Singer loved the idea. He carefully placed the bear on the windowsill, facing out. "There," he said. "Now he can see everything outside." Singer turned and went out the door like a shot. "See you up there," he shouted.

SINGER

Cory turned the arrowhead over in his hand. He reached back and felt the stone behind his ear. "This is getting kinda ... strange," he said to the magic bear, almost as if he expected a response. Then he set the arrowhead on the sill next to the bear. "Wherever the river takes you," he said, quoting one of Joseph's favorite sayings.

Stu was sitting with Singer on side-by-side stumps outside the lodge. Cory came up the trail. "Mornin'," Stu said.

"Beautiful out," Cory said.

"Can I tell him?" Singer asked, almost bursting.

"Go for it," Stu said, giving Singer a conspiratorial nod.

Singer sat up straight. "Okay. What do you call a cow that ... um," Singer tried to recall the word.

"Twitches," Stu whispered.

"Yeah. What do you call a cow that twitches?"

Cory rubbed his chin. "Hmm? Cow that twitches. I don't know."

"Beef jerky!" Singer blurted.

Cory laughed. "Did Stu tell you that?"

Singer nodded.

"Look what I made you," Stu said to Singer, reaching into the pocket of his plaid shirt.

"A bunny!" Singer reached for the dollar bill that was folded to resemble a rabbit. "How'd you do that?"

Stu smiled. "It's a money bunny. I'll show you how to make one after breakfast. How 'bout I keep him in his burrow till then?" Stu patted his pocket.

Singer nodded, taking Cory's hand. What an exciting start to the day. A new joke and bunny made out of a dollar.

"Before breakfast," Stu said, "I think we should go down to the lake and see if any treasures washed in from the storm."

"Treasures?" Singer said, bright-eyed.

"Sometimes the wind blows giant fish up on shore. Or big pieces of driftwood. Even other stuff. "

"Let's do it," Cory said.

"Yea!" Singer said, leading the way, skipping down the path, allowing Cory a few words with Stu.

"He doesn't remember a thing. Not the walking or the storm. I showed him the arrowhead. Nothing."

"Where'd you tell him the arrowhead came from?" Stu asked.

Cory chuckled. "I said you had a secret story about that."

Stu raised his eyebrows. "Did you now."

"C'mon!" Singer said, waving them on, halfway down the hill to the docks.

"He's a palomino pony," Stu smiled.

Cory waved back. "What do you make of it? I mean, how does something like that happen?"

"I guess it depends who you ask. Maybe he picked it up at the water's edge," Stu said. "Or maybe it happened just as he said." Stu and Cory shared a long look.

"Hey, what's that?" Singer yelled from the dock.

The men quickened their pace. Singer stood on the pier with one hand over his eyes to block the sun. The finger of his other hand was pointing to open water.

"Out there," Singer continued.

They stood on the end of the dock, looking through the hard glare on the water. The sun was low, shimmering on the surface like millions of tiny flashbulbs. Something was floating about 100 yards out. "What is it?" Singer insisted.

"Holy moly," Stu said to Singer. "Go get the net!"

"Huh?" Singer said.

"We're going out in the boat."

"Where's the net?" Singer wanted to know. He was so excited his feet were doing little more than moving in place.

"In the boathouse. I'll start up the boat."

"Wait for me!" Singer hollered as he ran down the pier to the boathouse as fast as his legs would carry him.

SINGER

The three of them throttled slowly away from the dock, Singer with the net at the ready. Stu didn't close the distance between the little boy and the mystery too quickly.

"What do you think it will be?" Singer's voice rose in anticipation. As they moved toward the floating object, Cory firmly held the back of Singer's pants as the boy leaned over the gunwale.

"Get that net ready," Stu instructed with mock seriousness. "We don't want to miss it."

Under the generous sun, the boat glided forward to a small ball, the size of a cantaloupe, bobbing on the lake's surface. The wet rubber surface shimmered in the light, rolled by gentle waves. It was blue with a red band and yellow stars. Where it came from, God only knew.

"Got it!" Singer said, almost going overboard. Water dripped off the net as he swung the ball into the boat.

Stu brought the throttle back to neutral. He opened his mouth in amazement. "Do you know what you've got there?"

"No," Singer said, eyes locked on Stu.

"That's a storm ball."

"Really?" The boy looked down at the ball in the net.

"Go ahead and take it out." Stu and Cory smiled at one another, watching Singer carefully free the ball from the netting.

"Wow," Singer said.

"Storm balls are very good luck, according to lake legend."

Singer looked up at Stu. "How did it get here?"

"We had a big storm last night. Legend says that every storm has a good side and bad side. The bad side comes through first, mean and damaging. But the good side comes after and has a silver lining. It leaves something good. An offering. You have to look for it. Sometimes it takes years to find."

Singer hugged his ball. "A storm ball," he said. "Can I keep it?"

"Yep. You found it, which means it was left for you." Stu's brow creased in thought. He tipped back his cap. "The original Indian words are more poetic than I'll do justice to, but they translate something like, 'In the storm's aftermath, what is swept across the water is not lost, it's found.'"

Singer didn't catch a word of what Stu said after hearing he could keep the ball. Which was fine. Because it was Cory that Stu looked at as he spoke. Rather than sorting through Stu's words in his analytical way, Cory watched the boy hugging his small treasure. The water had come to him in peace now, and he knew what he would do.

SINGER

Irrevocably, a force strikes, setting off a fracture.
But a fracture rarely takes a straight line.
Rising and falling, jagged angles tear along the path of least resistance.
Every turning point directed by the strength of what would not be splintered, would not be broken nor separated.

BOOK Three

AUTUMN 1985

For every action there is an equal and opposite reaction.

PART ONE

September

DULUTH

Cory's first official week of teaching high school ended with the 2:50 bell. Algebra II, his final class, was an honors subject for advanced students. They were bright, surely, but at this early stage, overmatched by the material, as well as Cory's unblinking pace. Keep your chins up, he encouraged, before providing enough weekend homework to assist them in the act.

Books slapped shut and the classroom emptied to groans. Except for two students, who lacked for weekend plans. Their motto: what fun is getting *all* your homework done on Friday night?

To watch a high school clear out on a Friday afternoon is to see something done faster than you'd believe possible by teenagers. A synchronized melee of voices lifted higher by weekend-spiked possibilities, the production line of crashing steel locker doors, the shrieking of tennis shoe bottoms pivoting for the exits. Fifteen minutes ago, these kids could hardly lift their heads. The final bell is a defibrillator on the dead of a Friday afternoon classroom.

Cory was done in. The weeklong combination of getting out of bed at 5:30 a.m. and the undertow of mental fatigue had taken its toll. In those first days, on top of the work, stands a fear of not connecting with the students and of not being fully prepared for teaching's responsibilities. *What if I fail?* Wresting yourself free of those early uncertainties knocks it out of you.

With his feet above the scratched drawer in front of him, Cory pushed back, balanced precariously on the back two legs of the desk chair. He closed his eyes to challenge his balance further—one of many such self-imposed physical and mental tests he'd administer throughout each day.

"Sleeping on the job?" a colleague asked, entering Cory's classroom. Cory kept his eyes shut, trying first to guess who had dropped by.

"O'Brien," he said, anticipating it was the English teacher. He opened his eyes to find he was correct.

"Jamie," the teacher corrected. "Last names are too impersonal for occupational use. Unless you're carrying cement blocks on a construction site."

Cory let his chair set down. "Maybe. But I don't make you to be a Jamie. What do you guys say in creative writing? It has the wrong timbre. O'Brien. Now that sounds like you."

"Suit yourself. But this creative writer says we go down to Grandma's and drink like Hemingway. See what that does to your timbre."

Cory puffed out his cheeks, thinking. "I'm going to have to take a rain check."

Jamie was a third-year teacher and he rarely missed an opportunity to remind Cory of his veteran status. All in all a good guy. Just a bit logorrheic for Cory's taste. "Come on, rookie. It's Friday. Happy hour with half-price beers made happier by half-price

AUTUMN 1985

burgers. There'll be a big group. Lisa's coming." His tone hinted at better than average possibilities.

Cory made it appear to be a hard decision. "Next time," he promised.

O'Brien frowned. "Famous last words." He rapped his knuckle on the wooden doorframe he leaned on. "Take it from a procrastinating novelist." Detecting no wiggle in Cory's final decision, he quick-stepped out of the doorway, footfalls swallowed by the hard marble hallway.

Cory surveyed the empty room, deeply breathing it in. There was the good smell of chalk meets body odor meets old textbooks meets hint of new-school-year paint. He'd left the white walls mostly empty thus far, not much for decorating. For one thing, he wasn't sure how much of himself he cared to display, and for another, he had acquired so little to put up. He had his freshman year Badgers hockey poster, the year they won the national championship. That was a collector's item, not as much for the season's accomplishment, but that was the year Joseph gave all the players plastic hillbilly teeth to smile with for the photo. Somehow, Cory preferred it in a cardboard tube. Or at least he always had. Maybe he would bring it in. He'd think about it. As it stood, the wall only held a Don't Drink and Drive poster that had gone up in every classroom. It was part of a new federally sponsored effort to reduce teen deaths on the road.

Cory needed some alone time. Students. Faculty meetings. Group lunches. It was baptism by fire. He had snuck off with his lunch to the school's front steps a few times, only to be told that's against policy. All the mingling and participation was working muscles Cory hadn't much developed. But he was willing to try, which is step one.

He rubbed his face. One more brain exercise, he promised himself, before he could call it a week. He sat up straight, focused on the Don't Drink and Drive poster and turned it into an anagram. *Dr Dan divot dinner.* Not bad, he thought, but a leftover k. *Rank dividend torn.* Close again, but one d short. Then Cory smiled, pleased to see he had some brainpower in reserve. He revised the anti-drinking slogan allowing for one additional e, but making it more befitting a math classroom: *Don't Drink and Derive.*

With that he got his things together. He snapped off the classroom lights, looking back at the empty desks, thinking of how far he'd come.

"Come here, Sir Dragon Slayer." Hanna opened her arms. She was still making up for lost Singer hugs. "Your princess calls."

Singer, caped in an old robe, used a cardboard tube from a roll of paper towels as his looking glass. "I don't spy any evil dragons." He slid the tube through a snug belt loop in the robe. "I'm coming." On his imaginary horse he galloped over to Hanna, who stood in the entryway.

She got down and rocked the boy in her arms. "There's my prince," she whispered.

Singer pulled away. "Mom, don't smush my sword."

"I thought it was your spyglass," Hanna said, touching the cardboard tube.

"Sword too," Singer informed her. "What am I doing tonight?" he asked, seeing she looked ready to go to the station. "Is Cory coming over?"

"He sure is," she said. "He'll pick you up at Ms. Kortuem's when he's done after school. I've got the news tonight, but then you know what?" Hanna looked at Singer for the answer.

"Weekend off!" Singer's lilting pitch captured the pure meaning of the words.

"Remember where we're going?"

"To visit Pat and Sheriff Harris."

"And where does Pat live?"

"On a farm with no cows."

"That's right," Hanna said "And he lives with two friends you haven't met named Meadow and HomeSky."

Singer giggled. "Those aren't real names."

"They are," Hanna told him. "They have different names. Just like you."

A light bulb went on just then for Singer. "I'll like them," he said, surely.

"I know you will," his mother agreed.

"And we get to sleep at Pat's farm?"

"Yep. He says he has lots of room."

"And we'll play with the Sheriff's puppy."

"We will."

"And play and play with nothing to do all day," Singer added joyfully.

"All day," Hanna said.

Back when they were making plans to all get together at the farm, Cory had put Singer on the phone with the Sheriff who told him he could play with his new pup if Singer would first play him a song on the piano. Cory sat on the piano bench with the receiver in his hand while Singer played *Rain, Rain, Go Away*. The Sheriff told him that now a sunny day for their get-together was a shoo-in.

"Do we not go to Sheriff's because there are bars on his house like a jail?"

"No, no," Hanna assured him. "His house is regular."

"Why are there jails?" Singer asked, suddenly serious.

"Oh, that's a talk for another time. Mom needs to get to work so tomorrow there will be nothing but fun." Hanna took full audit of Singer's wardrobe. "Are you wearing that to Ms. Kortuem's?"

Singer looked at his mother as though she must be crazy. "Yes. Her house is *full* of dragons."

The old makeup mirror was somewhat clouded on the right side, so sitting slightly left in the chair offered Hanna a sharper reflection. She unconsciously smiled as she worked her hair and makeup in the small dressing room of her news station, thinking about the fashionista makeup artists she watched flitting and primping about the anchors in Philadelphia. No wrinkle or blemish was safe. They used an airbrush. Generously. The older anchors called it their security blanket. Oh well. How happy Hanna was to be here, alone with her thoughts, in a cramped little room used by all the on-air women reporters and anchors.

Hanna's mirror had three descending light bulbs along each side, but the top-right socket didn't work. Someone, years ago, had glued the face of Greta Garbo on the bulb. Henceforth, this makeup station was fondly known as the Garbo mirror. When Hanna was promoted to weekly anchorwoman, she got the Garbo mirror. Her only addition was a four-by-six snapshot of Singer on Cory's shoulders wedged in the lower-right corner. Looking at it now, she kissed her finger and touched the image.

With her hair pulled back in a headband, she put the finishing touches on her mascara. Hanna paused, thinking about how surprisingly gracious Thomas Dickerson was when he got her note after her abrupt departure. She had explained that Duluth was the best place for her and her "little person," as Thomas chose to call Singer. Thomas rarely asked about her son, and when he did, he avoided using his name. Hanna had written that her rush to the airport was not so much fleeing from Philadelphia as a race back to her son, and the life she'd made with him. The thought of further delay, she had said, made her … homesick, she finally wrote, after holding the pen above the page for minutes, unable to produce a more apt word. She thanked him for the opportunity, never mentioning anything about the other anchorwoman she'd seen.

Cory and Singer had had a wonderful time with Darlene and Stu, but when Hanna learned of the sleepwalking incident, she was terrified. Immediately, she talked with her pediatrician, who had little more to offer than it could be a one-time occurrence or a phase he's going through or the beginning of a lifetime of such nightly patrols. Take special care to keep doors closed and locked after bedtime, monitor his behavior, and we'll go from there, she was told. It gave her little comfort as she and Cory followed his instructions precisely. In the three weeks since returning from

AUTUMN 1985

Lake of the Woods, there had been no recurrence, thank God, which opened up time for her to dwell on the origin of Singer's arrowhead and his mention of Joseph. These mysteries were outside the realm of a physician. The only person she could think to consult was Monsignor Kief. Cory agreed it would be good to talk to him, and Pat as well. These were among the reasons motivating a trip to the farm.

That incident aside, Cory came back from Lake of the Woods brighter, less stolen by preoccupation. Hanna was rendered speechless when he sat her down and said that if she wanted to go to Philadelphia, he'd like to go with her. He'd leave his commitment to the school and the athletic department, walk away from the cabin and the lake and go to the big city. He said you never know until you try, before taking up her hand and saying—out loud—that nothing was more important than Singer and her. Or had he put their names in the opposite order? It shouldn't matter—it didn't matter—nonetheless, she found herself wondering about the order. Order be damned, she resolved. This was a breakthrough. Cory Bradford had reached out and trusted something uncertain between the two of them.

Hanna told him how much it meant to hear his words, but she too had come to a conclusion during their brief separation: home was here. Home was with Singer and Cory and schools she knew and neighbors she waved to and grocery stores where people shook her hand and asked if she'd autograph their shopping bag and weekends off and peers who admired her and Neilsen ratings that didn't outrank family. Life was too precious to put on hold while a career bullied every personal decision. She was lucky, Hanna told Cory, to have built what she built and have this opportunity, now. She recognized her good fortune and ran back to it with open arms.

There was a sharp knock on the dressing room door. "Fifteen minutes, beautiful," the producer said as he passed.

Hanna snapped back to the here and now, finding her reflection. "Yikes. Not so much yet," she joked, shaking her hair out of the headband. "Look at that hair." She reached for the hairspray. "Cat stuck in tree; story at six."

As she tried to make something of her hair, her hand stopped mid-task. There was the snapshot of Cory and Singer in the corner of the mirror. It all crystallized for her as she remembered a fable from her youth: A dog happily carries his bone to the water. Upon seeing his reflection, he greedily opens his mouth, trying to snatch the bone in the reflection. In so doing he loses what he had to the bottom of the lake. Hanna took in her reflection, and again, the photo. She closed her lips before applying her lipstick.

Cory had his last sip of coffee. The gritty cold caused him to think twice before swallowing. Wincing, he returned the empty styro to the cup holder. The engine light of the old pickup had diffused, slowly receding into the dashboard panel after he shut off the engine. He left the keys where they were as he stepped out into the street.

Ms. Kortuem lived in a wonderful little house. All she had ever wanted was a front door and a few windows. She'd grown up in an apartment. For her, a multi-story facade with countless windows was nothing to aspire to.

Baking and children were her passions. What sweeter duet, she'd ask, to make a person joyous to be alive? Typically she'd pose the question while holding a decorative tray of just-out-of-the-oven treats in your direction. Your expected response was an affirmative nod and a reach. To not reach, to decline her baked goods, was to earn a look like you just tracked dog business across her living room carpet. Oh, take two, she'd say, behind a slight jab with the tray. The first one sets an expectation, she'd wink. The second brings you back.

As Cory came stiffly up the walkway he made two mental notes. Now that he was running five days a week to get ready to coach his JV hockey team, he shouldn't drive without an icepack. And, second, since he didn't have a trusted mechanic in Duluth, it was time to find the cause of that engine light. Supple's Service Station

AUTUMN 1985

in Baudette was reliable. He would try to get his truck over to a mechanic this weekend. He didn't want to be hauling Hanna and Singer around with a possible engine issue.

Ms. Kortuem turned over Singer, but not before Cory accepted three jam-filled sugar cookies dusted in powdered sugar. Yummy? she asked, before Cory could get the flaky perfection swallowed. He gave it a powdery thumbs up.

"What should we have for dinner?" Cory asked. Singer was swinging his backpack as they made their way to the truck. What a beautiful mid-September evening. Peak colors were a few weeks off but the maples were aflame in covetous shades.

"Homemade pizza," Singer said. "Half and half."

A gust of wind blew, sending leaves parachuting out of a tree. "A quarter for every leaf you catch," Cory challenged, pointing up. Singer tossed his backpack and his little legs took him onto the grass, catching the first one, but the second one he chased danced and swerved, falling to the ground before Singer dropped on top of it. "Got one," he said excitedly. "I'll save it for Mom."

"Make sure not to overrun those guys," Cory coached. "Focus. The eyes catch first, then the hands."

"Look. It's pretty," Singer said, breathing hard, holding his prize toward Cory.

Cory continued. "Look for the stem, not the whole leaf. That means you're focused."

"But the leaf is prettier." Singer looked up at Cory's face. "Are you mad at me?" he suddenly asked.

Cory blinked, relaxing his jaw. "No, buddy. I'm sorry. It is pretty. You're right." He took the leaf and spun it by its stem.

"Where did you get that? That line over your eye?"

"This?" Cory said. "That's a scar. Where a hockey stick clunked me."

"Did it hurt?"

"Nah. Not much."

"How come your helmet and mask didn't save you?"

"My helmet got knocked off right before the stick hit me."

"That's bad luck," Singer said.

"Yeah. But no more bad luck now." Cory swept Singer up in an easy motion and held him high aloft. "I've got my good-luck charm."

"Higher," Singer sang out.

"My super high in the sky good luck charm."

"Yay," Singer squealed.

"C'mon leaf catcher. Let's go eat. I'm starved."

Cory put Singer's backpack onto the passenger side floor.

"Can I ride on your lap?" Singer asked. "And steer, like with Stu in the boat?"

"Since we're only going two blocks, okay. Don't tell your mother. She doesn't like it when we live dangerously."

"Why?"

"Because moms and dads are different." Cory swung Singer up into the cab of the truck.

"Are you my dad?" Singer asked, looking perplexed. A child should never have to look that way upon asking that question, Cory thought. Hanna and Cory had never talked this through. Singer knelt on the seat waiting for his answer.

"Sort of," he said.

"What do you mean?"

Cory slid behind the wheel and pulled Singer onto his lap. "Here, sit this way for a minute." He reversed Singer so his back was against the steering wheel. "I'm not your official dad. Not yet."

"Why not?" Singer asked.

"Well, once your mom and I get married, then I'll be your official dad."

"When will that be?"

"I have to ask her first. And she has to say yes."

"Like when I ask if I can go on the swings?"

AUTUMN 1985

"Yep," Cory said. "Like that."

"I think she'll want to." Singer made a very confident face.

"I hope so."

"Will you ask tomorrow?"

"Mmm, probably not tomorrow."

"How come?"

"You are a little question machine, did you know that?" Cory tickled Singer.

"How come not tomorrow?" Singer said laughing

"Well, I have to get your mom a ring when I ask. A ring says we're going to get married. It makes it official."

"And then you can be my official dad?"

"Yep. Would you like that?"

Singer's face glowed. "More than a million milkshakes."

"Me too. More than five million fire trucks. How 'bout a hug," Cory said. Singer gave him one. "Wow, that's a biggie. Thank you. Now, face the other way and man the wheel. Let's go see if we have a pizza crust in the refrigerator."

"We got two at the grocery store," Singer told Cory.

"Remember, we can't tell Mom about her ring or getting married. It's our surprise. Do you think you can keep a secret?"

"Easy," Singer said. "I'll keep forgetting a little every day. Until it disappears."

"I like the way you work. Let's hit the road." For a moment, Cory thought about his teaching buddies at the bar having beers. "After dinner maybe we play two-deck Go Fish." Singer clapped as they pulled away from the curb. "Hands on the wheel." Singer's hands took hold. And Cory trusted it. He believed it. He gave into it.

"Hellooo?" Hanna asked quietly of the living room, feeling the relief of stepping out of her heels. The space was dark and empty except for the light thrown by the floor lamp next to the reading chair. Three library books were on the floor, as well as Cory's shoes placed neatly side-by-side.

"Cory?" she said, going quietly into the kitchen. The lights had been left on and it smelled of pizza. The dinner plates had dried in the rack, as well as the large aluminum baking tray used for homemade pizza. Hanna smiled, knowing how much fun it was for Singer to help roll out the dough and sprinkle on the mozzarella cheese. Her eye caught a glimpse of a hand-colored note. PIZZA IN THE FRIDZA. There was a red heart with the words THE BOYS written across it.

Hanna peeked in the refrigerator. A neat stack of pizza wedges was Saran-wrapped on the shelf. One of Singer's Tootsie Rolls sat on top. How such a little sight can make a person feel loved.

She smiled, taking the Tootsie Roll. Popping the candy into her mouth she realized she was so looking forward to seeing Monsignor Kief tomorrow. The Sheriff planned to bring him out to Pat's farm—HomeSky's farm, she corrected herself. It would be a great gathering. Hanna had a full heart of things to talk with the Monsignor about. A farm in autumn is rich with places to make conversation. Cory, too, had mentioned he was looking forward to a run with Pat. They seemed to have great talks along the way. How would HomeSky be? she wondered. Cory had seen her a few times since her return to Baudette, saying that each time she seemed more at home. What that poor woman had endured, Hanna didn't even want to contemplate. And Meadow. She had to be in her third trimester. Hanna thought back to her own pregnancy—what seemed forever ago, like it was another person who carried Singer, and in some respect, it was. She could hardly remember a detail. Nature has her way of erasing what might stand in opposition to repeat performances.

Hanna's stocking feet quietly ascended the steps. She peeked through the half-open door of Singer's bedroom. There were her two men, zonked out. What a week it had been for both. Each had their first full week of school, although Singer was only doing half-day preschool. Still, exhausting. They slept on their sides, facing her, Singer in front. His arm was tossed up to be in contact with Cory's chest. She approached the small bed. Her breath shortened

AUTUMN 1985

at the sight of family. It was like rain finding roots. The longer she looked on, the more headline stories of traffic accidents and house fires and corrupt politicians dissipated into nothingness.

Hanna stepped into the shower, relishing the heat and steam. Duluth is no stranger to temperature swings. A fall day can touch 70 degrees in the afternoon when going into the station at 4:30, and 45 degrees leaving at 11:30. Hanna reached for her loofah sponge, gently scrubbing a week of newscasting from her skin. She closed her eyes, feeling her neck muscles loosening—before nearly being frightened off her feet by the shower curtain sliding open.

"Care for some company?" Cory asked.

"Oh, God," Hanna said, her hands crossing her chest. "You scared me."

"Sorry," Cory half-smiled. "Heard the shower running."

"I didn't mean to wake you," Hanna apologized.

"You mean I'm not dreaming?"

She smiled. "Get in here, Casanova." Hanna opened the shower curtain a bit farther.

"Just thought we'd conserve water," Cory said, stepping in, immediately moving close to her.

"How environmentally conscious of you," Hanna said, slipping her arms around his neck. Their bodies came together under the spray of hot water.

"And I noticed we were getting low on soap, too." Cory took the thin white sliver and began to suds her shoulders.

"You're a regular boy scout," Hanna told him.

Cory gave her a dimpled grin. "Not tonight."

THE APOLOGY

Sheriff Harris was not known to be indecisive, especially around food. But today, how he hemmed and hawed. French toast? Too light. Biscuits and gravy? May as well call it blubber and gravy. Farmer's omelet? Had it three times already this week. Lu Ann stood tableside with her pen poised above the order ticket.

The Sheriff glowered. "Hell, I ain't felt such pressure since dropping trousers in line for my physical before shipping out to Korea."

Lu Ann showed no mercy. "Soldier up and order before my hand falls asleep."

"What's good today?"

"Thurgood, we've been through it." When Lu Ann started using his first name the Sheriff knew he was on thin ice.

"Well don't go and bite my head off. Okay … um, nah. Let's see …" Lu Ann leaned in for the order. The Sheriff tossed down the menu. "For cuss sake, I can't decide."

AUTUMN 1985

Lu Ann pulled out a chair and sat. She went from being testy with the Sheriff to wondering if something was wrong. "Sheriff, you've been eating here for how many years now?"

"Since you owned it. A hundred years. And for a time before that, too."

"Not like you to lock up around a menu."

"Yeah," the Sheriff agreed, pathetically.

"Okay, you need the Goldilocks special: not too much of this or too much of that, but just right. Mary Alice!" she belted out. "Bring a two by two by two. Scrambled, bacon, cakes. Please." She turned back to the Sheriff. "So what's on your mind?" When Lu Ann looked at a person, she got hold of you.

"Shoot, Lu Ann. I don't want to cry in my coffee."

"I brewed it strong. Might be for the best." She gave him an encouraging nod.

"Ah, hell. May as well get it off my chest." He took a swallow of coffee. "You know Private."

"Your pup?"

"Yeah. Well, he was a gift from my neighbor."

"You lughead," she said. "I know Kitty and the whole story of how she gave you a puppy and how you two were walking around in ridiculous-looking matching sweat suits and you had a argument right there in front of the Clancy house loud enough to wake babies."

"Well hell, that ain't entirely it. Who you been talkin' to?"

"Sheriff, I don't do talkin' here. I do listenin'. All that's old news. Tell me something I don't know."

The Sheriff craved a cigarette. For months that demon had lain idle, but since his falling out with Kitty, it was back at the door, smiling. "It's been pretty awkward, what with the two of us across the street. If our dogs need to stretch their legs at the same time, we find ourselves standing in our respective yards offering a small wave to the other. It's more like a wave that says goodbye than hello."

"What did you say to send things off the tracks?"

"Can't remember exactly. Some jackass comment about watching westerns by myself and being independent these many years and how some belt buckles don't go with a belt."

Lu Ann looked at him like he stepped on her foot. "Are you kidding me? A woman shares her time and compassion with you, and for her trouble, she gets belt buckle riddles. Maybe they put you under too long during that surgery and it killed off what little sense you had."

"Funny you should say so." The Sheriff fiddled with his coffee cup. "Between you and me, that surgery—the shooting—jarred me more than I thought. I shoved it back, no huge deal, right? I'm up and about, fine and all. But it has me acting kinda strange and thinking about stuff when I should be sleeping."

"You're not playing the pity card here are you, Sheriff?" Lu Ann watched closely for his reaction.

"No," he plainly said. But he had less command of that word than he was famous for. "I don't stand for excuses."

"Thurgood, you had a little brush with mortality back on the front step of that farmhouse. Don't you underestimate it. There may be some rebound from that. Now I'm not saying go over to Kitty's and blame the whole mess on that, I'm saying you should go over and apologize. Talk about some of these things."

The Sheriff chewed at the inside of his mouth. "Maybe I'm better off with things the way they used to be, before all these … developments. Before puppies and Kitty's drop-ins and feelings to step gingerly around. Hell, I don't know."

Lu Ann looked away, thinking. "Sheriff, can I take what the Monsignor calls the scenic route to my opinion of what you just said?"

"I'm listening." The Sheriff finished his coffee.

"You know HomeSky is back living at the farm with Pat and Meadow."

"Pat's in the barn," the Sheriff interjected, more for Lu Ann's sake than for accuracy.

AUTUMN 1985

"Right," she continued. "Well as I'm sure you've guessed, that's difficult for me. Hard to understand and look kindly on, to be honest. But if I take a decent step back, and get out of my own way, it's a difficult thing not to call beautiful. A baby's coming. There's a girl not much older than a baby with a safe place to have it, Home-Sky's there, who lost her baby, and Pat, now with the closest thing he's ever had to family sitting with him at the table. How can I look on that 'development,' as you call it, with hopes of altering it? I was left out. Why? I can't say. What's there is good, and it's not my place to wish malice upon it or hope to rewind it. Same goes for what you have with Kitty, that friendship—that companionship, it's good. It's wrongheaded to sit here and make a wish for it to disappear."

Lu Ann raised her eyebrows to the Sheriff. "I tell you what we're not going to do, you and I. We're not going to start a lonely-hearts club here and get fat on caramel rolls. I made that mistake once and it's good … for … nothing." Lu Ann's index finger came down on the table, tapping each of those words home as if with a ball-peen hammer.

"Now, here's what we're going to do," she continued. "I'm going to pull one of those pies out from behind the counter and you're going to go home, put on a dress shirt, and walk across the street to that nice woman's home, offer her some pie and apologize to her. And you're going to keep going over there until either I run out of pie or Kitty accepts your apology. Is that clear?" Lu Ann got up from the table and waited for her answer with her hands on her hips.

The Sheriff looked at her, seeing a side of her that either he had missed or she hadn't graced him with before.

"Don't look at me funny instead of answering," Lu Ann told him.

The Sheriff stood up, clomped over in his walking cast and wrapped Lu Ann up in a hug. The first such one she'd received from him. "You're a hell of a gal," he said quietly. "I'll thank you for that pie."

"Don't you go getting soft on me." Lu Ann wiggled free. "I have a strawberry rhubarb that just might do the trick." She turned and made a straight line for the pie case by the cash register.

The Sheriff called after her. "Make sure the crust ain't chipped." He did so to assure her that he wasn't getting too soft.

"Holy shingles," the Sheriff blurted, holding the wet sweat top up to his eye-line. It dripped into the washing machine, bearing witness to the fact that hot water most certainly can make colors run, red not the least of them. "What have you done?"

The Sheriff's game plan had imploded before getting off the ground. He had hoped to bring over an apology pie, as well as return the athletic wear, sparkling clean, so that Kitty could get her purchase price refunded. Now, the fragility of his brainstorm was as obvious as the red running through the white stripes on the jacket sleeves. The Sheriff turned the jacket around to look at the back and he wouldn't have believed what he saw had he not been holding the dripping evidence. The gleaming white silk letters that had once spelled PRIME TIME had been overrun by red dye. Now the back of the jacket said P I E ME. "As God is my witness," the Sheriff said.

Of the many possible interpretations of such a phenomenon, the Sheriff saw it as Amanda's permission slip from heaven above. Their marriage was cut short in years, but not in romance. She often left him notes to discover in a shirt pocket or a card under a pillow. He would march that pie across to Kitty. But the sweat suit, he'd leave behind. Call it collateral damage. Tossing it in the dryer, he cranked the control knob to 30 minutes. For once, discretion was the greater part of Sheriff Harris.

You can rehearse an apology till the cows come home, but when the door opens between you and the offended party, all memory of what you intended to say can vanish like a nickel at an orphanage.

"Yes?" Kitty finally said after 20 seconds of unbroken silence. The Sheriff stood erect on her door stoop, with something plated under aluminum foil. And, after lengthy deliberation, he had also

AUTUMN 1985

decided to carry over a late-blooming rose from his garden. Kitty looked at him and raised her eyebrows to spur him along. "How can I help you, Sheriff?" She couldn't help but be a tad amused by his impersonation of a fence post.

"I've come to give an apology but my wits have abandoned me," the Sheriff finally uttered, giving Kitty such a hangdog look that she, against her wishes, smiled.

"Would you like to come in and see if your wits have somehow preceded you inside?"

"I thank you," the Sheriff said. Kitty held the door. Once inside he didn't make much progress in the communication department. At the sight of their old friend, Hansel and Gretel's tails twitched back and forth with such tempo, one wondered if they might snap clean off.

"What do you have there?" Kitty inquired.

"I've brought you something. A pie here and a rose here." The Sheriff extended the rose when he said pie and the pie when he said rose.

Kitty giggled.

"I mean pie and rose," he said, getting his hands and words to synchronize.

"Do you mind bringing them to the kitchen? I'll get a vase for that beautiful flower."

The aroma of her home struck the Sheriff lame, yet he made his feet move, while trying to place its reminiscence. "Place sure looks nice," he said. And that stopped him. The aroma reminded him of his Amanda, how she had their home smelling after Tuesday and Friday cleanings.

"Let's see what's under that foil." Kitty cheerfully took a peek as they stood in the kitchen. "Oh my, beautiful. Is it strawberry?" she asked, excitedly.

"Strawberry rhubarb," the Sheriff said. "Fresh this morning from Lu Ann's."

"My favorite. Can I cut you a slice?" The high register of Kitty's tone got the dogs looking up hopefully.

"Are you sure it's no trouble?" the Sheriff asked.

"Afternoon pie. Absolutely no trouble." Kitty went to a drawer for the appropriate flatware.

"There's something I need to get off my chest first, if I may. Do you mind if we sit?" The Sheriff pulled out a chair for her. "Just two more days with this cast. I'd cut it off myself if it was an hour longer."

"Of course," Kitty said, filling a bud vase with water and placing the rose. She came over to take the chair at the kitchen table. The Sheriff fidgeted with the sugar dispenser. Sunlight streaked through the alcove window, which looked out on the tree-lined street, and to the Sheriff's house beyond.

"Quite a day we have out there," he started, eyes downcast.

Kitty settled in the chair opposite him and smiled. "A peach."

He was struck by Kitty's calm. "I've come to apologize." The Sheriff straightened himself, skipping the preamble, and looked her in the eye. "I was a long-eared horse the other day—or now it's been a few weeks—about the sweat suit and my being accustomed to, ah, a certain amount of space." He took a deep breath. "Fact is, though, I've sure been missing our walks and our time together. Private too has been missing you guys. That's what I'm saying here. I'm sorry about how I acted and how I took this idea of space and shoved it between us. That was not intended, nor is it desirable. You've been nothing but good and deserve better. I was wondering if we could try again. If you'd give me a chance to redeem myself."

Kitty's eyes sparkled, moistened by his heartfelt words. "Thurgood," Kitty said, "it takes a good person to swallow one's pride and come over like you have. I also want to add that I was less than stellar that afternoon, too. I know I can come on strong as old perfume sometimes, so where we ended up wasn't entirely your doing." The two of them held each other's glances for a long moment. Hansel and Gretel sat erect, their ears raised, taut as little tents. "I think we both got a little wiser from our ways and strays, and I'm glad to resume our friendship."

AUTUMN 1985

They sat at the kitchen table. An unsliced pie there. Sun draped on the chair backs. On the other side of the window glass, leaves showed red and orange and yellow highlights. They had spoken words, but had not affixed them with touch. The Sheriff reached. He laid his hand on hers. Kitty had of course seen his prosthetic fingers, but never felt them on her skin. She wrapped her hand around his and gave a squeeze. "What do you say I cut this pie?"

"Fine idea," the Sheriff told her, watching to see when she'd notice the plate that he had brought the pie on. It might be today. It might a few days ahead, as more pie was eaten. He'd let it run its course.

"Oh my," Kitty said, as the pie knife lifted a second wedge. "Where did you get this beautiful plate?" She looked at the Sheriff who, if she was not mistaken, was blushing.

"It was one of Amanda's," he said quietly. "I'd like for you to have it."

The second piece of pie nearly dropped off the spatula. "Oh, Thurgood, I couldn't."

A collector's plate was being revealed, wedge by wedge, below the pie: a Franklin Mint *Garden Cottages of England*. It featured a thatched cottage with candle-lit windows, snow on the roof, and a smoke curl rising out of the fieldstone chimney.

"I hope you'll accept. It collects dust at my place. I think Amanda would be happy to see it used."

Kitty took a deep breath. "Oh gosh, Thurgood. Now I need a tissue. If you'll excuse me." Kitty quickly left the table, taking a small detour as she did, to give the Sheriff a little kiss on the cheek. And as he would tell Kitty later, that small kiss had more tingle in it than Lu Ann's fresh strawberry rhubarb pie.

HAPPINESS

Oh, the morning. To share in its first pristine breaths is a gift, before others intrude with their speeding automobiles and barking dogs and bellicose ambition. Before such a morning, the word spectacular is obligated to genuflect. The prairie grasses at first-light, saffron and honey, are put ablaze by the lifting sun. The sky, soon thereafter, sun-glazed to a sapphire blue. The breeze, a whisper, the Great Spirit's sleeping breath.

These are days of September when the sun forgets itself and comes on with August radiance. A day that leaves you staring off at a distant ridge, pricked by a small dose of incapacitation, held by pumpkin-colored treetops and the distant grasses left greener in the dew.

HomeSky stood. Closed her eyes. Opened the gates to good thoughts. Walked through them to find Joseph, to find RiverHeart.

AUTUMN 1985

The life you live carries other lives forward.
The life you live carries other lives forward.
The life you live carries other lives forward.

Death is a relentless instructor. Every day, your son dies. Every day, your husband dies. You are never the same. Yet, what was cherished never wholly ends. A remnant is taken up and given breath through you. In their kindness, you walk. In their wisdom, you speak. In their laughter, you smile. You must collect happiness on the bare ground where they once danced. Only then can there be music to offset the screaming silence.

"Boozhoo," HomeSky said to the bees, the leaves, the ticks, the shadows, the stones, the wheat, the graves, the gnats. To bid hello in the truest sense is to greet all, not just the chosen.

Behind her, the spring on the screen door stretched and then shut with a light touch on its frame. "Hey," Meadow whispered, coming out the back door. She pulled down her swim team hoodie, but it rode back up her stomach. "Couldn't sleep. B was doing his wild rice harvest dance all morning." Meadow's hand went to her belly.

"Feel like walking?" HomeSky asked.

"If you're okay with the pace." Meadow came slowly down the front steps.

"We'll get there." HomeSky put her arm out and Meadow came in under it.

"Hook up the hay wagon," Meadow said.

Little more was said as they passed the barn and curled out toward the back pasture. Everything that needed to be expressed was said in HomeSky's arm around Meadow's shoulder. Peace rose out of the fields.

If daybreak made anyone happier than Private, the Sheriff certainly hadn't born witness to it. The moment the pup was out of his kennel, there was shuddering joy, wriggling and writhing under the Sheriff's large kneading fingers. Private would alternate between offering his withers or belly, flopping and rolling and groaning as he bent around the pressure of the Sheriff's hand.

"Let's get outside before you fountain yourself," the Sheriff said. Private gave himself a few licks, honoring his namesake, and then bounded after the Sheriff's leg cast, growling with pleasure when his milk teeth sank into the rubber heel.

Once Private hit the grass, he lapped the back yard like a Formula One racecar—ears pinned back, striding out with everything he had. On the third go around his paw found a patch of damp leaves causing his legs to whip out from under him. His tumbling into the bushes left him more surprised than hurt.

"Hey hotshot. Blew a tire there." The Sheriff laughed.

Private righted himself, shook, and sent out a high-pitched bark announcing his displeasure with the Sheriff's lighthearted response. Then he cautiously returned to the wet leaves, sniffing, hunching down, growling at the unknown adversary.

"Do your business," the Sheriff instructed. "Before somebody sees me out here like this." The Sheriff was standing in his robe. "Private. Business!" The pup was jolted into eye contact. The Sheriff hand signaled, showing him the approved corner of the yard that was, essentially, his bathroom. The pup made his way and commenced to do as he was told. Since his first paper-trained days, Private was carried to this spot, oftentimes in the act, and set down to relieve himself. After a few weeks he learned to associate the word "business" with the call of bodily functions—and the high praise of his master—with this square of grass.

Inside, Private sat as the Sheriff scooped his dog food. He remained in sit while the dog dish was set down. They looked at each other. "Okay," the Sheriff commanded, and the pup skittered across the linoleum to bury his face in kibble.

"Big goings on today," the Sheriff told him, sitting down with his coffee. Private wolfed down breakfast. "We're going for a visit and dinner to HomeSky's farm. You'll like it there. A new smell around every corner." Private looked up at the Sheriff a moment. "We'll pick up the Monsignor and head out around two. Going to be

AUTUMN 1985

taking Kitty with us, too. I called and asked HomeSky if they minded setting an extra plate. They were only too happy."

Private finished by licking the bowl clean, delighted to discover bonus kibble on the floor. He lapped them up, made an extended stop at the water dish, and trotted over to the Sheriff to lay on his side, sending a hind leg in the air, offering his belly. The Sheriff tried mightily not to look down. He glanced out the window. He took a lazy sip of coffee. He futzed with a loose thread on his robe. Then he snuck a peek. Private was waiting; his puppy eyes on full power. "Aw, crap," the Sheriff said, scratching the pup's full little belly. "That's hardly fair." Private's tail thumped the floor, proving once again what a mistake it is to make eye contact with a puppy.

Monsignor Kief was up and at 'em. His bed was already made, a sort of cotton-clad guarantee that there'd be no slipping back in. He'd been downstairs to the kitchen, twice, to make coffee—the first time he forgot to put water in the back of the coffeemaker. He reached for the radio on the counter, but decided against turning it on. It was his housekeeper's day off and he relished the quiet of a place to himself.

A single slice of raisin toast, the Monsignor decided, was just the thing to tide him over. Later, he'd walk up to Lu Ann's for breakfast. He took the toast, generously buttered, out the front door, stepping into the morning. Fall was there in the mellow settling of decay. Was it dignified for a retired Monsignor to stand beneath the curtain of a lifting dawn, robed, on his front stoop, with butter on the side of his mouth? He wasted none of God's precious morning considering such nonsense. Life touched his face, his hands, his eyelids; he took it in and breathed it out. "Good morning, Father," he said. "What a day you've made."

Upstairs he showered, shaved, brushed and flossed. His routine was completed by going heels up, as he called it, kneeling at the pedestal sink. His days began and ended here, had since he moved in over 30 years ago.

Halfway out the door on the way to Lu Ann's, he remembered he'd forgotten money. Yesterday at the hardware store, Monsignor

SINGER

Kief discovered he was down to his last dollars. Pat had asked him to pick up a paintbrush for finishing the barn loft, and he was 18 cents short, which was promptly forgiven. Monsignor Kief reentered his house and followed the aroma of toast back into the kitchen to the cookie jar on the counter. Stashed inside he found two bills folded by width, $10s, and one folded lengthwise and by width, a $20. "Looks like I'm buying dessert for anyone wise enough to know breakfast is a dessert meal." He patted the top of the cookie jar after returning its lid, and retraced his steps out the front door.

A hat and light jacket were a little much, the Monsignor realized, halfway through his five-and-a-half-block walk to Lu Ann's. He tipped his hat back and unzipped his coat. "You feel more like summer than fall," he told the day. "But I know you still have a few tricks up your sleeve." The elderly priest tapped his way down the sidewalk whistling a hymn. He felt in fine fiddle, but his hip had been grumbling at the weather of late. Pat had given him some stretches, and he made a mental note to start to include them in his morning routine.

As he turned the corner of Main Street, the sun kissed each cheek in greeting. Immediately, there was the pull of frying bacon. Most folks recognized Lu Ann's by the alternate filling and emptying of the neon coffee cup over the door. For the Monsignor, the sign was no less apparent, only olfactory.

His hand reached out, his fingers riding along the brick facade of the diner. The masonry was cool, but the sun would soon penetrate. He liked that thought: what the light finds it penetrates, leaving warmth within. He intended on delivering a mini-sermon on the point at the community table, but the cavalcade of aromas, the brass entry bell over Lu Ann's door, the shuffling and unfolding of newspapers, the murmur of welcoming voices, the tines of forks vibrating on plates—the sensory diner barrage—eclipsed his plan. The Monsignor was left with one singular thought: *what's the special?* He sent out a quick prayer to the patron saint of French toast.

"Hello flock," he proclaimed, his hand finding his coat hook, third one in, his name written beneath it. He removed his coffee mug from the peg, and hung his coat in its place. "I hope you've not been shorn *too* badly by this establishment's aggressive new pricing scheme."

Lu Ann stepped forward. "Now just a ding-dang minute." Between them, she and the Monsignor had a friendly running banter that was not unlike a play performed four times weekly in front of an audience of customers. "How is it a *new* pricing scheme if it went into place two months ago?"

The Monsignor blew into his empty mug. "It can't have been that long ago. No. Could it?"

"And you call a 10 cent hike on coffee aggressive?"

"Twice as aggressive as a nickel," the Monsignor's voice lilted. The customers oohed, scoring one for the Monsignor.

"I'm not going there," Lu Ann said, waving him off.

The Monsignor made his way to the community table, his hands using the shoulders of a few seated customers to guide him. "I would mention the 25 cent up-charge on the *previously free* shot of whipped cream on pie, but I fear if I do ..." he paused here, drawing his audience off their chairbacks, "the proprietor would rearrange the furniture on me."

The customers hooted and broke into light applause. The Monsignor sat, then rose for a bow, before again sitting.

"I surrender," Lu Ann said, waving an invisible white flag. Softer now she spoke. "I hereby announce a one-week moratorium on the 25 cent whipped cream charge on all desserts."

"Including hot cocoa?" the elderly, elegant Mrs. Carlisi asked in a voice richly tuned by morning's choir practice.

Lu Ann took a page out of the Monsignor's playbook and let the question hang. "Including hot cocoa," she announced.

The diner let out a second collective whoop! and went back to their food.

Lu Ann came over and joined the Monsignor at his empty table. "Ready to order, Hotspur?"

"Little lonely over here," he said. Typically the community table held at least a bachelor farmer or two chewing on their coffee.

"Such is the life of an agitator," Lu Ann warned him.

"And how are you on this Saturday?" Monsignor Kief brought his hands across the table. Lu Ann deftly moved the salt and pepper out of the way before giving his hands a squeeze. "Oh, okay," she said, trying to act cheery. "Honestly, it's different for me right now." She gave the Monsignor's hand a resigned pat. "Making adjustments."

Monsignor Kief had a sharp ear, not particularly in the way of hearing a napkin hit the floor from across the room, but more in detecting mood and intent. Lu Ann's comment said she wasn't ready to discuss Pat just now. Time and place, he knew, are the mixing bowl of a good talk. The Monsignor smiled. "I have a favor to ask, if you can spare a few minutes."

Lu Ann looked over her shoulder. "Nothing on fire at the present." She knocked on the table surface.

Monsignor Kief reached into his shirt pocket and unfolded an envelope. "I have a letter here from a man I met in St. Paul. Mick is his name. I wonder if you might read it to me? My housekeeper has the day off and we didn't get to it yesterday."

"O-kay," Lu Ann said tentatively. "Is this the same Mick who owns the diner where HomeSky worked?" Lu Ann's voiced tightened around the name HomeSky.

"That's the one," the Monsignor said energetically. "Here you are."

Lu Ann took the envelope. "You're sure?" she said.

"I shouldn't see why not. It's unlikely there are any state secrets in there." The Monsignor waited.

Lu Ann found a clean butter knife and ran it through the top of the envelope. She unfolded a single sheet of paper with the faint remains of a coffee ring on it.

"Letters are Christmas presents," the Monsignor said, rubbing his palms together.

AUTUMN 1985

Lu Ann's reading glasses hung around her neck from a pewter chain. She put them on, looking through a grease smudge. "I hate cheaters," she said wiping the lens. "Mortality hanging on your nose. Okay." Lu Ann smoothed the letter out in front of her. "Here we go."

> *Dear Monsignor (sorry, still not used to calling you Frank),*
>
> *The workday is just about to get cranking here in good old St. Paul. All's quiet. It's about 5 a.m. and before my first early birds arrive I thought I'd jot you a note.*

Lu Ann looked up from the letter. "Gosh he opens early. I thought 6:30 was bad."

> *Thanks, first off, for your last letter. I had never thought about kindness like that.*
> *I like that the more I think about it. About your question of how long have I owned my place, it will be 15 years this fall. Like being married, I guess. Happily so. Things are good here but I must say I do miss HomeSky. Just not the same without her, not by a long shot. I guess if you have a hole in one place, you have a patch in another, right? I'm not much for poetry—*

Lu Ann stopped reading. It took Monsignor Kief a moment to realize what she was must be doing. *If you have a hole in one place, you have a patch in another.* The words had found resonance. "I'm sorry," Lu Ann said, clearing her throat. She continued.

> *and should stick to my spatulas (pun alert!). Oops, just got a little coffee ring on my letter. Call it my official stamp and seal. Anyway, to the moment you've been patiently waiting for: your happiness triangle. Another good try. You still only have one right, and my clue is it's the one I thought you'd get. But don't despair, keep trying. Well, gotta go. First customer just walked through the door and he looks in desperate need*

of caffeine. Hello to HomeSky from me and the whole gang back here. She is missed.

Mick

"Darn it all," the Monsignor said. "I thought I'd be closer than one."

Lu Ann was distracted by the letter. "Sorry?"

"The happiness triangle. I can't seem to crack it."

"What is a happiness triangle, anyway?"

"Do you have a pen?" the Monsignor asked brightly.

Lu Ann always honored the waitress code: have two well-working pens in your possession. "I want that back," she said, handing one over.

"No, no. You do the writing. Get yourself a napkin."

Lu Ann pulled one from the dispenser. "Got it."

"Now draw a simple triangle."

"Okay. There's a triangle."

"Now put an F at each corner."

"F, F, F." Lu Ann did as she was instructed. She waited. "Now what?"

The Monsignor smiled. "Now you have it. According to Mick, what sits before you is the happiness triangle. If you can correctly identify the three words beginning with F, you have the secret to happiness right there on your napkin. Mick has an entire wall at his diner filled with napkins, pinned two and three deep, with customers' attempts to solve the riddle. No one's got it yet, Mick says.

"So," Lu Ann said, getting interested, "this Mick guy has the answer to happiness? What makes him so smart?"

The Monsignor took full advantage of the easy set-up. "He runs a diner."

Lu Ann smirked. "No. Really. What makes him the keeper of such secrets?"

AUTUMN 1985

Monsignor Kief leaned back in his chair. "Well, the story goes Mick is at the diner earlier than usual one morning. Jumps into his usual routine. Turns on the radio. Starts the coffee. Burns one piece of toast for himself because he says eating it burnt helps him wake up. Has a look at the newspaper. That kind of stuff. He wasn't feeling particularly happy, or particularly unhappy. Average early start to an average day. He pours himself a cup of coffee and when he sits down to read the paper, he knocks over his coffee mug. The counter gets soaked so he pulls out a pile of napkins from the dispenser and gets after it lickety split. When he finishes, he notices a part of the spill has seeped under his newspaper. One word is enlarged where the coffee soaked through. Guess what that word is?"

"I haven't a guess," Lu Ann said, a little skeptically.

"Happy," Monsignor Kief said, practically singing the word. "Almost as if it had been circled for him out of the sea of type. So he sits himself down, takes a dry napkin from the few remaining on the counter and writes the word happy in the center. Then he said three words came to him. Didn't know if he heard them on the radio. Didn't know if he had glanced at them in the paper. But from out of the blue, here came three words. He writes one on the top of the napkin and the other two in the bottom corners. Then he drew three lines, connecting the words. Just like that, he had a triangle with the word happy in the center. Then it dawns on him. All three words at the points of the triangle start with F. Coincidence? He said he really didn't know."

"Seriously?" Lu Ann asked. "C'mon. He never worked on this happiness thing before that?"

Monsignor Kief raised his eyebrows and said in a low voice, "'Never thought about it before in my life.' Those are his words."

"Sounds kinda far-fetched if you ask me," Lu Ann said.

"I must say, I met the man, although only for a brief time, and he's a straight-shooter."

"Well, it's interesting and all, I'll give you that." Lu Ann slid her chair back. "I better check on—"

"Here, the way Mick tells it, is where the story really gets good." Lu Ann sat her butt back in the chair.

"Couple minutes later a guy walks into the diner. A guy Mick says he's never seen before. Average enough looking fella. Sits down at the counter next to Mick, says good morning and orders a cup of coffee. Mick thinks nothing of it. Goes around the counter, fills him a cup. The man sees Mick's doodle on the napkin and asks what he's doing. Mick says it's nothing. Just fooling around with some words. Balls it up, tosses it in the garbage. They talked about normal stuff. Sports. Weather. Nothing particularly memorable. The guy finishes his coffee, leaves fifty cents. Says thanks. By the way, he says, you should keep that. Mick doesn't follow his meaning. Does he mean keep the fifty-cent tip? That napkin, the guy says. With the triangle. Mick pulls it out of the garbage and asks, you mean this? You got it right, the man tells him. Then he smoothes it down on the counter, perfectly smooth, like it's never been balled up. Spins it so the words are facing Mick on the other side of the counter. You got it right. The words. You'd be amazed how many get it wrong, he says. All wrong. He says go ahead and ask your customers. Give them a triangle, not the answer. Ask them to write the secret to happiness. *But* he says, they have to discover it for themselves. That's the *secret*. The guy nods and leaves. On his way out, he passes a customer coming in. A regular, who sits at the counter and asks Mick why the goofy perplexed look on his face. Mick looks up from the napkin. Has a sip of his coffee. Says he just had an interesting conversation with that guy. What guy? the regular asks. The guy you passed coming in. The regular says, I didn't pass nobody coming in. Mick makes sure he heard him right. Just now? You didn't see anyone? The regular said, just you, me, and whatever it is you're drinking in that coffee cup 'cause you're seeing things."

Monsignor Kief took a drink of water. By this time something could have been aflame in the kitchen and Lu Ann wouldn't have budged. "So then what?"

AUTUMN 1985

"He started doing it," Monsignor Kief said. "Just like he was asked. Beginning with that regular. He asked him if he knew the secret to happiness. The regular said he sure wished he did. So Mick pulled out a new napkin. Wrote the word Happy in the center, drew a triangle around it and started to write the first word on top. Got as far as the F when he remembered what the man had said: *They have to discover it.* So he wrote two more Fs, one each at the bottom corners, slid it to the customer and said solve this and you've got yourself the secret to happiness. Couple more customers tried it that day. Couple more the next. Now they draw their own triangles and show their napkins to Mick when they ring out. He says thanks, but you didn't get it. Tells them to keep trying, keep thinking about it. And goes over and pins their tries to the wall."

"No one has got it right?" Lu Ann asked.

"Not in the five years he's been doing it, Mick says. Not a one."

Lu Ann looked at her napkin. "Kind of a sad statement on society. Can you tell me what you put on yours? Would that be prying? Or cheating?"

"I think that's allowable," the Monsignor said. "The other napkins get put on the wall. Do you still have your triangle in front of you?"

"Yep."

"My top F was Faith. My left bottom was Friends. My right F was Fun."

"Sounds pretty good to me," Lu Ann said. "But what about food?"

Monsignor Kief sat straight up. "Eureka!" he shouted. "I didn't think of that."

"Mick owns a diner. I imagine food would make the list, right?" Lu Ann was beginning to enjoy this puzzle.

"So where would food go? And what comes out? Remember, Mick says we have one right."

Lu Ann thought for a moment. "What did his letter say? Something about getting the one he expected you'd get. I bet Faith is right."

Monsignor Kief jumped in. "Agreed. That means we have Faith and Food and only need one more. But how could friends and fun not be included? They're essential to happiness, are they not?"

"Maybe there's another word beginning in F that captures both. I don't know." Lu Ann shifted gears. "All I know is I'm getting the stink eye from Mrs. Quill who doesn't like waiting for her order to be taken." Lu Ann pushed away from the table. "Happiness will have to wait."

"That may just be the problem," the Monsignor said after her, only half kidding. He sat back in his chair thinking. *F? F? French toast starts with F. That would make me happy.*

AUTUMN 1985

MEADOW

"I'm kinda wondering about a couple things," Meadow started. She'd been quiet as they walked up the fencerow from the barn. The last of the alfalfa stood ready for harvest. She moved slowly, being both contemplative and "totally pregnant," as she put it. Meadow frowned. "I wouldn't call it wigged out," she continued, "but I'm fighting myself on some stuff." She looked at HomeSky. "Here." She put her hand over her heart.

The slant of the sun was kind to the adjacent field, accentuating its soft beauty. The morning's first long clouds had cauliflower tops and flat bottoms, like a cartoonist draws them.

"What is it?" HomeSky asked, stopping.

"I don't know." Meadow took HomeSky's hand and gave her a gentle tug. "Let's keep walking. I need it." She paused. "I think about B and his life … and how I will be thought of. I know. That's selfish. It's not about me. Adoption is about him."

Now HomeSky knew where the anxiousness resided. "You will be thought of wonderfully. Lovingly."

"Why? I gave up my child. My first-born."

"That is exactly why. You did the unselfish thing." HomeSky smiled knowingly.

"Did I?" Meadow asked. "Or does this adoption keep me the child? You're the adult. The adoptive mother has the real responsibility."

"Oh Meadow, there's going to be more than enough to go around. I'm not afraid of you shirking your responsibilities." HomeSky's words gave Meadow no peace.

As they walked, songbirds kept them company in the fenceline's thickets. "Will you hear me out on something, even if it sounds stupid?"

HomeSky said she would.

"When I got pregnant, my thinking was, I'm dead. Like, my old man, well you know him. So I'm scared, really bad. I couldn't think straight. But I knew we had to get out. That's where it went from I to we. I'm scared. We gotta get out." Meadow's frustration was building. "The Rez is like poison. Just little bits in your food, in the water, in the air. Might be too late for me, but I couldn't feed that to my baby. We ran. My one and only thought was adoption. Adoption, adoption, adoption. That's all. Can I somehow save this new life from the Rez? Then I get here and, wow, this thought strikes me: I'm not only trying to save my unborn child from the Rez. I'm trying to save my child from *me*. Give him up. You can't do this. You're not good enough."

HomeSky saw Meadow's bare arms ended in fists. Her jaw clenched on every word.

"I come here to your farm, to this serenity. One day turns into the next. First there's Pat. Then you arrive. I keep moving. Progress is made until finally, the adoption is going to happen. My dream is right here." Meadow closed her hand in front of her. She licked her dry lower lip. Her eyes were fixed at nothing. All she was seeing was her words.

AUTUMN 1985

"One morning, maybe two weeks ago, I'm walking to the mailbox. B kicks me in the stomach so hard that I had to stop. I'm on the driveway, you know, out by the mailbox, and I have a simple thought: *what if you're not so bad?*"

Meadow swayed noticeably. "Jeez, I'm getting dizzy. I should sit for a sec." Meadow went down to one knee, and sat cross-legged, the only way that brought her body any comfort. HomeSky sat next to her, steadying her.

"Are you okay?" HomeSky asked tensely.

Meadow nodded. She took a few short breaths and closed her eyes. "Yeah. Fine. The ground feels good. Warm." She pushed down on her knees, which stretched open her hips. "What a couple of oddballs we make." She gently placed her palms on the land and felt its goodness.

HomeSky also sat cross-legged, across from her. A hawk circled above. "He's probably wondering what we've found down here," she said, her chin pointing to the sky.

Meadow looked up at the hawk above, picking up where she left off. "What if it's not me that I have to run away from? Because that's pretty much what I was doing." The sky above opened her to speaking her most guarded thought. "What if I can be the mother to my baby?" Meadow's eyeline dropped from the sky and bore into HomeSky. "If I knew you'd be here. And Pat would be here. And all this that the Great Spirit has made for a child to get strong on. Maybe there doesn't have to be an adoption."

The two women looked at each other, knees almost touching, In that small space between them, years of pain stood ready to crumble to the ground.

HomeSky spoke. "You will be a great mother to your child. I will stay with you as long as you wish. I promise my undying support." HomeSky's smile was Meadow's smile. HomeSky's heartbeat was Meadow's heartbeat. "You will live for this child and, if asked, give him your very last breath. You will teach him to trust others as you have trusted. This land will hold you in her arms, and when you set your boy down, the earth will celebrate his feet with wildflowers.

SINGER

The birds will listen for his laugh. The stars will play in his eyes. And this sky will watch over you. I will walk behind you and beside you, not in front of you. You will be a mother, the greatest gift the Great Spirit can bestow. The hawk above will watch out for him, as he does now."

The two women titled their heads upward to the comforting repetitive chirp of the osprey, saying *here, here, here, here, here*. All was there, open and in front of them. Mother. Child. Friend. Hawk. Four became three became two became one, consecrated in sunshine.

AUTUMN 1985

ROAD TRIP

He slid out of bed, careful not to disturb Hanna. First light bumped against the east-facing bedroom curtains. Cory had folded a stack of morning wear—placed on the chair the night before—which he quietly scooped up. Slipping into the hallway, he dressed. In sweats and a sweatshirt, Cory pulled on his Wisconsin Badger cap and went to check Singer.

There had been no incidents of sleepwalking since Monument Bay, but the apprehension had hardly waned. In Singer's bedroom, Cory gave his eyes a moment to adjust from the hallway light. The boy slept burrowed under his sheet and light blanket. Grateful, Cory approached the shape, noticing that Singer was sleeping breech. "Good morning, good one," Cory whispered. He slid his arms beneath the bundle, carefully returning his head to the pillow, straightening the blanket at his shoulders, feet now pointing to the baseboard. The buttery smell of boy lay in the stillness. Cory reached to touch the warmth of his cheek; a few jewel-like beads of sweat rested on the child's forehead, brought on from being submerged in bedcovers. Dumbstruck, he stood there, terrified by his attachment to Singer. Cory removed his Badgers cap and snuck it under the boy's pillow.

What joy to go lightly out of a child's bedroom, to slip out on the wedge of hallway light and look back, to witness the sleeping child as the door comes closed, reaching with two fingers to keep it from striking the frame.

Downstairs, Cory started coffee. His body begged to run, but he had promised Pat they would go when he got to the farm. Cory knew his knee would bark plenty from that, the way they liked to push each other.

Everything was packed for the overnight. Cory would get breakfast going, and they'd hit the road quickly thereafter. But first, Cory sat at the kitchen table with his coffee and papers to grade. To his figuring, he had 90 minutes before he'd hear the scamper of footfalls overhead. As for Hanna, she was an immovable object until the last possible moment. She valued sleep over food any weekend of the year.

About an hour later, the sound of little feet dotted across the ceiling, wiping the frown of concentration from Cory's brow. He looked up from his algebra papers, tracing the footsteps as they moved toward the bathroom. Singer had been sleeping in big-guy underwear for a few months now, and was doing pretty well. After a short layover, the footsteps came bounding down the steps at a speed that made Cory wince. Into the kitchen Singer ran, wearing Cory's Badger cap backward. He put on the brakes, the hat spinning down over his eyes. Singer quickly pushed it back up. "What's cookin' good lookin'?"

"Good morning, ace" Cory said. "Come on over."

Singer jumped into Cory's lap. "We're going to the farm today, right?"

It took Cory a heartbeat to transition from the black and white of math to the full-on color of Singer.

AUTUMN 1985

"We are indeed."

"When can we go?"

"After breakfast and your mom gets up."

"Should I go wake her?" Singer was nearly out of Cory's lap.

"Whoa. Not so fast. Let's you and I eat. Your mom needs a little extra sleep. She had a tough week."

"Me too," Singer said, stretching the sleep out.

Cory took his hat off Singer's head. "Get washed up."

"Can I do it here?" Singer's eyes begged. "Scrambled eggs?"

"All right." Cory stood up. "Push the chair to the sink and hop up."

Singer started the faucet over the kitchen sink while Cory adjusted the temperature. The boy pushed up his pajama sleeves, turned up his palms and Copy put one drop of dish soap in each. "Egg, egg," Cory said.

Singer's eyes gleamed. He slapped his hands together and began to rub vigorously. "Scramble, scramble, scramble, scramble, scramble, scrambled eggs," he said with glee. The soap and water lathered nicely. "You too," Singer encouraged. Cory pushed up his sleeves, and dotted his palms with dish soap. At the sink, playfully, their hands came together. And Singer washed Cory clean.

With Kitty riding shotgun, a phrase she abhorred, the Sheriff made his way over to the rectory. They planned to get out of town by 10, but were running a few minutes behind. Monsignor Kief was big on promptness, something that will happen when you say a schedule of masses for 40-plus years.

"I'm having trouble keeping my eyes on the road," the Sheriff said, driving the cruiser right at the speed limit despite their tardiness. "What with how pretty you look today." Kitty had gotten her hair styled and colored a deeper brunette. Having the length brought up a titch gave her a youthful bounce.

She blushed. "What a nice thing to say. Thank you." They drove on in silence.

"You're quiet this morning," the Sheriff said.

Kitty turned to him. "Do you think I'm too made up for a venture to the farm?"

The Sheriff stole a glance. "Hell no." He was wise enough to know this question had to be put down forcefully.

Then Kitty got to the heart of it. "What if they don't like me?"

The Sheriff paused, leaving the impression he was contemplating the question. "Well, I'll just have to shoot them."

"Thurgood!" she said, slapping him on the shoulder.

"Nothing life-threatening. A leg or an arm."

"Seriously," Kitty said.

The Sheriff slowed for a turn. "Kitty, it's an impossibility. You're as easy to like as frosting on brownies. And these people, you won't meet nicer. I'm going to have trouble pulling you away is what." The Sheriff let that settle. "Okay?"

"Okay," she said, her tone brightened. "If you say so." She patted the Sheriff's knee, leaving her hand there a few extra beats.

The Sheriff pulled to the curb in front of the rectory. The cast was off his leg and he was moving pretty well. He double-timed it up to the big oak front door and leaned on the doorbell before letting himself in.

"Hello?" he called out from the entryway.

"In here," he heard from the great room.

"Sorry I'm—we're late," he said, approaching the Monsignor, who had a look of concentration on his face. He sat in his favorite high-backed leather chair.

"Ten Hail Marys and ten Our Fathers," he said. "Oh, before I forget, would you do me a favor?" The Monsignor patted the notebook on his lap.

"Sure." The Sheriff took a step closer.

"Jot down these words for me." He handed the Sheriff the pad and pen from his lap. "Ready?"

"Shoot."

AUTUMN 1985

"Friendly. Fortitude. Fidelity. Forthcoming."

"Interesting string." The Sheriff took a second, trying to decode them. "Is it wise for a Monsignor to be dabbling in F words?"

"Ah yes," the Monsignor said, getting stiffly out of his chair. "I'll tell you all about it in the car." He raised a finger in proclamation. "I'm on the brink of solving the secret to happiness."

Singer was playing the piano as Hanna had her last bite of bacon. She'd allow herself one slice, saying the sacrifice allowed her to savor it all the more.

"Is he too young for lessons, you think?" Cory asked.

Hanna set down her fork. "I asked Ms. Cuddigan at preschool. She thinks with his aptitude, he's ready. And he says he'd like to start. According to her that's the primary indicator. That, and sitting down to play unprovoked."

"We should get on it. I mean, listen to him." The music was hunt and peck with a simple beauty. The boy sang along, urging the right notes by singing to them until the piano matched. "Where does it come from, you think?" Cory asked.

Hanna shrugged. "I'm not over-the-top religious, but it's hard not to think he's been given a more direct gift than most of us have."

Cory agreed. "Have you ever watched his face when he sings?"

Hanna nodded as though she had spoken the words. "You see it too?"

"I'm not even sure how to describe it." Cory shook his head.

"It's like … he's not here," Hanna said, surprised by her description.

"Probably the closest thing to perfect we'll see." Cory stood to do the dishes.

Hanna came over and slid her arms around Cory. "Just leave those dishes, hunky cook." She kissed him tenderly. "I'm getting spoiled. Sleeping in. Breakfast waiting for me."

Cory stepped back after the kiss. "Get used to it." He gave Hanna a wink as he turned to go. She wanted him to stay. If not to lengthen the embrace, then to explain if he meant what she hoped he meant. But life had instructed Cory on the value of detachment. Evasion was survival—not just in sports.

Upstairs, Cory collected the overnight bags. One held Hanna and Singer's things. A smaller bag was packed with Cory's. He looked at his bag. Part of him screamed to leave it, another part insisted he pick it up. Cory unzipped the bag for maybe the fifth time since waking. There, inside a pair of folded socks, was a small velvet box.

AUTUMN 1985

BARN LOFT

The aroma of September hay is different than August hay: drier, sharper, a less fermented sweetness. Around it, the odor of barn wood had mellowed, the extreme temperatures and humidity now backed off. Pat opened his mouth to crack his jaw. He stood in front of his cot, arms straight up, careful not to stretch too far or too fast as to trigger a cramp. He quickly stepped into jeans and pulled on a t-shirt, rubbing the cold from his skin.

Invigorating. His loft accommodations were working out better than he'd imagined. Certainly, there was the occasional mouse dirt, bat droppings and visit from a rogue swallow, but mostly, he had the place, and his thoughts, to himself.

He rolled open the hay door and sat with his bare feet put out, hanging high above the ground. He thought of Joseph and how he would jump from here into the snow, drifted high against the west face of the barn. Joseph. Losing him was the greatest test he'd endured. When HomeSky left, it could have been even more devastating, but Pat relentlessly clung to hope, believing in her return. Hope mends what life breaks.

How close HomeSky came to never returning, Pat didn't care to know. It was far too close, he suspected. But the grace of God sent her back. To Pat. To Meadow.

"I love you, HomeSky," Pat whispered to the pasture winds. He had said this only a handful of times aloud to her, and that was years ago, before she'd left. Since then, he'd offered these words to the wind, too many times to count. Had the words found her, someway, somehow? Did she wake one morning to those words touching her?

To Pat's recollection, he had never spoken those words to anyone else but God. Maybe when he was very young and his parents were still together he had used them freely. As he grew, and ugliness filled the house and his parents finally ended it, the words *I love you* were as cumbersome as another language. Most recently, with Lu Ann, he, perhaps, was falling in love—an undeveloped love—a love of friendship that grew, but with no real direction or urgency or breathlessness. About this, he felt terrible. Would time arbitrate, bring them back together as true friends? Dear God, he hoped so. But his heart had gone to HomeSky. Viscerally. Perhaps, looking back on it, it was the first time he saw her, turning away from the window in the Sheriff's office to face the room. Why one is made to intersect with another under circumstances, dire or wonderful, can't be answered by scholarly means. It's compelled by a genius of its own.

Today, Cory and Hanna and Singer would come. Monsignor Kief and the Sheriff and his new friend Kitty, too. HomeSky, Meadow and he himself would greet them. Cory and Pat would run, just as they once had. What storms undid, conversations would knit together. Food would be cooked, as it had been. Laughter was invited and would join in after a long, listless absence. Singer's young feet would skip over the earth and he would point to things that age overlooks. They would be together as the evening sky slowly darkened. And togetherness would be their lodestar.

AUTUMN 1985

REG

A few weeks back, when the windstorm ripped through most of the northern part of the state and up into Canada, Reg got to thinking. Which for him was a dangerous endeavor.

He had a cache of old asphalt shingles in the garage. Leftovers from roofing tear-offs that habitually he'd take home, just a handful, different colors to match different roofs. After the storm, he had driven around town and dropped a few shingles in the bushes of Baudette's more elderly and vulnerable. It was follow-up time. He needed work.

Mrs. Cale was a kind and generous soul. Her husband had done moderately well in the lumber business, but unfortunately, was born with a faulty mitral heart valve. This went undetected until he was found dead at age 54 next to the bundle of 8x8 top-treated posts he was unloading at the city picnic grounds. He had volunteered to put in a playground.

In the 20 years since, Mrs. Cale had moved into town, found community there, bought a modest two-bedroom rambler, took to keeping tropical fish and a parakeet named Honey, and lived frugally off their hard-earned nest egg, some insurance money, and her social security check. Neither rich nor poor, she was the ideal prey for Reg. She had friends in town, but no family to meddle. And she was a good woman, which made her trusting. Reg had a field day with trusting saps.

After hearing the doorbell ring inside the house, Reg stood back from the storm door. He wore his working whites: t-shirt, bib overalls and tennis shoes that showed just enough paint splatters to give the impression he juggled a busy calendar of jobs.

The front door opened. "Can I help you?" Mrs. Cale asked pleasantly, still separated by the storm door.

Reg smiled. "Good afternoon. Mrs. Cale, correct?"

"That's right. Do we know each other?" she asked hopefully.

"Reg Cunningham, handyman. I was here last spring when your central air conditioning went out. How's that been working for you?"

"Oh yes. Mr. Cunningham. It ran good as new all summer."

"That's nice to hear," he said. "All my work is guaranteed."

"Yes. So Mr. Cunningham, to what do I owe this pleasure?"

"Well, I'm afraid I have bad news for you. I was driving by and noticed some shingles missing from your roof."

"Missing?" she said, concerned. "How?"

"You will certainly remember that storm we had a few weeks back. That wind did a number on roofs all over town."

"Oh, heavens. That storm gave me a fright."

"If you care to step outside I can point out what I believe to be the damaged area. Won't know for sure 'til I get up on a ladder." Reg came down the steps to make room for her to follow. Having purposely left his cane in the van, he tried to minimize his limp.

"Oh, would you look there," he said with mock surprise, pointing at her azalea bushes beneath the bay window. He went to the bushes and pulled out two pieces of torn shingles. "Here they are now."

"Are those mine?" Mrs. Cale said.

He examined them, testing their flexibility. "'Fraid so. Pretty brittle, too." A corner broke off. "Christ all Friday," he said. "Excuse my language, ma'am, but I haven't seen one snap like that in some time. Hope we don't need to do a complete tear-off."

"A what?" Mrs. Cale said, accepting a broken piece of shingle that Reg extended to her.

"A tear-off. Start over from the plywood. Feel how brittle that shingle is?" Reg solemnly shook his head. "Bad sign."

"How much would that cost?" Mrs. Cale asked, now worried.

Reg squinted. "Right around $3000 all told." Reg could tell by Mrs. Cale's reaction that that number wasn't going to fly.

"Three thousand dollars!" she said.

"Now don't you worry, Mrs. Cale. I think we can patch it for less than a third of that." Reg continued to flex the shingle. "Right about $950."

"Would my insurance cover it?"

"Pardon me?" Reg said, turning to her with his better ear.

"My insurance. Would it cover the costs?"

"Step on back here a minute. Let's have a look." They back-stepped onto the lawn until they were offered a full view of the roof. "As far as insurance goes, chances are you got a one-thousand-dollar deductible so it would do you no good to involve them. They'd just hike your rates. Nothing but thieves in neckties, those guys." Reg spat. "It's hard to see with the sun glare coming off the roof, but I think I see the trouble there near the ridge by the chimney flashing. Looks like a few shingles tore loose. I'd have to replace a small area up there to make it blend. You don't want an unsightly spot up there that everyone can see from the street. I think I could do it so you'd never even know it was patched."

"I'm not sure I see anything, Mr. Cunningham...?" Mrs. Cale held her hand over her eyes, trying to duck under the sun's angle for a better look.

"You need to know what you're looking for. *I* won't even know for positive till I'm up there. One thing's for sure, those shingles didn't fall from the sky."

"I guess so," Mrs. Cale said. "Will you be okay up there? I noticed your leg seems to be bothering you."

"That's kind of you to ask. I'll be fine. Years of experience."

Mrs. Cale looked at him. "When would you get started?"

"Right away," Reg said with no small amount of concern. "What you don't want is rain coming in there along that valley and working its way to damaging your ceiling. $250 down will get us started with materials." Reg looked back at the roof with a grave expression. "If you want to get your checkbook, I'll go to the van and write up the job and get you your receipt. That's Cunningham, three ns."

At the liquor store, Reg swaggered in, the conquering hero. He went straight to the cigar section.

The owner looked up from his *Playboy*. "Those are out of your league, Cunningham. Why don't you stick to picking butts out of the gutter?"

Reg noticed the magazine. "Sorry to interrupt your date. How's business?"

The owner grew suspicious. "Solid. Weekend stuff. Why should you care?"

Reg came over and placed a check down on the centerfold, strategically. "Don't want such a nice young girl to catch cold."

The owner grabbed the check and looked it over while Reg, an unlit cigar already in his mouth, strolled to the shelf of hard liquor. Impressed, the owner whistled.

Reg looked over the bottles of bourbon, grinning. "Can you cash it? Or should I have gone to Parker's where they do a decent book of business and have more than five bucks in the till?"

"This thing will bounce like a dead cat."

Reg laughed. "You calling Mrs. Cale a crook? She's an upstanding member of our fine community."

"What are you talking about?" The owner snapped the check and looked closer at the endorser.

"Mrs. Cale, dip-shit. Right there on the check."

The owner shook his head. "You idiot. This check is from Erma Gibbs."

Reg pulled out his wallet. "Oh yeah. Gave you the wrong check. Well that one will do. Had a busy day today."

The owner crossed his arms. "What kind of scam you running?"

"Phone is ringing off the hook after that windstorm." Reg shrugged innocently. "Can you cash it, big boy, or should I run down the street to a real liquor store?"

The owner squinted at the date on the check. The signature looked good. "As long as you're spending $50 of the $500 here, we're good."

Reg laughed. "You've got nothing to worry about. A hard day's work puts a thirst on a guy. Go get me a box. You'll have some carrying out to do."

Reg had one more stop to make before home. Saturday afternoon meant Dianne would be working at the Night & Day on Main. He could use another shirt or pair of slacks. His wardrobe was almost complete.

The white van pulled to the curb, rolling up enough for the tire to let out a squeal. Reg tucked the traveler pint under the seat and looked in the rear-view mirror thinking of young Dianne. So unscathed. He smoothed over his hair.

It was an oasis, stepping inside the shop, out of the glaring sun. Light music played, mixed with an aroma Reg associated with new and unblemished and folded. And there was Dianne coming from around the counter. Tall. Scooped blouse flattering her prominent chest. A leather skirt. How old? Seventeen? Eighteen?

"Well, hello Mr. Cunningham." She came over and touched his arm. "I thought I lost my best customer."

Reg shrank from the touch. "Nah," he said. "Just been awful busy out there. You know, after that windstorm a few weeks back."

Dianne's face became animated. "It was sooo scary. I thought the whole house was going to blow over." Reg loved how Dianne's front teeth crossed just slightly. And her nose wasn't perfect; had it been broken? "What can I help you find?" she said, ending the uncomfortable silence.

"Oh. Yeah. I think it will be slacks today. If you're not too busy."

Dianne threw her hair back. "God. It's been *dead*. Everybody's out raking leaves. I don't get it. What's the big deal about getting those things into bags? For my dad, wind blows one way, he chases them down with a rake. Wind blows the other, he chases them the other way. Slacks you say? To match your last shirt? Robin's egg blue, wasn't it?"

"Yes."

"Let's go have a look." Dianne touched him lightly on the elbow, guiding him after her. They went to the back, where the men's slacks were racked.

"What color do you think?" she asked looking over her shoulder, Reg following behind.

"That's a pretty dress," Reg said flatly.

Dianne giggled. "Oh, thank you, Mr. Cunningham. I bought it at a competitor's store in Duluth." She put her finger to her lips. "Our secret."

"Definitely," Reg said.

"Now, what's your waist size?" Dianne asked.

Reg stretched his neck. "Boy, I can never remember." He put his cane on top of a circular rack of marked-down shirts.

"Oh, it's nothing. We'll just measure again. Let me grab my tape measure."

Dianne got close to Reg and circled her arms around his waist with the yellow tape. He took a deep breath, pulling in not only his

AUTUMN 1985

gut, but the trace aroma of bubble gum and hair conditioner.

"Thirty-three and a half inches. You do keep yourself in good shape, Mr. Cunningham."

He patted his belly. "I could drop a few. Hard with my leg bothering me the way it does."

"How did it you hurt it?" Dianne casually asked.

A look disfigured Reg's face. Dianne took a step backward, wishing she hadn't asked.

"Work accident," he said hoarsely.

"Gosh, I'm sorry."

He looked at her. "You're not the one who's going to be sorry."

A chill crawled up Dianne's spine. "Um, how about we check that inseam. Make sure everything fits just right." She did her best to lighten the mood.

Reg brightened. "You're the boss."

They agreed on a nice pair of dark blue slacks. Dianne thought that color would go better in the fall and upcoming winter. "Let me get you a bag for these," she said, now that they were back at the front counter. Reg moved quicker than usual, positioning himself across from her, perfectly situated for the highlight. Dianne leaned over, reaching under the counter for a store bag. The neckline of her blouse fell open to give Reg full view of her ample breasts cupped in a lacy pink brassiere. "Now where is that bag?" she said, rummaging around. "Oh, there we are," she said, straightening. Dianne gave Reg a knowing smile. When working commission, a girl has to do what a girl has to do. "Will it be cash, check or credit card today, Mr. Cunningham?"

With his Night & Day bag in one hand, cane in the other, Reg came out of the quiet half-light of the store directly into the sharp-angled sunlight and practically tripped over a little boy preoccupied with his chocolate ice cream cone. He and his mom were coming from the next store over.

"Singer, be careful!" Hanna took the boy's free hand. "Please excuse us," she said, offering Reg a boys-will-be-boys smile.

SINGER

It took Reg a beat before recognizing her. She was Hanna Donnovan, from the news. Reg's mind moved quickly. *If that's Hanna Donnovan and that's her boy ...* he scanned ahead. *Cory.* Reg recognized him even looking at his back. A half block ahead, Cory reached for the passenger door of his pickup. "Not at all," Reg said, mussing the boy's hair. He turned and took a step in the opposite direction.

Cory pulled open the passenger door and tilted the seat up so Singer could squeeze through to his car seat in back. Reg set his bag down, got to one knee and pulled the bow out of his shoelace so he could busy himself retying it. He heard Cory's voice call to Hanna and Singer. With his shoe retied, Reg stole a look over his shoulder, watching Cory come around the bed of the truck and get behind the wheel. Reg stood and walked in the direction of the pickup. The truck's engine turned over and the backup lights came on. The parking on Baudette's Main Street had filled, leaving Cory pretty much pinned between two cars. Reg approached as Cory carefully worked his way out. The rear bumper of the old truck was rusted, dinged, with two bumper stickers, one on either end. The one on the left read Wisconsin Badger Hockey, the large W logo a sun-faded red. The newer brighter bumper sticker on the right read Duluth East Greyhounds with two crossed hockey sticks over a bold E. Cory's truck eased into the street.

"So that's where you are," Reg said, hanging back by the curb, watching the vehicle pull away. "Won't be hard to find that truck in the high school parking lot." He swung his shopping bag lightly at his side, as the truck distanced itself.

"I don't feel good." Singer said, from the back of the truck. "I don't want this." He held his ice cream toward the front seat.

"What, honey?" Hanna said. "Oh here, let me take that. What's wrong?"

"My head hurts."

Hanna unbuckled her seatbelt so she could turn for a better look at Singer. "Did you eat your ice cream too fast?"

AUTUMN 1985

"Should we pull over?" Cory asked Hanna.

"No!" Singer said more urgently than either expected. "Keep going."

Reg drank dinner. And dessert. He weaved out the front door, down the steps to the garage where he nearly fell trying to raise the rolling door. He gave it a good kick, this time succeeding in falling. Inside, junk stared back at him, stacked everywhere, sometimes as high as a stepladder. Like a labyrinth, narrow paths twisted and wound along the cracked concrete slab floor, allowing access to different areas of the garage. The summer dampness had retreated, but a sharp-edged whiff of mold and old tire rubber awaited him.

Reg headed to the center of the garage. In the dark of the space, the big desk came into focus under the garage light. He pulled open the drawer and found the pistol waiting. "Hello there," he said picking it up and pressing the gun's cool metal handle to his cheek. Reg nearly dropped the pistol as he fumbled to slide out the clip. "You're more loaded than me," he laughed, counting seven bullets. He stuffed the gun into his waistband.

GOING SOMEWHERE CUTIE? Reg flinched. The voice of Kemp pressed in from behind, hard and whiskered. Reg shrank, shuddering. COLD SWEETIE? WE CAN FIX THAAAT. Reg shook his head no. TIME FOR YOU TO LEARN THAT NOTHING GETS DONE BY THINKING ABOUT IT. TIME FOR SOME ACTION. Reg's ears burned, in memory of the injury. He clamped his hands over them, just as he had years ago when Kemp peeled his fingers away and filled both ear canals with glue from the schoolroom. He squirted it in and plugged them with toilet paper. The doctor was able to clear them eventually, but not without tearing one eardrum. NO REASON TO HEAR YOUR-SELF SCREAM BECAUSE NO ONE ELSE WILL. Reg jerked the pistol from his waistband and swung it violently left and right. He stumbled as he spun, pointing frantically at nothing. His mouth an ugly curl, spittle mixed with scratchy breathing.

"Action? You son of a bitch, I'll show you action!" In manic little hops, Reg swirled in a semi-circle, seeking a target. "Where are you?" His voice raged, ricocheting off appliances, boxes, shelves of old paint, car batteries, tires, standing rolls of used carpet. Finally, he flung his hands to the rafters and screamed, long and ugly. But it was 40 years too late. "There is hell to pay and I will not accept one penny less!"

Throughout the neighborhood, dogs began to bark.

AUTUMN 1985

THE FARM

"You feeling better, buddy?" Cory unbuckled the car seat and helped maneuver Singer toward the sunshine-splashed farmyard. The way the boy leaped to the ground and skipped away from the truck, gave Cory his answer.

HomeSky and Meadow came onto the porch and waved. Hanna waved back. "Why am I nervous?" she whispered to Cory, taking his arm.

"Just follow your son's lead," Cory said. Singer had already made it up onto the porch and was hugging HomeSky.

"I brought my magic bear. And my storm ball!" Singer said. HomeSky relished the hug.

"I don't think we've officially met," Cory said coming up the porch steps. He extended a hand to Meadow. "I'm Cory and this is Hanna." He smiled a dimpled grin.

SINGER

Meadow paused, distracted by the sight of Cory. He came with such a story, to meet him was intimidating. But there was something about him she trusted. A carefulness. It was unusual for her to be comfortable around a new face. And Hanna, oh my God. She was more beautiful in person than on TV. Meadow looked from one to the other, as all stood semi-stuck in the introduction, waiting for Meadow to say something. All she could think was *you're Cory the legend and you're Hanna the beautiful and I'm Meadow, the stretchmarked.*

"Boozhoo, welcome," she said. She shook Cory's hand, then Hanna's. "This is my son," she said, bringing both hands to her sizable belly.

"You look fantastic," Hanna said, meaning every word of it.

Cory's eyes didn't leave Meadow. *What is it about her?*

"Hey, hey!" Pat said making his way out of the barn, wiping his hands with a shop rag. "I thought I heard an old bucket of bolts pull in." He strode across the farmyard looking as happy as Cory had seen him in years. Cory came down off the porch to give him a back-clapping embrace in the yard. It was Hanna's turn to be surprised. Cory wasn't a hugger.

"What a day the Lord has made," Pat said, holding his palms up. "Don't tell anyone it's the end of September. Maybe the streak will continue." Pat spotted Singer. "Well! Who's that we have here?" He took long strides toward the porch.

Singer saw his opportunity. "It's me!" he said as he ran the length of the porch and leaped right into Pat's oncoming arms. Trust, in curls and sneakers.

"It sure is," Pat said. "Gosh you're getting big."

"Feel my muscles," Singer told him.

"You feel mine." Pat replied.

"Nice to meet you," Hanna softly said to Meadow, as they watched the Singer and Pat show.

"Thank you. You too," Meadow didn't know what to say next.

AUTUMN 1985

"I've never met a TV star before." The minute she said it she wished she had it back.

"Well, I wouldn't make too much of that. Take away the makeup and the teleprompter and we're all pretty much the same."

Meadow smiled, thinking there wasn't enough makeup in the world to ever look so good. "You have a beautiful child. He goes by Singer?"

Hanna looked over at her boy, who had now wrestled Pat to the ground and was going for the pin. "Thank you. Yes. Singer." She shook her head and laughed. "You wouldn't know it by looking at him, but he's all music."

Meadow nodded. "A name can be your story," she said contemplatively, looking not at Hanna, but at the child under his flounce of golden hair.

"Is there a story to Meadow?" Hanna asked. Meadow looked at her, the intensity of her eyes off-putting. "Not to my knowledge," she said. Truth be told, when Meadow first became a teenager she asked her father what her name meant. He was drunk. When he stopped laughing he said a meadow is a place a horse goes to shit.

Cory got their bags out of the pickup bed and HomeSky showed them to the guest room. This had been Meadow's room, but she volunteered to move to the smaller spare bedroom on the first floor. When HomeSky had helped move her things, she was struck by Meadow's austerity. A laundry basket handled all her clothes, backpack and few belongings. A second trip for her guitar had her moved out. It gave HomeSky pause, a warning of sorts. The untethered travel too lightly, recklessly, as HomeSky had when she left this very property. Reminder served, HomeSky redoubled her efforts to make this farmhouse also Meadow's.

"HomeSky!" a little voice shouted from the top of the stairs. It lifted goose bumps. To be asked for. Too many years had come between HomeSky and a high voice calling out in this farmhouse.

"Yes ..." she cleared her throat. "Yes, Singer."

"Come up and see my stuff." After a moment he added the word please, most certainly at his mother's behest.

Singer had his favorite pillow on his rolled-out sleeping bag. Resting on his pillow was magic bear. On the center of the bag was his storm ball, a small, inflated, bright blue ball with a red band and yellow stars.

"See?" Singer plopped down on the sleeping bag and patted it, urging HomeSky to join him. "Isn't this great?" He lay back in a sleeping position, hands behind his head on the pillow. "Mom says I get to sleep here but if I don't like it, Cory will, and I'll sleep up there with her." Singer pointed to the queen-size bed.

HomeSky stretched out next to him on the sleeping bag. "This *is* great," HomeSky confirmed. Hanna was unpacking a few things and putting them in drawers. She had finished her bag and moved onto Cory's.

"Who's this?" HomeSky asked, picking up the stuffed bear.

Cory darted into the room as Hanna unzipped his bag. "Oops, I'll take that." He all but pulled the bag out of her hands. "Have to get my running gear."

Hanna was surprised. "Okay. You sure are raring to go."

Cory nodded. "Long drive. I'll get changed in the bathroom."

Meanwhile, Singer was explaining magic bear to HomeSky—how he came from Lake of the Woods and how he could tell people things that hadn't happened yet.

"Really," she said. "That's a good kind of bear to have. Where did he get this beautiful necklace?"

"My friend Stu made it. Do you know Stu?"

"Yes. We've met a few times."

Singer handled the arrowpoint. It was tied around the bear's neck with a thin leather strap. "This is really, really old." Singer's eyes widened. "It's sharp, but it's made of a stone."

HomeSky had seen arrowheads; her grandfather had kept a few when she was growing up, but she couldn't remember one so entrancing. "Now I see where your bear gets his magic."

AUTUMN 1985

In the bathroom, Cory checked inside his rolled socks and found the small ring box. He looked in the mirror. "A couple minutes later, pal, and the cat's out of the bag." He cracked it open. His mouth went dry. The ring was equal parts beautiful and frightening. Cory smiled to himself. Shopping for it was a spectacle. He wanted to surprise Hanna, so he went alone. At the sales counter it was immediately evident he knew nothing about rings, or specifically what he was looking for. Then the double whammy struck: sticker shock multiplied by the cold sweats of a lifetime commitment. Cory was incapacitated. He was about to bail out when a particular ring caught the light just so and flicked him a glint. It was far too expensive. It probably wouldn't fit. He should shop a few other stores—but here he was, a few days later, in the bathroom, in a farmhouse on the land where Joseph grew up, in search of an adequate hiding place for that engagement ring.

Behind his ear, Cory found the stone braided in his hair. It was centering, its touch. His fingers, so close to the back of his ear, were amplified as they slid across the stone, providing something sure above the pester of uncertainty. The words from Shara's letter came to him: *Singer and Hanna are here to take you fast down the hallway.* Could it be so? Cory, twice flattened by the unapologetic shove of life. Upon rising, he encountered tragedy's unrelenting question: which direction to face? The past behind. The future in front.

Cory made a hiding place for the ring box behind the bath towels.

Upon returning to the bedroom, he found it empty. From downstairs there came the faint strumming of guitar chords blended with Singer's voice. Cory addressed the stuffed animal next to the storm ball on Singer's sleeping bag. "Well, magic bear, what's the word? Will it be yes, or will it be no?"

CONVERSATIONS

Forty-five minutes later, Sheriff Harris, Kitty, Monsignor Kief and a very excited Private arrived. The Sheriff hadn't stepped back on this land since the shooting. It would have been untrue to say there wasn't a twisting in his gut. "Here we are," he said with forced cheer.

"What a beeeautiful spot," Kitty said, not recognizing the tension in his voice. She went on in an enchanted tone about the farmhouse, its cupola, the surrounding fields, the view. And maybe that was for the best—the innocence of others—seeing something through their eyes.

Private leapt out of the back seat of the cruiser and began an investigation of smells so numerous he was yanked from one spot to the next. The Sheriff stepped out, uneasy. He tried to see only the beauty of the ridge that humped up to the east, with the stretch of trees riding along its back, the first autumn leaves lit like candles,

AUTUMN 1985

Pat tried to mask his surprise, but Cory was too astute for that.

"I know." Cory held up a hand as if to ward something off. "Doesn't seem like me. But it's not just me anymore. Plus, I hear myself telling my students and my players they have to get out of *their* comfort zones. You know?"

"Bravo," Pat said. "Dinner. Extraordinary. The perfect setting for a moment you'll never forget. Do you have a plan?"

"Sort of."

"What is it?" Pat was like a seven-year-old with his nose pressed to the glass of a toy store.

"Guess you'll have to wait and see." Cory winked at Pat.

"Ouch, that's harsh." Pat mock pleaded, "C'mon, I'm your inside guy. Your corner man." He threw a few air punches.

Cory laughed before switching to a more serious tone. "Actually, I was wondering if you'd be my best man."

Pat looked at Cory. *For real?* his face said.

Cory nodded. "I'd be honored if you'd be my best man."

Cory ran next to Pat with a smile on his face that Pat found difficult to label. The sun bounced in Cory's curls; he was keeping his hair longer now. A dimple sunk in his cheek. His gray-green eyes had a different intensity level to them ... more of a beauty.

"You look very content right now," Pat said.

"I know. And it scares the living crap out of me."

"I'd love to be your best man." Pat put his hand out as they ran.

Cory took it. Held it a moment. They came running down the gravel, perhaps no more than seven steps, hand-in-hand. Seven steps. They had traveled so far, yet became forever closer in that short distance.

Cory let go and stopped running. They had about a quarter mile of gravel until they were back at the farm. Pat's first response was to wonder if Cory had somehow injured himself.

Cory exhaled. "As my future best man, certified psychologist and overall keen observer of human struggles, can I ask you something?" Cory was attempting to keep the tone light, which led Pat to believe the opposite was coming.

Pat pulled up, hands on his hips, sweat streaming down his face and neck. "Yeah. Absolutely."

They walked down the empty road. Cory kicked a rock. "Are you familiar with the word anhedonia?"

Pat thought for a moment. "Sure. Give or take a few words, it's an inability to experience joy."

"I came across that word a couple years ago," Cory said. "It jumped out at me. I tried not to think about it, but there it was. Odd. Trying to dodge a word. Anyway, anhedonia. The word has been there since. With me."

Pat just listened.

"I think I might have experienced it … or might have it, for lack of the right clinical term."

Pat's thinking furrow creased. "Could be," he said taking the issue straight on. "But maybe not. I will tell you this. I'm familiar enough on the subject, having read and dealt with it with a few people I've counseled. What I do know is it's by no means a permanent condition."

Cory nodded. "I guess I'm less worried about that." Cory wiped sweat from his face. "I don't mean this literally, okay, but I worry if it's contagious. There's Hanna. She finds joy in the smallest, brightest little corners of the room that I walk past. I couldn't go through with this marriage if I thought I might take that from her. And from Singer."

Pat nodded. He could tell that Cory had been through his usual hard consideration on the issue. "Cory, you're a significant part of the joy in their lives. You are in that light that has spread to the corners of their rooms."

"I guess." he said. "I'm just worried. I have a hard time trusting this." He wiped the sweat from his face. "I'm not sure I have faith in tomorrow. I'm not what you'd call the luckiest person."

Pat walked next to Cory, letting him go on uninterrupted.

AUTUMN 1985

"There's an Ojibwe expression Joseph used once. I'll never forget it." Cory looked at Pat. "'Don't reach for a falling knife.'" Cory kicked a small stone to the weeds. "I asked him where it came from and he said his dad used to say it about a few of the kids on the Rez."

Pat stopped walking. His words had some bite to them. "You're not saying you're the falling knife?"

Cory returned his intensity. "Pat. Things happen around me. You've seen that."

Pat's face went slack. "Cory, things happen, period. They happen around you. They happen around me. They happen around the neighbor who's taking out his corn. How do you move on? That's life's question."

"Carefully," Cory said, just loud enough to be heard.

"That's fine," Pat said throwing his arm around Cory's shoulders and giving him a shake. "That's fine. Just keep moving, and make sure it's that way." Pat pointed.

They had come around the road's back bend. The last of the wheat was rolled in the front field, the cornfield they rented to a neighbor was ready for harvest, and centered in between was the farmhouse, in miniature, a quarter-mile in the distance, with its white paint luminous in the sun. Singer was in the sideyard chasing Private who bounded ahead of him, curling back to call the boy on, barks so exuberant that all paws left the ground. Hanna, Meadow and Monsignor Kief sat on the porch steps, soaking in the day. HomeSky filled a watering pail from the red hand pump under the sprawling oak.

"Keep moving toward that," Pat said. "Run, walk or crawl. You'll find the trust and the faith you so richly deserve."

Private turned and let out a lower pitched bark to the men approaching from the road. Hanna waved from the porch. Cory put up his hand and waved in return.

HANNA AND MONSIGNOR KIEF

The farm dipped to lowland out away from the house. Depending on the year's rainfall, the pond there would expand or contract. It had been a wet growing season, perfect for all with crops in the ground. The runoff pushed the pond's edges wider, past the cattail stalks. Hanna led Monsignor Kief down the gradual slope. Two mallards sprang from the water, the hen's raspy quacks making it clear the disturbance was not appreciated.

"Good day to you, too," Monsignor Kief said, his face lifting to follow the flight of the ducks. "Was there just the one?" he asked.

"Two," Hanna said.

"Ah, a perfect set-up to our conversation, I might imagine."

Hanna watched the drake and hen, wing to wing, getting smaller on the horizon. "Here's a good spot," she said. "The pond is just in front of us." She put down a blanket.

"I'm sure this sounds odd," Monsignor Kief said, "but the tang of slough sulfur is a smell I quite like. In reasonable doses." He accepted Hanna's arm as she helped him sit. "Ah, that's nice." The sun glowed on his face.

"I appreciate having some time with you," Hanna started, a bit haltingly. "I wish we had more opportunity to talk."

Monsignor Kief smiled. "Time is wild. As much as we try to domesticate it, it runs on." He paused. "I think the last we talked was back at Cory's graduation party, hosted flawlessly if I recall."

Hanna shook her head. "Oh, thank you. Can you believe it? Like you said, where does the time go?"

"Straight to your joints," Monsignor Kief kidded, adjusting his sitting position.

"How are you feeling?" Hanna asked.

"All things considered, great. One is lucky to encounter three score plus eleven years, and still be of reasonably sound mind. Not to mention, of reasonably solid foods." He laughed. "All kidding aside, I am blessed. But let's talk about you and Cory, shall we?"

Hanna was grateful for the runway to the conversation. "I sense I'm at an inflection point, I think they call it. Like at the cusp of something life-changing or life-confirming." She rubbed her arms as a shiver went through her. "I had a pretty big job interview over the summer, in Philadelphia. As it turned out they offered me the anchor desk for their prime-time news slot. Professionally, it was everything I could have dreamt for. But it meant pulling up roots, taking Singer out of Duluth, which we love. And there's Cory. His job. His life is here."

"Would he relocate with you?"

"He said he would, but even before saying so, I knew it was the wrong thing for us—I mean for Singer and me. I'm not sure how far *us* stretches. Where Cory ultimately is on all of this. I'm asking a lot of him, and I've told him so. He's 24. He has whatever future in front of him he wants. I have Singer, my future." Hanna thought about how to phrase her lingering doubt. "Is it wrong of me to ask so much of Cory? Is it selfish?"

"It's never selfish to ask," the Monsignor said. "It's only selfish to demand a certain answer."

"Monsignor, I'm not trying to turn this into a confession, but I do worry."

"About what, dear?"

"About me. About … I. Becoming too self-important. At the station, I get inordinate amounts of attention … people fussing over me … recognition in the community. It's easy to start to think the world revolves around you. It's frightening."

"The fact that you recognize it, and you're cautious, is good."

"There's so much superficiality in my profession. Staying thin. Makeup. Hair. Beauty queen nonsense."

The Monsignor nodded knowingly. "There are, you'd be surprised to learn, more than a few advantages to being blind. Among them is understanding that beauty is much more than skin deep." The Monsignor leaned back on his arms, stretching his legs so the sunshine could find more of him. "I hope you don't take this as overly preachy, but in my younger years in divinity school I was enlightened to something that I've since shared with many, many friends over the years." He sat up. "May I have one of your hands?" As Hanna reached out, the Monsignor turned her hand palm up. With his fingertip, he traced a circle in her palm. "It's not this that matters," he said. "This is what the mirror reflects, and the mirror reflects no depth. What matters is this." He touched the center of the circle. "Faith is knowing where beauty is."

Hanna closed her hand and smiled. "I'll keep that with me. Thank you."

"And try not to worry too much. Your true beauty is quite obvious to me."

It was a day of treasures. Small yellow butterflies lit on sun-warmed bare patches at the fringe of the pond, their butter-colored wings hinging open and closed. Others twirled down from above,

AUTUMN 1985

face-to-face, a butterfly kiss. White clouds, owned by no particular shape, whipped the sky. Tasseled corn rolled out like a blanket of green thrown over the field across the road. In the pasture just beyond the pond, monarch butterfly flags swayed in the breeze atop purple heads of alfalfa. All was as quiet as a door swinging shut. It was a day of mending.

"What do you miss seeing?" Hanna asked.

"Hmmm," Monsignor Kief said, a thoughtful smile spreading across his face. "I can still see things in my mind—captured like old photographs. I miss people's eyes, seeing into them. Everything is there. Our bodies fade around them, but the eyes hold bright, just as they were at 18 years old." Monsignor Kief adjusted his body position on the blanket.

"Is it too uncomfortable sitting here?" Hanna asked.

"Not at all," he said. "Do you mind if I now ask *you* a question?" The Monsignor patted Hanna's leg.

"Sure," Hanna said, trying to sound as though she were.

"Do you pray?"

"Oh," she said, "I wasn't expecting that." She sat up straighter. "I'm not too big on it, really." Hanna interrupted herself, "But I have asked God to help me to know if I'm doing the right thing, bringing Cory into my life—our lives."

"Excellent," Monsignor Kief said. "And God's reply?"

"Nothing."

"Are you sure?"

"I think so. Yeah."

"Well, God doesn't always wave back immediately."

Hanna looked at Monsignor Kief. His little smile gave him the appearance of being in on a secret. "What do you mean?"

"We wave at God. We say, hi God, I've got a question for you. Or we wave more earnestly: hey, there's something I need! And just because God doesn't wave back right away doesn't mean He's not listening. Some answers are meant to come by the scenic route. So, keep waving. Your answer will come."

"How long do I wait?"

"You wait for as long as it's worth."

Hanna took a long breath and let out a question from very deep inside her. "But what if Cory isn't right, and I'm wasting my time waiting for God to get back to me?"

"Do you feel like you're wasting time here? Now?"

"No," Hanna said assuredly. "But as you know, Cory has dealt with some pretty rotten and dark moments." She didn't know where to go from there.

"I know, dear." Monsignor Kief reflected. "But, but, Hanna Donnovan," his voice strengthened, "it is in the dark of God's pocket where sometimes you're closest to Him."

"So you think he'll be fine?" Hanna asked urgently.

"I do think he'll be fine. And you're a big part of why. And Singer. I think providence brought the three of you together."

Hanna nodded. "He is changed. Especially around Singer."

"Every child is heaven-sent. But your Singer was hand-delivered."

Hanna beamed. "He is something, isn't he? I've only had one so I have nothing to compare him to."

The Monsignor's eyebrows raised. "I have known many and I have nothing to compare him to, either."

AUTUMN 1985

SINGER

HomeSky and Meadow put out crackers and cheese and everyone, including Private, indulged. Pat took Singer for a quick tractor ride. Meadow opted for a nap. HomeSky and Kitty washed carrots and squash and soaked the wild rice in preparation for dinner. The Sheriff and Private ducked out for a long walk. Walks were still a bit uncomfortable, the Sheriff said, until the oil made it to his ankle. But he was continuing to lose about a pound a week and, all in all, felt more energetic than he had in years.

Meadow awoke to the low throttle of the tractor returning to the farmyard. She stretched and went to the window. "There they are," she whispered to B. "Your big guy pal Singer is steering right from Pat's lap." The two decided on one more circle around the yard before heading into the machine shed.

Downstairs, Meadow asked if she could help but HomeSky and Kitty shooed her away. She went out to the porch. A song flowed through her.

On the steps
In the sun
You can stay
You can run

You belong here
Stay with me
Here's forgiveness
In the tree

Climb in
Climb up
Tell the ground
You've had enough

Climb in
You will see
So far ahead
In the forgiveness tree

Meadow reached for her pocket. She was self-conscious in shorts, but the weather insisted on it. On her folded piece of paper, she wrote, leaning the page against the porch post. Meadow had scraps of songs everywhere. Some she could read, some were illegible even to her. The lead of the pencil rode up and down the page. Now and then letters were pushed out of round by the bumpy texture beneath, giving her words an organic flair she liked. "Just as long as you can read it later," she confided in herself.

"Meadow!" Singer shouted out, running toward the porch. "How's B? Can I feel?"

"Sure," Meadow said. The little boy leaned in, smelling of hay and sunshine. His small, perfect hands rested on her belly, his

AUTUMN 1985

head just behind them. "Wait for it now," she whispered to Singer. "Wait …"

Her baby kicked. Singer's mouth dropped open. "Did you feel that!"

"Yeah. Did you?" Meadow asked.

Singer nodded as fast as he could.

"He wants to come out and play with you," Meadow told him.

"Really?"

"Yep," Meadow said. "He's kicking to get out."

Suddenly, Singer had Meadow's hand, a gesture that nearly made her cry. "Come here," he said, leading her away from the house. He turned and pointed toward the roof. "Can we go up there?"

Meadow looked at the cupola. "Sure."

"I bet we can see for far away."

"Let's go find out." Hand in hand they went.

Walking up the stairs to the second floor, Meadow said, "Can I tell you a secret?"

Singer looked up at her with anticipation. "A keep-it secret or an everybody secret?"

Meadow smiled at his odd delineation. "More of a keep-it secret."

"Uh-huh," Singer said dutifully.

Meadow looked at his beauty and thought of her child climbing these same stairs in the coming years. The aspect of future had never frightened her because, what did she care? Now her mouth was dry. "I can't remember the last time I held hands," she told Singer.

"Really?"

"Really."

Singer asked, "Not even with your mom?"

"Not that I can remember."

Singer's brow wrinkled, then his eyes brightened. "It's good you're having a baby." He squeezed her hand tighter. "They're good at holding hands, starting with one finger."

The cupola was accessed from a pull-down ladder to the attic, and then from another smaller, narrower ladder to the windowed space itself. It was quite warm in the small cupola, despite the louvered windows being rolled out for ventilation. Pat had stationed an old wooden sitting chair there; Singer stood on it. Next to him, Meadow kept her arm around his waist as he turned a full circle, mesmerized in all directions. It was funny, Singer said, how teeny-tiny Monsignor Kief and Hanna looked on the blanket near the pond. As his head tilted up, he looked out at the ridge and began to hum. He stood almost as tall as Meadow on the wooden chair, leaning on her shoulder. At that, she began to softly cry, feeling HomeSky's loss of an adult child. If Singer knew of her tears, there was no showing. His humming became singing and it went up to the sky.

Meadow absorbed his Sun Dance song. His music went out for the next generation, for protection, so the young might find maturity, wisdom and a long, happy life. The Sun Dance music spoke. It told Meadow this was her good place.

AUTUMN 1985

DINNER

Bowls and plates of food were passed around the table. Everyone was encouraged to load up; there was plenty. Pat and Cory had barbequed two heaping platters of chicken on a large grill constructed of an old iron rain barrel cut lengthwise, with four poles for legs. Pat skewered a piece and told the table that this was where his and Cory's culinary abilities ended.

"When we were young," HomeSky said, passing the butternut squash, "in the fall we'd go to my uncle's farm. They'd rake the leaves in the farmyard, making piles as big as small sheds."

"Would you jump in them?" Singer wanted to know.

"We would. But they were mostly for the fall feast. My dad and uncles would shoot ducks. My mother and aunts brought wild rice from the lake, and potatoes and squash from the fields. We'd wrap the vegetables in aluminum foil, and bury them in the bottom of the largest leaf pile, get it burning, and keep adding to that burn pile all afternoon. By dinnertime, we'd shovel out the vegetables, cooked to perfection. Whenever I smell cooked squash or baked potatoes, the aroma of burning leaves comes with it." Pat looked at HomeSky. He had never heard that story.

"Before we begin this feast, we should say grace," Pat said. "We have so much to be thankful for. Frank, will you do the honors?"

Monsignor Kief bowed his head and folded his hands; the others followed. "Great and loving Lord, we don't stop often enough to acknowledge Your gifts. Thank You for today, for delicious food and amazing fellowship. Help us, every one, to pause, and open our gift called today in the light of the moment. Help me, and my friends here, not to put off our appreciation, but to live with a sense of now, and show our thanks by reaching out in love. Okay, God, please help me to say amen now before the food has grown cold and I've worn out my welcome. Because hospitality, as You know, is making someone feel at home even when you wish they were. Amen."

As everyone settled into dinner, Pat noticed Meadow had done little more than push her food around her plate. He leaned over. "Have I overcooked the chicken," he kidded in a whisper.

"No, no," she said. "It's great. Must have overdone it on the crackers and cheese." Meadow looked at HomeSky. HomeSky returned a rather furtive glance. Meadow picked up her knife, but dropped it, clattering off the plate. The unintended consequence was an all-eyes-on-her silence.

"Well," Meadow began tentatively, "now that I have your attention, I—we—have an announcement to make. HomeSky and I. Do." Everyone looked at her, which did little to advance her halting progress. HomeSky gave a nod—the tiny push she needed. Meadow swallowed a short drink of water. "That's a pregnant pause," she said. "So, deep breath... As you know, I'm having a baby soon, which is why I don't sit very close to the table," she delayed, trying humor to ease into her topic. "With Pat's help, we were able to get the BIA to certify HomeSky as the adoptive mother of my baby. Okay, no news there ..." HomeSky smiled at Meadow. Meadow

AUTUMN 1985

wiped an eye. "I'll try to keep all hormones in check, not start blubbering, but at this point, I've made a decision—with HomeSky, with her support—for me." Then, finally, she blurted: "I'm going to be my baby's mother." She looked at everyone around the table. "With lots of help from HomeSky. And Pat, too. I hope." Meadow let out a big exhale with eyes fixed on Pat.

"Truly?" He looked from Meadow's face to HomeSky's, and saw it was so. Pat went from astonished to elated. "I mean, we can do that, right?" he was thinking out loud now. Pat had spent so many months clearing the way for the adoption he'd all but forgotten that Meadow was 18, and completely within her rights to make this decision.

Pat slid back from the table, unable to contain his excitement. "*Now* I know what you two have been talking about on those walks of yours." He came over to Meadow and gave her a great big hug. "I hope you're still planning on staying here with your baby."

"Yes," Meadow said. "Yes."

"What's going on, Mom?" Singer wanted to know.

Hanna smiled at him. "Meadow was just telling us how excited she is to be a mother."

"I knew that," he said. "Can we eat now?"

"Yes, please," Meadow said. "Let's eat."

The meal was mixed with excited conversation about the baby. Cory watched Meadow, her transformation. She was a reserved girl, her eyes typically obstructed by her hair as she sank into her surroundings, observing. But to see her at the table now, excited, the center of attention, running two or three conversations, an angle of light had found her, revealing strength he hadn't previously seen in her face. For his part he did his best to participate, but his stomach was in heavy knots. He wondered if now was the right time. It was Meadow's moment, was it his place to intrude? The ring box bulged in his pocket.

They had proceeded halfway through dessert. If anything, Cory was further from asking Hanna for her hand in marriage than when he'd first sat down. What would be his first move—his gambit? Then he remembered gambit came from a word meaning tripping. Not exactly a confidence booster.

Everyone was focused on Meadow with her plans and next steps. How does one break into such a current of excitement with any grace whatsoever? *Maybe another time*, Cory thought. He looked around the table, struck by the faces there. Sheriff and Kitty talked to Meadow about a playground in their neighborhood with a pond for feeding ducks. HomeSky, looking so at home, Cory thought, like she had been when Joseph was at the table; now the object of her joy, Meadow, sitting across from her. Pat at the table's head, nodding, affirming, fork in hand but unable to get to dessert, so attentive to the conversation. Monsignor Kief, also busy talking, but not at the expense of his dessert. Hanna, looking beautiful and truly happy, offering to assist Meadow in any way she could, and Meadow, grateful, knowing that Hanna, a single mom, likely had some of the best advice of all. And Singer, looking directly at Cory. Cory raised his eyebrows. Singer continued to watch Cory, humming through a thin smile. *What a look on his face.* Cory winked at Singer. *It's almost like wisdom.* Singer nodded back. Cory glanced out the windows that lined the dining room. When he looked back, Singer remained surveillant.

Cory stood up from his chair, letting the act speak for itself. One by one the conversations dropped away. He waited patiently, his hands long gone clammy. "Meadow," he started, looking at her, "I too came to the table with news." Cory bit the inside of his cheek. "My apologies for changing the subject, but if I may ...?"

Meadow nodded, unsure what to make of Cory's formality. "Yeah, no problem."

Cory found the place inside him where years of composure were kept. A place he went to when athletics and academics and life put him on a stage, alone, and tested him mightily. He cleared his throat. He no doubt had everyone's attention. "HomeSky, Pat, this home, this spot, has been the setting of many plans and announcements. If you'll remember one Thanksgiving, Joseph and

AUTUMN 1985

I told you we were going to the University of Wisconsin to play hockey." HomeSky and Pat nodded. Cory rubbed his eyebrow. "I thought I was nervous *then* ..." he said.

"When I see Singer and Hanna here at this table, with all of you, I feel something, and I want to try to describe it by looking back, to our times here before." Cory knocked on the tabletop. "I understand that this isn't the same table, but it is." He looked at his surroundings. "I know this isn't the same house, but it is. And I know Joseph isn't here, but he is. Now that doesn't make much sense, coming from a person who likes things to make sense, but I think you know what I mean. There is completeness here. I've never felt it at another table." Cory looked at Hanna. Her face carried a little crease of concern in her brow. "I thought this table, this house, this spot to be *the* place to ask you, Hanna Donnovan, if you will marry me?" Cory took the ring box from his pocket.

Hanna's eyes grew wide and sparkled with tears. Her mouth parted. For the moment, all she could do was sit there and wonder if this was really happening. She nodded her head, and finally got out the words: "Yes. I'll marry you."

Singer was the first off his chair to join in the embrace. Cory, on one knee, slipped the ring on Hanna's finger. The three of them came together in a single hug. "Let me see your ring, Mom!" Singer shook with excitement.

Hanna had to spin the diamond so it faced up. "It's a little big," she told Singer as she squeezed the ring in place with her other fingers.

"Whoa. It's huge," Singer said, touching the diamond.

"The jewelry store said we could come in for a fitting, after the surprise," Cory explained.

"It's beautiful," Hanna said. "I love it."

By now the others had stood and gathered. All agreed. It was beautiful. HomeSky said a small Band-Aid and a cuticle scissors would have that ring fitting snugly for the time being. The Sheriff suggested a police escort home judging by the size of the stone.

Hanna extended her hand to Monsignor Kief. His fingers moved across the ring as he offered them both his congratulations and blessing. Meadow sat looking out the window, somewhere else.

The men insisted on washing and drying the dishes, but HomeSky stopped them there. She explained it was easier for her to put dishes away now than hunt for them over the next few days. Soon after, the Sheriff, Kitty, Monsignor Kief and Private said their goodbyes—Private cleaning all remains of dessert from Singer's face—before starting back for Baudette.

Things happen so fast, good and bad. Had all this good happened in the blink of an eye, as evening stepped in with its long-sleeve temperatures?

Hanna and Cory took Singer up to his sleeping bag for two books before lights out. Meadow went to her room to work on a song. HomeSky and Pat rocked quietly on the porch swing, watching the dusty sky go to dark plum, preparing to be pierced by the first star to wish upon.

"These are the sounds I didn't dare dream of," HomeSky said, parting the quiet.

Pat listened. Streaming through the screened front door, the faint strumming of guitar. From above, the low voice of a story being read slipped out the quarter-open bedroom window. The porch swing creaked as they rocked.

HomeSky turned to Pat. "Thank you for this. I thought all of this was gone for me."

Pat looked inward, thinking about what she said. Next to him, she was warm. "I called for you. To come home. I don't know how many times."

"I know. Thank you for not giving up."

"I'm not sure how to be close to you," Pat said.

HomeSky took his hand. They swayed ever so, forward, backward. "Time will show us." She brought his hand to her lap.

AUTUMN 1985

With Singer asleep, Cory and Hanna tiptoed downstairs and found the others in the farmyard. Pat had gone in to get Meadow, and turned off the porch and yard lights. Now the five of them soaked in stars.

"Unbelievable," Hanna said for the third time. "I've never seen so many. They seem closer. On top of us." She reached up as though to touch the sky.

Cory put his arm around her. "And the country woos another city girl."

"I'm not a city girl, exactly. Am I? Please say I'm not."

HomeSky spoke up. "Not anymore."

"Amen," Pat added.

Meadow took it all in. "It doesn't matter how many times you see stars like tonight. What's amazing is we're all seeing this light for the first time."

"Original light," HomeSky said. "The ancients call it *First Fire*."

Cory joked, "I felt a little under fire tonight." Hanna jabbed him with her elbow.

"I second that," Meadow said.

"You guys, seriously, did awesome," Pat said. "Big, big news, both of you. And sharing ... all of us together. What a gift..." Pat sometimes had a way of ending his sentences ragged, as if he hadn't quite captured his thought, but was feeling his way toward it. "Tonight was like using a candle to light other candles."

Their eyes remained cast upward to the sky at the endless throw of stars. Although none of them witnessed it, each of them had the same smile on their face.

The household slept. The front door had been left unlocked. Singer's sleepwalking took him to the ridge above the farmhouse, to the foot of the graves. He stood in the light of the moon, casting a shadow on the grass that the years had grown lush. His right hand was balled in a loose fist. Whether he sang or hummed or spoke, only the owls and the salamanders know. But there were voices and there was singing in the treetops. A breeze came up and gently lifted his hair. A portrait of peace, the boy smiled as he turned in the direction from which he came, hesitated, and then began his return across the pastures that brought him here.

Cory lurched upright in bed. The depth of his sleep was disorienting. *Where?* What a god-awful dream he'd had. Beside him, Hanna slept perfectly, her hair fanned out on the white pillow illuminated by moonlight. *Farmhouse.* The grogginess cleared. Cory drew his hand down his face. *Singer!*

He found the boy below the foot of the bed, sitting on his sleeping bag. Cory closed his eyes and gratefully exhaled. Quietly he made his way to Singer, careful not to wake him despite his wide-open eyes.

"Hello bud," he whispered as he sat down on the sleeping bag.

"Hi," Singer said back. He had magic bear upright on his lap.

"Do you need a drink of water?"

"No thank you."

Cory saw that Singer's hand was closed around something. "What do you have there?" He touched the top of his hand as if choosing it.

Singer turned his hand over and opened it. In his palm rested a native ceremonial button, the size of a fifty-cent piece.

"Can I see?" Cory whispered.

Singer nodded. "Uh-huh. It's for you."

Cory held it out to the moonlight. It was carved of bone, patinated by age, with three concentric rings of red-dyed porcupine quills woven through small holes around its center. "Are you ready for sleep now?"

Singer nodded passively.

Cory helped him slip back into his sleeping bag, stroking his hair. Singer closed his eyes and sunk into his pillow like he had never moved. The boy was fast asleep.

Cory came downstairs, finding the front door open, as he suspected he would. As he reached for it, someone moved behind him. He swung around to the adrenaline bloom of a thousand pins pricking his skin. It was HomeSky.

"Christ, you scared me," Cory put his hand to his heart.

"I'm sorry," HomeSky said. "I heard some moving."

"Singer. He was sleepwalking again."

"He was outside?" HomeSky's eyes widened.

"Yeah. I think so," Cory nodded. "By the time I woke up he was upstairs." Cory shook his head. "Can I show you something?" HomeSky said yes and followed him as he held open the screen door leading to the porch. "He found this tonight." Cory opened his hand as HomeSky stepped in the flood of moonlight to get a better look at the object in Cory's hand.

HomeSky's eyes adjusted. "May I look at it?"

Cory nodded.

Carefully, she took it. "A warrior's button." HomeSky turned it in the silver light. "From a war shirt." She frowned, examining it further. It was still dirt-smudged, although Cory had used a tissue to clean it. The colors were dulled by the years. "The bone is from the breastplate of a deer." Her finger traced the rings of red porcupine quills. "Every button tells a story." HomeSky looked up at Cory. "Singer had this?" she asked, almost disbelieving.

"It was in his hand when I found him. He was sitting on his sleeping bag upstairs."

"Strange. Where could he have been?" HomeSky looked out at the moonlit pasture that fell off into the dark.

"All I know was the door was open and his feet were dirty. What does it mean? What is its story?"

HomeSky studied the button. "If the quills are dyed white, it's for marriage. Yellow is harvest. Red, like these, is war."

"So it was worn in battle?"

HomeSky nodded. "But there's more than that. Three circles." She looked up at Cory, her face drawn. "The outer circle is anger. The next is suffering." HomeSky's finger traced around the inside circle. "The third is revenge."

PART TWO

November

WEDNESDAY

Reg's dirty white van slipped into the entrance. The midmorning sky pressed down gray and flat, leaving the high school parking lot in the dead light of November. Cars lumped one next to the other like giant sleeping dogs.

In the frigid air, white puffs of exhaust rose from the tailpipe of the rough idling vehicle. The van stopped to a shriek of worn-out brake pads. Reg squinted, leaning forward. In front of the first car in the row, a metal sign read: TEACHER OF THE MONTH. Reg had found the faculty parking area. He lit a cigarette and took his foot off the brake. His driver's side window, grimy and fogged, was rolled halfway down as he eased past the rear end of cars, looking from one bumper to the next to the next. Ten cars down he found his prize. A bumper with a Wisconsin Badgers Hockey sticker on the left and a Duluth East Greyhounds sticker on the right. The van's brake lights blinked on. Reg studied the old yellow pickup, his eyes tracing its outline, memorizing it. "Hello Cory," he said. He finished his cigarette and flicked it into the bed of the truck before pulling out of the parking lot into the empty street, then swinging the wheel hard so he could back up along the curb and park a quarter block away, the nose of his van facing the pickup. Reg reached under the seat and pulled out a bottle wrapped in a shop rag. He had a sandwich and a donut in a grease-stained brown paper sack. All he had to do was wait. For years, a single reckless thought had buzzed inside his head as directionless as a fly in a lampshade. Now, finally, he had his plan.

On Wednesdays, Cory had an open period between 10:15 and 11:15. He usually worked on his hockey practice plan, but today he was feverishly grading papers. Thanksgiving was just over a week away and his schedule was jammed solid.

Something caught his eye. Cory glanced up from his papers, sitting at a back table in the library. Someone had scratched I luv KT in the corner of the table. He shook his head. *What would drive a person to do such a thing?*

Cory hadn't talked to anyone at school about his engagement to Hanna, figuring once the ring came back from the resizing, it would present a less forced access to the conversation. But progress, if you could call it that, at the jewelers was so slow, perhaps they were using seismic pressure to reform the diamond to fit the smaller band.

In truth, Cory didn't have anyone to share his news with. He didn't really have friends beyond those at the table with him eight weeks ago. He liked his assistant coach well enough, a bit too loud and affable to be around too much, but a good guy. There wasn't really anyone he looked forward to telling. His mother, well, she would have plenty to say. But it would be about her and the difficulty of her situation: realtor and widow with no male support, financial or otherwise. Cory wouldn't bother to mention the check he put in the mail, month after month. He called it mother rent, but never aloud. Besides, Cory's mom had already said her piece

AUTUMN 1985

about Hanna, saying she was married to her career and needed someone to raise her child.

Cory shook his head. Back to math homework and the comfort of only one right answer.

Meadow lay on her bed staring at the ceiling. She squeezed her eyes shut. Her back had a scissors shoved in it, at least that's how it felt this morning. Yesterday, it was more like a burning hot golf ball was buried there. With legs up over her head, she tried to relieve a pressure point. "I don't have ankles anymore," she said to Boy. In the past month, since announcing her decision not to have her baby adopted, she'd begun calling him Boy. "Look at that." She pointed her toes to the ceiling. "No ankles. I have, like, flower pots where ankles used to be. No waist. No ankles. I will torture you in high school for this."

Her guitar lay next to her along with her songbook and a few false starts on scattered unfolded pieces of paper. "And I have no music-writing ability anymore. No concentration. I have to pee every 32 seconds." She rolled toward the edge of the bed, groaning. "Speaking of which."

Meadow came back to her bedroom-nursery, which was on the first floor. Everything had been set up to make the baby's room perfect and cozy, but life has a way of rearranging furniture. Pat had moved Meadow's bed down to this room after the doctor said climbing stairs, both up and down, was not a good thing at this point of the pregnancy. All had been sailing along smoothly, but the last three weeks were hell. High blood pressure put her on bed rest. Bed rest put her back out of alignment. And her twisted back made her left leg go numb. She told Boy this morning that the only thing worse than being 7 days overdue was being 8 days overdue. They watched the calendar and generally went stir-crazy. There was next to nothing to do. HomeSky was mostly at work; she was saving her vacation so she could help after the baby came. One or two days a week, Pat would sneak home at lunchtime, but the plant was running three shifts so he and the other manager were working right through breaks. Meadow kept mostly to bed and tried to keep her imagination from making too much out of the noises that an empty farmhouse makes when the November winds push while the temperatures pull.

Meadow picked up her guitar and went to the window. It was a day to write sad music and she tried to coax a song. *Think lonely, bleak, blustery.* As lousy as the weather was outside, and despite her physical pain, Meadow could summon not a melancholy lyric. She was happy. "The death of a songwriter," she said to Boy. "Happiness is responsible for the crappy state music's in."

She strummed the guitar, sing-saying the words.

In the spring of the trees
the rain found the gardens
and I let go
arms full of burdens

The wrongs go back
calendar years
like salt inside
seven million tears

Lay them down
to go to dirt
the pain, sadness
and the hurt

Lay them down
arms full of burdens
that makes the earth
that makes the gardens

There's rain
rain in the gardens
there's rain
rain in the gardens

There's rain
rain in the gardens

AUTUMN 1985

rain in the gardens
for you

Meadow peered through the glass as she wiped away a thin strip of condensation that lined the windowpane. Outside, the temperature dropped. The garden along the south side of the house lay tilled and fallow. The gray frosted soil, the proximity of winter, they tried, but couldn't suppress her warm smile. Soon she would be walking in the sun, teaching her son to count, the green shoots of lettuce and carrots their abacus.

When Cory pulled out of the school parking lot, Reg followed, not overly concerned about the distance between them. Surprise was on his side.

They only went a few miles before Cory made two left turns, putting him in a sprawling parking lot of the hockey arena. Near the doors, he took one of the Coaches Only parking spots. Reg laid back.

Cory certainly had his routine down. Quickly he had two sticks, a duffle bag and a puck bag out of his truck before disappearing into the arena with a slight limp. For the next 15 minutes, cars pulled in, some of the older players driving themselves and their buddies, while the younger players got dumped at the door by moms. Reg had no other choice but settle in.

"Son of a bitch," Reg snarled impatiently, checking his watch: 3:25. He had eaten his donut and drank enough bourbon to become groggy, but the sandwich didn't interest him. Any more of this and he was afraid he'd nod off and wake up to an empty parking lot. "What the hell." He slammed his van door shut and walked through the windy parking lot into the arena.

Reg pushed through a second set of doors leading to the rink. He stood by the boards looking through the plexiglass as Cory ran his team through a fast-paced backward skating drill. The stands were empty and as inviting as sitting on ice blocks. Reg went over to the rink manager's door and hit it a few times with his cane.

"Can I help you?" the manager said, his tone friendlier than his appearance would lead one to expect.

"Is there a place to watch that ain't so damn freezin'?"

"Sure is. Up them steps." The rink manager pointed. "There's a heated spectator's room. Looks right over the ice sheet."

"Good," Reg said, turning to leave.

"You here to watch someone play?" the manager said, making idle conversation.

"Yep."

"Who is it?" the rink manager smiled. "I know these kids pretty darn good."

Reg hadn't expected this. "Ah, my grandson," he said.

"Oh, nice. What's his name?"

"His name?"

The rink manager nodded eagerly.

Reg squinted. "His last name is Business. His first, Mind your own damn." With that Reg planted his cane and turned. He noisily made his way up the steps.

The practice went an hour and when the team left the ice for the locker room, Reg went back out to the van. Bitter wind blew up his pant legs every step back to the vehicle. Soon, kids streamed out the arena doors in t-shirts, with matted wet hair, standing around, talking.

"Dumbshit jocks," Reg sneered, with his van heater cranked. "Going to catch pneumonia." A short hit off the bottle put a pleasant quake through his system. Cory came out and said a few things before scattering the kids. Reg pretended to be busy as Cory's truck drove past.

Cory's cabin was just about 30 miles from Duluth. Reg kept note of the route and odometer reading on the flattened lunch bag in the front seat. Once Cory's truck was off the busier state highway, Reg hung farther back. He kept the yellow truck just in view on the county road, watching it turn at an intersection marked with a sign pointing to Pike Lake.

AUTUMN 1985

Reg pulled to the side of the road and sloppily jotted PIKE LAKE LEFT on the bag. He almost lost Cory on the single-lane blacktop that jogged left, then right around a large open field. Reg rolled to a stop, idling, his van in the center of the desolate road. "Where are you?" His eyes opened greedily when a quarter mile off, across the field, he saw Cory's truck heading away from him. Reg tried to close the distance, but by the time he got around the field to the curve where he'd last seen the truck, the road was empty.

Reg pounded the steering wheel. "Shit!" His head throbbed. With a shaky hand he pinched a cigarette out of the pack. Unlit, it remained between his lips as the van crept forward. Reg's head swiveled, peering down each driveway he passed. Occasional glimpses of a lake sparkled through the pines to his right, where mailboxes stood sentry at the heads of dirt driveways. On the fourth mailbox after the curve, the name BRADFORD, markered on a strip of cardboard, was neatly duct taped to its side.

"Home at last," Reg whispered, lighting his cigarette, inhaling lovingly. He drove one property beyond Cory's and turned down a narrow strip of driveway. If anyone was there to ask, he was a handyman working on a cabin on Pike Lake who took a wrong turn.

Squatting at the end of the curved dirt driveway was a lonely green cabin. Reg squinted through his windshield for a closer look. The place appeared shut down for the season. No car parked in the driveway, just a covered pontoon boat near the front entrance. The screen porch was wrapped with tarps. No smoke from the chimney. Reg got out feeling lucky. Even with the leaves down, the woods between the two cabins made it impossible to see through to Cory's.

Just to be sure, Reg knocked on the front door of the cabin. Zero sign of life; just wind biting at the trees. Somewhere in front, down by the shoreline, a crow shouted out the trespass. Reg angled across the property, heading for the woods in the direction of Cory's. Suddenly, he stopped. He straightened upright as if tapped on the shoulder. "Aren't you forgetting something?" he teased himself.

When Reg came back from the van, the pistol from the glove box was stuffed in his coat pocket. Darkness spreading rapidly.

It was a good tree to lean on, Reg decided. He waited, shivering, in the woods outside Cory's place until the darkness fully dropped, clearly showing Cory in the interior light, hunched over the kitchen table, grading papers. It's surreal to watch another human when you're separated only by a small distance and a thin pane of glass. You can make out how their hair falls somewhat to the side, how they leave their hand on the coffee cup even after setting it down, how they stretch a tired neck. Were it not for the window and the walls hoarding all interior sound, if not for the darkness between, you could be sitting next to each other as friends.

Reg crept closer to the front door, around the opposite side of the cabin. He found what appeared to be the bathroom window. A small double-hung, just large enough to squeeze through. He tested it, but it was locked at the upper sash.

The plan went into action. Reg reached into his jacket pocket and took out a tape measure. The rectangle of glass directly opposite the latch was six inches by ten. That's all he needed to know. Good as gold. As he crept back along the cabin, he stepped into a low spot, lost his balance, causing his cane to whip around and strike the side of the cabin.

Cory was exhausted. Hockey. The drive. Grading papers. Teaching all day. Plus he hadn't eaten. As he squatted to check the pantry for the pasta supply, a sharp BANG! came from the front side of the cabin. At first he thought something had fallen in the bathroom. He walked in and switched on the light. Nothing on the floor, so he checked the shower. Wouldn't be the first time the bottle of shampoo fell. Nothing there, either.

Reg's hand went into his jacket pocket and he pulled out the tape measure. "Shit." He jabbed into the other pocket and found the pistol. He could hear Cory's rustlings in the bathroom after the light came on. Reg pressed against the log cabin, his chest tightening.

AUTUMN 1985

From the corner of his eye, he watched weak light push through the half-drawn shade of the bathroom window, Cory's shadow moving behind it. Reg edged away. If Cory came out to investigate, he'd only need to come around the corner of the cabin and they'd be face to face. When Reg lifted his gun he was not pleased with how much his hand trembled.

Cory checked the front door. It was closed, unlocked as he left it. He figured, *what the hell,* wind was blowing pretty good, probably just a branch. But curiosity was always a part of Cory's active mind. He pulled open the front door to have a look.

Reg's mouth was dry and his heart was beating like he'd just stepped off the wrestling mat. He heard the front door click and swing open. If he tried to make it to the woods he would certainly be heard, if not seen. He backed up, along the log wall, away from the door, pistol held out. Shambling, he lurched around the corner to the dark lakeside of the cabin.

The goosenecked overhead light flipped on. Cory walked onto the front step. Stretching, he noticed the bread crusts he'd tossed out for the chipmunks were gone. In the yard, no sign of a downed branch. Maybe around the side. He slid his hands in his pockets as the wind blew through his shirt. He came around the side of the cabin. Nothing there, either. A light shone through the bathroom window. "So much for that," he told himself. He listened to the night. Trees swayed overhead, branches creaking. He looked into the starless sky. "Something's coming," he said. Cory went back into the cabin and locked it for the night.

Reg was halfway back to Baudette when his hands stopped shaking. He had pulled over at a rest stop and watched a man let two dogs out of his car before they made for the grass. Reg reached under the seat for the bottle and drained it. That's when the jolt hit him, and it wasn't from the alcohol. He had dropped his cane back at the cabin.

THURSDAY

Hanna awoke. Had she heard something? She rose on one elbow to find Singer sitting on the side of her bed in his bare feet and pajamas. The nightstand clock read 5:15.

"Hi there," she whispered, moving next to him. "What are you doing, sweetie?"

"Walking with a deer," Singer said, eyes open but fully asleep.

Cory had told Hanna about his conversations with a sleep-walking Singer. What Cory had said, and the pediatrician confirmed, was don't startle or attempt to wake him.

"Oh, a deer," she said with wonderment. "I bet it was a nice walk."

Singer frowned. "It was like Bambi. When the fire comes."

Hanna softly put the back of her hand to Singer's forehead. He was running a mild fever. "Do you want to come to bed with me?"

"I should stay with the deer," Singer said, getting upset.

AUTUMN 1985

"Let me get you a drink of water and then we'll see, okay?" Hanna took a deep breath.

"Okay," Singer said, allowing his mother to guide him to the top of the bed and put his head on a pillow.

"I'll be right back, honey," she told him. When she returned with a glass of water, Singer's eyes were closed, his breathing deep.

Cory had just finished putting his breakfast dishes in the drying rack when the phone gave him a start. Strange sound; Cory got so few calls, especially this hour of the morning. The faded yellow phone hung on the dining room wall. Would it be one ring and done? The second ring made him jump almost as much as the first.

"Hello?"

"Hi, it's me." Hanna said, rather rushed.

"Hi. Nice surprise. Is there anything wrong?"

"No, not really." Cory heard Hanna's hand cover the phone as she told Singer to go up and brush his teeth. "Sorry. Um … Singer was sleepwalking again last night. He had a fever. Seems fine now. It was so strange. I'm rambling. Sorry."

Cory slowed the conversation down. "Okay. So, no fever now. That's good."

"All seems normal."

"And I hear him playing the piano."

"Yeah. You know, this can wait until lunch if you have to get going. What time is it anyway? Sorry to call so early. I'm a little spazzed."

"No. No problem. I'm glad you called. Where did you find our little wanderer?"

"Sitting on the end of my bed. He said he was walking with a deer."

Cory listened.

"By the time I got him a drink of water he was asleep in my bed."

"Did he eat this morning?" Cory asked.

"Three pancakes, three pieces of bacon and we split an apple."

"Must have been quite a walk," Cory said, wishing he had the words back before he'd finished speaking them.

Hanna sighed. "I just don't know... Where does he go? Why?"

"Like the doctor said, it's probably just a phase. We just have to ride it out." Cory tried to sound confident. "So, what's on your docket for the morning?"

I was planning to go to the gym and then meet Sharon, but I don't know about leaving him with Ms. Kortuem."

"His fever is gone, right?"

"Yeah."

"Well, I'd stick with your plan. Right now, this is the new normal. He should be fine. If you make too much of things, sometimes you create the problem, you know?"

"Yeah. I guess. I just worry."

"That's understandable. You're a good mom."

"God, I hope so." Hanna switched subjects. "So you have a home game tonight, right?"

"Yep. 4:00 for us. 7:00 for the varsity. Is Ms. Kortuem still planning to bring Singer?"

"I think so. If he's up to it."

Cory shifted the phone to his other ear and held it with his shoulder. "Oh, I bet he'll be up to it. Big time."

"On top of all of this, I don't know if I can get home tonight between my six and ten. There's a ton going on at the station with the holidays coming."

"That's okay. We'll be good. Work on our cutting and pasting. No hockey. At least not in the in the living room."

Hanna laughed. "I know. I'm probably overreacting. Thanks for talking me off the ledge."

"No problem."

Hanna switched tones, speaking now in her most over-the-top suggestive voice. "By the way, do I get a roommate tonight? Because

AUTUMN 1985

I'm going to be married soon and we're going to have to stop meeting like this."

"You're not marrying that uptight math teacher, are you?" Cory asked. "Bor-ring."

"Can you believe it?"

"I'll be there tonight. Win, lose or draw."

"I like Thursday night home games very, very much," Hanna said, a tingle surging through her, leaving goose bumps.

"Nothing better," Cory told her. "Oh, one other thing," he added as they were about to hang up. "Singer didn't have anything in his hand when you found him, did he? He seems to collect things on his walks."

"Oh, weird. I meant to tell you that," she said. "He had a little twig, about the size of a pencil stub."

Cory had to get moving after they hung up; it was a 30-minute drive to Duluth, and then getting to the high school depended on how he hit the lights. But he was unusually distracted. Singer's collection of nighttime objects was bizarre. An arrowhead, a warrior's ceremonial button, now a twig. Cory went into his bedroom and pulled open the top dresser drawer. Beneath the socks, he found the button. He let his thumb trace over the three concentric rings weaved through it. He recalled the disturbed look on HomeSky's face when she explained their story: *Anger. Suffering. Revenge.* Rather than return it to the drawer, Cory took the button and put it in the front pocket of his backpack.

He had to get going. He quick grabbed his lunch out of the refrigerator. When he closed the door, the photo held there by a magnet stopped him. It was taken in the summer, at the campfire pit on the lakeside of the cabin. Hanna. Singer. Cory. Singer had his mouth open, pretending to devour the two toasted marshmallows on his stick. Cory leaned closer to the picture. He was struck by how relaxed he looked. He touched the photograph with his finger. "The picture of happiness," he whispered.

Outside the cabin, the day was a gray, dingy repeat of yesterday. He locked the door and checked the thermometer hanging on the tree. Twenty degrees. "It's too damn early for this," Cory complained to the wind, tossing pieces of a bread heel onto the frosted grass. A flock of geese came over the pine tops, low enough for Cory to hear the creak of their wings. They set their wings, preparing to land out on the lake. "Better keep going," Cory said. "That water might freeze tonight."

Under his scarred Carhartt coat, Cory shivered as he scraped frost off the truck's windshield. The engine was running, warming things up in the cab, barely. Among other things, the truck needed a new thermostat. But a first-year teacher's salary forces decisions. He made a mental note to buy some gloves and put a blanket in the cab. A steady hard wind gusted out of the north, off the lake. The top of the pines swayed and sighed in unison. Cory thought about last night's branch, or whatever caused the thud he heard. He blew into his hands, rubbing them. The cab of the truck was semi-inviting—at least it would get him out of the wind—but he decided to have one more look around the cabin. He backed up a few steps for a complete view of the old TV antenna on the chimney and roof. All clear up there. He went around the side of the cabin by the bathroom window, eyes scanning. Cory stopped so abruptly, his front foot slid on the frosted grass. Lying near the foundation of the log cabin was a cane.

Reg parked along the curb, the nose of his van facing the high school parking lot. He'd been there since 7:15 to see the faculty parking spots fill. There was no sign of Cory. At five minutes to eight, the bell rang. A minute later, Cory's truck blurred past Reg's driver-side window, and pulled quickly into the lot, taking the last spot available. Reg lit a cigarette as Cory stiffly jogged toward the side entrance, his backpack bouncing off his shoulder blade. "Coast is clear," Reg said, pulling away from the curb.

Yesterday's scrawl of directions on the lunch bag served him well. He had forgotten about the sandwich inside, which entertained him

AUTUMN 1985

as he rolled down the window and tossed the stale bologna and cheese onto the street. Reg laughed at the view in his side-view mirror: bread hitting the road, bouncing apart, flying bologna, the car behind him swerving as if to miss a land mine. The radio weatherman said things were going to get downright nasty, dropping to zero tonight with shifting winds blowing a blue streak tomorrow, bringing in freezing rain and snow.

When the van rolled into Cory's rutted driveway, the first thing on Reg's to-do list was to get his cane. Not only had he come to depend on it, but he didn't need it lying around, connecting him to Cory's place.

"What the fuck?" Reg had returned to where he was sure he dropped the cane, but all he could find was a small sinkhole under the eave where rain ran off the roof. He was sure that had to be where he stumbled last night. He checked the nearby weeds, even went around the cabin, tracking the way he had come in and left from the neighbor's. Nothing.

"Shit! Shit! SHIT!" Reg stomped his good leg like a third grader. Grinding his teeth, he wondered if Cory had found it, or had a dog run off with it? What? Then he decided it didn't matter. "The show must go on," he said.

Back at the van, Reg got his supplies and tools, making a few trips to the small bathroom window at the side of the cabin. He used a hammer to tap, tap, tap the center pane of glass above the sash just hard enough to break it without shattering. Reg used work gloves to carefully pull out the pieces of glass and put them in the cardboard box that held his tools. Then, reaching in, he unlocked the window and slid it fully open.

Using his step stool from the van, he got himself up and in the window headfirst, but there was no graceful way to lower himself down the other side. He tumbled in, arms unable to hold a partial handstand, his splayed feet dumping in behind him. White pain flashed as he flopped, one leg striking the toilet. He lay on the bathroom floor, thinking he broke his leg.

For five minutes Reg moaned, balled-up, ready to give up, go home and forget about all of this. What the hell was he doing anyway, on the bathroom floor of some guy from what seemed like a different life ago? That's when the voice of Kemp descended. YOU'RE READY TO QUIT YOU FUCKIN, LITTLE BABYASSED PANSY! AFTER THE BEATING HE PUT ON YOU? Reg shook his head, trying to say no, but his voice failed him. He covered his head with his arms. GET SOME GUTS. DO SOMETHING IN YOUR MISERABLE LIFE THAT CHANGES SHIT. YOU KNOW I KNOW WHAT I'M TALKING ABOUT. DON'T BE A FORGET-TABLE OLD DRUNK. LEAVE SOMETHING PERMANENT.

Finally the pain subsided to a dull ache. Reg sat up. No more Kemp. Pulling his pant leg up, he exposed a red knob raised on his shin surrounded by a blue pooling bruise. Reg got to his knees, then to one foot, and eventually to his feet. Whereupon he started laughing. At first, just a cough that became laughter, before becoming more regular, before snowballing into something sustained and jagged, from a place deep down and almost forgotten.

Pat re-jiggered his day at the plant to add a noontime window. He picked up the phone and called Meadow for the second time that morning. On workdays, he and HomeSky were calling the farmhouse regularly, knowing that Meadow could go into labor at any moment. "Hi," Pat said. "How's the patient?"

"Impatient," Meadow groaned.

"Hey, I'm coming home for lunch," he said. "Unless you're doing something."

Meadow was laying in bed, back propped up with pillows reading one of Pat's sociology books. "You're kidding, right?" she said. "What I wouldn't give to be doing something."

"Before you know it," he said, "before you know it. Do you want anything from the grocery store? I was going to swing by and say hey to HomeSky. What do you crave?"

Meadow let her head fall back on the pillows, closing her eyes. "I crave this child out of my body."

AUTUMN 1985

"Yeah," Pat said. "But food-wise."

Light static crackled on the phone line. "You know what I'd love?"

Pat listened on his end.

"Grilled cheese sandwich with American cheese, like those single-serve cheesy squares, two slices, on Wonder bread, cooked till it's almost burnt, with Tater Tots. And chocolate cupcakes."

Pat laughed. "Do you think for one minute HomeSky is going to let me out of the grocery store with that?"

"Just tell her it will induce labor."

"I'll do my best. I'm afraid to ask, but anything else?"

Meadow thought. "Some kind of mindless glossy fashion-gossip magazine."

It was almost as if she could hear Pat frowning on the other phone. "I thought you didn't go in for that kind of stuff?"

"I don't, but I'm desperate. I'm reading … *Behaviorism*, by … " Pat could hear Meadow shuffling around.

"John Watson," he finished her sentence. "Watson was the psychologist who most influenced Skinner."

"Never met him."

"Skinner. You know, the Skinner Box. Rat experiments."

"I must have been sick from school that day. But this book is interesting. How environment molds behavior. Makes sense. But I'm ready for something shallow."

Meadow had never read a magazine before she came to the farmhouse. In 18 years, not a one. She always told herself there was no reason to look at a life you'll never know. Beautiful, white, skinny models. Actresses with huge houses and swimming pools and perfectly groomed dogs and more cars than there was room on the driveway. And the ads. All the makeup and clothes and brands that she'd never own. Or a feature article about a girl so brilliant and talented that every college wanted her and every company tried to hire her. Why lie to yourself with page after page of that? But lately, a few magazines had found their way into her hands. She'd allowed herself to think maybe all those things weren't for someone else. Maybe if she didn't have them, her son could.

When Pat got to the checkout line with his handbasket filled, HomeSky looked at him like he'd lost his mind. "Not exactly what I'd call a well-balanced lunch," she said.

Pat pushed aside the bulk of the groceries and found a bag of mini-carrots. "What do you mean?"

HomeSky just shook her head.

"I can't help but spoil her rotten," he confessed. "I feel so bad with the pain she's in. Looks like they'll have to induce, huh?"

HomeSky began to scan the groceries through. "Doctor says tomorrow if nothing happens today. I've called home three times. How many for you?"

"Two. I can't stand it, her there alone."

HomeSky shook her head. "She really wanted to have this child naturally."

"Yeah," Pat said. "But it's probably better for everyone's health to induce, right?"

"That's what they say." HomeSky couldn't hide her disdain for Western medical practices, but she swallowed her criticism. Pat was plenty worried enough.

At the farm, Meadow insisted on getting out of bed to eat. She told Pat that the walk might get things going. That, or the ridiculous fat content in her lunch might do the trick. She ate half before pushing the plate away. "That was good, but any more will predispose Boy to being a fry cook."

Pat munched on his salad. "How 'bout I trade you some of this for some of what's left of that?"

"Deal," Meadow said.

"So, if it comes to it, are you feeling okay about having your baby induced tomorrow?" Pat popped in a Tater Tot, trying to reduce the seriousness of the question.

AUTUMN 1985

Meadow picked at the salad. "Whatever it takes. I'm so ready it's not funny."

"Good. Me too. But it kinda makes me a grandpa, which, don't get me wrong, will be a blast." He drained his milk. "I just always thought of grandpas as much older, with hairy ears and suspenders and Tootsie Rolls in their pocket for the children."

"Not in my culture," Meadow said.

"Yeah, true enough. Okay, good. I'm glad you're feeling all right." Pat switched to more familiar ground. "So you like reading about behaviorism, huh?"

Meadow chewed a carrot, thinking. "Sort of. There are a lot of words I can't figure out, but the main idea I agree with."

"The author's thesis," Pat threw in.

"Yeah, I guess."

"What is it you agree with?"

Meadow shrugged. "You know how I was joking about not predisposing Boy to Tater Tots by eating too many? Well I wasn't really kidding all the way."

Pat sat up straighter. "How do you mean?"

"What I got out of the book was where you are makes who you are."

"Is that the way it was written?" Pat wanted to know.

"Not exactly. That's my translation of the mumbo jumbo."

Pat was clearly impressed. "Meadow, that's great. It's a quite a skill to whittle a complex thesis down to a simple phrase."

"That's kinda what songwriting is."

Pat thought about that. "I never saw it that way. Thank you. I learned something today."

Meadow smiled shyly. She wasn't used to being the one doing the teaching. It felt pretty cool.

"Oh crap, I mean shoot," Pat blurted. "I have to get back to work." He started collecting the dishes.

"Don't sweat those. I'll get 'em."

"You sure? Doctor's orders are bed rest and no work."

"A little work won't kill me," Meadow said.

Pat looked at her. "Okay. But then rest."

"Yes, Grandpa," Meadow said, allowing a hint of a smile to break through.

"Yeow. Low blow. Call if you need me." Pat grabbed his coat and hat, and popped a Tater Tot into his mouth. "These things are terrible," he said before scooping up a few more for the road.

Meadow went to the window, and waved as Pat's car pulled away, leaving her with empty road. Something about the sight was final and sad. She closed her eyes, the pain in her back feeling more like it was wrapping around to her stomach. "You're lucky, Boy," she said. "To have him. To have this place to make you who you'll be."

As Meadow walked slowly to the kitchen and picked up the lunch dishes, a stab of pain caused her to turn toward it. She left the dishes and put her hands on the table, spread her feet, pushing her pelvis back, stretching. "Deep breaths," she told herself. Thirty seconds later, the pain subsided.

Stack of dishes in hand, Meadow went to the sink, started the water through a squirt of dish soap and looked out the window at the frozen front pasture. The color and feeling of the day reminded her of steel wool.

When the dishes were done, Meadow decided to lay down. Just for a second, she told herself, then she'd read. She fell fast asleep and a dream came to her:

Meadow walked down a narrow logging trail, the sunlight's yellow fingers pushing through the lush canopy of trees. Ahead, a white rabbit bolted over the rise, speeding directly to her, stopping. His eyes, oil-black, were empty of life, his sides rising and falling in exhaustion. "Stay here," the rabbit instructed. "I'll send him the other way." Meadow stepped aside and the rabbit ran away from her, fast as his legs would carry. Soon the rabbit returned, carefully

AUTUMN 1985

doubling back exactly the way he had gone. Again he sat at her feet, looking up at Meadow.

"Rabbit, what's wrong?" she asked. The rabbit crouched, laid his ears back, body tensing like a compressed spring.

"He's coming." Then he leaped with everything in him, airborne for 15 feet, off the trail, until he tumbled in the adjacent thicket. Into the woods he disappeared.

Just then a gray-faced pine martin came trotting down the path, nose to the ground, scenting. The only attention he paid to Meadow was to pass her, exposing his sharp teeth in an awful grin. He followed on, tracking the rabbit away from her, out of sight, where abruptly, he stopped. The scent of the rabbit had ended.

Reg locked the front door from inside the cabin, made his way to the bathroom, got his legs through the window, and lowered his feet until they found the step stool. As eventful as it was going in, the exact opposite was true when coming out. He smiled, quite pleased with himself.

With the window closed, Reg reached through the pane where the glass had been broken and reset the lock. From his box of tools and supplies, he took out the final piece of the puzzle. Taped between two pieces of cardboard was a six inch by ten inch rectangle of glass that he'd cut in his garage. He placed it gently within the thin wood muntins and held it in place by pushing in a few glazing points with a screwdriver. With his putty knife, he glazed the glass into place. It was easy work, so he lit a cigarette, keeping it between his lips, his hands busy with the repair. Reg mentally went through his plan for the last time, making sure he didn't miss a step: First he had turned off the space heater in the front room and its pilot light. Then he had switched off the breaker box and went to work on the light switch in the mudroom. Having removed the cover plate, he loosened the wires, and brought the ends close enough together to arc and cause a spark when the light switch was flipped on. Next he turned off the gas to the water heater so he could change out the on-off valve for the pilot light with a leaky valve. He knew it leaked because he had pulled it off a similar model a few years back. Why he had saved it, he hadn't a clue. With the faulty valve attached, Reg turned the gas back on and checked it with soapy water. Sure enough, little bubbles grew at the site of the leak, a telltale sign that gas was slowly escaping into the cabin. Then he had switched the breaker box back on so current was running to the light switch. He'd taken his tools to the van before locking the front door from the inside and going out the bathroom window.

Outside, Reg stomped out his cigarette, tapping the replaced pane of glass with his knuckle. "Air tight," he said with a snicker. He collected his things and finished loading the van. He looked at the log cabin. "Those things are going to fly like Lincoln Logs." A shiver of excitement thrummed through him. He'd brought a camera, and stood back far enough to get the small, one-story cabin completely in frame. With each picture he snapped, he said "before" and then pressed the button.

Every time. When Cory walked into a hockey rink he always thought, *someone could get hurt*. He reminded himself of the chance, or maybe the reminder was sent by the cold waiting for him inside the arena door. Or was it the stale lingering Zamboni fumes, or the echo of a locker room when a door opens and voices spill out? In this way, he lived in the proximity of old injuries. Not occasionally, but every lousy time. He'd shake it off, like a sudden chill. Sometimes what you love isn't altogether good to you.

Cory's JV team skated perhaps their best game of the season, which was saying a lot because they were undefeated. After lining up for the on-ice handshakes, Cory checked the stands and waved at Singer and Ms. Kortuem in the front of the Duluth Greyhounds cheering section. Cory held up 10 fingers, Singer mimicking the gesture. "See you in 10 minutes," Cory mouthed before he headed into the tunnel to the locker room.

Singer leaped into Cory's arms as he came up last from the rink. Family and friends were milling about in the entrance room of the

AUTUMN 1985

arena, waiting to greet the players. The boys were in single file, wearing neckties, the way Cory had been taught when he played for the Badgers. He told his team if they wanted to play college hockey they may as well get used to it now.

"Hey-ya superstar," Cory said to Singer, who was decked out in a Greyhounds wool cap and hoodie sweatshirt. "Nice outfit," he said, setting Singer down and taking his hand. "You want to carry this?" Cory handed him his coaches' dry-erase board.

"Could you hear us cheering?" Singer wanted to know, proudly holding the coaches' board.

Cory waved to Ms. Kortuem as she made her way through the crowd. "Thanks for coming," he said to her. "I could hear you guys cheering all the way on the bench." She was delighted to do it, having grown up in a huge hockey family herself.

Between elbow-wrenching handshakes from parents, Cory managed to find out that Ms. Kortuem had already been paid for the week, so they said their goodbyes. Cory and Singer were almost out the door before being intercepted by a particularly high-maintenance parent who wondered why his kid wasn't getting more ice time. Cory reminded the parent of his rule: if you had issues, Cory was available after the first practice of the month, every month. The parent continued following Cory, asking him if the rumor was true that the team was required to get cross country skis to improve conditioning this winter. How in hell was that going to work, the parent asked, with hockey already costing a small fortune? Cory said it was all explained in the letter he sent home with the kids— everything from what they were doing, to the fundraising event after Thanksgiving to offset costs. The parent followed Cory into the parking lot, offering advice on how to break the puck out to the center. Cory's temper was rising, but Singer's hand in his put things in perspective. Cory repeated that the time to talk about it was not now.

"What did that man want?" Singer asked, handing Cory the coaches' board as he climbed up into the back seat of the truck and buckled his car seat.

"Here's a marker. Do you want to draw up hockey plays on the way home?"

"Yeah!" he said. "Can I have red?" Singer asked, holding the black marker.

"You, my friend, can have both." Cory pulled the other one out of the pocket of his Greyhounds jacket.

"Was that man mad?" Singer asked, now halfway home with dry erase all over both hands.

"The man at the rink?" Cory looked at Singer in the rearview mirror.

"Yeah."

"Nah."

"He sounded mad," Singer told him.

Cory thought for a moment. "He's just concerned about his boy. Every parent says things in different ways. He probably just loves him a whole lot and wants him to do well."

"Oh," Singer said. "I bet your dad was like that, too."

Cory hadn't seen that coming. Wow. "Um, sure. It's hard to remember things from when you're little." Cory looked at his finger, the tip flattened, the disfigured nail.

"Did you and your dad play together like we're going to tonight?"

Cory looked back into the rearview mirror, seeing Singer waiting hopefully for an answer.

"Sure," he said. Cory couldn't think of a time he had not told Singer the truth. He switched the subject to pizza toppings.

Hanna was the consummate broadcast journalist. That's what everyone said. She had it all: BLTC. Brains. Looks. Timing. Composure. So when she broke down anchoring the 6:00 news, coworkers in the control room were stunned. But when it happened again at 10:00, they became worried. Luckily, the second time, Singer wasn't watching. He was in bed, fast asleep. The first time it happened he and Cory were having pizza in front of the TV. "Why's Mom crying?" he had asked.

AUTUMN 1985

The upbeat intro music to the 10:00 newscast wound down as Hanna said good evening. Everything seemed to be going along fine. Cory rubbed his eyes, glancing up from grading papers as Hanna led with more detail on the story that she broke at six. He was stiff from leaning over the coffee table in front of the TV, but if they were going to be work-free for Thanksgiving he had to "attack the stack," as his peers were fond of saying.

Not more than a minute into the broadcast, the first crack in Hanna's voice sounded. He straightened, his pen coming off the papers. The control room had switched to camera two, showing a photograph from the scene of tragic incident. When they went back to camera one, Hanna had begun to cry. Her eyes were looking away, tears sparkling. At the anchor desk, she sank into her right hand, her face covered by her palm, and began to quake. Her co-anchor had no response other than to drop his mouth open. Quickly, the director got them back to camera two, hardly an easier picture look at. It was the police photograph of the pond, with the small black mitten next to a hole in the thin ice.

It was the story of a young farm family that lived just south of Duluth. Yesterday morning, their seven-year-old boy was outside with his older sister as they finished morning chores. He was at a nuisance age, fond of hiding in the barn to leap out and scare her, or flipping off the lights while she milked. Nonetheless, his mom pushed him out to help. With her husband gone three days a week driving truck, the boy had to learn. It was how farm kids were taught family responsibility.

When the daughter sat down to breakfast, her mother asked where her little brother was. I thought he was already in, she told her. He must be upstairs changing for school. He wasn't there. What was his last chore? the mother asked. He had to open the cattle gate to let the cows go to pasture, the daughter said.

The mother didn't even pull on her chore coat, just went out the kitchen door and called for her boy, braced for him to leap out from behind the woodbin or some such nonsense. But he didn't answer. She walked quickly down to the gate, which had been left swung open. The cattle trail led out past the pond and to the pasture. The mother's eyes traced the worn path to the distant field, seeing the specks of cattle dotting the hill. She cussed her foolishness for not taking a coat when her eyes went to the pond. Ice had formed the night before. Twenty yards out, there was a gaping hole. Next to the hole, on the ice, was a small black mitten.

The mother screamed for the daughter to bring the neighbor. Upon returning, the daughter found that her mother had made it no farther than 15 feet out into the pond, where she had collapsed from hypothermia. They got her in blankets and to the hospital. She never regained consciousness. The daughter had lost her brother and her mother before the school bell rang for mid-morning recess.

The news director called shortly after the newscast to tell Cory that Hanna was fine, but just to be safe, and her objections notwithstanding, she was being driven home by a co-worker. The timing for Hanna to have a few days off was probably for the best, he told Cory. Reassure her that she's not to worry about what happened on the air, he said.

When Hanna arrived home, she was composed while Cory thanked the young man for driving her. When the front door closed, she began to shake. Cory held her, wishing he knew what to say. Every word that came to mind seemed inadequate.

After a few minutes, Hanna tightened. "I need to see Singer," she said. "Will you come up with me?"

They sat cross-legged on the floor, knees touching, shoulders touching, holding hands, watching Singer sleep. "He's so beautiful," Hanna whispered. "So peaceful."

Cory let go of her hand and rubbed her back.

"What I don't get is how can he be so peaceful with all the pain out there? It doesn't make sense."

"Maybe he is so peaceful *because* of all the pain out there. Maybe we need Singers to keep going." Cory looked at Hanna through the darkness and tilted his head as to say, *you never know.*

AUTUMN 1985

"I saw that little precious mitten on the ice, and that hole, and I thought about the mother, and what her daughter must have seen, and I thought about HomeSky's farm and her pond and how Singer played around it, and about what happened to you. I just lost it. How does a person remain professional at a time like that?"

"They don't," Cory said.

"I've reported hundreds of incidents, tragic, tragic things. I shed it. I forget it. Do my job. But not tonight." Hanna looked at Singer, then at the floor. "Every time I close my eyes I see that mitten."

Cory gave her back a final rub. "Why don't you take a shower, and then I'll scoop up Singer and we'll all sleep together. He should be the last thing you see before you close your eyes."

The still of the night never came. Regardless, Hanna slept deeply. Her reserves were emptied. Singer slept curled against her stomach. Cory lay on his back, eyes open, listening to the wind. It deflected off trees, the house, shook downspouts and lampposts. There was no restraining it. A storm was coming, that's what they said. Hang onto your hat, the weatherman warned. Freezing rain, then snow.

Cory got out of bed, went downstairs, made coffee and graded papers.

Reg's fingers drummed on the steering wheel. He had smoked his last cigarette two hours ago. The empty pint sat on the car seat next to his camera and a half-eaten pack of chocolate covered mini-donuts. The geese on the lake were finally quiet. For hours after dark, they had honked tirelessly, perhaps in anticipation of ice that was beginning to take hold of the water. The van was cold. Reg would run it for 15 minutes, and then shut it off for the balance of the hour. The dark that filled the driveway of the vacant cabin was thick and unyielding. Above Reg, the crowns of the giant white pines tossed and swayed in ancient resistance. But the coming force was committed, energy fed by energy. Inevitability does not make bargains. At 11 p.m., Reg started the van, snapped on the headlights and drove out of the neighbor's lot, passing Cory's mailbox on his way down the blacktopped road. Cory wasn't coming home tonight, he was sure of that now. To Reg's thinking, he was probably shacked up with his newscaster girlfriend in Duluth. But he'd be here tomorrow. Probably after school. And Reg too. Front row seat for the fireworks.

AUTUMN 1985

FRIDAY

There was an early moment of dirty sunshine before the gray swelled, stealing shadows, flattening vistas in every direction. The day had begun by taking dead branches off trees, and by the looks of it, the live ones would not be long spared. Oh, how the wind did howl. Trash cans toppled, lids somersaulting across the alleyway. Flags twisted around their poles. It was of the switching variety, this wind, calculating its angle of attack. Gas station paper towels were ripped from their dispensers. Candy bar wrappers were whipped across abandoned baseball fields, hung in the gallows of the backstop. Women lost their breath climbing the church steps with scarves knotted around their heads. It was a wind that jangled the key rings of landlords in apartment doorways, keeping them from lighting cigarettes. It was a wind that knocked the smile off of children's faces and chased dogs under the porch. It was a wind that ushered in deeds.

Hanna wrestled her grocery cart through the cold parking lot toward her car. Nearby, customers gawked, doing double takes, apparently astonished that a television newsperson actually did eat food. She had bags filled with the fixings for Thanksgiving. She, Singer and Cory would celebrate their holiday early at the cabin. It was their tradition, if you counted year two as the makings of a tradition. And Hanna did. She knew the notion of tradition was foreign to Cory, and he wasn't to be faulted. Parents plant the seed of such things in their children, or they don't. Hanna could hardly get Cory to recognize his birthday, let alone a holiday. To him, they were all just squares on a calendar.

Hanna got to the trunk of her car, where a woman approached. "Excuse me," she half-shouted over the wind. "You're Hanna Donnovan, the TV lady, aren't you?"

"Yes. Hello."

"I watched you last night. On the news. About that little boy," the woman said.

"Yes," Hanna said, starting to load her groceries into the trunk. She'd learned not to be rude, but to keep moving when the public approached. "Very sad. I apologize for not presenting the story better." She looked up and camera-smiled at the woman.

"Are you kidding me?" the woman said. She put her hand on Hanna's shoulder, to interrupt her from her task. "I was bawling watching it. I can only imagine how hard it was to talk about."

Hanna looked at the woman now. She was a head taller, strong-built, large, her wiry red hair cut short and uneven. She wore neither hat nor gloves, unaffected by the weather, but her eyes teared, maybe from the wind but likely not. There was a connection. "Thank you for saying so," Hanna told her.

"I have a confession to make," the woman said. "I try not to be judgmental—as you can see, I didn't quite make it into the Perfect Woman Club this year—but I always thought you TV types were just anorexic little robots wearing push-up bras and too much make-up. But you, I pegged you wrong. What you did last night on

TV was better than anything I've ever watched. Kid you not. Just wanted to come over and say so. Let you know you made me sit at the foot of my kids' beds last night." Then she got on with the practical. "Can I give you a hand with them bags?" To Hanna's surprise, she said yes. They got her groceries into the trunk, and then the woman was on her way.

As Hanna got behind the wheel, she watched the woman get into her rusted older model car. The woman climbed clumsily halfway into the front seat, reached over the seat and opened the back door from the handle inside. Then she got out, pulled open the dented car door and loaded in her groceries. "Maybe I pegged you wrong, too," Hanna whispered. She felt better. She felt way better.

Reg was at the last stop before leaving town. The barbershop for a shave and a haircut.

He'd been to the bakery for a bismarck, careful not to get any on his clothes, a novel concern for him. His slacks and coordinated shirt were selected from those hanging in his closet, choices he'd purchased over the past months. His black dress shoes had a high-gloss shine on the toes. His overcoat was dark, a wool topcoat he'd stolen off a hanger at a wake years ago, but never had occasion to wear. The van had been through the car wash after fueling. He cleaned and vacuumed the interior, even did the mirrors and the dash under the ashtray.

In the barbershop, the two chairs were full but no one was waiting. When the guys got one look at Reg they burst out laughing. *Who died?* they wanted to know. Reg only smiled and took up a magazine while he waited for a chair to open. Didn't know you knew how to read, one said. Hey, said the other, isn't this usually the day you're busy making earwax? Laughter bounced around the little room.

Reg heard it, but he didn't. Inside his head was a low roiling. Churning, billowing, it swamped the walls of the small crushing space where he had stuffed everything for so many years. Today, the guilty and the innocent would pay equally. He would see no flowers. He would touch no cheek. He would whistle no note. He would look at no sunset. He would smile at no odd thought. He would taste no sweetness. He would acknowledge no higher power. He would open no window to the morning. He would extend no apology. It was time. It was time. It was time.

As he left, he slotted a penny in the gumball machine and twisted out a red. His favorite.

Hanna had worked through most of her to-do list, yet she hoped it wouldn't start sleeting or snowing or whatever it was going to do; she had no time for it. Singer was at Ms. Kortuem's, and there was one last big thing to do before picking him up for lunch.

The Duluth shopping mall sat at the town's highest point. Forever Jewelers was there, and so, supposedly, was her resized engagement ring. What was estimated to be a "month-or-so" repair had turned into numerous apologies. Now, almost eight weeks after Cory's proposal, Hanna would get her ring back.

The manager of the store saw Hanna coming through the door, and scooted to the back, returning with a ring box. "Ms. Donnovan," he greeted her at the glass cases, offering his hand and a smile befitting a jeweler. "So good to see you." He rolled out a black display felt and cracked open the ring box. "I trust you're well. Now, let's have a look a this wonderful piece." He carefully plucked the ring from the box and placed it on the felt. "Cross every finger except your ring finger that it fits," he said, pleased with his airy disposition.

Hanna held her breath and slipped it on. It was a little tight but her smile showed that she loved it. Extending it out at arm's length, she viewed the ring, turning her wrist to catch the light.

"Careful you don't blind my customers," the manager continued.

Hanna brought her hand back in, spinning the ring slightly to test the fit.

"It should be a little snug. The barometric pressure is falling, which causes fingers to swell some. Gorgeous," the manager gushed.

AUTUMN 1985

Hanna nodded. She wished Cory could be here, but they had to divide and conquer if they were going to get everything ready and disappear for the weekend.

"Again, I'd like to apologize for the delay, but a piece of a lifetime is worth getting precisely correct. Of course there's no charge for the resizing. Your business is very important to us."

"Can I take it just like this?" Hanna said, holding up her hand.

"By all means. Just let me put the box in a bag for you." He reached under the counter. "There is one more thing ..." the manager began.

Now what? Hanna thought. "Yes." She tried to remain patient.

"Considering your status in the community, I was wondering if we might secure your permission to use your name in an endorsement. You know, something along the lines of ..." at this point he stretched his hands out like he was spreading words across a marquee: "Hanna Donnovan of Channel 6 News trusted her wedding ring to Forever Jewelers. Shouldn't you?"

Hanna took the bag he had set on the glass counter. "I'm not sure the station would appreciate my doing that," she said.

"Is it something you could check on?" the manager persisted.

"I guess I could," she said.

"We would happily throw in free cleaning on the ring for your permission."

"I thought the cleaning was part of the complimentary service package with purchase," Hanna said.

"Did I say cleaning? I meant to say we should be able to arrange for earrings or a small bracelet."

"I'll check into it," Hanna said. "And thank you."

"You'll get back to me then?" the manager asked brightly.

"Yes," Hanna told him, swallowing what she was thinking. *In about eight weeks.*

For the duration of the drive back to pick up Singer, Hanna could hardly focus on the road. Her ring on her steering hand somehow found light in the grim overcast day and sent it radiating.

Meadow's water broke while she was eating a bowl of Cheerios. In her words, it felt like a great gushing water balloon, followed by a smaller one. Luckily, neither Pat nor HomeSky had left for work yet. Meadow changed and grabbed her hospital bag while HomeSky called work and said she wouldn't be coming in. Pat stood with the front door open, car running on the driveway. Meadow calmly reminded him not to forget his lunch in the refrigerator as she pulled on her coat and went outside. Pat locked the door, before unlocking it to go back in for his lunch.

Pat went as far as the Emergency Room check in. When the paperwork was finished, Meadow assured him, again, that all was well, and he should get going to work. HomeSky promised to call if anything was happening, but it could be some time. He stood there not knowing whether to shout for joy, cry, or try a little of both. He was elated and frightened beyond words. They both gave him a hug and he was still standing there as they came with a wheelchair and rolled Meadow to the maternity wing. Don't worry, the nurse had told him as Meadow was seated in the wheelchair. It was hospital protocol.

The doctor on call came in and brusquely explained the plan like he was going down a checklist for a fishing trip. The nurse would be checking dilation regularly; possible need for inducement since the water had broken; C-section only upon complications; IV Pitocin drip; walk around the wing to accelerate early dilation; medication options for delivery; her regular pediatrician would be coming in after 3:00; extended labor typical with first baby. Meadow remained focused, nodding as he went. As he left the room, he bid her good luck and said he hoped she liked ice chips because they were on the lunch menu. She tried to smile but the pain in her back had migrated to her belly. She almost mentioned it but didn't want to be a bother.

Overnight, the lake beyond Cory's cabin had iced over. The wind beat across it, sending small branches skittering over the smooth surface like iceboats. A single goose had remained in the water too long and was now trapped in ice. Why had he stayed? Had a hunter wounded him? Was he weakened by sickness? Was he too old for the long flight south?

The answer was of no consequence to the eagle perched in the pine tree on the adjacent point of land. From one hundred yards away, the eagle could see every feather on the goose. When he'd drop out of the tree, swooping low, making his flight across the ice toward his prey, the goose would rise up, legs frozen in place, and beat his wings to a chaotic protest of honking and hissing. The eagle would land close and fly-hop around the goose, but there was too much wild left in the bird. The eagle would circle, terrorizing him, extracting precious energy from the goose, before the wind drove him back to his perch in the pine. He'd wait. The goose would settle back on the ice, exhausted. Until the eagle came again, like an arrow across the ice, and it would start anew.

Hanna and Singer had lunch at home. Hanna's job was the grilled cheese sandwiches and the fruit while Singer handled the potato chip and cookie rationing. He hummed as he got his eye down low over the small bowls, transferring two or three chips to make things even.

"So what's the plan again?" Singer asked for perhaps the twentieth time.

"You tell me," Hanna said. "You're almost done and I've only had two bites of my sandwich."

"Well," Singer said, extending his hands like a teacher beginning a lecture. "We eat, clean up, pack, go to your work where you talk for just a little while I make my puzzles, go to the grocery store for something you forgot, and then drive to the cabin. Cory might beat us there, might not, depending on when he gets his papers graded." Singer took a deep gulp of air. "Phew," he dramatically wiped his brow.

"Bravo," Hanna said, with light applause. "You only forgot one thing. We have to stop by Ms. Kortuem's for your magic bear."

"Oh yeah. On the windowsill upstairs."

She watched Singer eating his cookie. "What song are you humming?"

"Snail, Snail," he said.

"How does it go?"

He sang it for her.

Snail, snail
Snail, snail
What's the time of day?
One o'clock
Two o'clock
Time to slobber away

"Wow," Hanna laughed. "Let me guess where you learned that."

"Cory," Singer said. "He calls me his trouble door."

"Trouble door?" Hanna asked.

"Yeah. A singer who goes to places."

Hanna thought for a beat. "Troubadour," she said.

"Oh yeah," Singer said. "That's a tough one."

"Are you done eating?" Hanna asked.

"Yep-er-rini tall and skinny."

Hanna looked at her son. "Remind me not to let Cory feed you while you're not in my presence."

"No," Singer giggled.

She drew a little tap water in a plastic cup. "Here. Go water your lollipop plant before the train leaves the station." Hanna shook her head.

Singer jumped down, excited. His lollipop plant was on its second growth, almost all the way up yesterday.

On the windowsill, a plastic cup awaited with a lollipop pushed into the dirt. Singer shouted to his mother that a red one had bloomed, was it okay to take it? She said it was, but he already had his cookie so no more dessert until tonight or maybe for the car ride to the cabin, if he was good. Singer took the lollipop. The wind

AUTUMN 1985

shook the windowpane and the trees beyond waved, as if vying for his attention. He got up on his tiptoes and breathed on the glass, fogging it. Singer left a smiley face.

Pat had arrived at the hospital on his lunch break an hour earlier. He wished Meadow could have gotten a private room, but it was a modest hospital. A dividing curtain would have to do.

They were able to walk the maternity floor, Meadow pushing her IV stand with a drip of Pitocin to induce labor. But shortly after he left, the nurse grew concerned about the increased intensity of Meadow's back pain, and how it had dropped to her pelvis and radiated equally back and front. It could be back labor, the nurse advised, simple, yet uncomfortable, but just in case, they kept her restricted to her bed, connected to the fetal monitor fulltime.

Meadow drifted in and out of light sleep, startled awake whenever the baby's heartbeat caused an irregularity in the monitor's beeping. There were ice chips and smiles from HomeSky. You're doing well, the nurse would tell her, checking her dilation. Was there the vague recollection of the doctor's face? Were they concerned? Everything's fine, they told her. Great. You're doing great. We'll be ready to start pushing soon. Meadow closed her eyes. She could feel her blood pulsing in her temple, like war drums. Somewhere beyond, her baby's monitored heartbeat galloped.

Reg pulled in the vacant driveway next to Cory's and did a three-point turn to get the nose of the van facing out. He would have preferred the engine running and the heater on, but there was no telling when Cory would arrive. Conserve gas, he concluded. It was quieter there, off the blacktop, protected from the penetrating wind. Reg laid out his provisions. Pint of bourbon. Two packs of cigarettes. One bismarck donut. A camera. A pistol.

Hanna and Singer drove toward the cabin, singing songs. The road was gray, the trees were gray, the horizon was gray, yet somehow the diamond on her finger, not to be dimmed, found a sparkle in the ash.

The lake behind Cory's cabin was making ice as the wind ironed it slick. No longer was there a sign of goose or eagle. What conclusion they had come to was of no matter. It was as though they'd never been there.

Rubbing his eyes, Cory pushed back from his homeroom desk. Done. Fatigue was bested by anticipation. With the last of the homework finished, if he hurried, he might beat Hanna to the cabin. She had strung together a lengthy to-do list and said it was better for them to meet there than to attempt to coordinate schedules. Cory picked up the students' exams and tapped them on the desk, making a neat stack. He slid it forward, but not too close to the edge. A stapler went on top for safekeeping. Everything was as it should be.

Meadow writhed in a foggy dream. She was at a swim meet. The pool deck was warm and humid, but she was freezing, shivering in her swimsuit on the starting platform. The starters gun kept going off, BANG! BANG! BANG! but she didn't move. Her swim goggles had fogged. She put them up on her forehead and looked over at the starter. Her father had a gun. He was pointing it at her. She heard high-pitched screaming.

Hanna pulled into Cory's driveway, the frozen rocks and dirt popping under her tires. "We're here," she said softly, checking in her rear-view mirror. Singer had fallen asleep. He didn't stir. She reasoned he could use a nap, even though those days were past. It was going be late for dinner and late for bedtime with all the excitement. Sleep now was for the best. She found the key on the tree nail where Cory hung his toothbrush and small mirror in the summer. "Hello stinky cabin," she said, upon opening the front door. "Whew. You can use some fresh air, if you don't mind my saying." She propped the front door open with her first bag of groceries. Hanna got Singer next. She carried him in, doing her best not to wake him. He made a few incomprehensible noises as she laid him on the couch. It wasn't until reaching for the Hudson Bay blanket folded over the couch back that she realized how cold it was inside.

AUTUMN 1985

Covering Singer, she thought the heater must have gone out. Too many requests came at her at once. Should she get the groceries in? Get that front door closed to keep inside whatever heat there was? Or see if she could figure out how to light the dumb heater? One thing she knew for sure. She needed to use the bathroom first.

"What's going on?" Meadow cried, jolting upright. She had nodded off between contractions. Had she heard the doctor call code pink? The high-pitched screaming was the alarm on the fetal monitor. Last she remembered, things were fine. A crash cart banged through the door. Then another. She was exhausted from the last three hours of labor. But weren't contractions still stuck at three minutes apart? Wasn't dilation still only eight centimeters? More doctors ran into her room. Nurses swirled. The alarm continued to scream. HomeSky had said it was okay to close her eyes between contractions. You're at 10! She heard. PUSH! They cut off the belly-band that held the ultrasound disks in place. CODE PINK! What's wrong? What's code pink? HomeSky? Turn that damn alarm off! a doctor shouted. HomeSky! Right here, she squeezed her hand. Why did they pull the hospital divider curtain shut? What's happening? PUSH! The umbilical cord, someone said. It was around the baby's neck. Quick breaths. BEAR DOWN. PUSH! Pat was there too. What was Pat doing there?

Hanna read the lighting instructions on the side panel of the old space heater for the third time. She had a box of wood matches at her foot. From what she could tell, the pilot light was to be pressed and held down to be relit. Once that was done, the furnace knob could be set to the desired temperature. Simple enough. All would be warm by the time Cory arrived. She took a match out of the box, put the tip to the striking surface, and struck.

The concussive shock of the explosion rocked the van. Windows in the neighboring cabin blew out. Reg had fallen asleep, half eaten donut in his lap. "Holy shit!" he blurted in fear. Then pieces of fiery debris started to rain from the sky: a section of log, the legs of the kitchen table, copper plumbing. BAM! a burning lampshade crashed down on the van's hood, bouncing to the driveway. "Holy fucking shit storm!" His hands went up to his face, shaking in the realization. One large swallow was left in the pint. He took it down, but his hands wouldn't stop shaking, nor his legs, nor his chattering teeth.

Cory was getting close. The first of the snow was coming now, streaking horizontally on the northeast winds. He looked out over the final field that he would drive around to get to the cabin. How is it the wind blows invisible, so long unseen, until finally there comes something to give it shape, to reveal its magnitude? The snow was like a million tracking points, and the wind was there, as visible as a sheet pulled over your face.

Reg stood in Cory's driveway with his camera. The van idled roughly, driver's door open, wipers sweeping the wet snow from the windshield. It was surreal. Where the cabin had stood, he could see clear through to the trees, and to the frozen lake beyond. There was nothing left except foundation and the remnants of fireplace fieldstone. He didn't recognize the car parked there, paint peeled away, windows blown out. It wasn't Cory's truck. Reg surmised they must have all come out in her car. He clicked one last photo, climbed stiffly into the van and pulled out of the driveway. He turned onto the wet blacktop, accelerated, reaching for the objects as they slid on the car seat away from him. The camera. The sealed envelope. The pistol. There was one bullet in the magazine. For him. For the spot in his head where the voice of Kemp resided. Reg touched the gun just as the shock of a horn snapped his head up.

Cory pulled hard to the right. He was coming around the last turn leading to his cabin. Some idiot, looking down, was driving in the middle of the road. He pounded the horn, just eluding the front bumper of the van. As the vehicles passed, time slowed, their faces, large and animated, almost close enough to touch the other's cheek. Each saw the wide-eyed panic in the other as they narrowly missed. Cory pulled back the other way on the wheel, correcting as the truck fishtailed. He watched the van in his side mirror before it

AUTUMN 1985

disappeared behind a curtain of snow. Heart thumping, Cory exhaled. From where did he know that face? He drove on, his mailbox now in sight. Something about that face was distantly familiar. He put it aside. He was almost there now and nothing else mattered.

Some moments are too real. To compensate, the mind relegates them to a less damaging format, archived, like an old movie, a silent-running black and white, on a screen in the dark of our consciousness.

A man stood away from his pickup truck. He stared at the wreckage. Papers blew across the fresh dusting of driveway snow. A couch cushion burned in a tree. A little boy's shoe was overturned in the driveway. A cord from an appliance dangled in a bush. The man ran around the foundation of the cabin, screaming, primal, abandoned. He did so twice before falling to his knees. He pounded the earth. He pounded his face. Everything in his body demanded to know HOW? Then he stopped. The wind scattered sooty snow in his hair. He knew something then, clear as a picture he could hold. Instantly, his feet were under him, sprinting to the truck as only an athlete could. The truck fishtailed and was out of the driveway, onto the blacktop. His pursuit was unconditional.

"God damn you Reg Cunningham." Cory seethed as his truck accelerated down the blacktop. He had one chance.

The truck left the road, front wheels dropping off the shoulder, racing down the grade before reaching the cup of the ditch and roaring up the other side, launched airborne. So violent was the landing in the field that the windshield cracked in four directions. The truck lurched, almost tipping, before Cory accelerated, bringing the rear around. He stomped the accelerator to the floorboard, flying across the frozen ground. The cab was a paint shaker. Items were flung in all directions. Reg's van had to go around the field before reaching the road to the highway. Cory, by cutting across it, could reach the other side and be waiting on the road as Reg tried to make his escape.

The truck hurtled across the field, a dark blur slicing through the white. There was no going back. This field separated one life from another, separated love from hate, separated belief from godlessness. For every foot of ground the truck gained, Cory abandoned years of progress until his faith was lightened like objects ejected from the pickup bed. Finally, he was empty.

Meadow bore down. She felt a tearing. The crowning head came through, but the shoulders caught. She cried out. A nurse gasped. The baby's face was blue.

Like a panting wolf, Cory's truck idled. It faced north on the road where vehicles had to go south to make the highway. Wind. Snow. And out of the decrepit visibility, the van.

Reg was a half-mile up road, moving straight at him. Cory's boot went down on the accelerator. The tires burned. The engine found the harmonic hum of wide-open power. The distance between them closed as the speeds of both vehicles topped out. The van sliced down the middle of the road. Cory adjusted, now on the same course. The narrow orange speedometer needle was pegged to the right. Five hundred feet. Cory took one hand off the wheel. Three hundred feet. Cory's hand went to his side, releasing his seatbelt. Fifty feet. Cory grit his teeth.

She pushed her mightiest, glorious push. Such release, such complete and utter release! The shoulders came. The hips. The feet. Into the world, Meadow's baby arrived. But soundlessly.

The vehicles struck. Sickening. The guttural scream of metal crushing metal. Cory's head hit the cracked windshield, which yielded with little resistance. Out he came, shoulders, hips, feet—launched—a projectile of hair and blood and bone through glass. *He was there. The island. Airborne over the blue collar of shoreline, flung from the boat, cast from one life to another, thinking his singular thought: free.*

Surely, quickly, the umbilical cord was cut and unwound from the infant's neck. The syringe, inserted, cleared mucus from the airways. The blue baby was unresponsive. The doctor struck him on the buttocks, hard. And again. And again. The child coughed. Spit. Bubbles came from his tiny nostrils. The wail that came from his lungs as they opened ended the silence of the forsaken. In shrieking yelps, life came; its first beautiful searching voice. Doctors exhaled, eyes momentarily closed, then hands clapped shoulders. Nurses hugged. Bodies loosened and moved in grateful companionship.

Bedside, Pat held HomeSky's hand who held Meadow's hand. Congratulations mother. You did it. Her eyes squeezed closed, spreading tears to the corners. The three huddled, before making room for a fourth, as the infant was laid on her chest, held fast by the heat of gratitude. If there were more joy in a million pastures than in this tiny half-room, where could that place be, other than here, now, where love was born again?

SINGER

EPILOGUE

SONG

The car navigated the icy, night-befallen road. A husband was driving with his wife of 51 years. They had retired to live at their lake cottage where they read books and made fires and planned trips to distant places.

Out from nowhere, a deer bolted through a veil of snow onto the road, causing a chain reaction: the husband's foot sunk the brake pedal, his head swung in anticipation of impact, bringing his shoulders around, and his hands, and the steering wheel. The car fishtailed hard right, then left. As the vehicle made its first 360-degree spin, the man's wife saw that behind the deer walked a child.

The car was richly appointed with enough accident protection features to save passengers from almost any outcome, but the car never touched a hair on the deer. Harmlessly, they spun off the road, left stuck in the icy ditch.

"Did you see that?" blurted the wife, alarmed, reaching for the door handle.

"Nice buck," the husband agreed, finding humor—and finally the ability to exhale—in the midst of it all.

"There was a child!" She quickly left the vehicle.

The boy stood on the road. Jacketless. Curled hair matted down by wet snow. He was four, maybe five, she guessed, gauging against the size of her middle grandson.

"What in the world?" the husband said, coming through the pelting wind. He was told to hurry, go get the blanket out of the trunk. Upon his return, he found his wife kneeling on the icy road before the child. The boy was humming.

"He's sleepwalking," she told her husband. "Quick. The blanket."

They wrapped the child, around his shoulders and arms and over his fist closed tightly around something unseen. The car is stuck, the husband told his wife.

The man lifted the child, bringing him to his chest inside his open coat. The boy's humming rose up, louder, and became song before being taken by the wind. They were but a half-mile from their lake cottage. The husband reached for his wife's hand, sharing a resolute nod. Then they took the first forward step, and were no longer the same in the ocean of night.

In the frozen field, under a skin of snow, the notes found him. The sound pulled him up on his unbroken arm, where he listened through the unrelenting wind. When he was sure, Cory pushed with his functioning leg.

He had heard singing.

SINGER

READERS' COMMENTS

Readers value what other readers have to say about a book—as do I. While *Singer* is still fresh in your mind, please go to **fivefriendsbooks.com** and share your thoughts on this novel in the Readers' Comments section.

Thanks.

ACKNOWLEDGMENTS

Without friends, there are no stories. Without stories, our lives are brittle and narrow. So thank you, friends. Your enthusiastic support for *Fall to Grace* encouraged the writing of this sequel. And thanks to your recommendations, my book was introduced to new friends far and wide. To all who assisted in the editing of this novel, thanks. John, I appreciate your help with the cover design, among other things. And finally, Kelly, Sully and Teddy: you're the fizz in my soda.